In the Land of Winter

RICHARD GRANT

AN AVON BOOK

AVON BOOKS, INC.
1350 Avenue of the Americas
New York, New York 10019

Copyright © 1997 by Richard Grant
Front cover illustration by Mary Grandpré
Inside cover author photograph by Karen Strauss
Library of Congress Catalog Card Number: 97-18454
Visit our website at **http://www.AvonBooks.com/Bard**
ISBN: 0-380-79140-4

First Bard Printing: December 1998
First Avon Books Hardcover Printing: November 1997

BARD TRADEMARK REG. U.S. PAT. OFF. AND IN OTHER COUNTRIES, MARCA REGISTRADA, HECHO EN U.S.A.

Printed in the U.S.A.

WCD 10 9 8 7 6 5 4 3 2 1

"A SUPERB WORDSMITH . . . RICHARD GRANT HAS DONE SOMETHING PRETTY REMARKABLE."

Charleston (S.C.) *Post and Courier*

Pippa Rede is a loving single mother and young, contemporary witch struggling for subsistence in a frigid and wooded northeastern corner of our country. In her gray, enduring December, her beautiful, adored and adoring nine-year-old "elf" Winterbelle is Pippa's healing warmth—the only truly precious and irreplaceable thing in an otherwise disorganized, undirected, confusing and often hurtful life. But in the busy days before the highest, most glorious holiday in Christendom, her little girl is lost to her—stolen by bigots and zealots bolstered by the powers of official government who have labeled Pippa Rede a monster, leaving her homeless, jobless, and childless to face the longest, coldest nights of the year all alone. Yet, when all else has been swept away, there is still magic in the world. And in the dark, wild wood, at the very edge of the Mystery, Pippa embarks on a transforming inner quest, determined to unlock the strengths she will need to take on the vested omnipotence of the State in order to win back her Winterbelle and restore the rightness of the universe.

From Richard Grant—one of the most original and important writers of fiction in America today—comes a poignant, sad, funny, and altogether extraordinary work of power and purpose, with a heart that beats loudly and true.

"An imaginative and engaging book in which the harsh contemporary world is mingled with magic, in which fierce werewolves are less a threat than bureaucracy."
New Brunswick Times-Record

"Grant, in his warm and witty style, has written a winter's tale that tests the strength of spirit and reveals the truth and happiness of life and its precious moments."
Abilene Reporter-News

Other Books by
Richard Grant

SARABAND OF LOST TIME
RUMORS OF SPRING
VIEWS FROM THE OLDEST HOUSE
THROUGH THE HEART
TEX AND MOLLY IN THE AFTERLIFE

To
Deanie, the Good Witch of Nokesville;
Liz ("What the hell kind of witch am I?") of Coleman Pond;
Mary, my fairy god-ex;
Marc, a ghost;
and Pati, the princess that got away.

And to Matthew, Callie and Tristan: my elves.

I

as blood

He put his hand
Under his hood,
And saw a star
As red as blood.

—*Unnamed carol, quoted by G. K. Chesterton*

In the east she will place apples. A cluster of rowan berries. Geranium blossoms, fallen but still alarmingly scarlet. A photo of Winterbelle, showing rosy cheeks.

In the south, a big flake of birch bark, pressed flat. A sheet of bond paper with wishes inscribed. Breast feathers of a loon—white flecked unpredictably with warm gray—that she scooped out of a pond in the state park last August. A bowl of snow.

In the west: Pointy-fingered ivy cuttings. A "Vote Green" lapel button. 2 bayberry candles. Her salt-glazed Frey & Freya mug.

And in the north: A lump of charcoal. A perfectly good computer disk. Ashes from the Yule fire. A sea stone curvaceous and swollen like a goddess.

And the deep black
and long
December night.

The woman in the crimson scarf stared a long time at a display of seasonal greeting cards. Later (for what reason?) Pippa would remember exactly how she had stood there: locked into position, one leg firmly in front of the other—a stance you would assume at the start of a tug-of-war. Only instead of rope, the woman grasped card after card, opening, scrutinizing, all but sniffing them, before settling finally upon an angel tooting a long trumpet embossed in gold. Stars flashed above, one brighter than the rest, while below stood shepherds looking slightly delirious. Their sheep were puffy and insubstantial, like fallen clouds.

The card cost $2.50. For when you care enough to send the very best. The woman charged it to her account, whereby Pippa learned that her name was Carol Deacon Aaby, of Trim Street. Not a terribly active account: lilies at Easter and a basket for Memorial Day. Afterward, Carol Aaby did not leave the store immediately, but drifted over to the garden tools, where she interested herself in a trowel by Bulldog of Sussex. What could you do with that in the middle of a northern winter? Terrorize your geraniums, possibly.

4

Left again to herself, Pippa started to hum. *It came upon a midnight clear.* She swirled about the shop like a leaf held aloft by a dust devil. *That glorious song of old.* Around her, Rose Petal & Thorn had been in full holiday mode for nearly a month now, and what with the tsunami of customers, Chanticleer tapes looping like Möbius ribbons, track lights that glistened on silvery tinsel, and the smells of carnations, sweet fern, wax myrtle, lilies, pomander balls, rosemary clipped into topiaries and the plug-in crock pot filled with mulling cider, Pippa felt at the point of achieving some kind of out-of-body experience.

OOBE, she thought.

It was like a secret word, a seasonal incantation.

Oobe oobe.

Pippa plucked withering petals off poinsettias, spritzed the streptocarpus, scrutinized the undersides of orchid leaves for mites. She felt weightless, filled up with seasonal cheer, invulnerable to anything that might be waiting for her outside the spray-frosted door to Mill Street.

Christmas is magical, she thought. Whether you believe in it or not.

And Santa Claus was a shaman from Lapland, driving his reindeer south to browse in the uncut forests of Scandinavia, bearing strange and beautiful gifts from the North Pole (as his winter hosts would have thought) to secure a welcome at their hearths. Christmas trees are saplings of Yggdrassil, the cosmic tree whose branches flutter in the breezes of heaven and whose roots plunge deep into Hel, the icy hall of the Queen of the Dead. Even your nice plump turkey recalls the slaughter of livestock and consequent feasting known as *Wintersblöt*—winter's blood—the start of the cold season, a dangerous time when frost giants thunder abroad. The whole blooming holiday, when you get right down to it, is thoroughly pagan from one end to the other.

So it's okay to feel jolly with Christmas one week off. Even if you're not really a Christian. Even if you're really a—

"Excuse me," said a voice at her ear. So close that she almost pulled the trigger of her misting bottle in self-defense.

Her near-victim stood before her, smiling unawares. No taller than her unassertive chin: high-school sophomore, plus or minus. About him swirled a gusty, unsettled air, as though some errant child of the North Wind had penetrated the glittering warmth of the flower shop and might any moment breeze out again. Pippa felt she should catch him before this happened.

"Need some help?" she said pleasantly.

The boy rocked easily on the balls of his feet, forward and back, while his eyes danced about the store, touching on every sight but Pippa. His demeanor was jaunty, implying that it was nothing less than his distinct prerogative to occupy this space and exude these waves of youthful energy, fecklessness, and animal grace. His pants, rolled at the cuffs, were weighted with snow. Brown hair poked this way and that from under a floppy ski cap with a Kriss Kringle pompom on top.

Abruptly he wheeled on one leg, parking an imaginary skateboard. He peered straight at Pippa and said quietly:

"That was you in the paper, right? A couple of months ago?"

His eyes were chocolate with sparkles and his cheeks were cold and freckled, pink and brown.

Pippa glanced around, her cherry-red Converse sneaker with its one white star squeaking nervously on the sales floor. Why should she care if anyone was listening?

Beats me, she thought.

She cared, though.

"That was cool," the boy said. "I mean, I hardly ever look at the paper usually. But I thought you were great."

"You did?" said Pippa.

He observed her in little glances, between longer looks off to the side. Latent kidlike shyness coming out. Or perhaps he did not want his friends to catch him in conversation with a grown-up. "I saved it," he said.

She didn't get what he meant. She knew she was staring at the boy a bit more closely than was called for, under the circumstances. "So," she said, "can I help you with anything?"

"With my stepmom, how about," said the boy. He gazed down at his shoes, which looked too big.

This sounded like an accidental confidence—something he hadn't really meant to say. Pippa smiled, feeling parental.

"Sorry," she told him. "You're on your own there."

"Well, but—" He looked around again. "But see," going on quickly now, "there's this thing I wanted to, like, tell you about. I mean, I don't really *know* you or anything. Except for the article. But I thought—"

Pippa twitched her nose, Elizabeth Montgomery–style. The thing she remembered most clearly about her one and only appearance in the *Weekly Herald* was how terribly the photograph came out: herself, wearing a demented expression and a black cape borrowed from the Episcopal choir, mooning over a shadowed and cropped-off patch of rocky ground as though trolling for a lost contact lens, above the fairly oxymoronic caption: *Bringing long-dead customs to life.* The brief accompanying interview had been, to put it kindly, uninformative.

"I just wanted to warn you," said the boy, staring at last, and earnestly, into her eyes.

Pippa played back the conversation thus far as though it had been spoken in a language she knew only slightly. She took into account the boy's chocolate-mint eyes and his nose like a freckled fairy's. She could not decide how to think of him: as cute, or as beautiful. The question seemed to press itself with peculiar urgency, overriding the more obvious one which she asked anyway.

"Warn me about what?"

"Kaspian!"

Across the sales floor, Carol Deacon Aaby called out with dark fire in her eyes. She stared at the boy while pointedly failing to acknowledge Pippa.

"Kaspian?" Pippa said.

The boy gave a quick shrug, punctuated with a helpless raise of the eyebrow.

"That's me," he said. "Like the prince? Only with a K."

"Ah," said Pippa. "Well, it was nice to meet you."

He held out a hand that was warm against hers, palm to palm, and dry. Her own hand tingled with portent.

The woman across the room took a couple of steps their way. Her expression made Pippa drop the boy's hand.

"*Kaspian,*" Carol Aaby repeated. Louder now, with a certain note of menace.

"My stepmother," he murmured. Not shy any longer, if he ever truly had been. Grimacing, like a conspirator caught out. Then walking away.

Briefly he removed his hat, adjusted its position on his head, and for a couple of moments a confusion of oak-leaf-colored hair seemed to fill a great part of the store, swirling wildly around him and around Pippa and around Carol Deacon Aaby. His retreating stride was princely, even as the woman, tightening her own crimson scarf, took him under her arm.

Pippa turned away. She had the feeling there was about to be a Final Look—one of those things delivered over the shoulder while standing upon a threshold—and she knew that it would trouble her immeasurably if she happened to witness it. It would trouble her enough though she did not.

She held her eyes safely away until she heard the door swish open and then shut again. Snow drifted and settled with the calming of the air, and involuntarily, though Rose Petal & Thorn was quite thoroughly heated, her body gave a wintry shiver.

Meat, Pippa thought. Red meat.

And brought the cleaver down.

WHUMP.

To be exact, organically raised black Angus beef. Pippa thought it would do her good. She thought it would prove restorative. A shot of yang in this yinnest of seasons.

WHUMP. WHUMP.

The day was falling dark outside, without a breeze, so that frigid air slid down the hindparts of Wabenaki Mountain and puddled in the gloomy end of Ash Street, where Pippa lived with her daughter Winterbelle and her great-aunt Eulace in a groaning Shingle Style ruin. Through a sash as tall and narrow as a grandfather clock, its thick panes warped like glacial ice, Pippa gazed out at stubby, half-dead limbs of neglected lilacs and forsythia that appeared not quite motionless, but just perceptibly quivering with cold and spite. Inside, safe from them, home from work, reasonably comfy, and padding around in fuzzy slippers, Pippa was making a stew.

The slab of beef lay on a cutting board in the big,

saggy-joisted, high-countered kitchen. This part of the house was not well lit and remained, even at holiday time, predominantly cheerless. All its ornamental features (pressed-tin ceiling, scalloped cornices, scrollwork brackets under the shelves) had been painted uniformly white so long ago that they were now far along toward yellow, like the color cigarettes stain your teeth. A wood-fired stove that dominated one interior wall was huge and impressive but did not do anything well, except that its warming oven was good for incubating chicks. The refrigerator, whose curvaceous bulk recalled the 1939 World's Fair, stood rattling at a great remove from the other appliances, as though it might at any moment explode.

Pippa had made few improvements during the year and a half since her aunt—out of pity for Winterbelle, the official version went—had taken them in. Among these few were a programmable coffeemaker, a microwave oven and a bread machine (purchases instigated by an ex-boyfriend who believed in automating one's existence, wherever practicable). She sort of hesitated to get carried away because, after all, the place was her aunt's, and you never knew how far it was safe to go. She had learned that lesson in the fracas over the VCR. Eulace *preferred* to cross the room and punch the buttons by hand. To be exact, by thumb. She liked especially to time it so that the channel flipped just as the President (for example) was opening his mouth to explain himself. Then, as the slumberous old Magnavox blinked and retuned, Eulace would straighten with a look of pinched satisfaction, lurch back in strictly Pyrrhic triumph (because the hustle would have thrown her knee out) to plop on her padded deacon's bench, and declare:

"*He's* a fine one to talk."

—or something else whose very non-sequiturish quality put it beyond reach of refutation.

So much for the universal remote, a seemingly bullet-proof birthday idea.

The kitchen presented, however, a more ambiguous case. As to whose space it was, visitors might have supposed Pippa's. Not counting lunch (hardly an active philo-sophical category around here), Pippa attended to every meal. She was an artless, earnest, disorganized and incon-sistent chef; but her intentions were wholesome, and gen-erally speaking the little family went to bed with its tummies full.

The season of cold found her at a certain advantage: dropping ingredients into a bubbling pot was a thing she enjoyed, and there was little incentive *not* to muddle around the stove for hours at a stretch. She pared vegeta-bles with a folding knife made by artisans in Santa Fe too small for the job but a pleasure to open and close, and chose spices by an innovative method of color coordina-tion. With chicken, you wanted green and black: pepper-corns, rosemary, parsley, et alia. With beef, you went for yellow and brown. Ergo, over the cauldron of stew Pippa upturned plastic shakers of cumin, cinnamon, celery seed, dry mustard, turmeric, allspice, cardamom and clove. And garlic, not sparsely. If Pippa never got a date with a vam-pire, this weakness for garlic was why.

I'll have to settle for a werewolf, she supposed.

"How's your homework coming?" she called across the rolling expanse of pumpkin pine between the kitchen and the west parlor, whose oak beams and stolid Mission fur-nishings shone like polished amber before the dying glory of the sunset and the humbler charm of a small candelabra that Pippa (in a rare spasm of prosperity, once upon a time) had ordered from Pottery Barn. Winterbelle was going through a candle thing. In bed at night she absorbed (through mostly shut lids, apparently by osmosis) Pippa's mother's Nancy Drew collection by the light of a votive in a rose-red glass teacup, last of a vanished set. In the black & white guest bathroom, her own chilly girl's preserve, she combed her hair between a pair of single-taper sconces. And now it was homework by candelabra.

Pippa didn't know where it had come from or where it was headed; but she enjoyed candles, and the house could do with a bit of holiday cheer. Anyone's holiday. The more the merrier.

"There *isn't* any math," said Winterbelle.

Poker-faced. (Her tone of voice made Pippa look.) The girl's hair, pale and dry as beech leaves stuck to their twigs, bleaching in December sun, hung coarse and straight to her little shoulders. She wore an old t-shirt of her mom's as an outer garment over a turtleneck jumper. Here and there some extremity bulged with a warmer, a wrap, an extra layer of socks. It was hard to tell where the girl's actual physical substance began and the several protective layers around it left off. Pippa decided she was bluffing.

"What's 6 times 9?" she demanded.

"Mom," said Winterbelle, grimacing, "we're *finished* with multiplication."

"Oh? What are you working on now?" said Pippa.

The girl said, "Word problems," and promptly regretted it. Her mom discovered irrefutable evidence jammed into a secret pocket of her backpack.

"Two pages of this book that face each other have numbers that, multiplied together, equal 506. What are they?"

"I give up," said Winterbelle.

"No dessert," said Pippa.

"Oh all right. *Give* it to me."

Pippa gave her beloved miniature self a whump on the well-padded bottom.

"Mommy?" said Winterbelle, turning her elfin face upward. The symmetry of her features, nose and mouth and eyes, suggested the elder rune *Algiz*, used magically to petition the Valkyries. The Valkyries are thought to serve gods younger than themselves—battle gods no less—escorting dead guys through the upper planes; but who knows? Pippa suspected they had motives of their own.

"Yes, dear?" she said motherly, running a finger through the girl's hair which was thick and resilient as a broom.

"Can I wear your scarf to the Snow Festival?"

"My scarf?" said Pippa.

"*You* know." Winterbelle's face went from oversweet to faintly tart. Her chapped lips grew firm.

Of course Pippa knew: the deep (so deep as to be almost black) indigo silken square from which seven silver stars, the Pleiades, peeked out as you twirled and rearranged it about your shoulders. It was a simple thing, really, but it felt good, filled with subtle energies, and Pippa seldom wore it, preferring to use it as an altar cloth. She had elevated to an art form the arrangement of ritual objects on the fabric so that the stars shone through and the whole composition became precisely tuned to the cosmos. Like a tabletop Zen garden. Only interactive.

"I don't know," she said. "I kind of hate . . ."

"You kind of hate getting the vibes messed up," recited Winterbelle. "I *know* that. But I'll be careful. I'm a natural, you told me so."

"I don't know," repeated Pippa. Honestly she did not. "What is this Snow Festival, anyway?"

"Christmas," said Winterbelle. "Only they can't call it that. And it's not religious, only it's okay for students to wear religious symbols of their choice as long as they're tasteful. So I wanted to wear your scarf."

Pippa wondered if there were such things as tasteless religious symbols. But of course there were.

Severed heads.

Shiva screwing Shakti.

Stigmata.

"When's the Snow Thing?" she asked Winterbelle.

"The day of the Solstice," the girl said, impatient and stern. "You know: Yule?"

"Ah." At last, a term she understood.

Next month Winterbelle would be ten: a Capricorn with the Moon in her first house, Libra rising. Very cool, very psychic; though also with an odd Earthy spin that Pippa was not sure what to make of. Her daughter did not seem like an Earth creature. She seemed, if anything, like one of those amazing Russian gymnasts: girls as tiny and powerful as dwarves in their mountain caves, only able to leap, to dance in the air, to fly with arena lights shimmering through their invisible wings.

Compared to her spritely daughter, Pippa felt mundane and ill defined. Her own hair came up short of blond (the modifier applied most commonly was "dirty") and her features, though pleasantly formed, did not quite manage to be pretty, except in those hours when she was truly happy and a redemptive, all-forgiving light welled up from the bottoms of her eyes. Most days she did not feel like that and worked hard to avoid being seen as mousy.

Anyway, even the life of an air sprite is hardly peaches & cream. Pippa heard on public radio that those gymnasts were overworked by their trainers, forced to exercise hours a day, fed strange experimental diets, and given drugs to delay the onset of puberty; because once the womanly processes began there would be no dancing in the air any longer. Menstruation grounded you, it appeared: lowered your center of gravity, padded your muscles with adipose tissue, terrified you with mysterious cravings and dreads, and ultimately plugged you into those ancient, oceanic surges and dark, primordial seepings that revealed your true nature, or the nature of Nature Herself. Pippa sighed.

Still, she thought, Winterbelle had a couple of years to go. A couple of years left to fly in.

"Okay?" the girl pressed her.

And Pippa said, "Yes," though she had forgotten what the question was. In a way it didn't matter. Life was full of questions, and—for better and for worse—

"Yes"

had always been Pippa's answer.

Aunt Eulace said:

"More dirt food, I presume."

Meaning, organic produce Pippa could barely afford but purchased for many reasons, not one of which she felt moved to iterate over the dinner table. In her aunt's mind, the notion of photosynthesizing organisms growing in actual soil was laden with unsanitary, maybe scatological, connotations.

They were having soup. Vegetable noodle, ladled into salt-glazed bowls Pippa had gotten cheap at a pottery outlet tent sale. As each helping cooled, she stirred in red miso; you couldn't boil miso with the other ingredients because the helpful microorganisms would be killed. Eulace would not knowingly have welcomed the bacterium *Aspergillus hatcho* into symbiotic company with her digestive tract; but it would lower her risk of colon cancer anyway. Pippa foresaw her aunt living to a goodly age, then seizing up one summer evening while shouting at Bill Moyers.

"Try a spoonful," she told Winterbelle.

Eulace grunted, throwing doubt upon the wisdom of this. Her expiring perm leaned slightly to the left. There was something of Pippa's dead mother in her cheekbones, but nothing about the eyes. The mouth had distended downward over the years via gravity and dourness. The chin was, tragically, lost.

Winterbelle slurped: a positive sign, though Eulace did not hear it that way.

"Try not to eat so loudly," Pippa urged. Genuinely trying to be helpful.

"Some of these people in the cities," said Eulace, speaking in a code Pippa long ago learned to decipher, "don't even know how to cook. They get all their food out of cans they get free from the government."

Winterbelle frowned, regarding a chunk of something mysterious in the hollow of her spoon. "Is that true, Mom?"

Under the table, Pippa patted her daughter's knee. This too was a code. Winterbelle well understood it.

How freely we communicate! Pippa thought. Bridging the generations, one woman to another: Maiden, Mother and Crone. The timeless torture of dinnertime.

"I read in the paper," said Eulace, "about that woman who's suing the school board."

Which rang a bell with Pippa, though the *Herald* seldom got squeezed into her crannies of reading time. Right now she was picking her way through a book about the dark goddesses of Northern Europe, viewed from a postfeminist perspective.

"She *claims*," said Eulace, "that certain teachers are using New Age mind-control techniques to advance a hidden agenda of godlessness and One World ideology."

"Oh, for heavens sake," said Pippa. She couldn't help herself.

Eulace awoke to this incitement. "Well, it wouldn't surprise *me*," she said. "I've known for years these young teachers were off on some kind of tangent. It started with Peace. Then there was Sex Ed. Now that's old hat. And what they call Art in the Classroom is nothing more than pornography. You mark my words. There's something bad going on in these schools, and if this woman can drag it out into the open then I say, more power to her."

Pippa felt noodles lumping together near her heart. The soup could have used a hint of pungence, something mustardy, to draw the ingredients together. Things should blend, not stick out separately, she felt.

"Could you get me some water, dear?" Eulace asked her. Flashing, for the record, a smile that would have done nicely for Hansel & Gretel's stepmother, waving goodbye in the forest.

"I'll do it," Winterbelle volunteered, popping up.

This had to be a ruse. Once gone from the dining room, she was out of sight. She could be up to anything.

Pippa lifted the napkin from her lap; then she blew her air out and relaxed. Let the Maiden keep her secrets, as best she could. There was such a thing as knowing too much, shining too much light on things. The world could do with a bit more darkness.

Darkness and
mystery.

Daily-ritual-wise, her job at Rose Petal & Thorn suited Pippa to a T.

The store was about 10 minutes' walk from Ash Street, a couple of blocks past Winterbelle's school. The hours were reasonable, and if something weird came up, you could drag in a wee bit late. The boss, Brenda Cigogne, from Providence, didn't care how you dressed or how you acted, as long as you evinced some rudimentary grasp of the concept of style. *Personal* style. A girl is only as good as her attitude, was how Brenda looked at it. She had taken one quick glance (the only kind she took) at Pippa's pentagram earrings on what amounted to Out of the Broom Closet Day, one of those *rites de passage* that you have to get through sooner or later, and declared:

"I *love* Native Americans. All the *elements*." Rolling her eyes reverentially skyward. "Our society has grown so sterile. Young people today are so much more *sensible* than we were."

Anyway, Pippa found the pentagram earrings unbecoming. Too geometric for her. She preferred the organic swirls of Newgrange spirals and triskeles, inspired and imperfect things, living forms. She also had tiny Minoan goddesses, heavy pewter Trees of Life, Kokopellis, wolves howling, dolphins leaping, fairies dancing, a few permutations of the silver-and-turquoise motif, and many, many Moons. Any and all of which seemed more deeply spiritual to her than a five-pointed star inside a circle. Thank you very much.

As heresies went, that was as far as Pippa inclined. Otherwise she believed herself to be a run-of-the-bowling-alley sort of person. She did what felt right and tried to keep her karma clean. She taught her daughter to honor the Earth and respect all living things. Mostly she kept her mouth shut, except for that one time at Halloween with the reporter.

"Dear *God*," exclaimed Brenda Cigogne—her voice unnecessarily loud, given that it issued from only a few feet above Pippa's ears—"I do hope nobody comes in and *sees* me like this."

I.e., standing on a stool behind the counter, in the workspace where floral art was created, getting fitted out as a Bad Fairy.

Pippa said through gritted teeth (lest she swallow pins): "Quit squirming around."

"I am not *squirming*," her boss declared.

Brenda was active in the Theatre, a word she thought and spelled Continentally, and this year had gotten herself involved in a children's production of some well-loved tale (Pippa was not sure which; neither it appeared was Brenda), her role in which entailed being *most* put out at not having been invited to the presentation of the infant heroine. Her costume was beautiful, if a little bit over the top: opulent folds and layers of black moiré, spangled with foil sparkles in many colors, and sprouting from the shoulders two extravagant stems of a naked rosebush, the old-fashioned kind with thorns you could scrape barnacles off a hull with.

"Wow," Pippa said, in honest admiration, while Brenda shimmied and squirmed to get the dress down over her preened, sumptuous body. "That is truly great."

"Thank you, dear," the Bad Fairy said, accepting this, in addition to martyrdom, as her due.

Pippa pressed her lips tight, wondering whether her skills as a seamstress were up to the task of reshaping this garment into conformity with the flesh of Brenda Cigogne. One way or the other she needed the money. She sighed; then, hearing herself, added by way of explanation:

"I wish *I* had one of these."

"Where would you wear it?" said Brenda, turning this way and that.

"Probably nowhere. Just around the house." Pippa could see herself. Swishing from room to room. In the morning sunlight. Listening to a Gabrielle Roth tape, low Indian drums thumping out of Winterbelle's boom box, with these intensely antlerlike objects poking up from her shoulders endangering life and property. What a hoot.

"What a waste," said Brenda. "You could at least drive to Dan Dan's for a pizza."

Pippa laughed (careful about the pins). "I like that guy who works there. The one with the big eyes."

Brenda shrieked. Which seemed at first a surprisingly heartfelt reaction (perhaps a stab of jealousy?) but she then bellowed:

"Damnation. You *pricked* me."

A baker's dozen parakeets (including three especially nice yellow ones: Urd, Verdanti & Skuld) shrieked in off-key chorus from their cages above the sink. You could forget these birds for hours at a time, then suddenly the racket they made would overwhelm you, and you would be struck by the oddness of tropical animals existing at all in a place with long and dark and often joyless winters. Two hundred years ago, a real native parakeet had lived in the Carolinas, and Pippa reflected almost daily—whenever she noticed the captives—that *Amazonia carolina* would probably have made a better candidate for overwintering in Maine, had it not been hunted to extinction for no good reason at all.

"Keep still," she warned Brenda. "I've got to stick a couple more pins in."

"Hurry," Brenda fretted. "I just *know* that someone whom I do not wish to find me this way is about to come walking through that door."

Thwang.

Never question the prophecies of a fairy, Bad or not. Out of the gray December afternoon, trailing public-television tote bags and a Jack Russell terrier named Wøf, Mrs. James Willoughby Mallard swept into Rose Petal & Thorn, paused to compose herself, gave a few moments' thought to what she saw poised on a stool before her, and laughed: deep, loudly and long.

"What *are* you?" she asked in due course, drawing near the counter where a few stray petals of Oregon poppy (they shake loose so easily) made cheerful chiffon accents. A few of these, the pastels, might have looked nice pinned to Mrs. Mallard's subdued (to the point of being drab) tweed jacket: draw the eye upward from her jeans and, more bluntly, her boots, which were trafficking in slush.

"A public spectacle," Brenda said ruefully. "Hurry up down there, Pippa, can't you?"

Pippa could. But she preferred to go on mindfully, as before. She smiled toward Mrs. Mallard, who stared back with the lowest possible degree of expression: a bare acknowledgment that they shared a common evolutionary ancestor. Her attention was fixed on another (inner) object.

"Have you seen the *Herald?*" she asked. Down to business, now. Back to her trust-fund Bohemian self.

Brenda (who thought of newsprint chiefly as a medium for keeping cuttings moist) shook her head.

"Well, here it is," pronounced Mrs. Mallard. From a tote bag she produced the offending document. "Take a look at *that.*"

Pippa strained to see, though it was difficult hunched over as she was, with pins sticking out of her mouth.

Brenda scanned the page, moving her lips, until just past the headlines her patience expired.

"For heaven's sake, Mad," she told her friend, "don't make me *read* this."

"Oh, all right." Mrs. Mallard spun the paper on the counter and then patted it, twice, firmly. "It's that woman again. That, what's-her-name. The prayer-in-the-classroom person."

"Ah," said Brenda. She seemed reluctant to comment further. You never could tell when customers might be listening. *Real* customers, not habitual walk-ins like Mrs. Mallard.

"Now she's done with all that," Mrs. Mallard continued. "She's on to new and bigger things. A *satanic cult*, no less. A conspiracy of devil worshipers operating under our very noses. Respected members of the community leading sinister double lives. Children recruited through fantasy role-playing games. Unspeakable rites at hidden locations on the mountain. Drums beating in the middle of the night, animal remains, babies stolen and sacrificed. Dear God it just goes on and on. And mind you, not a *shred* of evidence.

Not a single witness. Just that one horrible woman. What *is* her name, damn it?"

"Carol Aaby?" hazarded Pippa. Connecting one thing with another.

Mrs. Mallard did not appear to have heard. "What amazes *me*," she said (not sounding amazed at all), "is that they keep *printing* this poppycock. That woman clucks her tongue and a full transcript appears next Thursday afternoon. Never a *syllable* of opposing points of view. Why are we so afraid of these people?"

"They're just big bad wolves," Brenda said, having scanned the store for members of the pack. "All huffing and puffing. Nothing better to do with their time."

"I suppose." Mrs. Mallard folded the newspaper and returned it to her bag.

Pippa said, "Didn't the wolf gobble up the first two pigs, though?"

"Not in the Scholastic Books version," said Brenda. "After that my boys lost interest."

"But in the real story," said Pippa.

"What real story?" said Brenda.

Mrs. Mallard shook her head. "The real story here is a determined assault on our tradition of tolerance. Sowing suspicion in the minds of people who really don't know any better. Pitting neighbor against neighbor, turning us all into a bunch of tattletales and snoops. It's about whether this is still a place where one can voice an opinion of one's own without being burned at the cross for it."

"The stake," said Pippa.

Mrs. Mallard nodded, distractedly. "It *strikes*," she declared, "at the very underpinnings of our democracy."

Brenda was no longer listening, preoccupied with her own underpinnings, which she anxiously had entrusted to

Pippa. For her part, Pippa identified with the little pigs. She said:

"So like, did she mention anybody in particular? Who's supposed to be doing these satanic rituals and all?"

"Well you see that's just the *point*. She leaves it all purposefully vague. That way one is free to suspect anyone at all. Or everyone. It could be you—" (nodding to the Bad Fairy) "—or me, or even Pippa here."

"Piffle," said Brenda.

Mrs. Mallard lifted her gaze, oratorically. "The *question* is, who has the nerve to stand up and oppose them? Have we run out of heroes? Do we have to wait for the whole ghastly process to play itself out, like the McCarthy era?"

Brenda shook her head in sympathy: aware that her friend was agitated, though perhaps not entirely clear about what. "Pippa," she suggested, "why don't you pour Mad some cider."

Pointedly, Pippa inserted one last pin. Meanwhile Mrs. Mallard helped herself to a cookie shaped like a Christmas tree, the same color they sometimes dye pistachios.

"Why are trees so cheap these days?" she asked of no one in particular. "It's as though the growers were desperate."

A parakeet uttered a sound like Bloit.

"Bloit," said Pippa back. "Bloit bloit."

"You talk to birds?" asked Mrs. Mallard, raising a single brow. The idea seemed to please her as well as to confirm certain suspicions.

"I talk to birds all the time," Pippa said. "And they talk back. Only I don't think we understand each other."

Brenda and Mrs. Mallard exchanged looks. They did not bother with being subtle. Suddenly Mrs. Mallard laughed. "That becomes more amusing," she said, "the more you think about it."

Brenda frowned, unwilling to hazard such an investment in thought. But the compliment paid her protégée appeared to hearten her. "Yes," she said. "Pippa and I do keep each other amused in here. We have to! There's no one else to talk to."

"Except the birds," noted Mrs. Mallard.

"*Exactly,*" said Pippa.

Brenda pivoted on the stool, inspecting her form in the mirror normally used to check floral arrangements for symmetry. "Well, girls. How do I look?"

"Wicked and cunning," said Mrs. Mallard.

"Pretty cool," said Pippa.

Brenda beamed for about five more seconds. Then she grabbed Pippa by the shoulder and launched herself floorward, returning to Earth with a grunt. Pippa blinked at a frightful thorn seven millimeters from her left pupil.

"I don't know how you keep your figure, Mad," Brenda Cigogne said, her eyes practically emitting dotted lines in the direction of her friend's stomach.

"A barren womb," Mrs. Mallard declared.

Pippa's attention sharpened immediately. Brenda's did also; both women watched the third, checking slyly for clues as to how Mrs. Mallard had intended this. With a hint of wistfulness? Perfectly serene? Proud of having attained a Certain Age, and then some, without the pain and the tumult of children?

Mrs. Mallard enigmatically smiled, puffing steam across her paper cup of cider, then gave them an expertly unreadable wink.

"Tell her, Pippa," she said. "If you want to keep your hips where God put them, don't let any little heads come shoving their way out of there."

Brenda scoffed. "That leaves *her* out, then. Pippa's daughter is almost as old as my youngest."

"Really?" Mrs. Mallard wrinkled her eyes with deepening intrigue. "You don't look old enough . . ."

To be what? Pippa wondered, as the sentence faded, unfinished. A mother? A grown-up? What? She knew it was something, that some part of her remained, in spite of everything, underdeveloped or incomplete, and that other people could see it, too. But what part, exactly?

She sighed. "I'm old enough."

And the other women nodded. Bored with the topic, probably. Ready to move on to something else. And who cared, anyway? It was all just women's talk.

"Listen to us!" Brenda said. "The three of us are a regular cabal."

"Coven," said Pippa.

"Once upon a time," Pippa said quietly, with absolute conviction, "the world was full of giants. And these giants fought with the elves for control of the seasons. They wanted it to be winter all the time, because they had thick skin and lots of hair and weren't bothered by ice and snow. Whereas the elves wanted summer to last and last. They needed warmth and sunshine to make the forest grow, so they would have a place to live. Every time the giants lay down to sleep, the elves would sneak out and dance and sing so the Sun would return and the Earth would come to life. Then the giants would wake and get all in a rage and stomp around knocking trees down with mighty blows of their hammers."

"Is this some kind of myth?" Winterbelle wanted to know. She lay curled in her cupboard bed, only her head and two small hands, clutching the comforter, sticking out.

"Shh," said Pippa. "Maybe I'm making the whole thing up just now. What difference does it make?"

"I just wondered. We're studying World Mythology."

"This isn't a myth," said Pippa. "So: It was about this time that the first humans appeared."

Winterbelle said, "From where?"

"From somewhere. Wherever they came from. The body of Mother Earth, I guess. Only they weren't humans the way we are today. They were more like gods. There was a clan called the Vanir, who were hunters and fishermen. They herded reindeer and they lived in the great northern forests. Most of the time they stayed out of the giants' way. They had dealings with the elves, but there was a lot of mistrust there. Some elves wanted to be friendly while others were mean. So mostly the Vanir went their own way. They had alliances where they needed them, all around the Arctic Circle. They learned magic from a horse god in Siberia. The tree spirits taught them woodcraft. And some people say they traveled all the way to Canada, which was ruled by a bear queen then, to learn how to work with leather and fur. In return, they taught the others the secrets of boatbuilding and navigation.

"Everything was fine until one year when the giants gained an advantage in their endless war. That year the Sun did not come back at all, and the Earth stayed frozen. After a while the Vanir had eaten up their food supplies and burned up most of their fuel. The situation was desperate, but no one knew what to do. The men wanted to go out and do battle with the giants, but the women were afraid they would get killed and things would be even worse Finally a young girl named Pathfinder had a dream in which she was lost in a terrible blizzard, when a great white wolf appeared before her. The wolf said:

" 'Kill me and you will learn what you need to know.'

"The girl didn't want to kill the wolf. She had no idea how to go about killing such a big strong animal. But the wolf was quite insistent and its will was hard to resist. So

Pathfinder picked up a rock and hurled it at the wolf, striking it between its huge yellow eyes. A hole opened up in the wolf's forehead, and all of its power came pouring out. It was like a river of warm milk, melting the snow and floating Pathfinder away very peacefully—sort of holding her up and rocking her gently to sleep.

"Well, the girl awoke and told her dream to some of the old Vanir women, the grandmothers. And the grandmothers talked among themselves for a while, debating what this could mean. One of the old women said this milk was the sperm of a god that would fertilize the earth and make everything fruitful. Another woman said, Forget the sperm, we need that wolf's meat. Still another grandmother said, If a white wolf spoke to *me* like that, I'd have a few questions for him. The girl Pathfinder said, I think the wolf was a woman. Finally the oldest grandmother of all, who was sitting back in the shadows listening to the others talk, cleared her throat and she said, Don't you know what that dream means? Well, listen and I'll tell you."

"Mom," said Winterbelle, in the very moment that her mother dramatically paused.

"Hm?" said Pippa. Full of her story, slightly breathless.

Winterbelle propped herself on one elbow, stretching the white cotton of her nightdress. "Could we hear the rest of the story later?"

"Sure, sweetie. You want to just go right to sleep?"

Winterbelle shook her head. Her eyes glinted in the darkness like pale planets. She said, "I want you to tell me about my father."

Which pretty well knocked the bedtime routine off its runners.

Pippa felt her heart grow warm and then cool, as though she had spilled tea down her shirt.

But of course, she thought. Of course. It had to happen sooner or later.

"Sure," she said, touching her daughter's arm, settling deeper into the cupboard bed. "What would you like to know?"

"Just *something,*" said Winterbelle. Her expression was thoughtful, but unfocused. She might have been collecting material for a private nighttime project, a do-it-yourself dream. "From when the two of you used to be together."

Pippa smiled. "You wouldn't believe how *little* it's possible to remember about a thing like that. It was really important at the time, though. I was in love, in a major way. And I was young. We both were young. We picked out candles at a gift shop. He wanted lots of different sizes and colors. We spent whole nights just watching them burn, snuggled up on the sofa together. He talked me into going out to Hawaii with him."

"You went to Hawaii?" Winterbelle frowned: this was a new one.

"No. *He* did. By that time we weren't together anymore. But he talked me *into* going. I mean, I agreed. I was ready to go with him. But it was winter at the time, see, and you'll agree to just about anything then. Anything to get out of winter. He didn't leave till the spring. And by then everything was different."

"You were pregnant with me."

"Not just. But you know that part of the story."

Winterbelle settled onto her back. She stared at the roof of the cupboard bed, whose opening was jigsawed out of birch plywood into the shape of swan wings. Pippa had painted the upswept feathers herself, in the folksy gay style known (at least in the shelter mags) as *rosemaling,* after her Witch friend Judith did the carpentry. It was totally neat.

"Time to go to sleep," Pippa said, kissing her daughter's

beautiful elfin nose, the warm hair above one ear, and a hand that clutched her as she was standing up.

"Mommy, talk to me some more," the sleepy girl said.

"In the morning."

"Now." Smiling, eyes closed.

"I love you."

"Love you too."

That was as much of a ritual as they had, the two of them. Yet when they lay in their separate rooms, their separate worlds and bodies, their two minds flowed somehow together, now and again, and it seemed that saying more, saying anything, had not really been necessary.

Just
nice.

Witching hour.
Watching hour.

Well past bedtime for worldly folks.
Weird. And worth the wait.

Now willows become witches, and walk.
Men become wolves; wolves men.
Monsters matter.
Worries worm inward; reason recedes.

Darkness doubles.
The Moon looks on: a mystery.
Mothers step out, stepmothers in. Godmothers guard.
Fairies fly. Wild Eldric rides.

Pippa creeps past Eulace's bedroom, down the curving stair, into a coatroom as still and cold as a tomb. She slides a black cloak over the scarf with seven silver stars. Gathers her bag. Unbolts the oaken door. Becomes a night thing, sliding without sound between shadows. Entering her element.

A screech owl shrieks, like a pain-crazed cat.

Welcome, Sister, Pippa interprets.

"Hey," she whispers. "Same to you."

The mountain rumbles down to meet her. Wabenaki: named for a nation nearly dead. Powerful people, once. Defenders of Vinland against Pippa's own distant kin. Their own word for the mountain meant Sees Across the Water. Now a thing that the mountain must have seen has swept the name-givers away. The place is a state park. Weekend wilderness, wheelchair-accessible. Camping by permit only.

For all of that, the mountain rumbles down, and no fence bars the Night Thing's stealthy ascent. Step at a time, up the slope along a path made familiar by many nights, unnumbered footfalls, Moons of many names and phases. This time, the waning sliver of Long Nights Moon rests hazily, barely risen, in a nest of fibrous cloud. Stars burn through like laser beams, surgically tiny and precise.

And the *cold:*

So cold, even trees must resent it. They bend and snap like whips, lashing the Night Thing for her trespasses. Press ahead, though. Up and up, Moonward, zagging like electric bolts, hands up on boulders, declivities where you remember purple trilliums blooming at Beltane. Ghost-gray lichens there glisten in the night. Frozen ferns underfoot, crunching. The snow has a dryness of Styrofoam, a fine sheen of chintz.

Beauty and loneliness.

Landscape with witch.

She had made her magic circle at a level place, a sort of plateau. Nothing big or fancy: a few rocks added to a ring already in place. Only two paces across; who knew what it was, or had been? Or who, first of all, had arranged it? The Night Thing assumed its stewardship, not knowing.

An Indian name for magician was motewolon. There were fairies called Negumwasucks. Even in Vinland, the

Little People lived furtively. The Night Thing, entering her consecrated space, got the feeling of stepping into a room where a long, long conversation had not even halted, just paused. It was hers to pick up; keep lively. Pass along.

You cast a circle with a wand, turning clockwise. You can also use an athame or ritual blade. The Night Thing, who had climbed far, traveled light and made do with her Santa Fe knife. Once the circle is drawn, none may enter or depart; only, by general consent, small children and cats. Witchcraft is, after and above all, a practical matter. Safe now, you can settle yourself, arrange your magical tools, call upon the local spirits, light a fire. Favored deities may be invited and those of malign aspect warned off. The Night Thing moved quickly from quarter to quarter, dispensing marvelous objects in their proper order, East through North: Red, White, Green and Black: the hand we are dealt of elements, seasons, primal powers, points of the compass, states of mind. The Night Thing was feeling sanguine, particularly. Premenstrual, perhaps. Anyway displaced.

She liked to hum or whistle while focusing her energies, awakening the spirits of the stones. Rhythms and tunes would arise in her mind, often by odd association. She did not let inappropriateness distract her. The most transcendent music she knew came from religions not her own: other people's graspings for their gods.

Pie Jesu,
Qui tollis peccata mundi,
Dona eis requiem.

Agnus Dei,
Qui tollis peccata mundi,
Dona eis requiem.

. . . The part about the lamb especially, with its hazy recall of a Middle Eastern blood rite. So very primal and intense.

She had brought Hanukkah candles, sticks of strong incense whose smoke stung her nasal passages in the icy air, a miniature cauldron of hammered brass to fill with snow and suspend above a pile of burning sticks. She had brought cake she made herself, from scratch, for the Negumwasuck. Wine for Freya, who enjoyed a bit of worldly indulgence. A wreath of bittersweet and sage, discarded from Rose Petal & Thorn when the berries began to drop.

She arranged these things and rearranged them—as though the exact placement of every object, the angle of drift of the smoke, the lumen count from the candles, together provided a means of fine-tuning the magical energies of the circle, the way you would twiddle with a radio transmitter. In a meditation class she had learned that the tiniest thought, projected at your deepest level of awareness, could alter the whole fabric of manifestation. So she imagined that the humblest spell, cast from a perfectly balanced circle, would ripple outward irresistibly, fetching up sympathetic waves from the Otherworld. And ultimately, of course, rippling back. Multiplied threefold, they say: you can believe that or not. Most witches do. It's like the Golden Rule with an enforcement clause.

She had no great plans for tonight. It was not a full Moon nor was it one of the high holy days, the Sabbats: Solstices and Equinoxes, Samhain, Midwinter, Beltane and Lugnassad. It was just a time, or a No-time, an interval between. Midnight clear, two days before Yule.

She had climbed up to her circle with the half-formed idea of sitting there and letting her mind come to rest, cracking open her awareness to the energies of the season, winter on the wax; but now that she was here and those untame energies were gusting through her, mixing with her own, she felt restive and unquiet. Insufficiently protected. Crouching low among the stones, she squirreled down into the warmth of her parka. She closed her eyes.

Worldly thoughts floated into her consciousness like smoke curling up from the village far below.

She thought of Brenda Cigogne and Rose Petal & Thorn. Holiday music. A glitter of tinsel. The worn carpet tracked with snow.

She thought of the older woman, Mrs. Mallard. Dryness of gin scratching the words in her throat.

She thought of Kaspian: the chocolate-mint eyes and cheeks as pink and white as a candy cane.

Lastly (and not for lack of trying to avoid it) she thought of his stepmother, Carol Deacon Aaby. Object of much attention, Pippa gathered. Provoker of controversies. Storm center of Pippa's swirling thoughts.

She raised a hand, sweeping it sideways, right to left: a gesture of banishment.

"Be gone," she commanded, and the spectre of thought obeyed her.

She opened her eyes again.

The world had changed.

It was always changing, of course. The Earth was caught in Time, cascading down it like a ball swept over a waterfall. But occasionally the change was more detectable; you could turn your head quickly and catch it at the corner of her eyes.

Pippa stared between the jutting bonewhite trunks of birch on the mountainside and out, immeasurably far out, above the rooftops of the village. Pinkish-white streetlights; the Congregationalist steeple with its illuminated clock; the row of crimson safety lights on the back end of a lonely semitruck, making its way northward, toward Canada. The world appeared in that cold moment to be an enchanted, sparkling place: as perfectly organized as a game board, with all the pieces assembled in their right places, waiting for the dice to fall.

Maybe that's what witches do, Pippa thought. Jiggle the world just a little, to influence the tumbling of the dice. Give a tiny tilt to the odds, the squint-eyed and coldhearted statistics according to which the physical universe is run.

The thought pleased her. Then it vanished; tumbled down the cataract. She had a sense of returning to herself, to her own body and her immediate situation.

Holy shit, thought Pippa. It's *freezing* up here.

She clapped her hands together and puffed up the pile of burning sticks. She hopped about, agitating her limbs. Then, laying her head far back, she gave a whoop: a full-throated holler that flew and bounced in the darkness.

And as she heard her own voice, echoing and strange, and saw the Moon burning low behind the fringe of fir on the mountaintop, and felt the North Wind at her shoulder, just waiting there, biding its time, she knew that magic was happening already: it was running through her veins; it was flashing behind her eyes; it was filling her and spilling out, joining the great living current. The magic made her feel warm, and lucky, and powerful, and able to share these things with the people she loved.

Thinking this, she raised her arms slowly, until they were aimed high into the blackness. She focused her will into the chakra or energy nexus that lies at the back of the throat. Then she packed all that will into a single wish that she spoke either loudly or quietly, or perhaps not at all, but commandingly all the same, into the attentive fastness of the night.

And the night heard
but it did not
answer.

The man's voice on the telephone said:

"Ms. Rede?"

—but for an instant Pippa did not recognize her own name. Not because of anything unusual about the voice or the way the words were enunciated; and not because she was unaccustomed to hearing herself addressed this way. No. Something else: a sensation that came out of the telephone handset not much different than a tingle of electricity, a low-amperage shock. And while it lasted, that was all she could feel.

"Ms. Rede?" the voice said again. Sounding puzzled now. She must have been silent for a strikingly long time.

"Here," she said. As though responding to a roll call. "Yes—I'm here."

"Ms. Rede."

Was this the only thing the caller (whose voice she did not recognize) intended to say?

Brenda Cigogne looked on, eyes arched, blatantly curious. Pippa tugged at the long cord of the handset, pulling the phone around the end of the counter, turning away. Into illusory privacy.

The voice said: "This is Mr. Martens. Calling from the school?"

"Oh of course." Though there was no reason she should have known this. The guidance counselor: a bland-faced man she had spoken to maybe twice. Never on the phone. Never while working at Rose Petal & Thorn. With customers and Chanticleer tapes and agitated parakeets complicating the task of understanding.

Pippa waited and Mr. Martens waited on the other end. Finally he said, "I'm calling to ask you . . . to ask your consent. Regarding your daughter. Ah, Winterbelle."

Sound of papers being moved.

Pippa experienced a chilly sensation around her neck, the way it feels when you suddenly unwrap a scarf. She touched it with a finger, near the jugular. Blood thumped. Everything was fine.

"What do you want?" she spoke into the handset. "My consent for what?"

Mr. Martens cleared his throat and (it sounded like) shifted his weight in a squeaky, institutional chair. "What we'd like to do," he said now gently, "is just have your daughter spend a little time with a lady . . . well, a psychologist . . . who visits our school from time to time. It's all quite informal. We'll be using my office and, ah, of course I'll be present. Just for the record."

Blood continued to thump beneath Pippa's finger.

"What record?" she said. "What are you talking about?"

Mr. Martens had found the pace of the conversation now. "Simply what I've told you. Ms. Rhinum—the psychologist—visits our school on a contractual basis. She's quite skilled and the children feel perfectly comfortable with her. All we'd like to do is have your daughter . . . Winterbelle . . . sit down with her for a few minutes. Half an hour at most. And just, explore some things. Strictly for her own benefit. And as I said, I'll be there as well."

Pippa began to move across the floor, away from the counter, tugging hard against the telephone cord. She felt sweat gathering on the plastic grip. "Is something the matter?" she said. "Has Winterbelle done something?"

"What would she have done, Ms. Rede?" said Mr. Martens. More gently than ever.

So now, thought Pippa, he's interrogating *me*. An old anxiety gripped her: the fear of saying the wrong thing, making a bad impression. It angered her, feeling this way. Being *made* to feel this way.

"Why won't you tell me what this is about?" she said. Her voice had gotten louder. Overcompensating.

"This is about nothing, really. Just a routine sort of thing we like to do now and then. If you will, a precaution." Mr. Martens had settled into the cadence of those recorded voices that prompt you to make a selection from the choices below. "We like to ascertain that our children are functioning well within the educational setting. That's what Ms. Rhinum is here to help us with."

"Ms. Rhinum is there?" said Pippa.

(Nothing.)

Pippa said, "Could I talk to her?"

"Ah—" Sound of murmured consultation, off-mike. "Ms. Rede, I'm afraid that, under the circumstances . . ."

Pippa had twisted herself around in the phone cord and was staring at Brenda Cigogne, though she barely realized this. All she registered was the look in her boss's eyes. Round, alert . . . alarmed? Feeling the blood reddening her face, Pippa turned away again.

"Look," she said into the telephone. "You need my permission for this, right?"

"Well, um, not actually." Mr. Martens took a heavy,

audible breath. You could almost feel the presence of another listener at his end. Co-conspirator. "No. Not under
these circumstances. But it would be helpful if you would
agree to cooperate voluntarily. That would be much better, I
think, for everyone. For Winterbelle especially. And for you."

Pippa felt her knees weaken. Sun poured through the Mill
Street window, giving the flower shop a hallucinatory glaze.

"Can't you just, *explain* this all to me?" Shocked, hearing
her own voice. So helpless and childlike.

"There's really nothing to explain," Mr. Martens
smoothly lied.

"I don't believe you," Pippa told him. Her voice was
stretched thin. "I want to know what you're doing with
my daughter."

"Now Ms. Rede—" Mr. Martens began, but she hung
up on him.

"Is something the matter, dear?" Brenda Cigogne asked
her. The concern in her voice was complex and, Pippa
thought, at least two-sided.

"Yes there is," she replied. Stepping back behind the
counter. Her feet moved in a jerky, uncoordinated way.
The telephone receiver felt weightless in her hand. "Something's the matter," she said. "Only I don't know what."

The afternoon cracked open. And through the hole poured
customers, music, floral arrangements, pallid sunlight,
Brenda Cigogne's animated and nonsensical chatter. A
dawdle of matrons sniffing at plasticky cyclamens. A skeletal, gray-skinned man so stooped with age that he might
have done better on all fours, who asked for "One *red*
rose, if I may, please," with overdramatized, Old World
gentility—then *charged* it, which meant filling out a whole
separate form, to the account of one Norbert Thiess. The
UPS man lugging crates of Iceland poppies shipped over-

night from a greenhouse in New Jersey. A rush order for freesias to be delivered to the credit-card center that had reanimated the carcass of an old mill across the road, in something of the manner of a zombie.

"*Here*, Pippa," Brenda said. She wrapped the freesias snugly in red tissue paper. "Run these over, won't you? There's no telling when Jacques will get back with the van, and the customer seems to be in a god-awful hurry."

"It's the breaks," said Pippa.

Brenda sighed. "That's a good way to look at it."

"No, I mean . . . they only get 30-minute lunch breaks there. Probably that's what the hurry's about."

Brenda rolled her eyes. The travails of the wage-slave class were unknown to her.

Pippa gathered up the armful of flowers and stepped out the door.

Cold possessed her. She was wearing her duck-down coat but had omitted hat and mittens, and now the wind swooping down off Wabenaki Mountain made her forehead ache and her fingers practically insensate. The sun was no help. It only made you squint. Pippa scooted across Mill Street, nearly empty at midday. The credit-card center sprawled over a couple of square blocks, but without an employee pass, the only way in was through the security door, way up the street and around a corner.

Pippa tried walking backwards, so that the wind caught her hair instead of her unprotected skin. It was not too difficult, if you could avoid thinking about what you must look like. Actually it was fun, like a game a kid might invent. (Pang: Winterbelle.) The concrete squares fell away as though a film were being run in reverse. Her shadow dogged her heels. Then

(!)

"—Oh," cried Pippa, regaining her balance after colliding with something or somebody in the middle of the sidewalk. And turning around, flustered, she recognized Brenda's friend and customer Madeleine Mallard.

"I *wondered* if you would," the older woman said, wryly. "And lo and behold, you *did*."

"Sorry," said Pippa. She glanced down shyly, into the bundle of flowers.

Mrs. Mallard smiled and shook her head. "What's that smell?" she said, peering at the red paper wrappings.

"Freesias."

"Oh, goodness. I can't *stand* to have those things indoors."

Pippa smiled, uncertainly. She had to deliver the flowers soon, before the cold shattered their petals.

Mrs. Mallard stepped aside. "I can see you're in a hurry," she said. "Run along now. Drop by and see me sometime, though. I'm on Church Street. You'll see it."

She held Pippa's gaze for a moment longer and there was something odd about her expression. Well, probably there was something odd about Pippa's too.

One thing more:

Just before turning off Mill Street—eyes stinging from the wind, ice forming at the corners of them—Pippa glanced a last time around and Mrs. Mallard was still standing there. Not exactly staring. Watching. Pippa waved but the older woman did not respond. Only stood there: a small dark spot, a shadow, in a blinding, frozen world.

"Nothing," said Winterbelle. "I told you. It was stupid. There were these, I don't know, six or eight or something cardboard boxes with words painted on them. And there was this stuff thrown all over the floor. And they wanted me to take the *stuff* and decide which *box* to put it in. It was like some kind of test. I mean you could *tell* what they were doing."

"What were they doing?" said Pippa.

Winterbelle wrinkled her tidy, upturned nose—her look of private contemplation—without looking at her mother. She was kneeling on the floor in her play area, laying paint in big, color-field swashes across an expanse of poster board. Pippa sat nearby in an old wicker chair, poking a needle distractedly into Brenda's costume. Bad Fairy fabric filled her lap. She watched her daughter carefully.

"They were trying to trick me," Winterbelle said.

"Trick you how?"

"How should *I* know?"

The girl looked cross. Beautifully cross. Candlelight (her regular accompaniment) flowed like molten amber from a phalanx of votive glasses arrayed before her, turning her pale features golden, her hair to perfect spun flax. There was no way to gauge her expression. It might have been saintly, conniving, sarcastic or blank. She was gifted, that way. Pippa herself had always felt totally transparent.

"It was some stupid shrink thing," Winterbelle said unexpectedly. "You know like one of the boxes, it said SECRETS. And another said THINGS THAT SCARE ME. And there was one called, I think it was WISHES or whatever. So I was supposed to, you know, pick up these mangy old dolls and toys and pictures and stuff that looked like somebody's *dog* had chewed them. I mean, you didn't want to even *touch* it. And they wanted me to put it in these *boxes*? So I said—"

Pippa realized, when her daughter paused, that she had been holding her breath. She let it out carefully, not wanting to interrupt. But Winterbelle had simply stopped talking. She was making big sweeps with a sponge drenched in some color that looked nearly black by candlelight. Maybe it was purple.

"You said what?" Pippa asked at last.

Winterbelle looked up as though she had forgotten what

they were talking about. Without changing expression—
as though her mind were elsewhere—she said, "Nothing.
But what I *almost* said was, *I'm* not going to pick this up,
I didn't put it down here. But I didn't."

Not purple. No: Pippa thought it might be some shade
of rust-brown. Tending toward red. A desert color. Winterbelle must be finished with her pink period.

"You didn't?" Pippa prompted.

Winterbelle gave a pleased-with-herself smile. "I just sat
there. I wanted to see how long they would wait. I figured,
well, gym class starts in a little while, and if I'm late
enough I might not have to dress out. I *hate* gym, especially
in winter. All we ever play is like volleyball, or we do
these bogus gymnastics. And the locker room smells like
this kind of, I don't know—poisonous *disinfectant* or
something."

Pippa smiled. She had to. Winterbelle's tenacity, the
fierceness of her opinions, awed and slightly terrified her.
Her own entire memory of fourth grade consisted of hoping she would not be called upon to read her book report aloud.

"So *finally*," the girl said, brushing her hair aside,
allowing her mother at last an unobstructed view, "they
kind of got what I was doing, I guess. Maybe they saw
me looking at the clock or something. So this lady, I
forget her name, but she said, What's the matter? Isn't
there anything you see that you'd like to do something
with? Anything you'd like to put away or get rid of? And
I said, No, I don't think so. And she said, How about *this*,
and she picked up this like gigantic plastic knife with fake
blood all over it. And I thought, Get real. So then she
picked up this little guy like a GI Joe, except he was
dressed in black with a hood over his face. And she was
like, What about this? And I said Uh-uh. So she got this,

I mean, *ugly* doll whose face was covered with spots like she had maybe smallpox or something. And I laughed."

"You laughed?"

"Well, what was I supposed to do? I wasn't going to *touch* it. I mean, it was like covered with *disease* or something."

Winterbelle was so vehement, so indignant, that Pippa began laughing herself. It began with a titter but then, when the valve was opened, the tension seemed to burst out of her, and she ended by rocking forward and back in the wicker chair, laughing loud and heedlessly.

"Oh, sweetie pie," she said. "You really are too much."

Winterbelle smiled and turned inward again. She studied her painting from as high as she could stretch on her knees, then reached across the poster board to retrieve a jar of bright, sunny yellow.

Suddenly she shrieked.

Pippa's body gave a sharp jerk: pure mommy reflex.

"Aaagh!" cried Winterbelle. "I *burned* myself!"

One of the votive glasses had been upset; the candle rolled across the floor, still burning, trailing melted wax.

"Oh my gosh," said Pippa, pushing aside the Bad Fairy costume, hurrying over to her daughter. "Poor sweet thing. Show me where it hurts."

Winterbelle held out a slender forearm: a patch of skin the size of a quarter was reddened but not blistering. Pippa tried to clear her thoughts, to remember what you were supposed to do in situations like this. Cold water? Aloe vera? Vaseline?

"Come on, honey," she said, helping Winterbelle to her feet. The girl moved limply, complaisant, still sobbing, holding her arm away from her as though afraid to look at it. "Let's just go down to the bathroom and we'll see—"

She halted because Winterbelle had stopped crying. The

girl's eyes were open and she seemed, for the moment at least, to have forgotten about her injury.

"Mom," she said. "Look what you've *done."*

Pippa followed her eyes downward.

A sewing needle, trailing black thread, was sticking out of her thigh. It was caught in her jeans and (Pippa realized) in the flesh of her leg.

She hadn't even noticed. She hadn't felt a thing, though now at the sight of the needle a jab of pain shot upward, causing her muscles to clench.

"God, Mom, that's gross," said Winterbelle. "You've got like, a *needle* sticking out of you!"

Pippa hastened to remove it, feeling embarrassed. "Come on, sweetie," she said. "Let's get something on your arm."

"Oh." Winterbelle retracted her arm and stared at it. She flexed the elbow, regarding the damage dispassionately. "It's no big deal," she said. "It's just a stupid burn."

"Come on anyway," said Pippa firmly.

Winterbelle shrugged and marched off along the hallway. Leaving her mom holding a sewing needle and rubbing her thigh.

And wondering
what it all
meant.

She thought she saw Kaspian on the village green. The boy's back was turned—she couldn't be certain it was him—and he was rocking from sneaker to sneaker as though the restless humors inside him would not settle out. Pippa believed that if you stared hard at someone the person would feel it and turn and look at you. But Kaspian (if it was Kaspian) did not turn. She watched his head tilt, his shoulders rise and fall. A tattered cardigan drooped to his knees. A faint westerly breeze fluffed the thick brown hair.

I am the mother of all things, quoted Pippa to herself. And all things should wear a sweater.

As she was walking away, hurrying toward Mill Street, late as usual, she felt a sensation like tickling or tingling at the base of her neck. She stopped and adjusted her scarf but the tickling continued. On an impulse she turned.

From half a block back, someone was watching her. Staring, you might have thought, though the eyes were hidden by distance.

Chocolate-mint eyes, thought Pippa, because she was sure it was Kaspian now. She held his half-seen gaze for another moment or two and then bustled onward, later than usual. Later than ever. The tingling did not cease at the base of her neck.

And then it began to snow.

The snow floated down at first in wide damp flakes like tiny pastries, sugar-white confections. As a girl and again as a young woman (leaving out the troubled time in between) Pippa had liked to capture flakes like that on her tongue, to taste them melting there, and she had invented her own old wives' tale about this: that for every snowflake you caught, there would be one day of happiness in the winter ahead. Now, in the half a block to go before she reached Rose Petal & Thorn, for the first time in many years, she held her tongue out and zigged this way and that along the sidewalk, hoping to squirrel away as much happiness as she could.

The results were a perfect metaphor. If you go chasing after magic, it blows away from you.

Only at the very end—standing on the threshold of the store, close enough to smell the cinnamon and clove from the cider crock—a single fat cluster of many flakes pressed together, spinning down like a maple tree's seedpod, helicopter-style, dropped cleanly into her open mouth and dissolved with a faint taste of steel. As an omen, it was ambiguous. Pippa almost wished she hadn't caught it.

Brenda asked about the Bad Fairy costume. Pippa hedged, though the alterations were almost done. She stepped past the counter into the packing and storage room, hooked her parka over its customary nail, and stared for a minute or longer at a shelfful of sleek, mass-produced ceramic vases, designed to contain one dozen sweetheart roses apiece, tastefully and disposably.

For no reason that she knew, Pippa felt like smashing

them. One at a time. Starting with the pukey washed-out celadon.

Late in the morning, the snow took on a fine, grayish, linty quality, coming from the west, off the mountain, dense as a dust storm. Public schools sent their students home at 1:00 p.m. and canceled the Extended Day program. Pippa spoke briefly on the telephone to Aunt Eulace, who was in no mood to entertain Winterbelle by herself. She doesn't *need* entertaining, Pippa thought, for her daughter was unusually self-contained and would be content alone in her room, painting pictures, or inventing exotic improvisatory dances. But she said nothing because she knew that what bothered Eulace was something rather different: not the fact of Winterbelle but the *idea*: a young girl alone at home while her mother was out doing who knows what. *Working*, Pippa had often pointed out (for they had had just this sort of conversation before), but with Eulace that cut no ice. A woman's place was with her children, Eulace strongly felt—and if no man was readily at hand to do the breadwinning, then whose fault was that? Why, the mother's own. You never *heard* of an unmarried woman raising kids by herself in Eulace's day.

So Pippa asked Brenda for the afternoon off. Brenda gave her the sort of look that Pippa knew she had every right to expect—four days before Christmas, Jacques out with the delivery van stuck in the snow somewhere, employees from the credit card center needing to be waited on *now*—then turned aside with not a mere shrug but a truly operatic swelling and collapse of the shoulders.

"If you feel you must," she sighed, as though Pippa had announced an intention to embark forthwith on a trek through the Himalayas.

"I'm home," she called to Eulace, dragging herself and a ton of encrusted snow through the kitchen door.

But her great-aunt was busy with one of those shows on which ex-somethings accuse one another of having done shameful embarrassing things.

Winterbelle was in her room taking a nap, Pippa's indigo scarf draped beautifully across her narrow shoulders. Pippa, giving in to a powerful instantaneous urge, leaned down and closed her eyes and held her face a couple of inches above her daughter's thin breast: breathing the warmth, the yeasty smell, that rose from the girl's perfect and precious body, wanting to touch her, to enfold her, to *memorize* her somehow. And insensibly also, wanting to weep.

It was just too much. The love, and the utter separateness.

Pippa straightened up and opened her eyes and looked out the window.

The snow had stopped. The sharp slope of Wabenaki Mountain rose shadow-upon-shadow, dreamlike, only partly visible, like something in a Chinese painting.

I guess I ought to think about dinner, Pippa thought. Would carry-out from the Hunan Wok be too much of an indulgence? And would it be worth listening to Eulace's inevitable diatribe about how you just don't know what those people put in their food?

Not until nearly the end of it, when darkness had fallen and Pippa was outside clearing snow from the sidewalk (paying special attention to the hazardous run of concrete steps leading down to Ash Street), did she realize that today had been Yule.

No good witch would have forgotten that. One of the eight high Esbats, pagan precursor to Christmas. A day when, back in the good old trailer-park days, her little circle of women friends would gather at dawn to spiral-dance behind the hedge at Judith's place. The circle was dispersed now, each of the women having gone her own way: lost to warmer climes, stupid relationships, graveyard telemarketing shifts, parenthood, Prozac and apathy.

Still, excuses aside, Pippa should have remembered. She should have made some observance. What the hell kind of a witch *am* I? she wondered.

Not a good one, apparently.

She laid her shovel against the porch rail, where a yellow bug-proof light cast a bizarre glow on things, and picked up her snow-clearing tool of choice: a grizzled broom, veteran of many blizzards. There was no other way, really, to get the sidewalk clean. And you had to do it early, before people trekked in and out and the snow got compacted. When that happened, you might as well give up until April, unless there was some freak midwinter thaw.

The problem was finding the right broom. Most of the things they sold in stores were too flimsy, too pliable: designed for light and carefree dusting-up around the house. What you wanted was a real, old-fashioned broom, worthy of the name—which after all referred to a stiff and resilient plant that was native to windy uplands at the edge of the North Sea. Whether they still made actual brooms from this plant Pippa had no idea, nor where you would obtain such a thing. For her own part, she kept an eye out at the Swap Shop, a little building of corrugated metal on the grounds of the 5-Town Recycling Center. Sooner or later, everything you really and truly needed turned up there. Or at least so it was for Pippa. Other women may have had fairy godmothers; she herself had a dump angel.

She clasped the broom fondly and firmly in her hands. She listened to the dry whisk as it hurled snow from the sidewalk, high and far across the buried lawn. The task was strenuous but relaxing, its rhythm as much a part of winter as the snow itself. Pippa's breathing and heartbeat fell into pace with the sideward swiping of her arms. Snow flew; sweat formed at her forehead; the air felt cold and welcome on her exposed neck.

She finished the job barely in time. No sooner had she made her way to the bottommost concrete step, harrying the surviving pockets of snow over the curb into Ash Street, than a small car of some nondescript grayish-brown—a wolf color—crunched to a stop directly in front of her. The driver's and passenger's doors opened together, and a man and a woman stepped out. Neither of them was familiar. Neither of them smiled.

"Are you Pippa Rede?" the woman inquired.

Pippa might have nodded or she might have said yes. All she remembered thinking at the time was that the woman's jacket was too small for her—a nice dark blue ski jacket, too good to throw away, but it did not quite fit around that large and basically shapeless body. The woman's face, its features and expression, were vague, perhaps purposefully so, and Pippa would later have trouble calling these to mind. But the coat she remembered. And a lapel button—something with a heart, a flower, a slogan.

BELIEVE THE CHILDREN

The man came around the front of the car and was the first to step up onto Pippa's immaculate sidewalk. *His* face she would remember. Long, shaven so close as to be almost shiny, with eyes that drooped in a look of perpetual regret, and lips that rolled inward and out again, damp and pink.

The shapeless woman stepped forward, crowding Pippa on the walk. "Where is your daughter?" she said. Demanded, rather. Her tone of voice startled Pippa, as though there was some urgency involved.

The man stepped cautiously between them. He was taller than both and he appeared to nod amiably, like a doddering relative, as he looked from one of them to the other.

"Ms. Rede," he said, his voice soft as though it had been treated with some tenderizing agent. "My name is Roger Wemble. I'm with the Department of Family Services. I've been asked to come speak with you—"

"Not here," the woman interrupted. "Inside. We need to see the girl. We need to see Winterbelle."

Pippa stared at the two of them, uncomprehending. The man appeared reluctant to meet her gaze, and when he did so it was only to smile apologetically.

"Might we go indoors, Ms. Rede?" he asked.

Pippa nodded dumbly. Turning about, she almost stumbled over her own broom. She led them up the walk, whose surface was dry and firm and quite free of snow.

She never thought to ask why.

The old house was dark and smelled of sesame oil. From the front parlor, loudly, came the sound of gunshots.

The woman with no shape and no distinct features drew up in alarm. Her eyes gyrated in their fleshy sockets. You would have thought she was about to run screaming through the door, or whip out a little aerosol can and Mace everybody. Then she seemed to understand that the gunshots were coming from the fat old Magnavox, faithfully amplifying a real-life-emergency-cop show. Eulace sat on her padded deacon's bench, glaring out toward the unlit hallway, where Pippa halted with their two unexpected visitors. For several seconds no one moved. No one spoke or did anything. On the television, members of an elite SWAT unit pounded a filthy drug dealer into pulp, which was better than he deserved.

"Maybe we ought to go, um—" Pippa motioned uncertainly toward the back of the house "—someplace quieter."

Eulace continued to stare at them. Roger Wemble and the shapeless woman followed slowly, perhaps reluctantly, as Pippa led them down the long hall, through the dining room where the worldly remains of Hunan Special Chicken lay about in paper containers, along with throwaway chopsticks and crumpled paper napkins.

"Sorry," said Pippa. "I haven't had a chance to clean up."

"Do you ever prepare your own meals, Ms. Rede?" asked Roger Wemble. He pulled out of his pocket a little electronic device, some kind of computerized notepad. Glancing up from this, he offered Pippa a make-believe smile.

She gave him no answer. She only stood feeling lost in a nonexistent storm, an imaginary white-out.

"Where is Winterbelle?" the woman demanded.

Roger Wemble pointed his plastic stylus at her. "Ms. Rede," he said, "this is Doctor Allison Rhinum. She is here in a strictly advisory capacity. I believe she has already met your daughter."

"I've assessed Winterbelle," the woman said, as though making a subtle but important correction. "That's the reason for this investigation."

"This *what?*" said Pippa.

Roger Wemble interposed himself. "How many people are domiciled in this residence, Ms. Rede?"

"This is a *home*," said Pippa. "Not a *residence*."

Sternly, Doctor Rhinum said, "Failure to cooperate, Ms. Rede, will be taken very seriously."

"Wait a minute," said Pippa. She held her hands up, shielding herself from further questions while she tried to get all this together in her head. "Could somebody *please* tell me what is happening here?"

Roger Wemble gave her the smile again. "We are making an official visit to your residence," he said—quickly, as though reciting something—"in order to determine whether or not your daughter, who has been found to be a child at moderate risk, is in fact healthy and living in a safe custodial environment." He snapped the lid of the notepad shut. "May we see her, Ms. Rede?"

Pippa stepped back. Literally stepped back. Flabbergasted: panicky.

"You are required to comply," Doctor Rhinum said, bearing down on her. "Should you refuse to comply, we are fully authorized—"

"The Department," Roger Wemble broke in, as gently as possible, "only wishes to determine whether Winterbelle is all right, Ms. Rede. That's what this is about. It's quite straightforward, really."

Pippa allowed herself to feel reassured not because there was anything comforting about his manner, but because she needed to. "All right," she said. "I'll go up and get her."

She turned to the back stairs, located through a portico on the other side of the kitchen. But the other two moved quickly to follow her. She looked around and there they were, poised beside the huge old woodstove, as though maneuvering to shove her into it.

"May we, ah . . ." Roger Wemble formed his words diffidently, as though anxious to avoid giving offense. "May we come with you? In order to learn in detail the conditions in which you and your daughter live?"

Pippa shrugged. She thought, Why not? They followed her through the kitchen, which was chilly, and up the winding back stairs. As they reached the second floor, the sound of Eulace's television was replaced by a rhythmic thumping or throbbing that seemed to emerge from the floorboards. Winterbelle's boombox, playing a Gabrielle Roth tape called *Ritual*. One of Pippa's own favorites. The air upstairs was unusually warm and dry, not by anyone's intent but because that's how the ancient heating system worked.

Hey, hey nah nah,
Oh, hey.

—chanted a woman's voice on the tape. An ecstatic voice: freely giving of its Dionysian energies. Roger Wemble and Doctor Rhinum met eyes with one another. Pippa felt like giving both of them a smack. Two smacks. One per smug, self-righteous cheek.

"Sweetie?" she called.

From the region of Winterbelle's bedroom, there was a stillness that Pippa found palpable. An abeyance; a suspense. That pesky girl was up to something, she could tell. An affectionate smile formed and withered at her lips.

"Where is she?" Doctor Rhinum asked, with clinical insistence.

Good question, thought Pippa. "I've been out shoveling snow for a while," she explained, but the Doctor only looked back as though she were dodging the question.

"Let's have a look," said Roger Wemble, "shall we?"

Together, Pippa leading, they trooped along the hall. They passed Pippa's room, where all was dark. Out of Winterbelle's doorway, a peculiar golden-orange sort of light glowed and flickered, seemingly in time to the music.

Ohhh, hey nah nah,
Oh, yey.

The woman sang with wilder abandon, the drums beat louder, and the golden light from Winterbelle's room rose and danced with them.

Turning in to the threshold, Pippa and Roger Wemble and Doctor Allison Rhinum beheld:

Two dozen candles of all sizes and types, flames licking the air, wax dripping and running on the floorboards.

A circle two paces wide formed by a coil of rolled-up t-shirts, braided together and laid out Ourobouros-style, beginning to end.

And within the circle, Winterbelle. The girl was quite naked except for Pippa's indigo scarf, which was tied low around her waist in something of the manner of a primitive skirt or loincloth, plus a profusion of jewelry in which the astronomical motif—sun and moon and stars—was a unifying theme, picked up also in the gold lamé ornaments of the scarf. Presumably this was lost upon everyone but Pippa.

"Surprise, Mommy!" Winterbelle shouted, seeing her mother at the door and not noticing until the next moment the two unanticipated guests. "Happy Yule," she added more demurely.

"What is going on here?" Doctor Rhinum wanted to know, and wanted to know *right now*.

Roger Wemble said nothing, but his plastic stylus poked energetically at the electronic notepad. His smallish eyes—pointed and shrewlike in the weird light of the room—darted here and there, appearing to take a particular interest in the shadowy depths of the cupboard bed.

Pippa crossed the room and punched the boombox off. Then she switched the light on. Immediately she regretted doing so, because now her daughter stood looking small and utterly exposed under the glare of a shadeless compact fluorescent bulb, and the whole situation was without context. It just looked *wrong*, was all. Abnormal.

"Mommy?" said Winterbelle. "What's going on?"

Pippa removed her parka and wrapped the girl in it. Winterbelle nestled in the folds of Gore-Tex and duck

down under her mother's arm; but then Doctor Rhinum
stepped forward and took the girl's hand and said:

"Won't you come with me, dear? I have some things I'd
like to ask you."

"No," said Winterbelle, tugging herself free. "I *won't*. I
remember you—you're that lady with the ugly dolls.
Mommy, I don't want to talk to her again."

Pippa pressed her daughter close. "She doesn't want to
talk," she repeated loudly, addressing Roger Wemble.
"Can't you see you've upset her? What right do you have
to barge into people's lives like this?"

Roger Wemble's smile had vanished. He said, "I can see
your daughter is upset, Ms. Rede, and I'm quite sorry about
that. But I can see a number of other things as well, and
I have to say that, on behalf of the people of this state, I
myself am rather upset as well."

"The people of this *state?*" said Pippa. "What have
they—"

Doctor Rhinum reached over and grabbed Winterbelle's
arm again—firmly this time, her big fleshy fingers wrapping themselves around the girl's thin wrist. "Come with
me," she commanded. "This is a very serious matter. Ms.
Rede, instruct your daughter to cooperate."

"Why?" said Pippa. Pleading, really. Sounding pathetic
even to herself.

"No!" Winterbelle cried, struggling against the large and
shapeless woman who would not let go of her arm.

Pippa tugged back but of course in the end she let go,
as mothers had always let go, and for the same reason.
Winterbelle was led squirming and kicking to the other
side of the room, where Doctor Rhinum unceremoniously
yanked Pippa's parka off.

"Ms. Rede," Roger Wemble was saying, practically oozing the words into her ear, "is it true that you have stated

to third parties on a number of separate occasions that you practice witchcraft?"

Pippa only half heard this. She watched in impotent rage as her little girl was turned this way and that, scrutinized like some laboratory animal.

"Is it also true," Wemble continued, "that you participate regularly in rituals of a Satanic nature, in which minors are subjected to treatment that may be regarded as humiliating, painful and/or injurious?"

Pippa turned to stare at him, aghast. But before she could make any response—even granting that such a question deserved one, which she was not sure about—Doctor Rhinum exclaimed:

"Look! Look at this. What is this on your daughter's arm, Ms. Rede?"

"It's nothing," said Winterbelle, reduced to whimpering now. "It's just a *burn*."

"It's just a burn," repeated Pippa, unable to think of what more needed to be said here, but feeling certain there was something.

"A *burn?*" said Doctor Rhinum.

"Let me see," said Roger Wemble.

Winterbelle grabbed up the parka and tried to cover herself. Pippa longed to embrace and shelter her daughter, but the large imposing bodies of two other adults stood between them.

"It's from a *candle*," Winterbelle said, still laboring to explain.

"From a *candle*," repeated Doctor Rhinum. She and Roger Wemble turned to look at Pippa across their shoulders.

"Well," said Wemble.

"I should think we've seen quite enough," said Doctor Rhinum.

"Yes," said Wemble. He consulted his electronic notepad. "Yes, I suppose so."

"Ms. Rede," said Doctor Rhinum, "would you step out of the room, please?"

"No," said Pippa. "I want *you* to step out of the room. I want you out of my *house*. Get out of here *now*."

Doctor Rhinum raised a large index finger. "Failure to cooperate," she noted.

Roger Wemble jotted this down.

"Now," said the Doctor. "Are you going to do as I say, or are you intent upon making matters even worse?"

"Worse than what?" said Pippa.

Wemble turned to Winterbelle. His look of artificial kindness was back. "Dear," he said, "why don't you get some of your things together? Doctor Rhinum here will help you. Look, we've even brought a nice bag—you can keep it for yourself. Do you have any special dolls or blankets or anything of the type?"

"What are you *doing*?" said Pippa. Shrieking, almost.

Turning from Winterbelle, Roger Wemble bore down upon her. "Now, Ms. Rede," he said. "I have some papers here for you to look at, which will explain your rights in this matter, and which will also clarify the authority of the Department to take summary action in cases where it is deemed necessary to do so. Naturally all these proceedings are subject to review and every possible care will be taken to ensure that the interests of everyone involved, not just the injured minor, are taken into account, although of course the child's well-being must be regarded as paramount."

"The injured minor?" Pippa said. Her lips resisted forming the words.

"I have other questions I must ask you," Roger Wemble

went on, "but if you like I can arrange for a client advocate to be assigned before we get into that."

"What are you doing?" Pippa asked, her body grown almost totally numb.

Only it was too clear what they were doing. Doctor Rhinum was going through all of Winterbelle's drawers, extracting a random selection of the girl's belongings and dropping them into a large nylon bag on which colorful dinosaurs cavorted. Roger Wemble was pressing a fat white envelope into Pippa's hand, all the while speaking blandly by rote about certain steps that must be taken immediately, for the good of all concerned, while others could follow according to what was learned in follow-up evaluations.

Pippa said, "Of *what?*"—choked out indistinctly through her crying.

"Of all the factors bearing upon your daughter's health and emotional security, Ms. Rede. Which will include the willingness of all parties to engage proactively in steps that may ameliorate the harmful environmental influences experienced by this girl."

Pippa's eyes lost their focus; the tall man in front of her dissolved into a blur.

"It's all in these papers," Roger Wemble said. "I hope you'll take time to look them over carefully. Now, if I could just get you to sign *here.*"

Pippa stared down at the legal-sized sheet and the pen being held out before her. She looked up to see Winterbelle, her face red and wet with tears, but not crying any longer, just moving with sluggish complaisance as she was instructed to put on this pullover, that pair of socks, glancing now and again across the room at her mommy as though afraid that even this—the fleeting eye contact—would be stolen from her. As indeed presently it would. After all requisite procedures had first been observed.

"You're taking my little girl away from me?" said Pippa. Tears ran into her mouth. Taste of primordial brine, the ancient Womb.

Roger Wemble looked up from his notepad and for an instant, maybe longer, a hint of something like sympathy could faintly be discerned in his eyes. "I'm afraid it's a bit more complicated than that," he began to say.

Then Doctor Rhinum moved in, filling Pippa's watery field of vision. "Get this woman out of here," she said. "Her presence is causing the child considerable distress."

"Allison, *please*," said Wemble, turning to her and evidently intending to say more. Only Pippa forestalled him.

"You *bitch*," she screamed, striking out at the shapeless woman with both hands, fingers digging like claws. "You evil *bitch*. You'll freeze in Hel by the time I'm finished with you."

Doctor Rhinum pushed her roughly away; she did not bother to reply. Bright red blood glistened from a gouge across her temple. She cast a dark look at Roger Wemble, who sighed and made an entry with his plastic stylus. Then he took Pippa by the arm and directed her—pushed her, really—out into the hall.

"Ms. Rede," he said with a certain touch of sadness. "You are only making things much harder for yourself. And for Winterbelle, I must tell you. Take my word for this. I've seen it many, many times."

"No," said Pippa. Openly weeping now. "No you have *not*. How can you *say* that? You've never seen me or . . . or—"

Or Winterbelle, she wanted to say. But the name would not come out of her mouth. It was simply not there.

It was lost.

II

as snow

In the bleak midwinter,
Frosty wind made moan.
Earth stood hard as iron,
Water like a stone.
Snow was falling,
Snow on snow, snow on snow—
In the bleak midwinter,
Long, long ago.

—*Christina Rossetti*

After midnight the sky cleared and the air became very cold as the Earth radiated heat into nothingness. At the peak of Wabenaki Mountain a north wind blew steadily though not fast, less than 10 knots, barely enough to dust off the greenstone knobs of Maiden Fell, alleged site of some tragedy. Ice swelled deep in secret cracks, straining to pry the mountain apart. A patchy, celadon grunge of lichen glowed on stones like nursery-rhyme cheese. In the village far, far below, Pippa lay awake with her eyes as ancient, impenetrable and icy

as any star
in that sky.

She got out of bed around 3:30, imagining that it was later, time to get a head start on breakfast before people were awake. A night light shaped like a fat frog, which for some reason had always been Winterbelle's favorite animal, glowed in the echoey black & white bathroom. The toilet seat was as cold as bone china. Pippa cried and cried, just sitting there. It was a tiny relief to sit, though she had been lying for hours: first cuddled in a fetal position with her back pressed against a large stuffed goose, for company, and then flat on her back until minutes ago.

The crying—wild, heaving, robbing her of breath—left her emptied, her insides a void. When she stopped, the plaster and tile rang with the violence of her grief. Pippa could hear a clock ticking on a shelf in the kitchen below. Hickory dickory dock. By now she understood that it was still night, hours from daybreak, but there was no way to even think about getting back into bed. It was easier to imagine that she would never go into that bed again, that horrible abode of waking nightmares.

The kitchen seemed possible. A place for her; a sanctuary. But when she went down to stand beside the lifeless

66

woodstove, with that old refrigerator humping malevo-
lently deep in the moon shadows and floorboards moaning
underfoot, cranky as ghosts, Pippa realized that what was
good and sustaining about the kitchen on a winter morning
were the things you did to take the chill off: turning on
lights and making coffee, popping things in the oven,
whipping pancake batter into shape, firing up the grill.
And packing Winterbelle's lunch. Chasing the girl away
from the television (left unattended by Eulace at such an
early hour) and using all means necessary, and then some,
to get food into her.

But Pippa was not going to do any of those things
this morning.

She might never do any of those things again.

The thought sprang upon her as though from elsewhere,
from outside, stabbing at her heart. Pippa wrestled it away
but it came stabbing inward again. She shoved back
harder; yet the terrible idea that Winterbelle might never
come home—that the girl was gone forever, that Pippa
had failed in the one thing she really cared enough to try
hard to do right—had gotten her in a death grip. Truly:
a death grip. Because if her little girl was gone, her life
was over.

Finally (a desperation move) Pippa squeezed her eyes
shut and ran her hand widdershins, counterclockwise, the
direction of banishing, around and around, tracing out an
invisible circle, filling it with imaginary light.

"Go!" she spoke aloud.

And this time, the terrible thought obeyed her.

Her heart lightened, as though a tiny ray of dawn had
found its way in.

Not much.

But it was a claim on some scrap of territory: the space within the boundaries of her Self.

After that, Pippa walked with otherworldly calmness across the kitchen floor to the radiator underneath the single tall window sash, its cast-iron piping painted white and gleaming dully, like the ribs of a long-dead and flesh-less giant. She lowered herself to the floor and scrunched her legs up tight against her rib cage. The long chain of her spinal column pressed itself between two hot metal ribs, uncomfortably. Smells known better to mice than to mothers rose from the dark places of the floor to enter her nose. Every single thing about the old house was alien and frightening to her. In a way she was glad of it.

She sat very still, breathing lightly, eyes wide but un-seeing. She prayed to the Goddess in a way that did not involve words or even ordinary, rational thoughts—not for anything impossible, for a thing she hardly dared to hope, but simply to remain alive and sane until morning.

To outlive this worst of all nights.

To not just give in to hopelessness

and let herself
crumple and
die.

Outside, in sunlight that brought no warmth, her broom stood propped against the railing of the front porch. Pippa took the worn handle and clutched it uncertainly through a padding of mittens: not wanting just to leave it sitting there, but unwilling to go back into that house where a part of her had died. Her legs, programmed to walk down the sidewalk, moved without her directing them. The broom was still in her hands. Finally the situation got pretty weird because she was standing on the curb of Ash Street with this battered piece of garbage from the Swap Shop in her hands, like some deranged soul who ought to be reinstitutionalized. Somebody's dirty white Jeep Cherokee crunched slowly by, and the driver, whoever it was—a neighbor she supposed—stared at her rather more intently than common politeness allowed.

As though he had never seen a witch standing around with her broom before.

Pippa shook her head. Above all (or nearly above all) she did not want to be pitiful. She swung the broom around hard and released it, letting it fly into the chaotically unpruned hedge of forsythia, where it stuck at a funny angle. An avalanche of new snow shook loose. Tiny dry flakes of it floated across the lawn, as though they were perfectly immaterial, sparkling cleaner and brighter than the sun. Some few of them reached Pippa and touched her face and disappeared there, leaving no trace, only a memory of frozen sweetness.

Magic, she thought.

Even when nothing else was left, when everything had been swept away, there was still magic in the world.

There was no sense in going to work.

Nor was there any sense in not going to work.

There was no sense left in anything; nor in not-anything.

It was so hard to breathe, because of the cold and a new aching in her lungs, that Pippa wondered if her nearly forgotten childhood asthma was coming back. *Let it come*, she thought.

Let it all come.

She shifted her backpack, stuffed with Brenda Cigogne's Bad Fairy costume, which was as finished as it was ever going to get, from one shoulder to the other. She peered at the world around her. A white, bloodless world, leached of meaning.

There was nothing anymore to be afraid of. Was there?

The village where Pippa lived was laid out in tidy, geometric lanes and blocks and neighborhoods in stubborn, Colonial-era defiance of the unruly contours of the planet. There were many possible routes to follow from the gloomy end of Ash Street to what remained of the quaint downtown shopping district: the pre-Wal-Mart, pre-credit-card-sweatshop center of village commerce. Yet of all possible ways she could have gone, Pippa took the route she always took—as though this particular succession of footsteps, however fatal, was foreordained.

She trudged over the sidewalks, mostly still unshoveled, that led through safe neighborhood streets where you didn't have to worry about your kid getting run over by a tourist in a hurry or by some local yahoo with a PAVE IT TO SAVE IT bumper sticker on his pickup truck. She turned up School Street, where a broad swath of asphalt had been painted in big yellow stripes (now buried under snow and rock salt) and there were blinking lights and a sign warning that you had entered a drug-free school zone. In this way, insanely, she came to stand before the entrance to the George Burroughs Elementary School, where a uniformed crossing guard in an orange safety vest stood with her arms raised, needlessly alerting motorists to the presence of vulnerable pedestrians.

Kids streamed everywhere. All sizes. Over- and underdressed, poor and pampered, beautiful and plain, dull and gifted and how Pippa had been, indescribably ordinary. Each of them, every little miniature person, was equally precious, miraculous, irreplaceable.

None of them was hers. None of them was Winterbelle.

Were they keeping her out of school?

Did they have her shut up in a room somewhere, a hard-edged place barely humanized by a few stuffed animals and a cute poster of a panda gnawing a spray of bamboo? Had the girl slept at all, or lain awake and wide-eyed and terrified like Pippa? What kind of nightdress had she worn? The pretty flannel one with the embroidered flowers around the neck? Had she woken from a bad dream and cried out for her mommy?

Was she crying still?

Pippa's body shook—she could feel it shaking as though it were a thing apart from her, the muscular spasms rising up from the bottom of her gut and spreading through her torso, all the way to her shoulders. She could not tell whether she was breathing or not. She was aware that people were looking at her. You could sense that.

Pressure on her arm came (she slowly understood) from a hand. The hand was attached to an arm in gray wool. The crossing guard. A heavy woman with raven-black hair, faintly mustached. Eyes that could gleam with friendliness, or not. Just now not.

"Can I help you, ma'am?" the woman asked.

Pippa felt (though she would never know for sure) that the crossing guard knew who she was. That she had been warned about her, told to expect that a certain agitated mother might come here, instructed as to how to proceed in case there was any trouble. Not that a woman like this would need much in the way of instruction. A woman like this (you could tell from the eyes, the creases at the edges of her mouth) had known trouble all her life, and was well practiced at stamping it right out before it got too far.

The hand did not move away from Pippa's arm. It remained there, ready.

"Is there anything I can help you with?" the woman offered again. Like she meant business this time.

Pippa fled. She felt as though she were wrenching herself away from the heavy, dangerous woman and running madly, blindly, escaping from the school and the swarm of other people's children and their happy high-pitched squeals and snowballs flying and mittens lost and knapsacks propped and forgotten against the chain-link fence. Why are schools surrounded by chain-link fences? To keep evil witches from snatching innocent little children away?

Pippa raged and she wept. She raged at herself for having walked past Winterbelle's school, and at the world for having turned so wholly and suddenly against her. She wept for everything she had ever done that was stupid, including allowing a dribble of sperm from a good-looking liar to bring into existence—into *life*—a grapefruit-headed bony squirming blob that had looked, somehow, insensibly, like it might like to be named Winterbelle, and that she had loved with helpless awful fleshly obsessive single-mindedness from the moment the jolly plump midwife had laid it out all covered with mucus and blood across Pippa's chest, where it blinked its eyes in bewilderment, kicked its tiny perfect limbs, and wailed.

Many years later that strange creature would reach up to her from the warm depths of its cupboard bed and call her Mommy. It would ask to be told another story, and another, and then to be told what the stories meant, and if they were really true.

It would kiss her and give her a birthday present it had made all by itself.

It would own cherished possessions (mostly of no objective value, like the empty plastic Tylenol bottle, the chipped Jemima Puddleduck teacup, the unclothed Native American Barbie). It would have secrets, dreams, and extravagant thoughts. It would invent real games to play with imaginary companions, and surprise Pippa's friends with sudden articulateness, and set its truculent little mouth in refusal to cooperate with well-meaning social workers, day-care providers, and most of all Aunt Eulace.

It would have a life.

It would belong to nobody but itself.

And then one day, it would be snatched away. Away from Pippa, away from the life that had been its very own. Stolen by large, imposing, all-powerful strangers and taken far, far away.

*   *   *

But not forever.

Pippa reminded herself of that. Or rather, reminded herself that she had made up her mind about that, and done a little witchy thing to enforce it.

She couldn't be sure whether she really believed in this—her decision, her power to make it real—or whether she was just engaging in New Age mumbo jumbo.

For now, it was all she could manage.

She had made it till morning. Alive, possibly sane.

Now the morning had come and she was part of it, and things were no better than they had been in the dark and aloneness of night.

If anything, they might be worse. Because the morning had come, and Pippa was still alive, and none of it made any difference.

And the stupidest thing of all was, she had left the old house in spite of it all. She had walked down the same sidewalks she always walked down. And she was going to work.

What surprised her (apart from the fact that she remained capable of surprise) was the feeling of safety, of at-home-ness, that came upon her as soon as the door swished open, admitting her to the fragrant hothouse environs of Rose Petal & Thorn.

Brenda Cigogne was thick in conversation with a gentleman who leaned on the counter, one elbow pressing flat a stack of flyers for a *Messiah* sing-along at the Opera House.

Come share the joy of the season with us!

the flyer said. It was signed by your friends at the credit-card center, who were underwriting everything in sight, pending approval of their permit to bulldoze a nearby mountaintop.

Brenda cast a quick gaze toward Pippa, though it was not certain whether she registered whom she was seeing, or simply was performing an act of small-business triage: customer/browser/teenager. Pippa fit none of these categories (or any category at all, she supposed) so Brenda merely nodded at something the gentleman at the counter was saying. He did not appear to need encouragement to go on talking.

On the endless tape loop, Mannheim Steamroller cranked out synthesized cheer at a tempo so frenetic that the thousands of gilded glass ornaments and miles of tinsel dangling about the shop seemed to quiver synchronically.

Pippa slipped into the storage room and there removed her backpack, then her parka. Out of the backpack she lifted folds upon folds of black moiré, untangled them from the jutting stems of a dead and varnished rose cane. The Bad Fairy looked a fright—more of a fright than it was meant to—so she glanced around for someplace to lay it out and smooth the wrinkles down. There was only a workbench used for potting up houseplants. As Pippa fluffed and patted the costume, she felt a small hard object beneath the many layers of cloth. She frowned.

A piece of her sewing kit? She groped after it but her fingers only met fabric and more fabric. Like the princess and the pea, she thought. One thing heaped on top of another.

Or actually, like Life.

At last, deep down, her nails scratched paper. More puzzled than before, she worked the mysterious object outward, squeezing it between her thumb and the finger known in certain small circles as Nameless (more widely as the Ring). She found it to be slightly pliant. *Cardboard,* she thought.

Out in the light at last, Pippa beheld a tiny box, the

size earrings might come packaged in. It was not exactly wrapped, but twined about with colored bits of string that Pippa recognized as having been left over from a weave-your-own-dream-catcher kit she had ordered from Hearth-stone for Winterbelle's last birthday. The sight of these pieces of string—but more so the realization that Winterbelle herself must have tied them, the thought of her daughter's beautiful nail-bitten slender fingers having *touched this box*—caused her to grab for her own middle, the empty place under the rib cage, to catch her heart as it fell there.

With infinite care she placed the box down. She touched it, straining to feel any subtle vibes or energies that might have been left imprinted. Psychometry, that is called. Apparently for some people it works. For Pippa it only strengthened the notion that, magically speaking, she was coarsened and dull.

She opened the box in a hurry then. The strings popped and she *did* feel that, jagged little pains like nerve fibers rending. Finally she lifted the cardboard lid and reached inside and took out a small piece of pale soft stone, light as soap. The stone was sculpted or at least chipped-at, making a kind of lumpy half sphere, one end somewhat stretched out and flattened.

At first she had no idea. Then she recognized for what they were the two black micro-eyes, dotted with the tip of a fine brush on either side of the flat, protruding head.

It was a frog.

More precisely it was a fetish: a totemic stand-in for Winterbelle's power animal.

And more precisely still, it was a present. A handmade Yule present for Pippa. Winterbelle must have made it and wrapped it and tucked it away someplace where she fig-ured her mommy would find it and be surprised.

"I'm surprised, honey," Pippa whispered. She let the frog rest on the upturned fingers of her right hand, bringing it close enough to place a gentle kiss upon its scrunched-up little face. "Oh, sweetie. I'm so surprised."

Brenda Cigogne in all likelihood did not guess (and might not have cared) that Pippa had been crying alone in the back room of the flower shop. But her gaze, both pointed and prolonged, upon Pippa's reemergence, did strike an interrogatory note, and it's true that a long time had ticked by during which Pippa had been hiding there. Trying to outlast a storm that would not abate. Finally giving up, lowering her head, plunging into it.

"Sorry," Pippa said, and left it at that. She stepped around to take her usual place behind the counter: unobtrusive, beneath the parakeets.

The talkative gentleman whose elbow had rested on the *Messiah* was still there. He smiled at Pippa in a quizzical way that she sort of recognized, though she could not think from where.

"Pippa," said Brenda, her manner uncharacteristically self-conscious, even formal, "I don't know if you've ever met Mark Portion. He's our local newspaper magnate."

The man's smile grew brighter though it did not quite lose the quality of *wondering* about something; and as the man stuck a big hand out at the end of an unnaturally stiffened white cuff, she remembered where she had seen him before.

Of course in a town this small you see *everybody*, sooner or later. And seeing a person once and then seeing him again a short while later does not mean anything at all— necessarily. But this was the same man who had driven right past her first thing this morning, at the wheel of a dirty Jeep Cherokee. He had been staring at her—not just looking—as though she were crazy. (Well, she *had* been crazy. But still.)

"Mr. Portion," said Brenda, a trifle nervous Pippa thought, "has just been telling me the most . . . well, I scarcely know how to say it. The most *alarming* news. I do hope it isn't true. It *can't* be true."

It was true, Pippa guessed. Whatever it was. In fact it probably was just scratching the surface.

"Very glad to meet you, Pippa," Mark Portion said. For a moment he seemed ready to tack on, *at last.*

She surrendered her hand to him, and he grasped it in his own larger one, perhaps to assure himself of her concentrated attention. He spoke in grand, oratorical style: "You know, in my position, I'm privy to certain . . . *information* . . . sooner than most people in town. And of course, sometimes the information does not turn out to be *wholly* accurate. Or in many cases you might say it only represents a certain point of view—so to speak, only one *aspect* of the story. And it's my job, Pippa—I make it my job—to get the *whole* story. After all, I have a responsibility to the people of this town. It's a sacred trust, Pippa, and one that I take very seriously."

She did not waste time wondering what he meant. Here were things she thought:

Mark Portion's facial muscles worked harder than was absolutely necessary, as though he were trying on lots of different expressions but couldn't find one that suited him. His smile especially bothered her because it was an Amway type of thing, about nothing. She did not like hearing her name repeated so many times by a stranger, as though he were laying claim to it. His brown hair was a little too long for how thin it had gotten. And why did somebody like this want to wear a tiny, almost invisibly thin gold hoop earring?

"I wonder, Pippa," Mark Portion said, the words oozing over her, "whether you might like to join me after work for a cup of coffee, maybe a bite to eat? That would be what, five o'clock or so? Unless you have other plans . . ."

Pippa glanced at Brenda who had ostentatiously occupied herself with tidying up spools of ribbons, Christmasy red and green, used for complimentary gift wrapping. What does this guy want me to say? she wondered. No, I'm free tonight, my daughter's been taken away so I don't have to worry about picking her up. Let's go get polluted!

"I don't think so," she said.

Mark Portion behaved as though he had not heard, as though her enfeebled voice left no impression.

"The Chowder House is a good bet," he said. "They put out a nice spread for happy hour. Of course I don't drink anymore, myself. But a hot bowl of soup is always welcome at this time of year, isn't it?"

Pippa glanced again at Brenda, who pretended to have forgotten her. A single parakeet chirped, plaintively, as though begging to have Mannheim Steamroller shut off.

"To tell you the truth," Pippa said to Mark Portion, "I had kind of a bad experience with your newspaper a while back. There was this reporter who interviewed me for like, *hours*. And then when the piece finally ran, all it was was this stupid-looking picture with some stuff that I never *said* printed underneath it. So I think maybe I'll take a rain check, if that's okay."

"It's certainly okay with me," Portion said. "But I wonder if that's really in your best interests." He scratched his neck, which looked irritated from being shaven too close. "Or, um . . . is your daughter's name Winterberry?"

Pippa's eyes stayed locked on the counter, where they happened to have dropped. A pair of scissors was lying there. You could probably kill somebody, even a large man, with scissors like that. It would depend on how deep you could jam them in. And how suddenly. The element of surprise would be crucial.

"Winterberry is a plant," she said, her voice grown hoarse. "It's in the holly family. My daughter is none of your damned business."

"That's true, and I apologize," said Mark Portion. He raised his hands: see, nothing up my sleeve. "But look at this from my perspective. Certain aspects of what ideally ought to be your own private life have now, unfortunately, become matters of official interest to the authorities, and therefore the citizens, of this community. It's just human nature, Pippa. And it's my *duty*, as a journalist, to report fully and fairly on local news, however unpleasant that duty may sometimes be. And in this case, I have to tell you frankly, I have no dearth of sources representing . . . what should I call it . . . the other side of the controversy."

"What are you *talking* about?" said Pippa. She was looking at him now. She had to, because otherwise she wouldn't have believed he was really standing there and saying these things. "What controversy? *What* other side? Don't you have any common decency at all? Can't you just leave people *alone*?"

Brenda Cigogne bustled over, shaking her head like a schoolteacher, a well-meaning disciplinarian.

Pippa realized she had been practically shouting.

"Not *here*," Brenda said crossly, looking back and forth between the two of them. "Mark, you're being a vulture. I suppose you mean well. But look—you've *completely* upset her. And here it is one of the busiest shopping days of the year. Now, Pippa—" (efficiently shifting her focus) "—why don't you take Mark up on his offer of a bowl of soup? That way you'll have something nice and hot to throw at him."

Mark Portion's face opened up in surprise; then he chuckled.

Brenda paused, looked at them for a moment longer: curious to some unreadable degree, but mostly satisfied to have restored a sensible and businesslike decorum. "All *right* then," she said, chipperly. "Now Mark, it's time for you to go and leave us in peace. It's *Christmas*time, in case you hadn't heard. Pippa and I have *work* to do."

Mark Portion nodded—disarmed now. He zipped his lightweight coat until the collar closed tight beneath his chin. His last gaze at Pippa was restrained, perhaps chastened. "I'll be at the Chowder House at five," he told her. "Join me if you feel like it. You look like you could use some protein."

But when he was gone it was no easier. Because now there was Brenda.

You cannot work side by side without talking to someone, or else a kind of unhealthy charge builds up in the air that is worse than the talking would be. If that is possible.

Whatever Brenda might have heard or not heard, thought or suspected or wanted to ask about, she kept her mouth shut. She was as good at that as she was at talking, when she chose to be. So after a while Pippa might have thought the whole thing was in her own head, a case of shame or paranoia; except that:

(a) Brenda had made the remark about "alarming news," and

(b) Every time Pippa turned around she caught her boss sneakily staring in her direction.

Well . . . but so what?

Was Pippa expected to bare her soul to everybody that looked twice at her? Did she have a civic duty to satisfy the whole town's morbid curiosity? Heretofore Brenda Ci-

gogne had not shown much interest in her employees'
lives, their personal affairs, their struggling little families.
And she was not exactly showing an interest now. Only
staring, in that funny way.

Anyhow, what would Pippa have said to her? What *could*
she have said? When she scarcely knew herself what was
happening. When she hadn't even glanced at the stack of
official papers—couldn't bring herself to—that that man,
Roger Wemble, had thrust into her hands. So she didn't
know, really, in a legal or real-world sense, what was happening to her. Much less what was happening to
Winterbelle.

She did know that Really Soon Now she would have
to come to grips with it.

She would have to do battle with those horrible people—with the whole world if need be—to get her daughter back.

Right now, though, she still felt a bit too much like
somebody who has just regained consciousness, who is
lying there between starched white sheets in the hospital
(or more like it, the asylum), trying to remember what
kind of accident or act of Nature or whim of the fate-
spinning Norns had hurled her, ass over teakettle, into this
unknown place.

She was not prepared, however, to spill *that* to Brenda
Cigogne.

So the strange charge built up and built up. Customers
came and kept coming. They grazed on cookies, sipped
cider, grabbed items off display tables and trudged to the
counter with them, seemingly without pausing to think
about it. Maybe that's what the holiday season does to
you.

Or maybe it was winter. One day old. Everybody
wanted to talk about the weather, and took care to state

their convictions on the subject with unusual passion, as though it were some matter of intense importance that you needed to take a stand on, like an impending election. Their attitude amazed Pippa, who could not remember anything about the day outside. She was even more amazed to hear her own voice among those chattering on and on about total snow accumulation, radiant cooling, the possible influence of global climate change, the popular overweight meteorologist on Channel 5. Her fingers tapped the computerized transaction-recording system, née cash register, as though more directly related to the machine than to her own starved and exhausted flesh.

She envied everyone.

She marveled at how *carefree* people were; how confident that Christmas would come and they would be safe at home with their families and peace would reign on the Earth. She wrapped their purchases and wished them a happy holiday. She even smiled when they wished her one too. It meant nothing; none of the things she saw or heard or did or said were real for her.

The only reality was the unseen: the invisible: the vanished.

So the day moved onward, like an enormous vehicle on which everyone obliviously rode. The parakeets squawked when Pippa was late feeding them. Jacques called to say the delivery van was stuck in someone's driveway. Brenda's blood pressure rose to record heights. Furtively Pippa removed the Mannheim Steamroller tape and placed it deep in a terra-cotta urn where it would not be found until Mother's Day. And in the middle of the afternoon—2:45 to be exact, shortly after public schools let out and the Extended Day program for the kids of working parents began—the door of Rose Petal & Thorn swished open and through it stepped Kaspian Aaby.

Kaspian of the chocolate-mint eyes, the freckles, the floppy brown hair. Kaspian who had stared at her in the park. Who had come to her one day and said, "I just wanted to warn you," but then had failed to do so. Not, probably, that any warning he had failed to deliver might have helped.

He did not meet Pippa's eyes. He stood before the refreshment table without taking anything. He shifted his weight from one silly untied sneaker to the other. It was obvious that he was waiting for her to approach him. Or was he? Was he aware of her at all? Was it his stepmother he was waiting for? (Pippa glanced around the crowded shop but saw no sign of Carol Deacon Aaby.)

Finally, furtively, Kaspian turned his head. His eyes leapt directly to Pippa's with incredible precision, as though some separate, secret faculty had guided them there. In his face she read shyness, maybe embarrassment; the boy looked down at his baggy jeans and then up again, as though he had no idea what it was that he meant to do here.

Pippa's reaction surprised and then, a moment later, saddened her. It took the form of a surge of motherly feeling, of unquestioning empathy, toward this kid who looked all at once so confused and self-conscious and totally out of his depth. She wanted to cross the room and touch his shoulder and reassuringly say *Don't worry, it's not your problem. Let the grown-ups deal with it.* But she could not do that. Because this boy had come a few days ago to tell her something, and now he had come back, and it was possible that he had more to tell. It was possible that something he knew and might say (or might not, if she handled this wrong) could be helpful to her. Helpful to Winterbelle.

And she could not let him go before finding out about that.

"Hi," was all Kaspian said, when Pippa came to a halt a step away from him. She could feel Brenda's Cigogne's gaze on her back, and she tightened her shoulder blades, fending it off.

"Kaspian, right?" she said. Just to get things started.

The boy nodded quickly. He sort of smiled, then blanked it out. An air of surreptitiousness hung about him like a badly arranged costume. The Young Prince, disguised as a simple village boy.

"I'm due for a break," she said—the least of the lies she had told today. "You want to, um . . . go get something?"

Kaspian shrugged, looking hard through the plate-glass window, though there was little to see there: the long windowed wall of the credit-card center; a blur of sunlight; passing cars.

She led him like a puppy out the door, dressed exactly as she was—unwilling to risk losing him by going for her parka. The cold wind off Wabenaki Mountain pressed through all the gaps of her saggy, home-knit sweater.

"Where to?" she asked him. She guessed that he would not want to go anyplace where his friends would see him. She wasn't even thinking about the stepmother. Not just yet.

He shuffled indecisively. He looked scared and she felt sorry for him, though she tried to clamp down on that. However hard this was for him, it was harder for Winterbelle. That was the thing to focus on.

They ended up at Zaddik's Bagel Bakery, one of those eternally jinxed business locations that, the last time she looked, had been a Mexican food carry-out. The color scheme was still desert tan with lurid turquoise squiggles and orange rays. Even the furniture was the same. The difference was in the air: hot with the smells of cinnamon, scorched onion, peppery chives.

Pippa sat them down at a round café table. Neither spoke of getting food, nor indeed of anything at all.

Abruptly, Kaspian raised his eyes and looked at her with overpowering, kid-style sincerity. "I heard about . . ." he began, then dropped his gaze and said just, "I'm really sorry."

Pippa gave in then and did what she felt like doing, which was to touch him and tell him it was all right. It wasn't his problem.

"You don't know," he said, shaking his head earnestly. She waited for him to elaborate but he did not care to.

She sighed. She did not want to press him. It was awful that a kid had to be involved in this. And yet, one way or another, a kid was. At least one. As gently as she could she said, "Is there . . . was there anything you wanted to tell me about? Anything more?"

He nodded without looking at her, and for a few moments he did not speak. Then he said in a voice that was flat and forced, the way you talk to a parent or maybe a teacher who has scolded you, "Have you ever heard of QROST?"

Crossed, it came out, the way he pronounced it. Yet somehow she could tell it was an acronym, a made-up word. It sounded like any number of things—a drug, a band, a religious movement. In the end she decided that no, she had never heard of it.

"It stands for quasi-ritualized occultic sexual traumatization," he said. He spoke in an entirely uninflected voice, as though the complex phrase had no particular meaning, no emotional import.

Pippa felt a wave of pure cold move into her, settling low in her abdomen. "It does?" she prompted him. She tried to make her own voice as flat as Kaspian's, but could hear the failure, the quivering.

"Yeah." He squirmed in his seat, looked at the walls, the white-board menu. "It's this kind of a . . . like a syndrome, I guess. They say it's happening all over the place, only you don't hear a lot about it in the media. See, we had this guy visit our church a couple of months back and he did this whole slide show and lecture on it. He said they've got a lot of it out where he comes from. Out around Tulsa. That's a town in Oklahoma."

Pippa nodded. "Tulsa, Oklahoma," she said. She meant it to be encouraging.

Kaspian nodded back. "So this guy said, out in Tulsa they've developed this new technique for helping people tell whether they've been victims of QROST or not. And it's a really promising technique because a lot of people can remember. That they *have* been, I mean. And this guy gave a three-day seminar in the church meeting room to teach people how to apply this technique here. To our own loved ones."

Pippa had a terrible, terrible feeling that she knew where this was spiraling down to. She shut her eyes and could feel it plummeting there. Down, way deep down, into a place that was cold and white and full of death. She opened her eyes again and saw turquoise squiggles and hot orange stripes and a yellow splotch of Mexican sunlight.

"So your stepmother took this seminar?" she asked him.

To her surprise, Kaspian shook his head vigorously. "She didn't *have* to." (Something new in his voice: a hint of what? Dry and scathing, like the surface of an emery board.) "She could have *taught* the seminar, probably. But a lot of other people did. Signed up for it, I mean. It was a hundred and seventy-five dollars for all three days. The third day was when you learned the actual technique."

A lot of other people. Just now Pippa did not want to hear about other people; her life felt quite full of unwelcome strangers. She raised one small hand, examining its thin fingers that looked bony and white as though X-rayed by the fluorescent ceiling lamps. Kaspian watched her with bemused attentiveness. Kids are always interested to discover grown-ups being strange.

"And it worked for them?" she asked him finally. "This promising new technique? It helped them remember?"

The boy nodded. He seemed eager now to tell her more, to tell her everything. "See, there was this girl—I mean really she's, well—this girl I know." But Pippa's raised hand signaled him to stop. He blinked at her, confused, maybe afraid.

"What about the man?" she asked him. "The guy from Tulsa. Has he gone back?"

"He's left, that's all I know. There's kind of a circuit, I guess. I think this is what he does for a living."

"The Fix-It-Up Chappie," Pippa said quietly.

Kaspian knew for sure she was strange by now. He didn't even bother to ask.

"It's from a Dr. Seuss story," she told him anyway. *"When every last cent of their money was spent, the Fix-It-Up Chappie packed up and he went."*

"Ha," said Kaspian. "That's it, I guess." He waited a moment, as though out of courtesy, then said, "Anyway, there was this one girl. I mean, there still *is*. She's a couple of years older than me. And this . . ."

Words drifted toward Pippa but she was unable to grasp them, to make them make sense. Feeling depleted, she took a long slow breath and held it down. She tried to draw the strength, the *prana*, out of the air in her lungs. She imagined the *prana*—a cleansing white light—entering the tiny blood vessels and from there dispersing evenly through her body. There were questions she wanted to ask, crucial facts she needed to learn. But instead what came into her mind was an image of her tiny Yule present: the hand-carved frog fetish, light as soap. Behind this she saw, or imagined (though the clarity of the vision was greater than *imagined* suggests), the innocent, delicate fingers that had fashioned it. The warmth and the moistness and the little-girl stickiness of those hands. Zaddik's Bagel Bakery appeared insubstantial around her, translucent, hazy and bright as the steamed surface of a mirror. Kaspian Aaby looked alert, somewhat surprised, as though she were behaving strangely. Or *not* behaving: sitting there stunned, irrational, dumb with loss. He could never have understood what she was feeling, or why she was afraid to feel anything more, even the slightest thing. Nor would she ever have tried to explain it, to him or to anyone.

She stood up beside the table. She did not know why she was doing so: to leave, or to test her ability to move; or maybe her body had simply done this all on its own, the way it did so many other things.

Kaspian hastened to his feet—adolescent gallantry jumbled with concern, even alarm, in his eyes.

When she lost her balance he tried to catch her, to hold her safe and steady. But he was too late, or too small, or maybe the cause was hopeless.

She heard the gasps of people at other tables, and then she heard nothing. Saw nothing. Knew nothing but emptiness, a blank and ghastly pallor,

where once there had been
a sort of life.

"Not good," said Brenda Cigogne, shaking her head, as though the question were one of a lapse of common sense. Regrettable, but easily avoided in the future. "Fainting in a *taco* place." She shook her head again. "And a *teenage boy* there with you. Not good at all."

Pippa could hardly disagree. "It's a bagel place now," she pointed out, but Brenda of course (and perhaps wisely this time) ignored her.

"You look a complete fright," Brenda said. "You're not *pregnant* again, are you?"

This roused Pippa, the way smelling salts do, obnoxiously. In the storage room of Rose Petal & Thorn, a combination of dull lighting, stacks of cardboard shipping cartons leaning dangerously inward, a backdrop of metal cabinets the color of auto-body primer, and—at center stage, sprawled like a dead scarecrow over the potting bench—the Bad Fairy costume, all taken together, created a persuasive illusion of having descended to the Underworld of the low-paying service industries.

"What do you mean pregnant *again*?" she asked. Because Brenda hadn't been anywhere in sight the first time around.

Nobody had. That had been what made it so—to use her friend Judith's favorite sarcastic expression—*queen-sized*.

"You're not, are you?" said Brenda sternly.

Pippa shook her head.

"Well, thank God for that." Brenda glanced across her shoulder, out toward the bright precincts of the sales counter, where Jacques the French-Canadian-Passama-quoddy-Indian delivery person stared at the computer like callow Arthur sizing up Excalibur in the churchyard. You had to wonder when he was going to give the thing a good yank, just to see what would happen. Brenda scruti-nized Pippa with a mother's brisk and matter-of-fact though not uncompassionate eye. "Will you be all right?" she asked.

Pippa did not know the answer. She was not going to say Yes just to keep up appearances. Appearances had, after all, as Brenda did not fail to point out, gotten quite bad enough. She just kept still where she was slumped in the old padded chair, next to the dead scarecrow and feeling akin to it, only less fearsome, until Brenda decided the matter for herself.

"I better go look in on things," she said. And without a second glance or a second thought, she was gone.

The sun went down a little after 4:00. It was stone-dark by 4:30. Pippa got off work at 5:00. The best way back to the old Shingle Style house, if you wanted to avoid any sight or reminder of George Burroughs School, espe-cially the outbound crawl of cars bearing other people's kids home from Extended Day, was a steep side road called Yew Street that ran past a graveyard full of tall granite obelisks and an elaborate limestone sepulcher with carved angels, or something, getting badly eroded by acid rain.

Tall trees grew here and there, splendid when their limbs were heavy with snow, naked and distant-looking tonight.

Long Nights Moon had collapsed into a singularity of shadow.

A cycle had ended. Which meant that another had just begun, too faintly to discern without specialized instruments. Pippa's mind was too blunt for the job. But as any witch knows, you work with the tools at hand.

It was not a spooky graveyard. Pippa had tried before to imagine it that way—even once persuading the other women of her circle to scope out the place as a possible site for their Samhain ritual. Pippa herself had no ancestors to get in touch with there; but an old boyfriend of hers— years later and older than Winterbelle's dad, but the same general type—had a story about a great-great-grandfather killed in some war. The story was not about the lamented gent himself but about a picture hanging in the family house somewhere, showing him in full sepia-toned mufti looking *exactly* like the odious teenager in *Kids*—the one who goes around infecting virgins with HIV. You couldn't *believe* the resemblance, Pippa's boyfriend had said.

Knowing what she now knew about men, and the villains of stories, and stories in general, Pippa had to wonder exactly how much of this was bullshit. And even assuming the answer to be about 99 percent, then what gritty piece of Truth lay at the center, like the thing inside an oyster, giving the bullshit someplace to accrete around?

A couple of the other women had liked Pippa's graveyard idea but most of the group was too New Agey for that. As witches went they were the incense & strawberries type, preferring to call themselves Wiccans while clutching their holy Llewellyn paperbacks. *Barbies on broomsticks*, as Judith would say. So their Samhain ritual had happened in the usual place (at that time, a weedy patch of ground

Pippa was squatting on, living in a nylon yurt) full of affirmations and positive healing energies directed at All Living Creatures that are Part of the Body of the Mother. And whipped cream and a cherry on top.

The things you do—the places you live!

Yet you survive, somehow. Mostly.

Whistling past the graveyard. Pippa thought it would be good—a show of pluck in the face of overwhelming odds—if she went whistling past the graveyard through the icy blackness of a late December night. But no melodies came to her. At least nothing plucky. Chestnuts roasting on an open fire wouldn't do. "Toyland" made her weepy in the best of circumstances. She was most of the way up the steep slope, Mount Wabenaki blotting out the stars all in front of her, when her brain was invaded by an ancient Beach Boys dope ballad called either "Hang on to Your Ego" or "I Know There's an Answer," one or the other being a previously unreleased track. The lyrics were so insanely 60esque that you had to stop and think about them, marveling that a whole lot of people, in California at least, had once *thought* like that.

Despite herself—despite *Winterbelle*—Pippa momentarily smiled.

She got rid of the smile immediately, and buried the remains of it (though the stupid song would not get out of her head). She would never admit to have smiled at a time like this. No one could forgive such a thing.

She must carry the secret to her grave.

At the gloomy end of Ash Street, the old house stood wrapped in a suspicious cloud of solitude. Pippa kept still by the foot of the sidewalk, whose dark contours were partly scumbled by drifts of snow as coldly luminescent as starlight. Her broom was nowhere in view. The only illumination came from three tall uncurtained windows in Eulace's front parlor, which held one small plastic candle apiece, backlit by the otherworldly indigo of television.

She felt a premonition of something. Shadowy presences stirring in the imaginal cloud. Pippa was pretty good at receiving premonitions but not at decrypting them. Until it was too late of course, and then what difference did it make?

Some witch she was.

Sighing, she trooped up the sidewalk letting the empty backpack slide down the arm of her parka. A blitz of wind off the mountain—now so close and overwhelming you no longer saw it, only felt the gravitational mass of it hulking there—threw her hood back, snapping hair in front of her eyes. An omen? A warning? A brusque, comradely welcome home? Call it in the air.

In the front hallway Pippa shut the door but didn't turn the dead bolt. Eulace preferred that the door be kept locked—locked and barred, like a fortress to hold at bay the plague that ravaged the countryside. Pippa thought her great-aunt watched way too much crime-related television programming, and wasted her energies railing at nonexistent enemies. To the extent that Eulace believed in an unseen, liminal world, her belief focused upon a depersonalized spirit of Evil that ranged across the land, suckling on such things as drugs and abortions, lenient judges, homosexuals, and people with kooky ideas. She would not have identified this spirit as Satan or anything like that. She was essentially nonreligious, as Pippa understood her own mother to have been. No, it was more a philosophical thing: her anger at the loss of certainty, of fixed and known and widely accepted truths. Everything about the modern world (including, Pippa believed, Pippa) just pissed her off.

She looked pissed off right now—catching Pippa by surprise, lurching out of the dim recesses at the back of the house. Her uncomfortable-looking shoes squeaked two highly individualized squeaks as she swam into focus, like an interlaced GIF taking form on a computer screen. Only at the very end, when Eulace came to a halt—close enough to tap on the shoulder with a broom, say—could Pippa read the old woman's expression.

It was secretive but filled with unmistakable triumph. As though she had just witnessed a particularly good public burning.

"Hi," said Pippa, for lack of anything better. She started to mention supper—how she'd whip something together in just a minute—but the memory of there being one too few people in the house to cook for turned the words to poison in her throat.

She blinked her eyes, astonished at the power of this terrible thing, now nearly a day old, to stop her heart from beating, to bring the face of Death so close to her that the stench of the Hag's breath (she fed on rotting corpses) made Pippa retch.

She blinked again. The Hag retreated—though you knew she was out there, biding her time. For now, Aunt Eulace filled the role well enough.

"So they took her, did they?" Eulace said. Her voice was loud in the quiet hall, easily drowning out the TV, where the overweight meteorologist thought we might get a little more snow by the time Santa takes off. Eulace added, "I wondered when they would."

Pippa felt herself struggling for breath; but at least she was breathing. "You wondered . . . what?"

Eulace came nearer. One shoe squeaked; the clock on the kitchen shelf hollowly ticked; a commercial for GM trucks began with a twang of country rock.

"It was only a matter of time," Eulace told her. "The way you live. That crowd of so-called friends of yours. Believe you me, I've seen it coming a *long* way off."

Pippa felt for the first time in her life, or maybe the second, an impulse to cause bodily harm. She flinched away from it, bringing a hand up in front of her face.

Eulace (who must not have understood the peril she stood in) pressed closer still.

"They asked me for permission to search your living quarters, and *I* wasn't about to tell them No. *I've* got nothing to hide, that's what I told them. As far as I'm concerned, you can go take all that stuff and you can do whatever you want with it. Enter it in as evidence. Exhibits A through Z. My heart goes out to that poor girl, is what I said. The mother, now, she was always a wild one. Just like her own mother before that. Fruit of a poisoned branch, as the saying goes. But maybe it's not too late for the girl. My heart goes out to her. That's all I have to say."

Pippa pushed outward. A violent clash of feelings swelled like hot blood behind her eyes, blinding her, and she staggered to the base of the staircase where she groped for the stolid old post. Eulace's voice seemed to follow her but she could make out no words. The premonition she had felt tickling within her as she stood on the sidewalk had exploded, blasting her insides to a chaos of messy protoplasm. She sat on the cold toilet seat in a kind of swoon, black and white tiles swelling and contracting as though the bathroom were an organ she was being digested by.

It passed.

Everything passed by her finally, as it had been passing for quite some time.

She was alone: all but bodiless, or rather disembodied:

sundered from the physical connections that had made her life and Life Itself seem to coincide.

She was insane, or maybe just shorn of the crazy illusion of sanity.

She was far, far away from the gloomy end of Ash Street—soaring with nameless birds of prey above Wabenaki Mountain, immune to the parching wind, perfectly serene in the fastness of the sky.

She was kneeling in an Art Deco bathroom, puking nothingness into a bowl as cold as bone china.

She was a witch without a broom.

A ripped-open heart without a chest to bleed on.

Call it in the air.

What do you do in a situation like this?

Really, tell me.

WHAT DO YOU DO?

You stand outside your daughter's bedroom.

Your daughter has been taken away from you by child welfare authorities who believe you have been abusing her.

Your daughter is the only precious and irreplaceable thing in your otherwise disorganized, undirected, confusing and often hurtful life. You have tried to be the best mother you could be for her. Walking away from relationships because the guy, though you loved and lusted after him et cetera, did not seem like good stepdad material. Enduring the humiliation of the AFDC application and review process; the waiting room full of torn women's magazines and dirty toys; the prying and officiousness of the caseworker; the home visits of the welfare nurse, full of condescending instruction about the food pyramid, basics of first aid, the advantages of breast-feeding. Begging for one shitty job with terrible hours after another. Making the best child-care arrangements you could. Taking a shot

at weird enterprises like growing and harvesting and de-
cocting magical herbal preparations—bath oils, love po-
tions, any stupid make-a-wish thing—then trying to sell
them in little hand-labeled vials through the CoOp, because maybe if you can make a go at this it will allow you
to spend more time with your daughter. Failing, miserably.
Getting accepted to that state program that got cut last
year, where you could go back to school and learn something useful in today's economy. Computer graphics, for
example. Sketching flowers and fairies on a WACOM tab-
let. Whoopee doo. And now with the funding killed, cop-
ping a day job at Rose Petal & Thorn. Which believe it
or not is the best job you have ever had, the gig at the
lesbian bookstore included; although there at least, in lieu
of a dependable paycheck, they welcomed little squirming
Winterbelle as sort of a gender-role statement, professing
not to mind the mess she made, the books she chewed,
the ruckus at naptime. Firing you anyway, though.

Little squirming Winterbelle.

So beautifully bloblike in her infancy. Helpless hopeful
eyes peering up at you. Wanting only your love. Your all-
important motherly approval. And you tried to give it to
her, give it always unstintingly, though now you cry and
cry to think it had not been enough. Nothing would ever
come close to doing justice to how wonderful and loved
and wanted Winterbelle had been—nothing you could
have done or given or said. But at least every day you
could keep trying. Keep hugging the silly thing and kissing
the soft fat place in the middle of her cheek. Taking her
little hand and pressing it flat against your face. Nuzzling
her under the tiny tiny arm—so delicate, you could imagine it snapping just like a stalk of celery—treasuring this
smallness and this fragility, vowing to keep it safe.

Failing again.

Failing this time, finally, maybe, forever.

So now you stand here in the door of her room. The room is a mess. Clothes lie where people have dropped them. Toys have been picked through. The deepest corners of drawers have been pawed roughly at, closets torn open, everything examined and enumerated by unknown hands and eyes.

Who had been here, asking Eulace for permission to *search their living quarters?*

The only clue was the odd phrasing itself, as quoted by her great-aunt: echo of an alien voice. Pippa thought she heard in it something legalistic, rather than merely bureaucratic. Police, then, as opposed to child welfare authorities? Calling while Pippa was at work, saving themselves the hassle of a warrant?

Pippa took a few cautious steps into the room and then paused again. She thought about the way people who have been robbed often say they feel "violated"—equating robbery with something more intimate and horrible, like rape.

Pippa did not feel that way. Her daughter's room was a mess, but she felt actually bizarrely *apart* from it all. It was rather as though a fierce windstorm had forced its way through the old rattling windows, knocked the furniture around, spilled clothes on the floor, and then gone, the way wind does. You could not really feel one way or another about that; it was too obviously impersonal.

Which is just how this—the wreck of Pippa's life, the smashed detritus of all her years of adulthood—seemed to her as she stood there.

It was not as though she felt nothing. She felt many things; felt them too deeply to separate and analyze and name. But the feelings were part of her flesh, inseparable from her very essence. They had nothing, or very little, to do with *this*.

What *this* was was something apart, something foreign and dangerous and maybe unstoppable. Larger than human-sized. Like a winter storm.

A winter storm might kill you. If you failed to act to protect yourself, it certainly would. But it was not killing *you*, in any personal way. It was just raging with cold and death because that was its nature.

Pippa stood there feeling half-dead, because as a mother she had no choice; she was obeying a timeless law of Nature on a par with the speed of light, the phenomenon of radiant cooling of a body in space. When your child is gone, your life and your future go with her: so Nature has decreed.

So what do you do?

What do you do in a time and a place like the gloomy end of Ash Street, three days before the highest and most glorious holiday in Christendom?

You bend over as women always have bent, as they will go on bending, and you go about straightening the place up. You shed tears because it is in your nature to shed them. The tears do not distract you, though they make it difficult to see.

You accept the unacceptable.
You go on.

In the phone book she looked under Attorneys, and read "See Lawyers." The listings began on page 101 and petered out on 107. The number of possible lawyers to choose among was daunting.

Upon closer study Pippa found that most of the listings bore out-of-town addresses. There were only 13 lawyers in the village itself. Most appeared simply as names, though others had taken out display ads describing their practices and their qualifications in detail. She eliminated right away the man whose bachelor's degree was in Mechanical Engineering. Also the one whose office was across the street from Dan Dan's Positive Pizza Scene, where she had had one of her shitty jobs.

What were you supposed to think about in picking a lawyer? The only people she knew who had ever needed lawyers were women friends who, in series, had gotten divorced, and had basically handed the same attorney down from one to the next. Judith explained, after it had been her turn, that this person's primary qualification was that he was, quote, One tough son of a bitch. Pippa crossed him out.

It did not occur to her until this point—seriously narrowing it down—that some of the lawyers would be women. They tended to have nice old-fashioned names: Susan, Emily, Miranda. Two of them ran modest little ads, the yellow-page equivalent of sensible shoes. Of these, one noted "Evening hours available," which Pippa thought was considerate, while the other—beneath a sketch, in red, of a cozy-looking farmhouse—promised "Traditional legal services in a relaxed rural setting." Pippa wanted immediately to make an appointment with this woman, if only to sit in her farmhouse, drinking tea. But the address was way out of town, and Pippa couldn't imagine offhand how she was going to get there. Hitchhiking did not seem advisable, and she wasn't yet ready to reawaken some dormant friendship to ask for a ride. Doing so would require an explanation, and she didn't feel up to that.

Back to the list, then. One by one she sounded out the names and contemplated the way each attorney had chosen to describe his or her services. One display ad, half a page large, emphasized "Domestic relations," which were further broken down as follows: Divorce, Custody, Adoption, Abuse & Harassment, Paternity. Pippa was not sure that this was where she belonged. An adjacent ad more soberly described "General practice of law, including family problems, divorces, and child custody." She felt more comfortable with this—"family problems" struck her as suitably nonjudgmental—except that an inch farther down, the list extended to "Criminal representation and trials."

Pippa stared out one wide corniced window, where the day had barely gotten past the ghostly blue of predawn, though it was already 7:00.

The question was, she guessed, what exactly did she need a lawyer *for?* If it was simply, or mostly, to help her understand the system, the nature of the problems she faced, then that was one thing. If it was to charge into battle as her champion, lopping the heads off child-welfare types and freeing Winterbelle from captivity, that was another. And if it was something even more drastic (there remained, after all, Kaspian Aaby's half-delivered message about something called QROST), then maybe one tough son of a bitch was not a bad idea, after all.

Unwillingly she looked down at the phone book again. Her eyes dropped cleanly, like a lawn dart, onto a two-line entry that said:

**Arthur Torvid, Counselor at Law,
Old Tannery, Top Floor**
Protection for the people—
Expert in 1st Amendment issues

Pippa thought she knew the name from somewhere. A vague image of a business card, reproduced in the monthly program listing for the community radio station, formed in her mind. This must, she supposed, be the local hippie with a law degree, dedicated to saving the world one victim at a time. Until now she had never considered that such people had much raison d'être in a place like this—where, after all, the closest thing to a civil rights issue was the occasional Jewish kid who had trouble making up a spelling test because some country teacher had never heard of Rosh Hashanah. Suddenly things were revealed to her in a new light.

Waiting for the law-office answering machine to pick up (it was still only 7:17 in the morning) she experienced the feeling you have when you finally roll up your sleeves and embark on some burdensome chore—going through heaps of your daughter's old clothing, for example, deciding what can stay, what might be sold to the woman at

Away We Grow, and what is condemned to the Goodwill bag—and having put the thing off for so long, you feel a surge of energy and confidence just from having broken through your own inertia.

"Hello?" a voice said loudly in her ear.

"Oh—sorry," said Pippa. She eased the phone away from her mouth, and was halfway toward slipping it gently back in its cradle, but the impoliteness of hanging up on a wrong number would have bothered her for the rest of the day. The Three-Fold Law, et cetera. So she brought the phone back and said:

"I'm sorry to bother you. I guess I dialed—"

"Whom were you calling?" the voice asked her. Brisk, almost commanding.

"Oh, um—" Pippa had forgotten the name. "I was trying to call a lawyer's office. I must have—"

"Arthur Torvid?" the voice said.

"Yeah." (Somewhat relieved. At least it was a common mistake.) "Do you get a lot of calls for him?"

"Most of them. I'm Arthur Torvid. What can I help you with?"

Pippa felt off-balance. Unready for this and unsure, now, whether she really wanted to go through with it. What kind of lawyer was answering his phone at the crack of dawn?

An old hippie lawyer, she guessed.

"Well," she said, not having planned how to explain herself, "it's kind of a long . . . well not really a *long*, but kind of a weird . . . I don't know. It's about my daughter."

"Custody thing?" said the brisk voice on the telephone. "Spousal kidnapping? You know paralegal counseling services are available pro bono through New Hope for Women."

He spoke *awfully* fast. Especially for this hour of the

morning. Pippa wished she had a cup of coffee to sip, something to get her brain geared up.

"It's hard—" she began again.

"Hard to talk with Ma Bell listening," Arthur Torvid said. "Of course it is. I understand. Why don't you come over?"

"That's what I wanted to do," said Pippa. "I mean, I was calling to make an appointment."

"Great. You've made one. Come on over. Are you calling from in town?"

"You mean—come over *now?*"

"Now or whenever," said Arthur Torvid. "Now would be fine. I've been up for hours."

She thought she detected a shade of amusement in his voice.

"So have I, actually," she said.

"Aha." Arthur Torvid did not sound at all the way she had expected. "So. Do you know where I'm located?"

"The Old Tannery?"

"Top floor," he said. "Door's always open. And you are . . . ?"

For a moment, she didn't get what he was asking. She was . . . ? Kind of the question of her life, there, really.

Then she got it. "Oh. Pippa Rede."

"Beautiful," said Arthur Torvid.

The Old Tannery was set partly on piers overhanging a narrow, dark, fast-moving river. Buntings and snow geese sometimes took refuge there. Pippa looked and saw nothing but frothing water channeled between huge granite blocks, their faces glazed with ice: an outstanding place to kill yourself. The building had gotten a facade-lift sometime in the 80's, but true to the spirit of that decade the appearance of progress masked a far-advanced state of underlying decay. Inside the narrow front stairwell, the air held the bracing tang of carcinogenic insecticides, and as Pippa climbed to the third and topmost floor, it also grew stiflingly hot. She closed her eyes for a moment, lowered her head; she did not want public fainting to become a habit. Something was the matter with her blood sugar, she supposed. The obvious answer was to eat. She would do this soon, she promised. Just now the sadness of cooking anything, of being alone in that cold kitchen, was too heavy to bear.

On Arthur Torvid's office door, pinned by two thumbtacks, was the business card she remembered from the radio station flyer. It repeated the slogan from the telephone book: Protection for the people. Pippa knocked lightly at the big door—then, aggravated at how feeble it sounded, she turned the handle and stepped in.

The office looked like somebody's back room, a place where you drop things until you figure out what to do with them. Most of the clutter came in the form of reading material: novels, law books, magazines, newspapers, a year's worth of unopened mail. There was a big desk with a computer, a boxy DOS-type thing like the ones at the public library. Pippa wondered why a hippie lawyer didn't use a Macintosh. An *old* Macintosh.

She jostled her backpack off. She was aware that schlepping things around in a backpack was not a totally grown-up thing to do—in fact she had gotten the idea from Winterbelle, back in first grade. But it was so much *easier* than carrying a heavy purse. And it left your hands free. A witch ought to have her hands free. You never know when a stray newt might need its eyes plucked out.

Arthur Torvid appeared, without fanfare or even footsteps, in a narrow opening between bookshelves that must actually have been a door, two-thirds blocked off. He was of medium height, with black hair shooting sideways

around a wide bald spot, and a belly that protruded like
something he was proud of. His eyes were dark and intense. He wore khaki pants and a sage-green polo shirt
that said, in tiny tasteful letters, Ohio Hempery.

"Pippa Rede!" he declared.

She nodded.

"Welcome to my lair. Pro forma apologies for the
housekeeping, offered and accepted I'm sure. Now let's sit
down, shall we?"

It was a little hard to keep up with him. He bustled
over to his desk and motioned Pippa toward a selection
of unmatched seating alternatives: a slumping leather chair
that looked like a giant aged Birkenstock, an uptight
Windsor sort of thing, and a folding deck chair whose
canvas sling sported a bright-colored jungle motif. Pippa
chose the last; she supposed this placed her immediately
in a certain category of clients.

"What kind of help do you need?" Arthur Torvid asked.

Before she could think of how to answer, he ducked
under the desk, scrabbled for something on the floor, and
finally stomped the button on a power strip. The computer
fan revved up, and when Torvid reappeared, his face was
illuminated by an unhealthy grayish glow, like the light
from a storm cloud, coming out of the monitor.

Pippa found this disconcerting and arguably discourte-
ous. She looked away, gathering her thoughts, and noticed
on a side wall, partly covered by a framed diploma from
(it looked like) Golden State University, a large poster of
Dennis Hopper riding a motorcycle. In this well-known
image, young Hopper faces the camera extending promi-
nently the finger known in certain small circles as the
Enchanter, and in larger ones as the Bird.

Pippa looked at Torvid again. She was worried now.

"What kind of a lawyer are you?" she asked.

"What kind do you need?" he said quickly. "I'm pretty flexible. But look, if it's not a good match, I'll send you to somebody that's right for you. Don't let any of this stuff—" he waved around the office "—put you off. I can be professional when I need to be."

Pippa considered this. She decided to believe him.

"It's about my daughter," she said. "They took her away."

Arthur Torvid leaned across his desk in her direction. His face squinted somewhat. It was as though her words were so faint, they didn't quite make it across the room and he was reaching out to coax them the rest of the distance.

What a foolish, small, ineffectual person I must seem! she thought with dismay. *Poor Pippa.*

"They who?" asked Torvid, a new sharpness in his voice. "They as in . . . the Authorities?"

Just the way he said this word, with a pained sort of precision, made Pippa feel that she might, after all, have come to the right place. She nodded.

"The Child Welfare Gestapo," Torvid pronounced. He leaned back, faced the computer screen, and punched a series of keys with rapid, energized strokes. "What was it—some neighbor turn you in for abuse and neglect? Were you home-schooling? Is there a coparent seeking custody? Any sexual-preference issues here? It's important that I know the whole story."

This is going to be difficult, Pippa thought. Number one, he talked too fast—he *thought* too fast—and number two, he wouldn't take his eyes off the damn computer, as though he was waiting for her answers to scroll out there.

"What are you doing?" she finally asked him.

He tossed a glance at her; then something he saw made him turn and look more deliberatively. All at once he smiled, with what seemed genuine good humor, and looked in that moment like Larry of the Three Stooges.

"Sorry," he said. "Just checking my e-mail. It's an addiction, you know. I'm on a couple of civil-liberties mailing lists. There's a case going on now in Wisconsin, schoolteacher suspended for kicking a DARE officer out of her classroom. Very stimulating discussion."

Abruptly he bent under the desk and flipped the power strip off.

"All right, Pippa Rede," he said. "Let's start at the beginning. I'd like you to tell me everything about your daughter. And about yourself."

His voice was still sharp, but his eyes had gentled down, and Pippa wondered if the brusqueness might be a sort of cover. A cover for what, there was no telling. She bet that somewhere on the premises she would find a small plastic bottle of selective seratonin reuptake inhibitors. If not Xanax Itself.

"Well," she said, "I guess the beginning is, I'm a witch."

Arthur Torvid did not react to this in any way. None: not even a nod. Pippa concluded that in this man's world, a declaration of witchhood did not even register on the weirdometer.

"My daughter's name is Winterbelle." She now felt strangely, preternaturally calm. "She's nine years old. She'll be ten next month. And I want her back so badly. I really can't see any point in living if I can't get her back. That's the truth. She's the only thing I care about."

At last Arthur Torvid gave her a nod.

"They came to my house . . . I don't know why. I think some woman named Aaby might have—"

"Carol Deacon Aaby," Arthur Torvid broke in.

"Yes. I think."

His expression slowly changed, acquiring a look of ferocity.

Pippa said, "It wasn't just *her*. I mean, there was this child psychologist woman, and a man named Wemble. Wait a minute." She reached into her backpack and pulled out the stack of official papers. It was a relief to flop them down on Arthur Torvid's desk: transferring the burden to his stocky, confident shoulders.

"Ah!" he exclaimed, pouncing upon them. "Yes"—flipping rapidly through; could he possibly be *reading* that fast? "Yes, yes. Yes yes yes. I see, I see."

In other circumstances—meeting him as a customer, she a waitress, for example—Pippa thought she might find this man amusing. His stiff hair wagged while his head bobbed like a frog in water, and his thick hands with stubby fingers had a way of *jabbing* at things, quick little thrusts and retreats, as though he were living in a world principally populated by evil snakes.

"So it says here," Torvid said, lowering the papers and peering across them, "you are entitled to supervised visitation for a period not to exceed one hour per week, at a time to be arranged. Have you called to arrange that?"

Pippa shook her head. She didn't want to admit to him, not yet at least, that she had not even looked at the terrible documents.

"Good," he said. "Don't."

"Don't?" she said.

"Don't call. Don't make any arrangements with these people. If you do, you're buying into the basic premise that they have a *right*, a *power*, to control your access to your own flesh and blood. Understand? Our attack is going to be based on the principle of family sovereignty. We're going to argue that the seizure of your daughter was illegal, unconstitutional, prejudicial, harmful to the common good, and exceeding the limits of the State's authority. To do that, we must not acknowledge that authority in any way, explicit or implicit. Do you follow me?"

Pippa did, she thought. "But um, couldn't we just argue that I'm innocent?"

"Of course you're innocent!" Arthur Torvid fairly shouted, raised his eyes toward the water stains in the ceiling. Then he lowered his gaze, and his voice. "You *are* innocent, aren't you?"

She nodded.

"You don't, let's see—" his eyes skipped across the sheet before them "—*abuse, mistreat, torture, grossly demean, inflict bodily harm upon, culpably neglect or otherwise allow damage or injury to be suffered by* your daughter?"

"Does it say I do?" aghast, asked Pippa.

Torvid tossed the papers away from him, as though they were of no consequence. "It's just language. Boilerplate. They have to stipulate to a judge that certain conditions have been fulfilled in order to justify seizing custody of a minor. The conditions are specified in legislation and by administrative rule. After they've gotten their provisional okay, they dig deeper into the specific case and trump up some sort of customized list of allegations that, believe me, will sound even worse. This they use to justify continued possession of the child pending a formal court proceeding, which normally occurs after a couple of months. They need time, see, for their staff shrinks to brainwash the kid into thinking, or at least stating for the record, that the parent is Satan himself."

He looked at her, perhaps to gauge the impact his words were having. Of course there was no way he could tell that from Pippa's completely blank and frozen demeanor. The only way she conceivably could have done justice to the emotions that raged within her would have been to run shrieking around the room, yanking books off shelves, punching out the glass of the computer display, and devouring the large glossy picture of Dennis Hopper.

"One good thing," said Torvid, "is there's no mention here of QROST. Did they say anything to you about QROST?"

Pippa said, "No, but um—"

"Good. At least things aren't as bad as they could be. QROST is what they pull out when they *really* want to burn somebody."

"It is?" said Pippa. Weakly, as usual.

Arthur Torvid waxed solemn. "It stands for something— Quasi something Occultic Sexual something. I could look it up. Major league bullshit of the highest order, I.M.H.O. But it hasn't yet been thrashed out in the courts, so there's a lot of room for them to play with it. But don't even think about that. It's not mentioned in these, pardon the expression, *documents* anywhere. Now, listen: has this gotten out to the media?"

Pippa described briefly her brushup with Mark Portion. Torvid turned his eyes ceilingward.

"Mark Portion." He appeared to reflect at length, or to await divine feedback. "What a guy."

Without warning he leapt to his feet. His stocky torso appeared to expand still further, to occupy a great part of the already full room.

"Pippa Rede," he declared, "we have a busy time ahead of us! We're going to take on the vested powers of the Government and the State. We are going to rattle the almighty Authorities in their seats of power. *And*"—enunciating one word at a time—"*we are going to prevail.*"

Pippa watched him, feeling as removed from these inspirational words as though they had been delivered by a tiny figure on a television screen. She did not feel inspired.

She was not sure whether to believe him. But she did feel hopeful, maybe, at last, a tiny bit.

"Have you ever done this before?" she dared to ask him.

"Never," said Arthur Torvid, without a smidgen of self-doubt. It was remarkable, really. "Always wanted to, though."

"I guess here's your chance," said Pippa. "And one other thing. Could I—I mean . . ."

"Money." Arthur Torvid looked at her in a funny, knowing way. "Am I right? You're going to ask about money."

She nodded. Obviously he had done *that* part before.

"You don't have much money, Pippa Rede. Isn't that so?"

She nodded again.

"Then I won't ask for money. Robin Hood was right, you know. As quoth the bumper sticker."

Pippa actually could not believe she was hearing this. "I could pay you *something*," she said. After all, there were considerations of karma.

"Of course you can," said Arthur Torvid. He thought for a moment and then added, rather slyly, "You're a witch, you said."

"Kind of a witch." She backed off a little because lately she was having some doubts about this.

"Then I will be happy," Arthur Torvid said—and indeed, he looked happy—"to accept payment in kind."

A message was waiting for Pippa when she arrived, 20 minutes late, for work at Rose Petal & Thorn. Brenda Cigogne handed her the little slip of yellow paper. Wordlessly: making a point of it.

The message, in Brenda's bountiful handwriting, said:

Please call Mark Portion. Says its urgent.

Pippa wondered whether the apostrophe existed anymore. It had when she was in school. That seemed a long time ago now; a different era. She dragged the phone cord as far as it would stretch, into a corner of work space under the parakeet cages.

"I *told* you," she reminded Mark Portion, when he got around to picking up his end of the connection, "I don't want to talk." She hoped the quavering in her belly did not make it as far up as her mouth.

"Listen, Pippa," the man's deep and unctuous voice said, after a pause. "I've got a newspaper to put to bed. Try to understand where I'm coming from."

"Why don't *you* try to understand?"

There was silence on the line. Like, Your request is being processed. Please hold. Then Mark Portion asked pleasantly, "How do you feel about Satan?"

"*What?*"

"Do you practice your witchcraft alone? Or as part of an organized group? Do you have contact with other organizations around the country?"

It sounded like he was reading from a list. While Pippa thought about hanging up on him, he added in the same blithe tone:

"Just stop me if we come to a question you'd care to answer. Have you ever participated in the ritual slaughter of animals? To what extent do your rituals involve the indoctrination or initiation of underaged children? Are you motivated chiefly by the desire for personal gain or power, or do you have a broader social agenda?"

"Stop this," said Pippa. "Please. Just stop it."

"I want to *help* you," Mark Portion said. His voice in the telephone ached with sincerity. "I want to help any young mother in your terrible situation. And of course I want to help your daughter too. What I need is *information*. That's my job, Pippa. To *inform*. To bring the truth to light. Help me discover the truth, Pippa, and the truth will set you free."

An inspiration seized her. Turning halfway about, looking back into the cheerier regions of the flower shop, she told him, "I think maybe you ought to talk to my lawyer."

She felt pleased with herself, the more so as Mark Portion did not immediately reply. Parakeets jumped about on the aluminum bottoms of their cages, like ecstatic drummers.

"Who is your lawyer?" Mark Portion finally asked.

"Arthur Torvid," said Pippa.

A noise greeted this: not exactly a syllable, perhaps a sound generated by the nose.

Mark Portion said, "Arthur Torvid?"

Pippa had nothing to add; she sensed that something was wrong here.

"Let me guess," said Portion. "The sovereign citizen defense. Government has no authority to regulate the lives of citizens, in whom all constitutional authority is vested. Something like that?"

"No," said Pippa. Though the word *sovereign* did register in a familiar way.

"Well, let me make one little suggestion, if I might." Mark Portion paused, then continued bluntly: "Get a second opinion. You're in trouble enough as it is."

"Why?" she said.

But the connection was broken. Mark Portion had hung up on her.

She supposed she was the sort of person people did that to.

"I'd like you to meet NoElle Deacon," Brenda Cigogne said. She pivoted with a certain flourish, like an m.c. pre-

senting to the audience (in this case Pippa and the parakeets) a young woman who appeared recently to have
stepped out of some old-fashioned girls' school and into a
cosmetics commercial. Shining long swirls of blond hair.
Perfect teeth arrayed in a beauty-queen smile. A Kirstin
Scarcelli dress & sweater ensemble, suitable for church so-
cials. Waist and legs like a Disney cartoon heroine. Pippa
felt an irrational, angry desire to rip through the folds of
ramie-cotton blend, checking to see if this android came
equipped with simulated genitalia.

Why am I being so hostile? she wondered at the back
of her brain, seat of the prehensile 12-step impulse shared
by all women.

"And you must be Pippa," the android said, stepping
forward with one set of dishwater-free fingers tipped with
long pink nails proffered to be shaken.

Pippa took the hand and found it cool to the touch.

"I've heard," of course NoElle Deacon added, "so much
about you."

Pippa looked toward Brenda for some explanation. Her
boss was behaving oddly; though who was Pippa to talk?
Apparently self-conscious, Brenda Cigogne said:

"NoElle is the daughter of one of our regular *customers,*
you know. Of course I hadn't *seen* her since—goodness.
How long could it have been? Since before you went off
to—"

"B.J.U.," NoElle helpfully said. She seemed determined
to hang on to Pippa's hand until Pippa herself dropped it.
Which she did then.

Brenda went on, "So when NoElle showed up this morning and asked if we needed any help—she's just home for
a few weeks, over the Christmas break—well I thought,
you know, it's been so dreadfully *busy* lately. And
you . . . ."

She looked helplessly at Pippa. As though expecting her to fill in the blanks. Pippa pressed her lips shut.

"You seem so *distracted*," Brenda moved on, past the awkwardness. "Anyway, so I hired her. You can show her some of the things you do—think of her as your *assistant*. Just for the next few weeks, of course."

"Next semester starts on the 18th of January," NoElle said. Perkily: wanting to be useful.

Pippa's brain clouded. The 18th of January was Winterbelle's birthday. Her face felt hot and her fingers cold. She wondered if she was losing it.

"I'm sure we'll get along just fine," said Brenda Cigogne.

"Like a regular family," said NoElle Deacon.

Her smile at Pippa was 100 percent opaque. There might have been anything or nothing behind it. There was no particular reason for Pippa to hate her.

The wind turned and the weather changed. It was always changing, of course. Especially in winter, it never truly settled down; the great cycles and metacycles ground against one another like unmeshed gears. Tides rose and waves crashed on unseen shores. Storms brooded like newborn colonies of wasps, a thousand miles away, then swarmed with implacable fury, then as quickly were gone. Sunlight came down warm and blessingly one minute, cold and mocking an hour later. The winds never stopped. Even if the computerized weather map on Channel 5 showed an airscape totally at rest, you knew that Wabenaki Mountain was busy cooking up a climate of its own.

By late morning the breeze had moved all the way from northwest to south. Warmer and moister air floated in, struck the side of the mountain, and rose upward into collision with the high-pressure ridge that girded the summit like a defensive fortification. Strange, roiling clouds of

ocean-gray took form. Snow materialized as though magically conjured, like fairy dust, upon the slopes. Pippa
stepped out onto Mill Street, unsure how to go about
surviving her lunch hour, and found herself staring up at
the mountain in a kind of dumb, half-aware, mesmerized
fascination.

For a minute or longer her mind seemed to empty of
its own thoughts and to feel instead the thoughts of another being, out of another time—perhaps the mountain
itself, dreaming of summer. The illusion extended to her
sense of smell: she breathed a sour, organic, ancient stew
of seawater, rotting kelp, driftwood pickled white. Even
when her mind returned to itself—back to the oppressive
present tense of Mill Street—the smells lingered on, and
Pippa supposed that the new flow of air had traveled all
the way here from some distant sun-warmed sea.

If so, then little airborne microbes would have come
with it. Invisible hitchhikers, looking for a place to crash.
They would be dying now, freezing, their membranes rup-
turing. Billions and trillions of unseen, anonymous deaths.

Did the Ocean mourn them?

It was hard to think so. It was hard to believe, really,
that such infinitesimal, rudimentary, nonindividuated forms
of life had any moral weight on any conceivable scale.

And yet if you were a witch you had to believe that
they did. You had to believe that the fleeting existence of
every single bacterium—every virus, protein strand, whatever—meant *something*. It owned its tiny share of the Meaning of all creation. Because every cell was part of the body
of the Mother. The death of any part, however tiny, must
be counterbalanced by a birth somewhere, just as your
own dead skin cells flaked off and were endlessly replaced
by newly divided cells arising out of your flesh. Winter
and death and darkness and retreat were only half of the

story: somewhere else, summer and life and light and growth must prevail.

That's how witches see the world. As all of a part, intimately connected. Perfect and beautiful; rounded and whole.

Pippa found now, however, that although she shared the vision and believed it, it had lost its power to inspire her, to nurture a sense of awe or of serenity. In fact, it did something quite different: made her feel insignificant and small. As powerless as a microbe. And as expendable.

She could hardly imagine herself getting to the end of this day, feeling the way she did.

Many days, of course—especially during this darkest time of year—she got the feeling that she couldn't go on. Couldn't keep doing all that was required of her, bear the responsibilities, endure the humiliations. Probably everybody feels like that. Yet everybody, at least most of the time, trudges out and does what they have to do anyway.

Pippa didn't think she could do it anymore.

She couldn't imagine going back inside Rose Petal & Thorn and making small talk with customers. Listening to the harebrained banter of Brenda Cigogne. Murmuring "Same to you" when people wished her a Merry Christmas. Wrapping gifts.

All she wanted to do was curl up in a ball somewhere, let the cold and the darkness and the final serenity creep over her.

Out of the flower shop stepped a small, underweight gentleman so badly hunched over that he seemed to crawl on all fours as much as to walk. Pippa watched him with a feeling of unwilled tenderness—compassion that she no longer felt for herself—and she followed his slow, halting progress along the sidewalk with curiosity, right up to the moment when he paused a couple of paces away from her.

She thought she might be blocking his path and moved to get out of his way. But he would have none of that. He took one more step in her direction and then—painfully, it seemed—raised one arm which held two small cone-shaped paper parcels, the sort that single roses came wrapped in.

"Please accept one of these," he said, with a mellifluous voice like some forgotten B-movie actor, "with my compliments."

"Me?" Pippa said. Pretty sure that there must be some mistake.

"If you please," said the old man.

His face, a sort of wolf-fur-gray, twisted partly sideways and partly upward so that he could meet her eyes.

"I am a friend," he said, "a very *old* friend, of Mrs. Madeleine Mallard. Who sends you her compliments and best wishes. Please," he added, rather imploringly, "do take a rose."

A rose, thought Pippa. One rose. It was mysterious and beautiful. She took one of the parcels from the old man's hand, in part to keep him from having to stand there any longer with his arm hitched up.

He sighed and lowered himself back into what must have been his accustomed position, bent over and staring at the ground. "Thank you," he said graciously.

"Thank me?" said Pippa. "Gosh—thank *you*."

She opened the top of the paper cone and saw that the flower inside was white: the gentle white of milk, with just a hint of creamy yellow at the vortex of furled petals.

"It's wonderful," she said. Really meaning it.

"Roses," the old man said, dreamily.

And then he was going. Hobbling but somehow sure of himself, confident of his direction and his purpose.

Pippa envied that.

But then she thought, as she watched the old man turn the corner onto Church Street and vanish in the holiday crowd, that there was no reason for envy. Because she herself had a purpose, a very certain one, though the way to achieve it was far from clear. In a funny way she felt as though it was this—not the rose, but the realization, the remembrance—that the poor old man had given her.

Winterbelle, she thought. That was the reason to go on, to live till the end of the day, then through the night, and on and on, however long it took. Forever, if necessary.

Thank you, she mouthed without sound into the shadow of the old man's absence.

Then for the first time in how long, she had no idea, she got herself a decent lunch. To give her the strength to face what must inevitably come, and the good sense

not to wonder too much
what that
might be.

On December 24th, the *Weekly Herald*—winner of many local journalism awards before its publisher attended an out-of-state management seminar and, upon returning, fired two reporters, the photographer, and the copy editor—published a special holiday edition billed, in antique lead type above the masthead:

CHRISTMAS THE WAY IT USED TO BE!

With all the women busy in the kitchen, Pippa supposed.

Sure enough, an accompanying low-contrast photo, stretching across most of the front page, showed a 100-year-old scene of falling snow, pointed firs, rambunctious dogs, and a team of men and older boys wrestling a massive freshly cut Christmas tree into position on the village green. A long-since-vanished gazebo was visible behind them, and part of the mill that was now a credit-card center. The Congregationalist steeple had not yet gotten its clock; the bank sat where it still sat; a hardware store occupied the present-day t-shirt emporium. On the whole

122

what was striking to Pippa was how little really had changed.

Squashed at the bottom of the page was the article she was looking for, and dreading. Its headline said:

FEARS OF OCCULT ACTIVITY GROW
AS OFFICIALS WEIGH RESPONSE

Pippa shut her eyes tight, afraid now to read any further. And yet, of course, she had to look, the way she guessed you would have to look if you were present at an execution. It was just too horrible, too unbelievable, to keep your eyes away.

At first, she did not find herself anywhere at all in what followed.

"Drums beating wildly," the article began. "Weird howls in the middle of the night. Shadowy figures leaping around a bonfire, deep in the woods. And in the morning, mysterious clues to what diabolic rite may have been carried out while local residents huddled in fear and confusion behind locked doors."

Say *what?* thought Pippa.

"These lurid accounts were among many to be heard by a reporter on Tuesday night, at an informal meeting to discuss reports of widespread occult activity in the area. The meeting, organized by a group of concerned residents headed by Carol Deacon Aaby, was held at the First Church of Mankind's Destiny Among the Stars. Among those in attendance were several local citizens living in the vicinity of Wabenaki Mountain State Park, who reported hearing and seeing some of the peculiar activities noted above, as well as psychologist and cult expert Dr. Allison Rhinum, who spoke and answered questions concerning the prevalence of what she termed 'quasi-ritualistic' practices, especially among youths and other disaffected members of society.

"No representatives of the law enforcement community were present, but a source in the Police Department stated to this reporter that an ongoing investigation of the matter has yielded, thus far, only circumstantial, if tantalizing, evidence. 'You've got some strange-looking objects,' this source revealed, 'and you've got something spilled on rocks that looks like it might be blood. And you've got clear evidence of candles being burned.' Upon questioning, the source acknowledged that reports have been received from anonymous informants concerning 'specific individuals who may be involved in illegal behaviors,' and that these reports are being 'vigorously pursued.'"

Pippa felt a tickle on her wrist, which she took to be a manifestation of nervousness. She scratched hard, then looked down to discover that she had smooshed a little brown spider.

"Oh, I'm sorry," she said, lifting the spider on a finger before her face. "I'm sorry, little guy."

When the world is out of balance, all creatures suffer: a point of witch's doctrine, if there is such a thing.

Pippa had no desire to read on. But the article continued with or without her.

"Officials at the State Park expressed surprise at reports of possible wrongdoing on Wabenaki Mountain. They did report, however, that they had issued a permit to a local group known as Manely Men to hold monthly gatherings on park property. No details of the nature of this shadowy organization were available at press time.

"In a case that authorities believe may be related to far-reaching cult operations, Mr. Roger Wemble of the Department of Family Services, also in attendance at Tuesday's meeting, stated that the Department had recently intervened to remove a child from a home in which, in Wemble's words, 'evidence strongly suggested a pattern of systematic abuse, both psychological and sexual,' which he further characterized as 'typical of occult organizations such as Sisters of the Moon, which rejects the entire structure of Judeo-Christian morality.' Efforts by this reporter to locate or contact Sisters of the Moon for comment have thus far proved fruitless.

"Details of the child-custody case mentioned by Mr. Wemble are confidential under departmental guidelines. The *Herald* has, however, obtained the names of the persons involved and is attempting to investigate the substance of the charges. To date, the alleged perpetrator has refused comment. However, this individual's attorney, Mr. Arthur Torvid, spoke briefly by telephone to a reporter. In that conversation he stated in part:

" 'If you think Christianity is the only ball game in town, you ought to get out more. Didn't you hear Cybill Shepherd give thanks to the Goddess when she accepted her Golden Globe? And don't forget that even a raving Satanist is guaranteed the freedom of religion under our Bill of Rights. If you don't like it, you ought to go live in Georgia where they burned the Bill of Rights a hundred years ago.'

"The Police Department spokesman declined to comment on whether the individual named in the above child-custody case is the target of any investigation."

That was all.

There was no follow-up on page whatever. The *Herald's* editorial policy did not allow articles of such length— above all not in a Special Holiday Issue, where it might compete for attention with important advertising.

Pippa could not help but think, as she tore the newspaper into strips the size of supermarket coupons, that now everything was as bad as it could possibly be.

Immediately she wanted to take it back. Because sure as Hel, as soon as you even *think* a thing like that—as soon as you presume to put a cap on Nature's power to inflict pain and suffering as She damn well pleases—you will be proven wrong. Because things can always

and probably will

get worse.

Solidly in the door of Rose Petal & Thorn, Brenda Cigogne stood waiting for her. Waiting to *pounce,* you might have said. She gave no sign of intending to budge her sizable figure so as to allow Pippa to enter.

"I'd like to speak with you," Brenda said. Her resolute tone did not entirely cover an underlying tremble: it was the same voice she used on rare occasions when a customer's account got so long overdue that Something had to be done about it.

Pippa could hardly refuse to be spoken to. She could hardly, in point of fact, move. She was standing with the door hydraulically pressing itself shut against her calves and the hot, cidery air blowing out at head level. Brenda looked as momentous as the front end of the store's delivery van, to which Jacques had affixed a plastic wind guard proclaiming, in reverse lettering that you could read in your rearview mirror, WE GO ANYWHERE!

Brenda on the other hand was going nowhere.

"Pippa," she said, in that very particular voice, "there have been stories. Bad stories. About you."

Pippa wanted to say, So what? But that would not have sounded the way she meant it. So she said nothing.

"I didn't *want* to believe them, Pippa," Brenda proceeded, with hesitation. A bad sign, using Pippa's name a lot. "But *now* I'm afraid . . . after everything that's happened . . . well, I just can't think it's good for the store."

"For the *store?*" (Genuinely unsure she had heard this right.)

"The terrible *publicity*," Brenda went on. "And you know, right here at *Christmas*time. Which you know is the most important retail season of the year."

"The take is higher on Mother's Day, actually," Pippa said. Why she said this no one would ever know. It was true, but it made her sound . . . what? Cynical? Contemptuous? Something awful.

"Oh, Pippa." Brenda shook her head. "We've known each other for quite a good while now, and we've worked together . . . I simply don't know what to say. Sometimes you can *think* you know someone, I suppose, but then it turns out that you don't have any idea. What they're *truly* like, that is. Of course we all have our secrets. Some of us more than others. And maybe it's better if it stays that way. If the secrets never become known."

"She's been talking to you," said Pippa, "hasn't she?"

"Who?" Brenda Cigogne shrank back, as though something in Pippa's voice frightened her.

"Carol Deacon Aaby," Pippa said. The syllables shot out like spittle.

"I don't see what *that* has to do—" Brenda caught herself. She was at any rate not a liar. "Yes, Pippa, she has. But you certainly can't go around shooting the messenger, can you?"

"It depends," said Pippa. "It depends on the message, I think."

"Then tell me it isn't true," Brenda said, her voice rising in challenge. "Tell me they haven't had to take poor Winterbelle away. Tell me you aren't practicing witchcraft. Look me in the eye and tell me that, and I'll believe you."

Pippa could not figure out how to go about this. She must have looked like a blithering fool, opening her mouth and closing it again, finding no adequate words. No magic formula.

"It *is* true, then," said Brenda. Sounding, perhaps, more relieved than regretful.

"Some of it," said Pippa. "I mean, it's true I'm a witch—but not like *that*. It's like kind of a . . . a Nature thing. Fertility and balance and cycles and so forth. Look, there are *books* you can read about this."

"Books I can read?" exclaimed Brenda, as though the idea were unspeakable. "Pippa, we're not talking about something that happens in books. We're talking about real life. A *little girl's* life. A little girl's *soul*."

Pippa practically sputtered: "You think you have to tell me about that? I'm her *mother*, for—"

"For what?" Brenda eyed her with a certain shrewdness. "For *God's sake*, is that what you were going to say? But that's not really appropriate, is it? Under the circumstances."

Somewhere in Pippa's brain, an important connection broke. Access to her logical, reasonable, 2 + 2 = 4 faculties was abruptly cut off. The only thing left was a boiling cauldron of emotion.

She squeezed her eyes shut and tried to hold the hot tears inside.

"Please," she said. "Please don't do this."

"I'm sorry, Pippa," said Brenda. And she did sound sorry. But it was too late, apparently, for any of that to matter. "Really, I *wouldn't* do it except that—well, you know as well as anyone. I've got a business to run. I can't afford, *now* of all times, to frighten off my customers. You have to consider people's *beliefs*, don't you? And Pippa, people in this town take certain things Very Seriously. Christmas being one of them. Christianity another."

"Yeah, well," said Pippa, her eyes drying up of their own accord. A bizarre steadiness took hold of her. "They kind of go together, don't they? At least that's the way it *used* to be."

"Yes," said Brenda; she had no idea what Pippa meant, nor did she care to. "Well, so you understand, then. I'm only thankful that NoElle came along when she did."

Pippa thought about that. It did kind of make sense, didn't it. Kind of fit into the overall pattern.

"Hey, you know what?" she said, pursuing a strange impulse.

Brenda looked at her worriedly.

"You still haven't paid me for the Bad Fairy costume."

Until now she had totally forgotten this, and even now had very little idea why it mattered.

Brenda almost gasped. "Is *that* all you're worried about? Money? At a time like *this*?"

No, thought Pippa. Compared to what I'm worried about, that doesn't even rate. But she had gotten into this now and there was no way to get out.

"I figure about five hours total," she said. The words came out not at all feebly: another surprise.

Brenda hustled as fast as Pippa had ever seen her move—no, faster—and grabbed a handful of bills out of the petty cash drawer. Fearfully, it seemed, she counted them into Pippa's palm, like a timid sales clerk making change.

"In spite of everything," she said, her voice now audibly quivering, "I *do* hope you'll be all right. And I hope you have a Merry Christmas."

"A *what?*"

It was too outrageous. Even Brenda could not think of

anything more to say. Pippa stared at the bills in her hand and started to turn and leave. Arresting herself in midstep, she looked back at Brenda with what must have been an exceedingly wacked-out, even downright demented, smile.

"Break a leg," she wished the Bad Fairy.

Brenda threw up her hands and fled inside her store, like someone who has been cursed.

So, thought Pippa, as she stepped slowly, like an animated corpse, through the bustling streets at the center of the village. Now I'm fired.

Well, it's not like it had never happened before.

It's not even like it had never happened at the worst possible time.

When Winterbelle was about 6 or 8 months old—at the height of tourist season, when you could never find an affordable place to rent—she had gotten sacked from a spot as live-in housekeeper at a B&B. The hours had been atrocious and the pay almost nonexistent, but it had given her and the baby a place to sleep. Aunt Eulace then had not been in a mood to acknowledge her existence, so Pippa and Winterbelle ended up crashing in the basement of her ex-boyfriend's parents, who in other respects appeared to hate her. The best you could really have said about that experience was that it hadn't killed them. From where she stood now, Pippa might add that things could have turned out worse. In those days at least you could get on WIC and AFDC and food stamps and somehow pull your life, or a reasonable facsimile, back together. Now she supposed you and the baby could just die in each other's arms, a morally beneficial lesson for the wayward and unrighteous.

All around her people moved with an air of collective purpose. They carried bags and pushed their children, out of school for the holidays, before them like well-loved but troublesome sheep. Pippa tried not to look anyone, especially the kids, in the eye. Her overriding fear was that one of the kids from George Burroughs School would recognize her and ask where Winterbelle was, whether she was sick or anything.

And Pippa didn't know! How could a mother not even know where her 9-year-old daughter was, or whether she was all right, or how she was spending Christmas Eve, or anything else? It went against all sense of rightness and order in the world. It defied the most sacred tenets of Nature, in which Pippa believed if she believed in anything. Which she was not at all sure about, anymore. Compared to that horrifying wrongness, getting fired from Rose Petal & Thorn was hardly even worth thinking about. Pippa decided she would not think about it, ever again; and to her surprise she found that this was possible. Brenda Cigogne's face blurred in her memory. The glittering insides of the store faded to something like the ghostly, meaningless after-image of a dream.

Freed of that, at least, she walked a little faster along the sidewalk of High Street, a crowded nexus of boutiques and upscale souvenir shops and restaurants. For most of her life she had lived within walking distance of this place; yet now she felt slightly stunned at the sight of it; she felt as though she had somehow been transformed into a foreigner, ignorant of local customs and unfluent in the native dialect. She stared at the decorations on light poles—bright green wreaths of balsam fir tied with gaudy red bows, trailing tentacles of golden twine and shiny foil stars. From a third-floor balcony at the Old World Inn, an ensemble of high-school musicians wearing their marching-band uniforms blared out carols of the mostly secular sort: "Frosty the Snowman," "Rudolf the Red-Nosed

Reindeer," "Silver Bells." Here and there foot-weary shoppers paused to watch them, bending their heads back and squinting upward like eyewitnesses hoping some potential suicide will go ahead and take the plunge.

Am I being cynical? wondered Pippa.

Well, how could she not? It was practically the only refuge left to her.

"Hey, Pippa," someone said nearby.

And since there was no way to simply vanish, Pippa lowered her eyes to meet those of her friend and fellow witch, Judith Loom.

Judith you had to hand it to. She had chosen to greet the consensual holiday in full regalia: black flowing overcoat that at first glance resembled a cape; a startling overapplication of eye makeup, featuring a field of sparkles against a cobalt background, curling well up onto her temples; two or three pounds deadweight of sterling silver jewelry, studded with fake gems, hanging from half a dozen piercings; a jauntily floppy beret, with scarlet quills; and animating the whole affair, coiled around her neck, a tame and overweight ferret named Ashera.

"Merry meet!" Judith declared, so loudly that foot traffic on the adjacent several squares of the sidewalk jolted to a halt. "Bright blessings on this eve of the Xian feast!"

She pronounced *Xian* in three syllables, delivered with a certain icy hauteur.

"Hi, Judith," Pippa mustered the oomph to say. It was not, she thought, so much that Judith was larger than life. Or stranger than life. It was that she seemed to represent some alternative *version* of life—a clue as to what other species might have arisen in lieu of *H. sapiens*, had evolution gone a little differently.

"Great *Goddess*," Judith proclaimed, her voice if anything getting louder. (Which was cool, because the more passersby stared at her, the less they would notice Pippa.) "Did you read the fucking *paper* today? Can you even begin to *believe* it? Why don't they just put up some scaffolding in the middle of the village green? Then instead of a Yule fire, they could have a nice Witch-burning."

The way Judith said *witch*, you could hear the capital *W*. It was an ideological thing, like hearing a union-labor type going on about Workers. Pippa guessed you had to admire it. She just wished, now and then, you could reach over to Judith and push the NORMAL button. She glanced around the sidewalk and estimated that no more than about 15 people were eavesdropping on them.

"Yeah, I saw it," Pippa practically whispered.

"*Saw* it?" cried Judith. "Is that *all*? Let me tell you what *I* did. I faxed copies to the Ontario Council for Religious Tolerance—"

"Isn't that in Canada?" said Pippa mildly.

"We *all* ought to be in Canada. Then we'd have health insurance. *And* to Witches Against Negativity and Discrimination. That's in California."

"Wow," said Pippa. She felt as though none of this had the slightest bearing upon her, personally. How could it? How could *anything* a person like Judith Loom did or did not do relate to her? Much less to Winterbelle.

"I wish," Judith said, rather haughtily, "that *I* could feel as complacent as *you* obviously do. Of course, you choose to practice your faith discreetly—which is your perfect right. But *I*—I am out there on the front line, by my own choosing. I *flaunt* my religious preference. And I don't care what *anybody* thinks!"

If only that were true, Pippa thought. Then Judith might not be here shouting in the middle of a crowded sidewalk.

"Hmph," came from someone quite nearby: a dark-haired woman weighted with gaily wrapped packages. Recognition grew by slow degrees, like a fever coming on: this was Carol Deacon Aaby.

Pippa's face felt hot. Some instinctual level of her being caused adrenaline to seep into her bloodstream, as though she had glimpsed an immemorial adversary.

Carol Aaby did not stop or make a point of looking in Pippa's direction, but the way she carried herself—shoulders determinedly set, shopping bag raised in a protective position on one side—suggested that she too was responding to a primordial prompting, a presentiment of danger.

"I'm not going to eat you," Pippa said, her voice reined in but audible, should anyone choose to hear it. Judith took no notice, but Carol Aaby perceptibly flinched. Ashera, the ferret familiar, adjusted her position on Judith's neck for a better view, as though the mention of eating had aroused her. Then Carol Aaby quickened her pace. She moved ahead through the assembled bodies on the sidewalk with the urgency of a diver stroking hard for clear air. One-minded, desperate, suffocating.

Pippa took a step to follow her.

The motion grabbed Judith Loom's attention. She had been stroking Ashera's head while continuing to talk—something about an Esbat party on the next Full Moon, what to bring for the ritual beforehand, people they knew who might or might not come—and now she stopped and held Pippa with a quizzical look, as though she were dimly aware that Pippa was up to *something*, but could not have told you what.

A short distance up the sidewalk, Carol Deacon Aaby turned and—with the barest backward glance—ducked into a shop called Enclosures. Bed & bath accessories for the coccooning set. Above the door hung a plush, fabric-art panel depicting a buck reindeer in red flannels, smoking a pipe, puffs of china-white chintz rising between his single-malt-amber antlers.

"Well," Pippa said, "I guess I better get going."

As though an alarm had sounded, Judith's eyes bored into her: a canny look there, amidst the mad sparkle and kohl. Without knowing what Pippa was doing, how she was feeling, what kind of ordeal she was suffering, Judith had only her subtlest sense—the witch's gift for scrying— to rely upon. But that sense must have informed her that some mysterious agency was afoot.

"Sister," she said, in a horror-movie whisper. "What is it? Are you in danger? Do you need my help?"

Pippa opened her mouth to say No. But she could not do so honestly. Honestly, she did not know. Could Judith help her? Could she possibly help Winterbelle? *No*, you would have to think . . . and yet, who could say? Things are connected in ways we do not know.

She shrugged. "I'll give you a call."

Judith's hand shot out. Bracelets jangled like sleigh bells. Fingers heavy with rings closed around Pippa's small wrist.

"There is Something," she said. Her voice now was stupidly overripe, like a storefront fortune-teller. Madame Stolichnaya, Reader & Advisor. "I can *feel* it."

"That's cool," said Pippa. "You've got a gift."

All she could think about was getting away from this crazy woman and away from the teeming sidewalks. She wanted to be someplace quiet where she could think—in her slow, groping, terrified way—about the things that were happening in her life. Carol Deacon Aaby. Unemployment. Other people's holidays. A 9-year-old girl without a mommy.

"Talk to me," commanded Judith.

And Pippa, whose only answer all her life had been

Yes, looked at her harebrained, exotic, suddenly interested friend and told her
   "No."

The door to Enclosures opened. Pippa stepped into a world of teapots, crisply folded linens stacked in antique cupboards, Crabtree & Evelyn soaps, painted glass Christmas tree ornaments, intricately carved Black Forest clocks, and tiny jars of English jams, Irish oatmeal, and clotted Wisconsin cream. The lady at the counter looked up at her. Creased parchment-dry lips into something like a smile. An invisible sound system played something suitable. Haydn, Pippa guessed. Or Handel. One of them.
   It was the other side of the looking glass. Pippa did not know the most fundamental rules. She could never have gotten a job here in a million years.
   She did not see Carol Deacon Aaby anywhere.
   Enclosures was compartmentalized. A stair rose to a loft stocked with sensuous negligees, elegant toiletries, Mexican glass decanters from which to dribble scented liquids into your bath. But Pippa couldn't picture Carol Aaby's skin in direct contact with slinky underclothes. She turned to the back of the store, where a mullioned glass partition demarcated a tiny, make-believe bedroom.
   The place was fit for a princess—a fairy-tale princess—all the way to the magnificent four-poster bed trimmed out with silken gonfalons, lace-edged cotton sheets, puffy pillows encased in white-on-white, needlepoint snowflakes. It was all so perfectly chaste: you could not imagine an actual *body*, with its warmth and smells and discharges, flopping down here. Ergo, ideal habitat for Carol Deacon Aaby, whom Pippa finally ran to ground there—trapped, staring back between bedposts, with an expression not far short of open terror.

Pippa moved in on her, circling the bed.

"*Don't*," the other woman told her, almost hysterically. She raised high her shopping bag, enlisting it as a shield. "Don't come any closer. Get away from me."

Pippa halted. She stood at the foot of the bed, a quadrant of white silk lying between the two women like an empty game board. In a voice as frosted and featureless as those sheets, she said, "Why are you doing this? You don't even know me. And I bet you've never *seen* my poor little daughter."

Carol Aaby's eyes shot this way and that. They found no help.

Pippa went on more loudly, "How can you possibly do this? I mean, to another woman? Another *mother*. How can you just . . . like, *attack* somebody like this? What makes you think you can just go in and totally screw up another person's family?"

Carol Aaby appeared to muster her fortitude, to buck herself up. Still holding the shopping bag before her, she faced Pippa straight-on.

"How dare you talk to me that way," she said.

"How dare *I*—" Pippa could not believe this woman. Not even a little: she was as outrageously implausible as this bedroom.

Carol Aaby must have sensed an opening. "You have no *right*," she said, "to threaten decent, God-fearing people this way. I've a good mind to report you to the authorities."

Pippa was amazed at this: the woman's knack for turning guilt and fear into righteous indignation. She said, "I'm not threatening you. I'm just asking you why. What's the matter with you? I mean do you really think it's *right*, what you're doing?"

"I am doing *nothing*." Carol Aaby now dared to take a tiny step forward. Closer to Pippa, but also closer to an escape route, the opening to the main sales floor. Her fingers were white where they gripped the handle of her bag, bulging incongruously with gaily wrapped gifts. "I am doing what I believe is right."

Which is it? wondered Pippa. It can't be both.

She said, "Don't you believe I love my daughter, just like you love your own kids? Don't you think we're even *people,* like you are? Don't you think we *matter?*"

Carol Deacon Aaby gave a discreet snort. "I believe all people are sinners. And yet through the grace of Our Lord, all people are capable of redemption. *Know ye the truth, for the truth shall set you free.*"

Pippa felt like she had been hearing that a lot lately. She thought for a moment, trying to remember where.

Carol Aaby took another step. The two women were close now. One tall oaken bedpost between them.

"I just don't understand," said Pippa, "how a person can be so mean."

"You are the Devil's pawn," declared Carol Aaby. As if that answered the question.

Pippa laughed. She had no idea why. The impulse vanished even before the laughter—thin, rising from the back of her throat—had fallen silent.

Carol Aaby looked scared again. More than that: wacked-out.

"What's the *matter?*" Pippa thrust herself forward, getting into the other woman's space. "Never heard a witch *cackle* before?"

Carol Aaby made a small noise, a whimpery squeak, like a cornered animal.

"You *ought* to be scared," Pippa said, pressing in on her. "You're *right* to be. Because you've hurt me so much—and Winterbelle, you've hurt my poor little girl—that I could just . . . I could really—"

Carol Aaby's eyes opened wide. Then they darted sideways, toward the exit. She was freaked, maybe, but not immobilized. She was not going to stand still while Pippa laid some infernal curse upon her. Flying into a sudden, ill-coordinated frenzy, the woman swung her shopping bag at Pippa, driving her back. Then she drove for daylight. The path she took—the only one open—was across the four-poster bed, that expanse of virginal silk. While Pippa watched in amazement (it would have been comical, slapstick, under other circumstances) Carol Aaby clambered onto the bed and clawed her way crabwise across it, trailing the shopping bag behind her, spilling packages assorted in size and shape, until she reached the other side and fairly tumbled down onto the floor. She picked herself up and fled. There was no looking back, no thought of retrieving the lost presents.

The parchment-lipped lady at the checkout counter watched Carol Aaby hustle out onto the sidewalk, setting a door harp aclang. Then she turned her head slowly to stare at Pippa. The force of that gaze was such as to render further action—crossing the store, seizing Pippa brusquely by the scruff of her neck—superfluous. Meekly, Pippa stepped out from behind the bed. She felt like the governess in *Fanny and Alexander* (a beautiful, magical movie that she and Winterbelle rented at Christmastime, every year until now) confronted by the two stern moms with feathers flying all over the nursery. Only instead of curtsying apologetically, she lifted her undistinguished little chin a bit higher, and in no big hurry set off toward the door.

Directly in front of her—the last package dropped in Carol Aaby's hasty retreat—lay a small, cubical box wrapped in pure white glossy paper, tied with a ribbon of gold as narrow as a shoestring.

Pippa couldn't have told you why, instead of just stepping over this, she bent very quickly, so fast even she hardly noticed, and plucked it up.

The box was heavy for its size. She hefted it up and down in her left hand, holding it away from the lady at the counter, and in about two long seconds she was out on the street.

The crowds were still there. The ensemble of high-school musicians still belted out carols from a balcony of the Old World Inn. The daylight was as pale and translucent as an ice cube, just as it had been before.

Nonetheless it seemed to Pippa that the world was different in some way. The people in it had changed, some-how. Pippa included. And the package in her left hand, that weighty little cube, seemed to vibrate—to *ring*, like a railroad track before the train pulls into sight—with secret, premonitory energy. Maybe it was just the scary thrill of holding something that had once belonged to her enemy. Or maybe it was something else. What was in the box? An expensive hunk of jewelry? A chocolate Santa?

Or a powerful talisman, something Alexander would covet. An amulet. A golden scarab. A lamp you could rub and get three wishes. Which would be two more than Pippa needed

to get everything
she could possibly
want.

Yew Street was empty and, at a glance, lifeless. The sun moved in and out like a gull navigating between asbestos-textured clouds. A southerly breeze whipped long canes of alder, growing out of a gully by the roadside, wildly about Pippa's head, like whips. In the background, Wabenaki Mountain, its face in midday shadow, swallowed the landscape and distorted her sense of perspective. Today of all days, the graveyard *did* look spooky. Not that Pippa was spooked. But you had to appreciate the atmosphere.

She was not sure where she was headed. Home, perhaps—but that was getting to be an ever more tenuous concept. What could a home be if Winterbelle was not there? If it held neither love nor respite nor sanctuary?

Her mind was packed full, though it was hard to say with what. Not *thoughts*, if by that you meant anything that could be put into words. And not *feelings*, exactly, either—for though she was drowning in them, her mind was not where they seemed to be located. Everywhere but. And for sure not anything like purpose or understanding or resolve.

With the whole world, maybe. Pippa's mind was full of

141

the world and all its weirdness and all its wounds. Not simply her own. Her own and everybody else's too. Being a part of everything meant that everything was a part of you—didn't it? So if everything was fucked up, then *you* were fucked up especially bad, cosmically bad. Beyond all recognition.

Still, there was a pattern to it. Not mere chaos. A certain order, the way there is an order to the wildest storm, a regularity in the way giant waves come crashing on the shore. Pippa felt in some subterranean way that if she could recognize this pattern she might anticipate the waves—when they would fetch up, what kind of damage they would do. How much of life they would sweep away. She might take preventive action. Salvage something.

Here is one example. Pippa found that in her mind, amid all the tumult, certain words from the *Weekly Herald* had begun to repeat themselves, like a scratched CD belting out the same maddening phrase over and over and over. Most of the article she had (thank the Goddess) forgotten; but these few little pieces were stuck inside her. As she walked past the old graveyard, slower and slower—finally coming to a halt—she listened hard to those words banging against her inner tympanum.

And in the morning, one of them ran, *mysterious clues.*

Strange-looking objects, ran another.

Evidence of candles being burned.

Something spilled on a rock that might be blood.

On the whole, banal stuff. Very much in keeping with the scary, sensationalist tone of the article.

But it seemed to Pippa that unlike the rest of the piece, which consisted in varying proportions of paranoia and bullshit and rumor-mongering, these isolated bits were *about* something. Something definite. A specific place. Real, objective things that some person had looked at.

You had to read between the lines; but it was not hard to figure that, probably by accident, somebody walking through the woods had stumbled upon a place where pagan-type rituals had been performed. There were quite a few such places to Pippa's personal knowledge, and undoubtedly many others. The rocks, the candles, the spilled wine: it was all cookbook stuff, straight out of Scott Cunningham. *Wicca 101*, as Judith would say. Any broomcloset witch could read a couple of books and order some "magickal tools" from Abyss; and from there it was off to the races.

Yet it was not any broom-closet witch whose precious beautiful daughter had been snatched away.

And it was not any cookie-cutter ritual site they had been talking about in the newspaper. The clinching detail, Pippa felt, was the rock. The blood, or something like it, spilled there. That was a Real Thing. You could kick it.

Pippa bent her head back with difficulty—the tension in her body had concentrated itself around her neck and shoulders, locking them in place—and tried to decide where on that tall, furrowed, snow-caked slope her sacred circle lay. From down here everything looked different. Everything was a muddle, whereas from up there, peering out from the ledge, everything was perfect and orderly and clear.

Pippa wanted that clarity. She needed it.

Lucky for her, witches always wear sensible shoes.

She had never approached the mountain from this direction, but it did not take long—twenty minutes of sustained, vigorous scrabbling—for her hands and feet, operating as it seemed independent of conscience direction, to find their way onto a fall of boulders whose rounded, weathered skulls wore a skin of green-gray lichen and sprouted whiskers of evergreen fern no taller than your ankles, crinkled up to prevent desiccation. In this place of ancient, glacial upheaval, Pippa felt secure. She was back on home ground.

Usually she came up the mountain by night, in the waxy glow of a Full Moon. Winter sunshine was harsher though also, strangely, colder-seeming, as though it were not just failing to deliver heat but actually draining away some of yours. It came from a place so low in the sky that all the densely packed atmosphere it had sliced through to reach the Earth must have depleted what warmth it started out with, leaving only a washed-out umberish blur like a water stain on enamel. Then when heavy clouds blew over, the light dropped even further, to the dimness of early dusk, a vaguely frightening sudden gloom.

Wind pressed up behind Pippa, who was bent low, almost crawling over the rocks, and her backpack kept riding up on the smooth nylon of her parka. Her entire hands, not just the fingers, inside their Polartec mittens, were painfully cold.

You had to will yourself *not* to notice these things, to snip the connection between the outside world and the way it made you feel It was like retreating inside your body membrane. Or drawing your head back under the roof of your shell. Winter would kill you if you didn't resist it but that was not going to happen: you just made up your mind about that.

When Pippa got to the first ledge, some distance around the curve of mountainside from her circle, she rested long enough for her breathing to settle down. The village below looked like the trimmings of a fancy electric train set. Shadows stretched long and purplish from the tidy houses. Evergreen hedges appeared black. Shade trees were like fractal images generated at random by a screen saver: their naked branches getting smaller as they ramified outward, until they merged with the backdrop of snow. From his magical sleigh drawn by long-suffering reindeer, this is what Santa Claus sees.

It was a tawdry little world in many respects. Pippa turned away from it. She began moving again, this time making her way from one great rock to the next, taking big steps, leaps almost—continuing this way horizontally and westward. The village shifted beneath her until Ash Street came into view: big old houses and empty lawns and fat-bodied sedans, the whole Aunt Eulace milieu. Pippa did not hate it from up here. She did not envy its old-fashioned comforts, resent its insularity, cringe at its prejudices. Ash Street was tiny and distant now; it had no power to affect her one way or another.

Pippa started moving again and at last she recognized her circle, her hand-me-down sacred space. It was slightly above her, farther up the mountain at a place where the ledge jutted to form a precarious bluff. The biggest of the circle's stones (in the south—the one she called the Altar) stuck up well clear of the snow and acted as a sort of navigational aid, a monument to sight in on. Pippa made for it directly, scrambling in and out of ruts, impatient now finally to *be* there, to receive the circle's cold blessing.

Then at the last moment—only a step away from the place she thought of as the Gate, a gap between two portal stones in the east—some peculiar force rose up to hold her back. A sense of wrongness, of slumbering energies aroused. Anger not her own.

Pippa came all the way up to the opening, the Gate, and she peered beyond it into her circle. And she saw:

In the north, a flat rock scrawled upon in black, as though by a wide-tip laundry pen, with the outline of a cross and the slogan BURN IN HELL.

In the west, her salt-glazed Frey & Freya mug cracked into shards. The red wine it had held—her gift to the Goddess—splashed and frozen over a rock. Looking surprisingly much like blood.

In the south, a piece of white paper, upon which once wishes had been inscribed, overwritten with obscenities.

And in the east, amid rowan berries crushed to pulp, a crumpled photograph of Winterbelle. The little girl's once rosy cheeks turned to brown, as though a match had been held under the print but—saved by the wind or the punishing cold—it had refused to burn.

At the sight of her daughter's face, discolored, Pippa gave a soft cry.

She had not felt invaded or violated or personally attacked when strangers had torn through her rooms, pawing all her possessions. But she felt that way now.

She felt as though somebody had *stomped* her—kicked her right in the solar plexus—causing imaginal lights to fire crazily in her brain.

Breathing became hard. She felt dizzy and closed her eyes, struggled just to remain upright.

All the while she told herself that these feelings were out-of-context, disproportionate. That when you make your sacred space on publicly owned land, in the middle of a state park, you have to accept the risk of casual intrusion. Even of vandalism. Just like, when you practice witchcraft in modern America, you have to expect that many people, most people perhaps, are going to get the wrong idea. They will misunderstand, and some of them will misunderstand in a major violent way. Pippa knew and she accepted those things. Or at least she figured there was no sense getting upset about them. It was just the way things were.

Nonetheless she felt violated. She stood there for many

long seconds, panting in shock. Then with an effort of will she stepped through the Gate, into the middle of her desecrated circle. And stood there: not even looking, just feeling the awful, idiotic cruelty of what some bigoted know-nothing had done.

Or at least, *part* of what that person had done.

Because the other part, and maybe the worst, was to go back down the mountain and talk about it. To Mark Portion, or the police, or some other God-fearing soul. Because in the vandal's mind, the crime here lay not in having trashed someone else's holy sanctuary. It lay in the sanctuary itself, the impulse to seek the Divine within it. The true criminal was Pippa herself.

The wind blew hard. Clouds were forming thickly now, and at the corners of her eyes Pippa glimpsed isolated flakes of snow, dancing in a chaos of cross-drafts.

She began crying again. Tears came out of her these days without any warning, and often without obvious cause. Pippa could not tell whether her circle was really what the tears were about.

More probably they were about, you know, *everything*. Pippa's whole life melting down around her—not *just* losing Winterbelle, though surely that was enough, but the whole train of disaster that dragged along in its wake. By now circumstances had gotten to be too big and too complicated to struggle against. So that's what it was, then: Pippa was crying in defeat.

She lowered herself slowly, fearing that her knees might buckle and send her headlong onto the rocks, until she was kneeling before the big stone in the south: the Altar.

South was where the icy goddess of winter made her home. Its color was white and its element was air: freezing, parching, passionless air. Facing that way, with the wind whipping the tears from her face, Pippa felt like a hapless little fairy cowering before the Snow Queen.

"Is it me?" she asked aloud.

She was speaking (she guessed) to the terrible goddess Hella, ruler of the frozen Underworld. She couldn't image who else would be listening.

"I mean I know life isn't fair and the rich get richer and assholes cross the finish line first. But I mean, have I *done* something? Is this just me getting punished for not being, you know . . . regular?"

She sat and she waited. The Goddess spat snow in her face.

"Yeah, thanks for nothing," said Pippa.

She *knew* it was ludicrous—kneeling here on the frozen ground, blabbing like an insane person. She knew that. And yet . . . a thing can be ludicrous and still make a certain kind of sense, can't it? To Pippa, this little conversation with the Hag was, if anything, overdue.

"I guess you hear this from everyone," she went on. "I mean, sitting down there with all the souls of the dead hanging around you. Nobody thinks they deserve what they got. But come *on*—I'm not even *dead* yet. And what I *really* want to know is, Why Winterbelle? You can't tell me *she* deserves any of this."

Hella's face is conventionally imagined to be beautiful on one side while the other side is covered with dead and putrefying flesh. Pippa couldn't say how accurate this was. But she supposed it would kind of wreck your outlook on things. It would make you wonder, Why isn't one of the *gods* sitting down here instead of me? Why do all the shit jobs get assigned to women?

"I hear you," said Pippa, momentarily sympathetic.

And *another* thing. (This is the imaginary Hella speaking.) If I'm supposed to be the goddess of the dead, then why do dead *warriors* get to party with the Valkyries in Valhalla? Why am *I* stuck with all these like, deceased accountants and housewives and whatnot? If you ask me, the whole thing is a crock.

"Cauldron," suggested Pippa.

Whatever.

Pippa shook her head. "Tell me about it," she said.

The wind whirred through barren oak limbs, which quaked like bursitic arms. High overhead a raven cruised the sky, looking for a carcass to scavenge. As Pippa watched, the bird uttered a series of chortling, throaty noises— sounds you wouldn't expect a bird to make. She had heard about a witch somewhere, way out in the country, who had trained her raven familiar to talk.

Had the raven, she wondered, repaid the witch by teaching her to fly? It would seem only fair.

But life isn't like that.

Is it?

"Here," said Pippa, struck by a thought. "I think I've got something for you."

She squirmed out of the backpack and opened the zipper a few inches. Out of it she extracted the little cube of snow-white wrapping paper. Its weight seemed to have doubled since she snagged it from the carpet at Enclosures.

"Just a little something to cheer you up," Pippa told the Goddess.

She laid the box carefully on the Altar. When it touched, it made a clunking sound, as it had done on hitting the sidewalk. Metallic, Pippa thought. But this time, in a different acoustical gestalt, the sound was higher-pitched, more delicate. Bell-like.

Pippa just had to know. She had to know what it was she had stolen. Which is a way of saying, she had to know what Carol Deacon Aaby first had purchased, then dropped. The two of them were connected now. Perversely, cursedly—like two sides of the same Moon.

Carefully, she untied the gold ribbon and peeled back the wrapping paper. Inside was a sturdy cardboard box that said *Hecho en Mexico*. And inside that, finally, swaddled in cotton, was a silver sleigh bell.

Pippa drew in her breath. The bell hung from a short leather cord and looked exactly like the last picture in *The Polar Express*, one of Winterbelle's favorite books. (Those wolves! racing through the forest beside the train; their glowing yellow eyes!) Pippa gave the bell a gentle shake, and the most beautiful sound in the world emanated with the purity of light made audible, shining and dancing through the air.

Did the world change, in that moment?

Pippa waited with her breath held tight. Then she felt stupid and gullible and she exhaled.

The world changes in *every* moment. Everybody knows that. And most of the time, especially lately, the change is for the worse.

With reluctance, but also with satisfaction—because it *was* a gift fit for a goddess, and probably nicer than poor Hella was used to—she laid the sleigh bell back on the Altar stone. For several moments she stared down at it, wondering.

What could a marvelous object like this have to do with Carol Deacon Aaby? What unknowable internal process made that seemingly cold and hostile and anger-filled person pick this lovely, simple thing off a shelf somewhere? What buried part of her responded to the magical chiming? Was it a present? For whom?

Mysteries.

The day was getting darker and darker. Snow came

down more assuredly now. From where it circled, just beneath the lowest clouds, the raven said:

Call. Call.

"What?" said Pippa. "You mean *caw?*"

"No, *call*," repeated the raven, testily.

"Oh."

Pippa stood up in a hurry. She had very little experience
of this kind of thing, but her general understanding was,
when you start getting messages from wild creatures of
the woods and the sky, then either your medication is
badly in need of adjustment, or Something Big is starting
to happen.

Pippa's supply of Zoloft had run out a long time ago,
and she couldn't afford to get the prescription refilled. So
it was probably not that.

"See you," she said to the terrible Hella, patroness of
victims and of women with dead-end jobs. "Thanks for
listening. I guess."

She left the circle and started down the mountain with
what might have been imprudent haste, considering the
dangerous footing. But after all, it was getting to be afternoon on Christmas Eve, and she had a telephone call to
make.

The big Magnavox was tuned to Court TV: the case of a
Texas man accused of shooting his son's history teacher.
An improper reference to the Alamo allegedly was
involved.

"Are there any messages for me?" Pippa asked loudly—
not that her voice gave the Magnavox much in the way
of competition.

"You expecting any?" asked Aunt Eulace, without turning
around. You could hear the niggle of suspicion in her
voice.

On-screen, a defense attorney was displaying the murder weapon for the benefit of the jury. It had a barrel as long as a cattleprod.

"Ladies and gentlemen," the lawyer said, "let us bear in mind that the constitutional right to keep and bear concealed firearms, as further guaranteed under the laws of the great state of Texas, are not at issue in this trial."

"Okay," said Pippa. "Well, I'm just going to be using the phone for a few minutes. Then I'll see about dinner."

"Don't bother," Eulace said.

Meaning what? Pippa walked back to the cold kitchen and lifted the aged black handset from its cradle. She remembered the number from back in her AFDC days.

"Family Services," said a voice at the other end—adding, as an afterthought, "Merry Christmas."

"Thanks," said Pippa. "Can I get, um, Roger Wemble on this line?"

"You *can* . . . " the telephone woman said, beginning what Pippa recognized as the standard runaround.

"It's important," she cut in. "It's about my daughter. Winterbelle Rede?"

There were moments of silence, a disturbed kind of silence, while the woman evidently consulted her computer screen.

"Ah," she said, "I see. Well. Let me put you on hold then, may I?"

Like Pippa had a choice. She could not hold her body still while she waited. Her feet moved across the floor and her belly started to tremble. What am I doing? she distantly asked herself.

"Ms. Rede?" said the unctuous voice of Roger Wemble, the Child Welfare caseworker.

"Hi," said Pippa.

"We were wondering," said Wemble, "when we would hear from you. I gather from the *Herald* that you've retained, ah . . . legal representation?"

Pippa didn't want to get into that. "It said in those papers you gave me," she said, "something about, supervised visitation? And I was supposed to call to make arrangements?"

Wemble said nothing at first and then, noncommittally, "Yes?"

"So I'm calling," said Pippa. "To make arrangements."

"Ms. Rede," said Roger Wemble, "it's Christmas Eve. Ordinarily I wouldn't even *be* here at this time."

"Lucky me, then," said Pippa. "Look, you don't have to tell me what day it is. I'm calling because . . . well I mean, Winterbelle isn't exactly a Christmas *person*. But I kind of thought, shouldn't I be able to see her tomorrow, anyway? So she doesn't have to spend Christmas alone?"

"She won't be spending it alone," Roger Wemble said, quickly and officiously. "We have made *excellent* foster-care arrangements, and she will naturally be celebrating the holiday along with the rest of her custodial family."

Pippa's blood ran as thin as black water in a winter stream. "*I* am her family," she said.

"Of course. I refer to her *custodial* family. Who are providing her with all the care and attention that you presently cannot."

Pippa wished she could get her hands on that cattleprod.

"Can I see her or not?" she asked, as sanely and reasonably as you can imagine.

What a fake-out.

"Ordinarily not," said Roger Wemble. "Ordinarily, at least one week's prior notice and scheduling are required.

But since it *is* the holiday—as long as some kind of supervisory presence can be arranged . . ."

"What does that mean?"

"That means, I must find somebody who is authorized by the Department to be present when you are in the company of your daughter. Someone familiar with the regulations concerning such visitation."

"Regulations?" Pippa felt like vomiting. "No, please—I don't want to know. Just try to *do* it, okay? It's really . . . "

Really what? she wondered. A matter of life and death? Or even more vital than that? A question of the rightness of the Universe?

"I'll have to make some phone calls," said Roger Wemble. The way he said it, the business of making these calls sounded like the most onerous task ever borne by a human.

"That's your job, isn't it?" said Pippa.

She regretted saying it, pushing things too far; but after a pause, she heard Roger Wemble sigh.

"I'm afraid it is," he said. "It didn't used to be, but it is now. Budget cuts, you know."

"Yeah," said Pippa. Budget cuts. She did know.

"Are you at home?" Wemble asked.

"I don't know," said Pippa, distractedly. "I mean, yeah. I'm right here. I'll be waiting."

Wemble clicked off.

Pippa turned around to find Eulace standing in the shadows of the dining room, where she could easily overhear every word.

"If *I* were them," her aunt said, "I'd just tell you, No thanks, mind your own business, thanks, and leave it go at that."

Pippa was too astonished to remember to hang the

phone up. A faint recorded reminder came on while Eulace was lurching herself back toward the parlor.

" . . . *ask the Operator for assistance,*" the voice was saying.

"Tell the operator," said Pippa, dropping the handset on the counter tiles—not *quite* hard enough to shatter—

<blockquote>

"I'm taking care of it
myself."

</blockquote>

Xmas morning.

Wouldn't you know, the sun was shining. The sky had turned a particular cobalt you see on posters advertising expensive vacation packages, only there it is a sea—the Aegean, say—being alluringly depicted. In the last hours before dawn the temperature had dropped to about minus 15° F. Cars with decent batteries would still crank up, while those belonging to the kind of people Pippa knew would just sit there, clicking, as if surprised at what you expected of them.

She lay in bed the longest time. Eulace moved about the dark old house first above and then below her. Pippa could hear her great-aunt hunting for things in the kitchen: coffee that you didn't have to grind, a box of Pop-Tarts. Nondairy creamer. *White* sugar and not that sticky dirt-colored stuff. The television popped on and the theme of *CBS This Morning*, taken from the musical *Oklahoma!* rose through the floorboards, followed by a medley of holiday favorites performed live by a brass quintet in the studio. Pippa wondered whether she was depressed. If you stay in bed an awful long time this is often a symptom of depression; it's one of the things they ask you about when you sit stiffly in an uncomfortable metal chair at the Department of Family Services, trying not to make a bad impression. You don't want to come off like a welfare mom, so you say "No" when they ask if you find yourself spending a lot of time in bed. In Pippa's case this also happened to be true—she was a basically restless person, which had something to do with how she found her way to the DFS office to begin with, running off and getting pregnant et cetera. All of which made her unwillingness to get out of bed this morning the more unusual.

She had taken to sleeping in Winterbelle's cupboard bed. A tiny bit of the girl's warm, breadlike smell still lingered in the sheets and the pillowcase. Pippa liked (and hated! but could not resist) pulling the covers up over her head, breathing the confined air underneath, and imagining the small beloved body that had lived and grown and dreamed and played in this magic-filled place. She found in an irrational way that she could relax here (and only here), just as though Winterbelle were really, impossibly, present. Was this sick? Pippa didn't know or care. Until her daughter came back, she was living here for the two of them. Keeping it warm; keeping it safe.

The supervised visit was set for 2:00. It could last up to an hour, or it could be terminated early. Roger Wemble had been very clear about that. The authorized representative of the Child Welfare office would decide, on the basis of "how things go."

How did they expect things to go? Did they expect Pippa to start chanting satanic curses, or pull out a boom box and play hypnotic white-noise tapes while she brainwashed everyone in the room? Really, these people were too much.

But she pushed her mind away from them.

The only thing she needed to think about was Winterbelle. Seeing her, being able to touch her again, telling the girl that no matter what, her mommy was going to make sure, she *promised*, that everything would come out all right. They would all live happily ever after, somehow. And that was all that mattered, finally. No matter what indignities were involved, how many or how grievous the insults might be, how infuriating the injustice, Pippa must keep her mind on the happy ending to come. And she must tell Winterbelle to do the same. That way, together (even though apart), they would get through it.

The sun moved around, pushing shadows ahead of it, and Pippa wondered if she was going to stay in bed until it was time to get ready for the appointment.

She was about to decide Yes when the telephone rang.

The sound made Pippa shiver. Eulace almost never got phone calls; and as for Pippa, she could not conceive of who would be calling her on Christmas morning that she really wanted to talk to. She listened while Eulace clomped across the kitchen floor below, then spoke briefly—no more than a couple of words—into the handset. For a few seconds there was nothing more. Then, the most dreaded sound: the heavy tread of footsteps on the winding back stairs.

Eulace came only partway up and shouted over the remaining distance.

"It's for *you*," she announced, with a trace of pleasure. Confident, perhaps, that the news would be bad. "It's one of them that's been calling."

Pippa sat all the way upright. Cool room air swirled around her back. "*Who's* been calling?" she wondered aloud. But Eulace was out of earshot, clumping down the stairs again.

Reaching the kitchen with a bathrobe twisted around her and Winterbelle's fuzzy frog slippers, which perfectly fit her feet, Pippa picked up the telephone like an un-known, possibly dangerous object.

"Hello?" she hesitantly said.

"Pippa Rede!" a man's voice exclaimed. "Where have you been? This is Arthur Torvid."

Pippa exhaled in relief.

"Your attorney?" Torvid added, as though she might have forgotten.

"Yes," she said.

"I just wondered if you were still there," he explained. "Long silences on a telephone make me uncomfortable."

Long silences? This guy's internal clock must be overwound.

"Listen," said Torvid, "I've got big news for you. The Human Relations Task Force has agreed to investigate your situation as a possible case of religious persecution."

"The who?" said Pippa.

"It's an independent advocacy group. Very top-drawer bunch of people. They promised to get a team up here to start fact-finding within a few weeks."

"A few *weeks?*" said Pippa. "Fact-finding? I'm sorry, Mr. Torvid, but I'm not sure—"

"Call me Arthur," he said. "Please. And you have to understand, this is a very busy organization. Especially these days, the way things are going in this country. It's a definite break that they consider your case worthy of attention."

Pippa wondered if Arthur Torvid had any idea how this sounded on her end of the line. "That's really cool," she told him. "I'm glad somebody thinks my daughter is *worthy of attention*. Really. But shouldn't we be . . . I mean, I don't know, *you're* the lawyer . . . but shouldn't we be maybe, going to court or something?"

"No no no," said Arthur Torvid. "Not *yet*. Don't you

understand, that's the *last* thing we want to be doing right now. We've got to mobilize public awareness, build a groundswell of opinion. Start at the grass roots. Going to court right now would be tantamount to saying, Yes, we acknowledge that you have a right to take this girl away from her mother, and we're begging you—*begging* you—to *please* out of the kindness of your official hearts, which let me tell you is a real oxymoron, to give her back again. No way shape or form, Pippa. Not while *I'm* driving the boat."

"Maybe I should be driving the boat, then," said Pippa.

"What?" said Arthur Torvid. (Perhaps she had spoken too quietly. More likely, as was usually the case, she had simply failed to make an impression.) "Listen, have any DFS thugs gotten in touch with you? Have they asked you to come in for an interview, or gotten you to sign anything?"

"Not exactly," said Pippa. "I did talk to—"

"Finest kind," Arthur Torvid said. "Keep it that way. Don't play their game, because you can't win. No matter what you do or don't do, say or don't say, they get ammunition out of it. You smile, you're living a fantasy. You don't smile, you're hostile and uncooperative. Hear what I'm saying?"

How could she not? Pippa said, "Could I talk for a minute, please?"

"What?" said Arthur Torvid. She supposed this was her chance.

"I'm going to see my daughter," she told him. "I've scheduled a visit—a supervised visitation—for this afternoon."

"You've *what?* Pippa Rede, Pippa Rede! This is the worst thing you could *possibly*—"

"Would you shut up?" she said.

And *thwang*. For once, the magic of human speech worked for her. Arthur Torvid fell silent.

"It's Christmas," she reminded him.

"You don't *believe* in Christmas."

"I believe in everything," she said. Somewhat surprising herself, because she had never thought of it this way. "I just don't believe *only* in Christmas. That's what people don't get. How you can believe in more than one thing at a time. But I do. So anyway, it's Christmas, and I don't think a little girl should be alone at Christmas."

"She's not *alone*," said Arthur Torvid. "I'm sure they've got, you know . . ."

"Right. Make-believe parents and brothers and sisters and a pretend Christmas tree and presents and the whole nine yards. It's such bullshit. I want Winterbelle to know she's got a mommy."

"Of course she's got a mommy."

Pippa thought that Arthur Torvid, in his impatience with her, sounded like a headstrong little boy. An only child, to be exact. She wondered if *he* had a mommy. Probably too much of one.

"I can tell you don't have kids," she said.

"Actually I have two," he said, surprising her. "A boy and a girl. They live in Nevada with my ex-wife. A *systems design consultant*."

Pippa could hear saliva being discharged as he enunciated this. It was a strange concept for her, too. Everything is strange, really. The world is full of mystery and shadows and things that will never be known. You have to remind yourself to marvel at that, now and then. Otherwise you might develop a know-it-all mentality. Pippa told him:

"Look, I'm going to do it. I'm sorry you don't approve. It doesn't *matter*, but I'm sorry anyway. I wish we could see more eye-to-eye on things. Do you want me to look for another lawyer?"

"Don't get another lawyer!" Arthur Torvid almost shouted at her.

The outburst must have startled him as well as her. He was quiet for a few seconds. Then he said:

"Pippa, this is a big case for me. An important case. It's so much involved with the things I believe in, the things I wanted to practice law for in the first place. I *want* to represent you, Pippa. I *want* to help you get your daughter back. Believe me, I'm committed to this. You won't find anyone else as committed as me. I'll fight the bastards until blood comes oozing out of their Xerox machines. I know I'm unconventional. But ride with me awhile, you'll get the feel of it. And you'll start to see results, Pippa Rede. I promise you that."

Pippa said, "Hang on a minute."

She lowered the phone from her mouth. Something was going on here and she needed a breath or two in which to think about it.

Arthur Torvid was asking her—*begging* her, as he would have said—to be on her side. Like a kid wanting so badly to be picked for the softball team. She was not accustomed to being in a position like this.

She kind of liked it.

She liked also the sort of amusingly kinky image of blood oozing from a Xerox machine. She pressed the phone back to her head.

"Okay," she told him. "You can be my lawyer. Now let me go see my little girl and quit whining about it. Okay?"

"Absolutely," said Arthur Torvid.

When Pippa hung up, she felt more like a real witch than she had for days.

It's pretty obvious, Pippa thought, why unhappy people choose times like Christmas to off themselves. The peace-on-Earth vibes are so intense, and so obviously coming from *elsewhere*—outside your own head, that is—that the pounding sense of wrongness can drive you crazy, and there's only one way to stop it. Ergo: bang.

But no bang for Pippa. She might pace and obsess and feel as though her stomach were digesting itself, but she must hold herself together somehow. She tuned Winterbelle's boom box to the community radio station, on whom you could usually count to do something inappropriate for the season, such as broadcast their thirteen millionth rehash of the evils of Vietnam on Veteran's Day. Today, natch, one of the station volunteers had hauled in her kids and their tape collection to inflict further joy upon the listening audience, and if there was *one thing* that might possibly nudge Pippa over the edge it was Burl Ives's sing-along rendition of "Holly Jolly Christmas."

In the old house on Ash Street there was no such thing as silence; turning the radio off only meant listening to the groaning of Eulace's TV, currently receiving the combined righteousness of the Mormon Tabernacle Choir. In the end—the end coming about 11:45—there was nothing to do but get out of there. Aunt Eulace shot her a little *mal de ojo* on her way to the door, but Pippa was well protected against that: she carried the little frog fetish in one pocket of her twill pants, where she could caress it from outside, through her mittens. In the other pocket she had tucked her own present for Winterbelle.

For weeks, in secret, she had been building and furnishing the World's Tiniest Dollhouse: a sort of homespun Polly Pocket, nested in a flea-market wooden jewelry box that she had painted flowery scrollwork on. The box opened to become one wall and the floor of a cozy witch's kitchen. There were Popsicle-stick rafters from which hung a sprig of heather, a bundle of rosemary leaves, and shriveled red mushrooms; a squat little stove glued together from real brick fragments, complete with a cauldron made of a copper thimble smeared with soot; a raven in a cage; a cat whose long sleek hair had been clipped from one of Barbie's ethnically variegated friends; shelves stocked with jars of weird-looking stuff; a wooden mortar and pestle big enough for the resident Baba Yaga to ride about in; a black robe and tall pointy cap impaled on a hat rack of plastic bones—all of this scaled down so that it could be squeezed, albeit with difficulty, into the pocket of Winterbelle's jeans. The only thing missing was the witch.

Pippa had made a witch too. In fact she had devoted such punctilious attention to the poor creature's clothes and hairdo (hideous, yet somehow homey), that she felt sure now Winterbelle would perceive in the gaunt little figure her mom's low-self-esteem self-portrait, and feel sad.

Outside, in the marrow-cold and sun-bright air of midday, she weighed the time left to kill in order to arrive at the address Roger Wemble had given her precisely at 2:00. A detour through the state park was out of the question, now that her refuge there had been fouled. Strolling downtown or drinking coffee at the Stop 'N' Go entailed the risk of bumping into someone she knew. Residential streets would be full of children trying out their new sleds. So what was left? The graveyard?

Well, why not, she thought. Spend her Christmas among the silent majority. In deference to Hella, whose high season was at hand.

Pippa had to smile, grimly, at the amazing place her head had gotten to.

The trouble is, there isn't much doing in a cemetery on Christmas Day. Pippa tried reading gravestones, but found no poetry in the old country names. They were too much like the names of people she knew—the Ebens and Sarahs, Tooleys and Ilvonnens having passed through the generations like distinctive nose shapes. What was worse, her eye kept getting drawn to dead babies: Ashley Jane Sepe, fourteen days old, and Brandon Gilbert Eugley, who died a week short of his second birthday. Was it possible that in the days when early childhood mortality was so mercilessly common, people felt differently toward their kids? That they held back some critical part of their emotional investiture, as a hedge against bereavement? Pippa tried to imagine what that could have been like—watching your little girl playing out the kitchen window, calculating the odds of her ever getting old enough to menstruate.

She shuddered. She looked up and around, wishing hard to be distracted. And what should she see, trolling up Yew Street, but the Rose Petal & Thorn delivery van.

You could *not* be mistaken about this. It was a white Toyota with twining, voluptuous rose canes painted all over its flanks, making leafy brackets around the shop's name and telephone number, the FTD logo, and the slogan WE GO ANYWHERE! that Jacques had hand-lettered backwards above the grill. The van cruised hesitantly along the empty street, then, as though making its mind up, turned through the perpetually open wrought-iron gates of the cemetery.

The long driveway was plowed, more or less. Still, Pippa would never have risked it in the delivery van. She guessed this was why Jacques was forever getting stuck in places so off-the-map that Triple A had to call back two or three times to get the directions straight. In her perverse curiosity, she did not think to duck behind a gravestone. Now she realized she was standing right out in the open while the Rose Petal & Thorn-mobile came valiantly lurching and spinning in her direction.

Then it stopped. The door opened and Jacques, the French-Canadian-Passamaquoddy delivery person, stepped out. He wore boots up to his knees, an East German Army officer's jacket, and a hat with ridiculous rabbit-fur earflaps. Under his arm, securely tucked like a football, he carried a long white cardboard box, tied with a golden ribbon. The kind of box that roses are delivered in. No doubt about it, Pippa thought. Jacques is on the job.

Jacques was one of those people who, though you see them every day, you never learn anything personal about. Pippa knew from the emergency-numbers list thumbtacked behind the counter that his last name was Pollock. She knew that he was from somewhere farther north, and had drifted down this way looking for a job. She knew he had worked at Rose Petal & Thorn since before Brenda had moved up from Providence with divorce settlement in hand and bought the store; though there were months when he did not seem to work at all, and others that Brenda spent vowing to replace him. That was the limit of what Pippa knew.

Jacques came wading toward her through the snow, which was roughly midcalf-deep. One of his front teeth was missing, which Pippa noticed because he was smiling.

"Hey ya, Pip," he said.

At last, thank the Goddess, someone who did not greet her with Merry Christmas. "Hey, Jacques," she said.

By the logic of the occasion, one of them would now almost certainly say, What are you *doing* here? Pippa did not want it to be Jacques, because she did not want to answer the question. On the other hand, she did not want it to be her, either, because then Jacques would reply, I was about to ask *you* the same thing. So instead she blurted the first alternative chitchatty thing that came to her mind, which was, inanely:

"Long time no see."

Jacques tilted his head to one side. His eyes were jolly;

working on holidays seemed to agree with him. "Since yesterday?" he said.

His accent was somewhat flat, but with a soothing elongation of the vowel sounds, as though he spent a lot of time singing lullabyes.

Pippa must have given him a weird look, because he quickly added:

"Hey, I heard about you getting fired. You're lucky. Congratulations."

He seemed to mean it. At least, she could read nothing like sarcasm in his face. "Why lucky?" she said.

Jacques exclaimed, "Cause man, it's *winter*." He stared off toward the mountainside, taking in the big vista. "There's so much to *do* in winter. I keep trying to get fired, but the Stork won't go for it. Guess one of these days I'm going to have to quit, and let her hire me back come spring."

Pippa followed his eyes along the slope of Wabenaki, as if that might help her get attuned to this unusual point of view. She said, "Who's the Stork?"

Jacques looked somewhat abashed. "I mean Brenda. Cigogne, you know? That's just a name we call her."

"We who?"

Jacques shrugged. "Me and the parakeets."

"Ah," said Pippa. She almost laughed. "You talk to them too?"

He shook his head. "Mostly just listen. They're funny, sometimes."

"Yeah," said Pippa. She thought, Well, who knew?

Jacques glanced at her, maybe to see how she was taking all this, and appeared gratified to find her smiling.

"So, Jacques," she said, "what *are* you doing out here on Christmas Day?"

"I was about to ask you the same question," he said.

"I figured."

He nodded. He did not seem to expect an explanation. This attitude—not expecting things, taking what comes—was a pleasant change, Pippa thought. She resolved to cultivate it in herself.

"I just got this one delivery," he said after a while. From under his arm he produced the long white box. "Same as every year. Dozen white roses, to the Thiess site."

"The Thiess site," Pippa repeated. The name meant nothing that she could recall. Yet it struck a note of authenticity: *site* being the euphemism Brenda Cigogne preferred when talking about somebody's grave. Hearing it now, in this peculiar setting, made her irrationally wish she had her job back.

"Want to come?" said Jacques. He motioned off toward a corner of the cemetery where some of the older, less standardized tombstones were set into a slope that was thickly shaded in warm months by flowering crabs. A quince hedge ran along the black iron fence beyond them, and in back of everything you could see the shadowy contours of a small relict woodland.

They trudged through the snow, in and out of drifts that had built up on the windward side of granite blocks. Jacques appeared perfectly content to keep silent, but for some reason—maybe as simple and pathetic as loneliness—Pippa did not want that.

The Indian half of Jacques interested her. She sort of expected Indians to be into some kind of traditional Native spiritual thing; yet she knew that really most of them had been Christianized for generations, and were often more devout than the typical white person. Still, she guessed it never hurt to poke around a little.

"So do you, um, do anything special on Christmas?" she asked him.

"Sure do," Jacques said readily. They were about halfway up the slope now, and he stood for a moment looking around, searching for the Thiess site in this stark, all but featureless landscape. "Got an ice-fishing trip planned with my cousin Spear."

"Your cousin *Spear?*"

Jacques said, "Sort of a cousin," as though that were the issue. "We grew up together. Actually what it is, we both had the same aunt we kind of lived with."

"Ah." Pippa wondered if this did make sense. "That's interesting—I live with an aunt, too."

"Probably not like this one."

"Probably."

Jacques spotted the place he was looking for. "Come on," he told her. Quite familiarly now. Pippa liked it when people just accepted you. She wondered if this were a general feature of the economically disadvantaged.

Jacques led her over to a large squarish tombstone of pink granite, not the usual gray kind quarried around here. The inscription in large sans serif lettering said:

NORBERT THIESS
1883—

"What does that mean?" said Pippa. "Doesn't anybody *know?*"

"What it usually means," said Jacques—opening the long white box, fluffing the green tissue paper inside apart with surprising deftness, what with his bulky leather work gloves—"is that they ain't dead."

Pippa laughed but then she stopped. She might be a witch but she was not into anything like *that*. "But I mean really," she said.

"Yeah," said Jacques. "Really."

He bent down and he lifted the dozen long-stemmed roses out of the box and laid them just so, slanting diagonally, their perfect half-open buds fanned apart so you could count them all, across the snow that covered the grave. The flowers appeared creamy, almost yellow, against the dead-white backdrop.

"Who sent them?" Pippa said. Her voice had fallen, not by intention, to nearly a whisper. "I mean, is it the family or something?"

"*Sends* them," Jacques corrected her. "Same thing every year. Christmas Day, got to be. Long as I've been working, anyhow."

Pippa nodded, impatiently. "So, who?"

Jacques searched the wispy cirrus clouds forming in thin lines high above the mountain. "Think it was Mrs. Mallard," he said at last.

"*Mad* Mallard?" asked Pippa. Though of course, there could be no other.

Jacques chuckled. "That's a good name. Have to tell that to the parakeets."

"They've heard it," said Pippa, half-mindedly.

Jacques turned to face her. "You want to go do some ice-fishing? You might like my cousin. He'd like you, too."

"Gosh, I—" Pippa was surprised; taken aback, really. Then she reflected that this was undoubtedly a great compliment, being invited to join in the family Christmas. Or whatever it was. "I'm really—thanks a lot. Honestly. But I've kind of got a . . . kind of a meeting I've got to go to."

Jacques smiled agreeably. "You'll have to meet my cousin later, then," he said. Adding: "Spear."

"Spear," said Pippa. "Yeah. I'd love to. Anyway, tell him Hi."

Jacques nodded and that's how they parted: with no
further wasting of words.

And no Happy New Year, either.

The sign in front of the house, flapping on its bracket in
the westerly breeze, read:

ALLISON RHINUM
CERTIFIED THERAPIST
ABUSE AND RECOVERY ISSUES
"IT'S NEVER TOO LATE TO HAVE A HAPPY CHILDHOOD"

As long as she lived, Pippa supposed, she would remember this perky little slogan. She supposed that on her
deathbed it might very well flash one last time through
her mind: *It's never too late* . . . Then nothingness.

The building itself, far from the dire and impregnable
fortress it had become in her mind, during these past 24
hours or so since Roger Wemble had recited the address
over the telephone, was nothing more than an ordinary
Craftsman-style bungalow of the kind you see everywhere:
single-storied, half-shingled, casement-windowed, with
trim painted a middle-of-the-road royal blue, neither festive nor somber. Pippa had arrived seven minutes early,
despite everything, and had to walk up and down the
block several times until it was 2:00 exactly. She wished
she had gone to the bathroom somewhere.

There was no bell to ring. She squeaked open an aluminum outer door and knocked on the hard blue surface
underneath. Blood raced through her arteries, ferrying
every kind of biochemical stress marker to places that had
no use for them. Her reddening face, for example. Her
fingers that shook so badly she could barely control them

enough to pull her mittens off. The skin of her hands was alabaster-white, and looked aged, translucent as a palimpsest. That's how she was caught—staring at hands that madly quaked—when the blue door opened suddenly wide.

Doctor Allison Rhinum, a highly regarded specialist, stood filling up the open space, which became warm and scented of mothballs. There was motion behind her, deeper inside, but Doctor Rhinum imposed herself on Pippa's attention. Her face looked puffy, the pores of her nose filled with beige powder. Yellowish incrustations at the corners of her eyes suggested a cold, or some allergic complaint. She wore a black crew-neck sweater that emphasized the bulginess of her neck, ornamented with an aggressively large and primitive necklace of Yoruba fertility charms.

Ordinarily Pippa did not pay all that much attention to other people's clothes. Something strange had happened to her mind, a speeding amplified attentiveness.

"There is to be no physical contact," Doctor Rhinum said, in a nasal voice.

"No . . ." Pippa could barely hold the woman's gaze. She probably looked shifty, staring this way and that. "You mean, I can't touch my own daughter?"

Doctor Rhinum had spoken her piece. She turned and left the doorway empty, which Pippa guessed would have to do for an invitation.

The front hall was wide and ran all the way through the house, ending in a narrow stairwell—lots of wasted circulation space, but plenty of room to hang coats and kick boots off. There were at least half a dozen sets of these, in all sizes, on a thick coir runner. Scarves and hats hung from a row of hooks. A bright red plastic toboggan stood propped on end against a wall, near a door leading off to the right. This was a building that kids lived in, or at least frequented, Pippa thought—marveling at the idea, which seemed so unaccountably strange to her.

"I trust Mr. Wemble informed you," Allison Rhinum said, "that this visit may be terminated at any time, at my sole discretion. Is that clear?"

Pippa loathed this woman so intensely that even to *nod* at her felt like something that would get you contaminated. She dipped her head slightly.

"Come with me," the Doctor ordered, turning away.

Pippa breathed in and out, steadied by the knowledge that she was guarding a Secret, albeit a totally irrelevant one: the beautiful, transcendent memory of a dozen creamy white roses lying in the sunshine, on top of the snow:

"Can I take my coat off?" she said.

"What?" Allison Rhinum almost barked. Her whole being, shapeless as it was, radiated a weird sort of anger. Not even at Pippa, so much, it appeared, as at something larger and more impersonal. Some unseen and possibly nameless Evil. With which Pippa, evidently, had gotten mixed up inside Allison Rhinum's mind.

Pippa slipped out of her parka, which she hung on a nearby hook. Underneath she was wearing a simple wool skirt and yellow turtleneck, pale so as not to make her face look too sallow. She held the backpack close, cherishing the little present inside it. That was a mistake, perhaps. Allison Rhinum stared down at it.

"What do you have in there?"

"Is that any—" Pippa caught herself. Of *course* it was none of Doctor Rhinum's business. But then, neither was Winterbelle, which had not stopped them from stealing her away. "Only my stuff. It's like a purse, you know? Except it's easier to carry. I mean, in winter and all."

Allison Rhinum sniffed. You could hear the phlegm in her sinuses. She pointed to a doorway and Pippa stepped into a room decorated with garlands of balsam fir, a bowl full of bright round ornaments, and a plastic tree. The tree was hung about with old-fashioned decorations of the kind you might help your kids make, as a household project: strings of popcorn, pictures of snowmen and Santa Claus and holly sprigs cut out from magazines and glued onto cardboard backing, red construction-paper candles spouting yellow flames. There were a few uncomfortable chairs and a coffee table. No lights were on, and the sunlight passed wanly through lace panels hung by thumbtacks across a box window.

"Wait here," Allison Rhinum said.

Then Pippa was alone. Alone in this strange and yet familiar-seeming bungalow. Keeping an appointment to see her own precious daughter on Christmas Day. Holding insanity at bay with arms that were weak from hunger and cold, shaking with terrors that rose from deeper inside Pippa than she ever wanted to look.

She was a practical-minded person. She felt no need to understand how the world worked. She only wanted to live her life and be happy in the years she had to share with Winterbelle. Now she was forced to grapple with things both within her and without that she could not even find words for.

She did not hear footsteps, but suddenly turned to find Winterbelle standing just inside the room. Allison Rhinum loomed, three times as large, like a fleshy mountain, close behind her.

"Hi, Mommy," Winterbelle said.

"Honey," said Pippa. "Oh, sweetie—"

Her body moved without anything like rational intention, covering the distance across the room in no time at all. Winterbelle stepped forward and raised her arms to meet her mother's—but Doctor Rhinum moved into the space between them with the bulky efficacy of a football lineman.

"We *talked* about this," the woman told Pippa, who bumped into her.

Threefold Law or no, Pippa thought, this woman is going to pay a price for this. A heavy and painful price.

She backed slowly away, finding a chair with her hands and blindly lowering herself into it.

"Hi, Mommy," Winterbelle said again, emerging from the shadow of Allison Rhinum with the brilliance of the sun coming out. She stood nervously, almost on tiptoe, but seemed to understand that she was not supposed to get too close. "I've missed you."

Pippa's eyes filled with tears—she no longer resisted this, because it would come anyway, and it would pass—but through the watery blur she examined her daughter for signs of . . . of anything. Just signs.

Winterbelle wore a dress she had nearly outgrown, a pleated cotton party dress with a frilly collar and sleeves, leaf-green, very Christmasy. She looked pretty in it, and tall, and Pippa was so proud of her; though in another part of her mind she wondered whether Winterbelle had picked out the dress to wear today for herself. It did not seem exactly like what she would have chosen. A bit too . . . confining. Or was Pippa wrong; were there things about her daughter she did not understand? Had Winterbelle changed already in these past few days that she had been gone? Such things happen so quickly, Pippa knew. Kids can become like strangers, large and mysterious, if you take your eyes off them.

"I'm so glad you came," said Winterbelle. "I told them you would come."

"Oh, sweetie." Pippa wiped her eyes. "Of course I came. I've missed you—oh, I've just missed you so *much*."

"I know you have, Mommy. It's all right."

Allison Rhinum was not looking at either of them. Yet you could feel the heaviness of her attention as though it were a huge piece of cloth draped over everything in the room.

"Here," said Pippa. She unzipped her backpack and felt inside for the World's Tiniest Dollhouse. "I've got something for you."

Winterbelle drew in her breath, remembering: "Did you find the frog?"

"Oh, yes, sweetie, I did. Thank you so much. It was so beautiful. I've got it with me—right here."

Pippa tapped her pocket and Winterbelle glowed with pleasure.

"I carved it," the girl said. "I was *planning* to do a wolf—because you like them?—but I kept wrecking the nose, and the tail kept breaking off. So I did a frog instead. I hope that's all right."

"It's perfect, sweetie," said Pippa. "I just love it. Now, here." She drew the present out. It was not exactly wrapped—the wooden jewelry box was beautiful in its own way, so she had just circled it with a strip of ribbon, tied and retied into a nice plump bow. "I made you something, too."

Winterbelle stepped eagerly forward. Again Allison Rhinum moved faster, blocking the girl's path.

"Let me see that," she demanded. She held out a hand, thick and strong-looking, that looked as though it spent most of its time clutched into a fist.

"It's a gift," said Pippa, "for my *daughter*." She allowed the merest fraction of her resentment to show. "It's just a—" (lowering her voice to a whisper) "—just a *dollhouse*, for heaven's sake. *Please* let her have it. Please."

Doctor Rhinum glared down. "This was not part of the arrangement," she pronounced sternly.

"What *arrangement?*" said Pippa. "I've done everything you and Mr. Wemble told me. Do you have to object to *every-thing?* I mean, can't you just draw a line somewhere and *stop?*"

"That is exactly," said Allison Rhinum, "what I am doing."

But she stepped back, a full pace, clearing the path for Winterbelle to accept the present from her mother, and Pippa felt as if she had won at least one small victory in the sad, long war.

Winterbelle took the little box and held it near her face and stared at it with her eyes so wide, she seemed to be trying to press every detail, every nuance of this moment, forever into her memory. Her long slender fingers moved cautiously to loosen the ribbon, undoing the bow first and then pulling the whole thing away and tucking it into the sash on her dress, unwilling to consign it to the floor. After that for a number of seconds she rotated the box and looked at it from various angles, touching with a fore-finger its miniature gold latch. At last she eased the lid up.

Her mouth opened. She stared into the witch's kitchen as though it were an entire newly discovered continent in the palm of her hand. Pippa could see the girl's radiant blue eyes, focused intently, darting from one tiny object to another. Winterbelle appeared to be holding her breath. With her free hand she raised the lid a few degrees more, so that the dollhouse wall was perpendicular to the floor.

Then she looked slowly up at her mom. She said, one syllable at a time, "It is so *awesome*. Especially the stove. I can't believe you *made* this." She took a step toward Pippa, then caught herself. A bright wet dot materialized in each of her eyes. "Thank you, Mommy," she said huskily. "I love you."

"Oh, sweetie," said Pippa, "you're welcome. I love you, too. I'm so glad you—"

Unnoticed, Allison Rhinum had been edging in on them. She leaned over Winterbelle, staring down into the dollhouse with an expression that you might have classified as simple curiosity, or nosiness, except that it was somehow more menacing than either of those. Without much ado—as though the gesture had no particular import—she reached down and scooped the present out of Winterbelle's grasp. She examined it briefly at close range, then snapped the box shut.

"Hey," said Pippa. "Be careful with—"

"WHAT ARE YOU DOING?" shrieked Winterbelle, with an instantaneous violence that startled both grown-ups. "Give that *back* to me! *Give it back now*, you troll! You big fat ugly pig—that's *mine!*"

Allison Rhinum gripped the dollhouse in one large hand. She turned to Pippa, absolutely ignoring Winterbelle, as though the girl were safely locked behind a soundproof partition.

"Well," she said, "I can see that I was correct. It was a mistake to allow you to come here and traumatize this child. And I must say, it was a *major* error in judgment on your part to utilize this interview for the purpose of furthering your daughter's cultic indoctrination."

Pippa started to say, "I am *not*—"

Only Winterbelle threw herself into a kind of frenzy that Pippa had never seen before. It was as though, shamanically, the girl changed suddenly into a frightful predator, maddened with hunger—an eagle whose talons ripped at Allison Rhinum's face, or a mountain lion rending with its teeth, seizing gobbets of flesh and spewing them out.

At the same time she was just a little girl—littler than nine, a gangly preschooler, sleepless and dazed and terrified and angry at everything, at a world she could not understand—beyond the reach of soothing or hugging or calming down, so furious and out-of-control she must be physically restrained.

"No!" cried Pippa.

"I hate you!" screamed Winterbelle, striking again and again at Allison Rhinum's face. Kicking her shins. Scratching. Biting. Ramming with her head. "I hate you I hate you *I hate you I hate you I hate you I hate you*"—blowing out of her like the scalding discharge of a pressure cooker.

"Sweetie! Stop it!" Pippa shouted, though she knew it was useless. "You'll only make things worse."

Allison Rhinum endured the assault for so long, you had to think maybe her nerve endings were coarsened or only partly operable. Or else that this sort of thing had happened to her so many times before, she understood (in a strictly cerebral, nonempathic way) that the best thing to do was let it run its course.

All at once her entire body responded. She spun upon Winterbelle, seizing the girl by both wrists and lifting her up off the floor with—what could you call it?—a clinical, dispassionate ferocity. She let the girl dangle that way, at arm's length, kicking and shouting futilely, until at last, after a long ten seconds or so, Winterbelle stopped moving altogether and just hung limp. Exhausted, trembling, soaked with her own sweat, like a creature dragged out of an icy stream.

Allison Rhinum lowered the girl to the floor, where she bunched up in a miserable pile, like laundry. Then Winterbelle started to cry. Not a loud or wracking cry—just pitiful sobbing. A sound of pure, overwhelming childhood misery and hopelessness.

Pippa would never lose her direct organic connection to this living creature. The cytoplasm of her own body had subdivided to produce the egg that Winterbelle had grown from. The girl's flesh had been Pippa's flesh, and it remained Pippa's flesh, with minor genetic sequencing inserted by the handsome dad, last seen bound for Hawaii. When Winterbelle got sick, Pippa felt her symptoms. When she was happy, Pippa laughed. When she was angry, Pippa's blood pressure rose. The illusion that a mother and child are separate, mutually distinct individuals is so transparently stupid that to believe it you have to possess the soul of a sewing machine, or maybe a computer, like so many people do nowadays. Pippa was not one of them.

She told Doctor Allison Rhinum, "If you do this to her again"—her voice calm in a way that it had, perhaps, never been before—"I am going to destroy you. Completely destroy you."

Allison Rhinum stared back with an expression Pippa could not name. Not hatred. If possible, something even more elemental than that. More deeply rooted in the limbic, reptilian brain.

Well, the feeling's mutual, Pippa thought. Whatever it is.

"Winterbelle," she said. Looking down at her daughter with no longer a sense of overwhelming compassion and sympathy—for while she felt those things, of course, she understood that the situation had gotten beyond the reach of them. What she felt chiefly was a sense of resolve.

Winterbelle lay curled on the floor whimpering like a weary infant, ignorant of what exactly it wants or needs, conscious only of the general truth that it wants *something*, needs it badly right now.

"Winterbelle!" Pippa said, more forcefully. She had to have her daughter's attention.

At last Winterbelle looked up. A wounded-animal look in her eyes.

"Mommy," she said. Her voice was strange, croaking. "Mommy. Save me."

"I am going to save you," Pippa said quickly—though not quickly enough to keep the sight and the sound of her daughter in that moment from haunting her forever.

(Save me.)

"Sweetie, I promise. Mommy is going to save you. Mommy is going to come and get you and take you back home. Only right now—listen to me!—Mommy has got to leave. As long as I'm here, it's going to be worse for you. Don't try to understand—it's a grown-up thing. Just listen to your mommy. I've got to leave because there are some things I need to do. But then I'll come back. And I'll save you. I'll take you back home. Just *believe* me, okay? And wait for me, sweetie. Just wait."

Allison Rhinum began to speak before Pippa had even turned away from her daughter on the floor. She spoke rapidly in a nasal undertone. Pippa tried not to listen but the words clung to her like damp scraps of paper. *Suspension of visitation rights. Formal custody hearing. Official notice. Investigation. Scheduling. Right to counsel.*

Abruptly, Pippa whirled and slapped her.

Slapped her hard, and loudly, on the bulging fleshy cheek.

Whhaappp.

The sound was so sharp, so immensely gratifying, that Pippa imagined it hung in the air for quite a few moments.

Allison Rhinum was, during the course of those moments, too flabbergasted to speak.

By the time she recovered herself, Pippa was out in the
hallway. She was yanking her parka off the hook, hurling
open the door, going out into the blinding white void of
winter, a land whose mysteries no one has plumbed.

"I can have you arrested and charged for that," Allison
Rhinum said behind her.

"Go ahead," said Pippa.

"I can make things *much worse* for you."

"Oh, really?" Pippa looked back. She noticed that the
little dollhouse was no longer in Allison Rhinum's hand.
She must have dropped it, or set it down, in her shock
and anger.

(Had Winterbelle snatched it back? Did she have someplace to hide it? Were such things too much to hope?)

"Hey, look," said Pippa, "I'm sorry I had to hit you.
Really. But see, I *had* to. So go ahead and do what you've
got to do. I guess I'll be seeing you."

And she turned and left, and she heard no more just
then from Doctor Allison Rhinum.

And it was perfectly true, she thought. She *had* to slap
her. Not for herself. For Winterbelle. *Loudly,* so that Winterbelle could hear the smack. So that her daughter could
play it back again and again, whenever she needed to
remember.

Because Winterbelle had to know that her mommy
would fight for her. Her mommy would hurt anybody who
hurt her precious little girl. And she would be back, just
like she said she would. Come Hel or high water.

Or more likely
both.

Trees Cracking Moon fattened, a crescent that rose while the sun was still high and went down before midnight. Pippa felt the moment of its setting though Wabenaki Mountain lay between them. She seemed to be growing acutely, even painfully, sensitive to things that she had never much thought about before. Television commercials, for example, in which she now detected certain governing attitudes toward the people watching them. The most terrible, overheard through the walls of the old house on Ash Street, were those aimed at a mainstream family viewership: attractive well-adjusted kids nagging good-naturedly until Mom or Pop agrees to give them the product in question. Then, smiles all around. Pippa wondered how many of these plastic TV kids were anywhere near as jolly as they looked. What kind of childhoods did they have, schlepping from talent agents to cattle-call auditions? Why did the sight of them make her feel so hopeless? How could she go on without Winterbelle another minute?

In the village, children played with their Christmas toys, raised hell, tossed powdery snowballs that disintegrated in flight, dashed across streets without looking, modeled extravagant ski caps, and roved in small bands, feckless and bored. Rose Petal & Thorn unfurled a nylon SALE banner Pippa could see NoElle Deacon through the plate-glass window, looking smiley and bloodless and fake, like the TV kids. There were not many customers. Pippa lingered on the sidewalk, halfway expecting to see the ancient, hunched-over gentleman who had one day offered her a single rose. He did not appear, and she wondered what the fuck she was doing. A boy across the street turned out not to be Kaspian Aaby. A loud voice behind her came from someone other than her friend Judith.

Pippa guessed she was lonely. She guessed she was sad. Near the police station, in midsidewalk, she caught the eye of an acquaintance from back in her days of participation in a local eco-activist group that called itself the Street Players. Deputy Doug—the only part of his name she could remember—stared at her for a moment over his coffee mug. Then he set the mug down on the concrete and trotted between parked cars in her direction.

"Hi, Doug," she said, smiling extra hard.

Doug looked this way and that. He was mostly bald though still fairly young, early 30's. Harmless, scrawny-limbed, country-boy type.

"Heard about your problems," he said in a way-too-quiet voice.

Pippa wondered, Heard professionally? Or just through the grapevine?

"You got a lawyer?" Doug said.

She nodded, feeling the fear creep through her insides. The shadings and nuances of fear—irrational dread, chronic anxiety, raging terror, et al.—were among the things she had gotten acutely sensitive to. "Why?" she summoned the courage to say.

Deputy Doug shrugged, jerking his shoulders. His uniform made him look uncomfortable. "There's some heavy shit going down, and I don't want it to land on you. Okay?"

"What does that mean?" said Pippa.

Doug looked furtive, as though his life among the pettiest grade of criminals was getting to him. "There've been . . . *reports*. Most of them anonymous. Crazy shit, you wouldn't think anyone would believe it. But it's kind of a smoke and fire thing—there's been so *much* of it. It's gotten to where, somebody will write in saying, you know, I heard such-and-such at my S.L.A.A. meeting—"

"My what?" said Pippa.

Doug blushed. "That's Sex and Love Addicts Anonymous. I'm just using it as an example. What I'm saying is, no matter how ridiculous a thing might sound, you can't do *nothing* about it. Especially if you keep hearing the same stuff again and again and again. Know what I'm saying?"

Pippa shook her head. "What stuff?" she said.

"Talk to your lawyer," Doug advised. And then he was gone—*poof*—like a well-intentioned but out-of-it fairy.

Arthur Torvid's office had received a spot of brightening up in the form of a Christmas cactus in a plastic pot, wrapped in gold foil. The blooms of the plant—an alarming mixture of fuchsia-purple and scarlet—were pretty well shot. Pippa sat very still in the jungle-print deck chair, waiting for Torvid to get off-line.

"Sorry," he said finally, giving his monitor a farewell slap. "Bit of a flame war going on. Lots of recrimination and name-calling."

"Who started it?" asked Pippa.

Torvid hesitated a moment, then tossed his head to the side, dismissively.

A confession of guilt, she thought, if ever I saw one.

"Bunch of pro-government fascists," he said. "As though organized political parties have ever accomplished anything. I tried to explain to them—"

"Could we talk about me?" said Pippa, hearing apology in her voice and hating herself for it. "Please?"

"Absolutely," said Torvid. He stood up and came around to the front of his desk. He wore a sweat-gray warm-up suit whose pizza stains did not look fresh. "What can I do you for?"

She said, "I just ran into a friend of mine—well, sort of an acquaintance—outside the police station."

"Ah, yes!" said Torvid. He nodded as if these facts were well known to him.

Pippa went on, "And he told me to come talk to *you*."

"Best advice you could have," Torvid agreed, with some enthusiasm. "Always good to have a friend on the force."

"He's not really a friend," said Pippa.

Torvid wasn't listening. He perched on the desk and began kicking his feet, congenitally restless. "I've been thinking, Pippa Rede," he said. "The best defense is a good offense. Maybe what we ought to do is initiate aggressive proceedings."

"What do you mean?"

Torvid nodded, evidently much in agreement with himself. "We'll begin with a writ of habeus corpus. Demand that your daughter be produced in court along with a compelling explanation of why it is not in her best interest to be returned to her natural birth parent immediately. Then we'll follow with a suit requesting that all pertinent records be made public. Simultaneously we'll petition the court to order that your daughter receive independent counseling and evaluation by an expert of our choosing, and we'll follow by attempting to have that Rhinum woman decertified. Our final step will be a civil action seeking unspecified damages, to be calculated on the basis of psychological harm incurred, disruption of normal development, irreparable trauma, and so forth—you follow me?"

Pippa shook her head. She stood up and lifted the Christmas cactus and said, "This needs water. And you've got to give it sunlight or it will die. I want to leave my daughter out of this as much as possible. I don't *want* her dragged into court. I don't *want* to sue for unspecified damages. I don't want there to *be* any damage."

Arthur Torvid opened his mouth. Then he closed it and nodded. "I see your point. Points."

Pippa said, "Why did Deputy Doug say I should talk to you?"

Torvid sighed. Then he came out with it. "They're investigating you for involvement in a pattern of ritual abuse. There's talk of a grand jury. Indictments, police raids, rounding up other members of the ring."

Pippa felt one of the advanced gradations of fear coming on. "Members of the *ring?*"

Torvid surprised her by practically jumping up from the desk. He stood more or less eyeball-to-eyeball with the young Dennis Hopper.

"I *know* it's bullcrap," he said boisterously. "You don't have to *tell* me it's bullcrap. I even think you don't have to tell *them* it's bullcrap. What I'm afraid, though, is that the D.A.'s office figures it'll be easier—easier politically— to let a jury do the dirty work for it. Let a *jury* decide the charges are without merit. That way, the D.A. can go back to his constituents and say, Look, I did my best. She's got herself a tricky lawyer who knows how to work the technicalities, what can I say?"

"Great," said Pippa. "So a year from now, I get out of

jail because my tricky lawyer works technicalities. Meanwhile what happens to Winterbelle? And what happens to her when it's over?"

Arthur Torvid turned his back on Dennis Hopper. He looked calmer, somewhat closer to the way you expect an attorney to look (except for the warm-up suit). "If they go ahead with this," he said, "you can kiss your daughter good-bye. To begin with, she'll be placed in permanent foster care. To end with, you'll be lucky to be allowed to see her for two hours every other weekend, even after your acquittal. Once you're on the List, you stay on the List. You get me? Due process does not apply here. Your name will be placed in a national data registry. You will be a Reported Child Molester for the rest of your life. We can sue, and we can win, and you can live comfortably off the settlement. But your daughter is gone."

Pippa cried. She cried loudly and it was not just about what Arthur Torvid was telling her. It was not even just about Winterbelle. To a great extent it was about her own powerlessness—tricky lawyer or no—in the face of something huge and formless and impersonal: a shadowy Presence that seemed always to have been there, dangling at the corner of her awareness, waiting for the moment to descend.

"Listen," said Arthur Torvid. He stood next to her, close enough to touch, and for a moment actually touching. One of his hands lay awkwardly, for two or three sobs, on one of her shoulders.

She looked up at him, tried to clamp down on her crying.

He said, "I didn't mean that's what is inevitably going to happen. I'm sorry if it sounded like that. I was just answering your question: **What *if* these** terrible things happen? It's my job to see that **they *don't*** happen, they're not *allowed* to happen. That's why I advocate getting aggressive. Make the first strike, try to catch them with their pants down."

Pippa shook her head. It had gotten way beyond her ability to grasp, even in fuzzy outline. She did not know whether to trust Torvid's judgment. Nor did she know of any alternatives. She had run out of questions, objections, preferences—the whole kit.

"I guess," she said, struggling to come up with some words that worked, "I guess maybe you ought to do what you think is the right thing."

Torvid patted her shoulder. She could hardly imagine a situation in which this gesture would be welcome, or even acceptable. Yet in a perverse way, it was welcome now. It was a relief to be condescended to.

"Don't worry," said Torvid. He stepped away and appeared to be staring at his computer, maybe longing to get back to the flame war going on in some netherworld where there were only virtual casualties, no bleeding bodies on the ground. In fact, no ground. He looked at Pippa from a distance that seemed unbridgeable. He said, "We're going to kill them."

And Pippa for once
did not feel troubled by
the witches' 3-Fold Law.

On the Feast of the Innocents, two days after Christmas, Pippa came home in the afternoon after walking around town all day, purposelessly, just to keep from sitting still, to discover some kind of meeting in progress. She could tell it was a meeting and not just a gathering of friends because, first of all, as far as Pippa was aware her great-aunt Eulace *had* no friends in any recognizable sense, and secondly, the half dozen people in the front parlor were hunched forward in chairs that had been drawn into pow-wow formation around a padded chintz ottoman, on top of which papers were arranged. The papers appeared to be maps. The people ranged from ancient & decrepit down to about 45. All of them raised their heads—twelve eyes among them—when Pippa entered the house, knocking snow off her boots.

She was so surprised, she could not help asking:

"What's going on?"

"This," Eulace informed her, sniffily, "is the Road-Naming Committee."

"For Enhanced 911," a gentleman added, brushing something imaginary off his lapel.

Pippa did not know whether to smile or nod or what. "Don't the roads have names already?"

"Not that anybody *agrees* on," said Eulace. She sounded quite stern about this. You would not want to get into an argument about road names with her in such a frame of mind.

"It's very important," a lady emphasized, the youngest of the group, "that everything be standardized. That way the police can respond to *any* 911 call, even if the caller is unable to provide an exact location."

Probably this was all in Pippa's head, but she felt as though the people in the room were staring at her with a couple of degrees too much intensity

"I like the ones named after trees," she said meekly. And she was turning to slink decently out of sight when Aunt Eulace, her tone somewhat barking, called after her:

"I'm tired of taking all your phone messages. Why don't you call this Mr. Andor back so he'll leave me alone?"

Pippa turned briefly, failed to gain any further clues from her great-aunt's full-browed glower, and packed herself off to the kitchen, which, she guessed, was where she belonged.

What phone messages? she wondered. To the best of her memory, Eulace had never willingly conveyed a hint of anyone's having tried to get in touch with her. Much less actually made note of what the person had been hoping to say.

Besides, she didn't think she knew anybody named Andor.

She saw the note, then—a leaf of plain paper, squarish and white, positioned with exactitude at the center of the cutting-board—with a special kind of surprise: the kind where you wonder why you hadn't noticed it coming, just before the 2x4 smacks you in the eye

"Dear Pippa," the note began, and at this salutation Pippa stopped.

Dear Pippa. She could not imagine Eulace speaking these words. They were therefore just a formality. But her great-aunt was not and had never been given to formalities. Therefore something was screwed up.

She guessed she better sit down. The ladder back of the kitchen chair came all the way to the ventral lobe of her head. The squarish white note fluttered in her hand like a scrap of institutional toilet paper.

"Dear Pippa," it said. "Someone named Cliff Andor has been calling here day & night and wants you to call him back *as soon as you get this message.* Please do call as I can't stand hearing the sound of his voice one more time."

There followed, in block print overwritten for emphasis, a number in area code 707. Pippa decided not to waste time wondering about it. The note went on:

"This brings me to what I really wanted to talk to you about. I know that things have been hard for you lately with the Child Welfare people finally coming for Winterbelle. But you must see that everything happens for a reason, and in the long run things tend to work out for the best. You never should have had the child to begin with, and at least this way she can be given all the things that you could not. While of course I'm quite sorry for you, I have never believed you were well suited for taking care of a young girl let alone yourself and a young girl too. Maybe someday you and Winterbelle can be together again and we'll all laugh about it! And in a hundred years none of it will matter anyway, as we'll all be dead.

"You and I have had our differences over the years since your mother passed on, but I believe I've always tried to do what is best and what I could according to the lights which I've been given. I never believed anyone should have things handed to them on a silver platter, but when I saw that you and the poor girl could barely keep a roof over your heads, I was happy to offer you mine. I've never asked for thanks and I do not do so now. I only ask you not to expect that the free ride is going to last forever.

"I know you've got people in the area who will be happy to let you stay with them, at least it has always worked out that way in the past, all the way back to when you and your mother were fighting and you so much as up and moved out. I trust this is still the case. In any event, I'm letting you have a little more money in addition to what I've already provided to help you get going on your own two feet. Don't think that I'm throwing you out onto the streets because I'm not. You're welcome to stay here whenever you need to—family is family, and in the end every one of us is as guilty of sin and ignorance and vainglory as any other.

"Do believe that I sincerely wish you well.

"Your loving great-aunt—"

Pippa turned the note over. Taped to the back of page 2 was a bank check for fifty dollars.

She wondered several things. What is vainglory? *What* money had Eulace already provided? Suppose we're *not* all dead in 100 years? (Winterbelle, at least, had a shot.) And how far exactly did Eulace think Pippa was going to get with fifty dollars?

Mainly, though, she thought: If this is really happening—getting evicted, on top of everything else—why don't I feel bummed out about it?

In fact Pippa did not feel awful at all. The note seemed to her too idiotic to have that much of an impact. It didn't deserve to affect you, one way or the other. Coming home and finding all her remaining possessions out on the front lawn would have been one thing. This piece of paper was nothing. In the context of Pippa's life, it hardly made an impression.

She strode back out to the front parlor, intent upon telling her aunt something to this effect. In front of the guests, who now obviously could be seen as a crude form of self-protection, like hostages. But as she stood in the hall, not yet within eyeshot, and heard the Road-Naming Committee muddling ahead with their worthy endeavor, it just didn't seem to be worth it. Let them rename the damned streets. Let them change Aspen Court to Credit Card Cul-de-Sac. Who cared?

Pippa walked up the stairs, stepped into Winterbelle's old bedroom, crawled into the cupboard bed, drew the covers way up, and lost herself in bottomless sleep.

Waking up, she felt worse.

Where *was* she going to live now? And on what?

There was more than fifty dollars, of course. She still had a final check coming from Rose Petal & Thorn, and there was a chance of picking up some temporary work doing postholiday sales and inventory. She could drop off an updated resume at Wal-Mart, if she could figure out how to get there. And as a fallback, there was the secret emergency stash of $20 bills tucked into a coffee-table book about gardening with perennials. This was what she thought of as her private health insurance plan: each 20 (plus an extra 5 from somewhere) equaled one visit to the Community Clinic that the doctor with a big red beard held in his office every Saturday morning, or two bottles of Echinacea Extra at the CoOp, or a prescription for Winterbelle's ear medicine Their worst winter so far, praise Freya, had cost seventeen 20's. Witches on the whole are a healthy lot.

Outside it was already dark. Dinner hour had come and

gone, and Pippa got the confused feeling you have when you wake up at the wrong time—as though you're not where you belong, you've missed out on something. The big old house had settled into suspicious silence, like a forest where all the small, easily digested animals have fallen quiet. Pippa's own footsteps sounded menacing, setting off a chorus of sympathetic groans from the aged floorboards while she moved from place to place, opening drawers and closet doors and wondering how you went about a thing like this. Leaving with no destination, packing when everything of genuine value has been already taken from you. Finally she zipped wide the opening of her backpack and dropped in handfuls of the sort of stuff you take on a camping trip—toothbrush, unopened cake of soap, oversized t-shirt to sleep in, a couple of paperbacks, a box of tampons, extra sweater, socks, a noisy wind-up alarm clock, her sewing kit, and a butane lighter. The rest would just have to wait. Eulace would just have to wait, too.

She clumped down to the kitchen, where a fluorescent under-counter light cast a moonish pallor on things. It was the kitchen, really, she hated to leave behind. Such a big, impractical, homey, comforting place. She wished she could wave her wand and transport the whole thing, like Dorothy flying her farmhouse, away to a kind and peaceable land. Maybe Canada, only with shorter winters. As a compromise between impossibility and nothing, she looked around for a piece of kitchen gear that would fit in the pack—rejecting the butcher's cleaver as too dangerous, pots as too bulky—and decided upon the mortar of cast stone and its handworked wooden pestle. These had been expensive and she would not put it past her great-aunt to drop them off at the Swap Shop first thing next morning.

All this weighted the backpack down more than she had intended. But it was done, and when she stepped out the front door for what she supposed was not *really* the last time, though it did feel that way, she took a breath of air so cold it seemed not so much to fill her lungs as to freeze-dry them, and she nearly tumbled down the porch steps in an overwhelming surge of relief, of release, of unanticipated freedom.

How weird, she thought, gripping the rough chipped rail.

The old house behind her seemed like an enormous weight that had fallen at last from her shoulders. In comparison, the backpack was light as a snowflake. Pippa could hardly believe it—her own absence of sentiment, of regret. She felt a raw edge of fear in her stomach, but that was not much different than the way you felt when embarking on any unfamiliar thing. A journey. A new job. A fresh relationship.

For the longest time, trooping down Ash Street toward the center of the village, peering in windows at Christmas trees still up and bright, the watery blue luminence of TV screens, she was untroubled by any question of where her feet were taking her. *Away*, was all she needed to know. She was leaving Eulace's house behind and going away.

The village was silent yet had a lively feeling about it. Holiday vibes. Trees Cracking Moon was melon-yellow, a waxing crescent about 40 percent full, high in the southwest. Traffic noise from the highway a few blocks off sounded much more distant than that. It came steadily, though. People were moving through town. The credit-card center never slept. Probably there were tourists who made a big thing of this, coming to a quaint little postcard village way up north to drink cider by a hearth, while the blizzard raged and the hired help scuttled around. Pippa couldn't blame them. Half the town—or say a third, seriously, of the people *she* knew—depended on the tourist biz in one way or another. Even Judith made seasonal money doing readings for people who couldn't make it home to their regular psychics.

Pippa's brain was on fire in a compressed way, like a teeny nuclear reactor running at full power, all that hot stuff sizzling dangerously within its containment vessel. All things to her looked dazzling, streetlights bright and streaky, automobile flanks as slick as mirrors, people on High Street walking stiff and upright yet gracefully, swiftly, like actors in a black & white movie. *Holiday Inn,* with so much busyness and dialogue to get through between production numbers. The village actually felt like that to Pippa—like a striking and sophisticated confection, full of life on a certain level, though the life was alien and your relationship to it was strictly one-way; you could no more snuggle up with those professional people in front of the hearth than you could cut a rug with Bing. But it was entertainment.

Across the village green, the Congregationalist church glared white and its steeple clock was backlit orange-pink, like the moon in neon. Pippa stood in front of the Opera House, staring upward. The clock said 9:17. It felt much later. The strident *pitta* energies of midnight were already kicking in. You don't feel them so much when you have kids because you're long asleep, or else too tired to notice.

But Pippa didn't have a kid, just now, did she? So here she was out on the streets alone hours after nightfall, catching a *pitta* buzz. One of the big twin doors of the Opera House opened behind her and a provident draft of warm air brushed over her.

There must be a show going on. Pippa peered through the plate-glass door and saw a sandwich-board kind of thing set up just far enough inside so you wouldn't collide with it, with a sign that announced

SLEEPING TALIA
A FAMILY TALE IN TWO ACTS

Pippa frowned for just a second. Then she got it. Brenda's play with the Bad Fairy. Too much. The show had started over an hour ago. It almost seemed worthwhile to sneak in and take a look-see—check out her costume-fitting under the revelatory spell of stage lights. This was the kind of thing you have to do on impulse, so without giving herself time to think Pippa yanked on one of the big twin doors. And stepped into a Family Tale.

The Opera House had no ticket office; just a big empty lobby, whose every surface seemed to be padded in some variety of wine-red fabric. There were mirrors and chandeliers and you would have said the whole thing was just too tacky, except that Pippa had been once to the Kennedy Center in Washington and that was worse. She climbed a winding staircase, figuring to make her entrance in the shadowy rear of the balcony, where teenagers sat to grapple.

Onstage there was lots of commotion—thumping and yelling and clattering of props—so when Pippa squeaked the door ajar, nobody turned a head. Below, in blue lighting that stood for darkness, half a dozen actors commingled in a land of painted firs. At its center, under a moon-gold spot, beautiful Talia lay fast asleep. She was a Rite-Aid blonde, with red spots on her cheeks. Above her, distraught, Prince Charming pined. The Prince looked a little small for the part. His costume brushed the decking

as he addressed himself to the audience, lifting his eyes
toward the gallery.

It was Kaspian!

She almost laughed in the surprise of recognition. Kaspian, looking cute and brave in his oversized tunic. Drawing (awkwardly) a real sword of shining steel. Chocolate-
mint eyes glinting. He declaimed:

> *"Whoever laid upon yon Maid this foul*
> *Enchantment, let her know that I am on her trail!*
> *And she shall pay a heavy price—for from*
> *This day I shall not rest until I turn*
> *The Spell upon its Maker. Mark my vow!*
> *That she shall know the taste of her own Craft*
> *Ere all is done. But now must I to breakfast."*

The boy-prince arrayed himself and his costume and
weaponry and made as though to exit. His retinue likewise.
Only next a whirry sound (as of harsh wind) shook the
painted forest, and the pool of yellow moonlight curdled
to blood red. A thunder-board rumbled. The actors (except
Kaspian) shuddered in fear and sought refuge.

In the midst of all this, from somewhere way down in
the orchestra, a camera flashed.

Two beats—then onto the scene stepped the Bad Fairy.
Brenda appeared almost supernaturally animated as she
wagged saucily downstage, like Liz making her entrance
in *Virginia Woolf.* Her eyes overarched themselves.

"I *do* mark your vow, dear Prince," the Bad Fairy said,
in a loud generic Old World accent. "For through my Dark
Arts, I can take many forms, and I have been spying upon
you some while already, hidden among the boughs."

Kaspian made a cute wiggly shudder, affecting discom-
fiture. The Bad Fairy had him on the run.

"You are foolish indeed," she said, "if you dare to contest me in matters of Craft. And yet—" (vamping) "—there are yet other, softer Arts, in which you may prove a ready pupil. Come you with me, and I shall lead you to my secret Bower amid the timbered Waste."

Holy cow, thought Pippa. Kaspian better watch out, back in the Green Room.

Down in the Dark Forest, the Prince rallied.

"Nay, upon my soul!" he said, his sword erect. "I shall not make this profane liaison with you."

He accented the first syllable of *profane*, which caused the iamb to come out right but led Pippa to wonder if Kaspian had ever heard the word spoken in its usual context before.

The Bad Fairy wasn't accustomed to taking lip, especially from Princes who haven't started shaving. She bristled in an oddly literal way—rose canes wagging dangerously from her shoulders. Pippa thought the effect was kind of funny but unnerving too. Brenda did bring to her role a verisimilistic lack of compunction.

Pippa sighed. She guessed she had seen enough.

In nearly total darkness she slid along the wall, feeling for the doorway. Her fingers touched the handle. But just as she was pushing through, another hand fell on hers and she took a quick breath and drew back. Before her, a tall shadow, formless as Peter Pan's cutout silhouette, gasped loudly enough to hear—

"Mary Margaret!"

—in a carrying contra-tenor.

Pippa was less rattled, evidently, than whoever *this* was. She slipped out the door, holding it open behind her.

Into the mezzanine stepped a striking and lanky-limbed individual so deliciously trashy-looking that Pippa's first impression was: preoperative plumbing-change candidate.

But it was more complicated than that. The . . . *man*, she guessed . . . peered down a long aquiline nose at her. His skin was latté-colored and his hair black and curly. He had too many piercings to count. He wore a velvet jongleur's cap, a purple waistcoat with starchy white ruffles, several rings per finger, *skin*tight pants that stopped just below the knee, black silk stockings, and tap shoes.

"*Mercy*," he breathed, rapidly patting his sternum. "Are you trying to *wreck* me for *days?*"

"Nope," Pippa said. "Just leaving early. Same as you."

She could barely take her eyes off. The tall man was about the same age as her. He glided across the mezzanine to stare down into the lobby below.

"Isn't this place wonderful?" he said. Sounding much calmer now. "It's so *filthy*."

Pippa hardly knew what to say. "Are you from around here?" she tried.

The tall man pirouetted with one hand clasped over the lower half of his face, fingers splayed like a fan.

"It *shows*," he said, "doesn't it?"

Pippa cautiously smiled. "I kind of got the impression that you wanted it to."

He bowed his head in shame. "Hella help me! *That* shows, too."

"Who?" said Pippa.

The tall man frowned—at **last, an** ordinary expression. "Who what?"

"Who *help* you?" said Pippa. "You said somebody help you."

"Dear me," the man said. "Don't tell me you haven't heard of Hella?"

Pippa quit smiling. "As **a matter** of fact, I have."

"Oh, good." The man **glanced** over the railing **again**. Worriedly, she thought. "Then you must join me immediately. We shall find someplace to sip brandy in this town, if such an establishment exists, and we shall exchange unpleasant opinions about this so-called play. Please, you *must*—any friend of Hella's is a friend of mine."

Pippa could think of worse things to do. In fact, under her present circumstances, she could hardly think of better. "Okay," she said. "I guess."

"Oh, wonderful. Now, dear, let me ask you one teensy favor. Would you—" the tall man looked paler "—would you mind terribly, helping me down this awful stair? Just hold my hand. I'm so petrified of heights."

Pippa stepped forward, trying to figure this. The guy and his whole shtick. "What were you doing on the balcony, then?" she asked him, holding out a forearm for him to adhere to.

The man said (as though this should have been perfectly obvious), "Why, because I love to look *down* on things!"

Pippa did not laugh. At the bottom of the stairway she tightened the parka around her neck and glanced over at her strange companion. "Aren't you wearing a coat?"

"They didn't tell me," he said, "it was going to be *cold* out here."

That's ridiculous, Pippa thought. "How does the Sea Puppy Pub sound?"

"Indigenous. Is it close?"

"Everything's close." She paused by the door. "By the way, my name's Pippa."

"Oh, *is* it?" said the man, as though this were truly interesting. He made a comical bow—much more exaggerated than anything onstage—and when he came back up, a stiff lilac-colored business card had appeared in one of his hands.

"And *I*, my lady," he said (the card bore him out on this), "am Glyph And/or. *At* your service."

*   *   *

"So exactly what," Pippa asked him, "is Witches Against Negativity and Discrimination? I mean, is it *you*, or are there other people involved?"

Glyph And/or stared at the low beams that traversed the ceiling. He was not ignoring Pippa, exactly. He was off on a tangent.

"What really gets me," he said, "is this automatic equation of Magic with Evil. I mean, check the scene. The Prince shows up and here's this Princess, right? Lying fast asleep. He doesn't even know she's a Princess. How could he? All he knows is exactly one fact: she is beautiful. Well, and two: she's in some kind of unusually deep sleep. And from this he deduces A, she's under a horrid spell, B, through no fault of her own, and C, the perpetrator is a woman. Specifically, D, a Witch. And so he vows to seek vengeance, and we in the audience are expected to cheer him on. Am I right?"

Pippa didn't know. She held the lilac business card like a wine list, flipping it over and over, consulting it, though it continued to say (and not say) the same things. W.A.N.D., she read again. Very clever. What does it *mean*, though? Who is this person, and what is he doing here?

"And here's another thing," said Glyph.

"Is your name really Glyph?" Pippa asked him.

He stared down his high-ridged nose at her. "Is your name really Pippa?"

She slumped against the dark oiled wood of the booth, wishing more warmth from the cheerful fire across the pub radiated this far.

"Oh, I'm sorry," said Glyph, leaning forward. His eyes, deeply made-up, had the eerie quality of lunging out of the shadows at you. "That kind of thing, that foolish little play, just sets me off. I know it's a weakness."

Pippa shrugged. "It's a hobby, I guess. To tell you the truth, I was having a little trouble with the Princess."

"Yes?" A plucked and accentuated eyebrow rose. "How so?"

"Well, I mean—what *about* the Princess? She sort of gets lost sight of, doesn't she. The Prince takes one look at her, and he sees she's this perfect-looking zonked-out blonde, so he makes up his mind to like, fuck her. Then next thing he's off on some big macho thing against the evil witch."

"Yes!" Glyph rolled his eyes. He looked immensely gratified.

"I mean, it's like the Princess doesn't have any role to play except to lie there and be fought over. *She* doesn't have decisions to make, or responsibilities to deal with. And this struggle she's in with the Bad Fairy has to be fought by some charming hero instead of her. You know what I mean?"

"I *do*," Glyph assured her, reaching across to take her hand. His fingers were long and his wrists unusually narrow, a trait given emphasis by the ruffles at the end of his sleeves. "Anyway, who's to say the Witch isn't perfectly within her rights? For all the Prince knows, Talia might be a lumber heiress who wants to clear-cut the Enchanted Wood. The Witch is fighting to protect her home and her way of life."

"Actually she's a Bad Fairy," said Pippa. "And I think it comes out later in the story that Talia has broken some kind of magical prohibition."

Glyph made no effort to mask his disdain. "Magical prohibitions are stand-ins for the unexamined taboo structure of the dominant class. Her only crime was choosing *not* to behave in the way that was expected of her."

Pippa wasn't sure, but it seemed to her this Glyph was

able to switch sides pretty fluidly. But maybe that went with the territory—wherever the territory was.

Their waiter checked on them. He was somebody Pippa didn't know, a kid with scraggly facial hair. Glyph studied him with a detached, apparently purely theoretical interest. Pippa declined a second glass of white wine, but Glyph commanded:

"Bring us *both* a brandy. In the largest *possible* snifters."

"Yes, sir," said the waiter, a little worriedly.

Pippa wondered if she should mind that *she* never got called ma'am, while somebody like Glyph And/or—surely the weirdest-looking customer the Sea Puppy had seen this month—rated a sir.

"Where did you come from?" she asked him.

"Califia," he said.

"How'd you get *here*?"

"Oh, my dear—" (rolling his eyes) "—don't even make me *think* of it. I will say this: the *best* part of the trip was the final three hours en route to this *charming* little nest of hysteria from a City that Dare Not Speak Its Name, and *that* was on a Trailways *bus*. Which I am happy to report, came equipped with video monitors and was showing a Jodie Foster movie."

"Ah. Which one?"

Glyph shrugged. "I kept the earphones off. But I felt *comforted*, knowing that the bus line had attained the level of *civility* Jodie Foster implies."

Pippa smiled. "I guess W.A.N.D. doesn't have a big travel budget, huh?"

"Honey, W.A.N.D. doesn't have enough money to rent a broom. Everything is done strictly on a volunteer basis." He paused while their brandies were delivered, complete with wiry candleholder contraptions to warm them on. "I regret to say, I'm doing this all on my own."

"Your own money?"

He nodded, a little cautious now. The money thing, Pippa thought. Guaranteed to produce instant awkwardness. This, plus the bus ride, gave Glyph And/or a boost up her credibility scale.

She asked him, "So do you, um, have a place to stay?"

"Is that an offer?" Quickly, then, he brushed his hand back and forth; *only joking*.

"As a matter of fact—" Pippa figured this moment was as opportune as any to give him the rundown.

But Glyph became distracted, digging about in his waistcoat pockets. "I've got the name of this contact person, somewhere. Judith something."

"Loom?" said Pippa. "Judith *Loom*?"

"Exactly." Glyph called off the search. "You must know her. The Wiccan world is a small place."

"This village is even smaller than that."

"So I gather," said Glyph. He dipped his head, approaching the brandy with due deference. Then he lifted his eyes, which now seemed large and full of fluid, mooning at Pippa compassionately. "I'm so sorry, dear, about your poor daughter. Really I am. Of course I can't directly relate, having no kids of my own. But enough disclaiming. Of *course* it's dreadful, anybody can see that. Look at you: there's tragedy plastered over your face."

Pippa sucked in rather too much brandy and fought off a coughing fit. She nodded, her eyes watering—not crying, just watering. Glyph looked at her in a way that made her wonder if he suspected her of faking it. In fact she sometimes suspected herself of that, the past day or two. The Horrible Thing had become part of her life so that she no longer even thought about it all the time—the way you don't spend every minute reflecting that, for example, the ceiling of your bedroom is too low and it makes you feel claustrophobic. Not that you ever stop *feeling* claustrophobic. You just stop thinking about it, and after a while you lose your concept of a ground state, an ideal place where the feeling does not exist. It was something like that with Winterbelle. Yearning for her, anguishing over her, had become a more familiar condition than having her, which was almost forgotten.

"Excuse me," said Pippa. "Were you saying something?"

Glyph shook his head, sympathetically. "Now then," he said. "About your friend Judith. I've been trying to reach her for *days*. I wonder if there's some technical difficulty with her voice mail."

"It's just an answering machine," said Pippa. "$29.95 at Reny's."

"Whatever," said Glyph. "The upshot is, I haven't the foggiest idea where I'm going to hang my hat. And in my case, that's a big problem."

Comic relief: his floppy jongleur's cap was bangled, vividly colored and of great proportion. Pippa smiled at him.

He smiled back. They looked at one another, comfortably enough. It seemed as though the two of them had been talking a lot while listening only for certain things—personal key words—so that only now were they pausing to consider the implications of bumping into one another like this, on a cold and lonely and unprecedented night.

"Yeah," said Pippa, picking up where they left off, "well, Judith's got a kind of high-complexity lifestyle."

Glyph's eyes, pivoting upward, made it unnecessary for him to respond, *So who doesn't?*

"She kind of comes and goes," Pippa said. "I mean she does have this house-sitting gig, for the winter, but . . . "

"That's nice," said Glyph. "I wish I had a house. And a yard and a dog."

"Wishes come true," said Pippa.

He sighed. "In *family* tales. Out here in reality you need all the magic you can summon just to keep wolves from the door." He finished his brandy and set the snifter down. "Which is where I came in, approximately. Your friend Judith faxed me an article from your local newspaper, and I took the next coach out of Dodge."

"Thanks," said Pippa. "I didn't even know Judith had figured out it was me."

"She hasn't," said Glyph. "I called her on the phone and asked her to describe the local Wiccan community, and as soon as she got to you I thought *Bang*. That's the one. The poor hapless thing."

"Is that how Judith described me?" Pippa knocked back her own brandy, which sank luxuriously through her vitals.

Glyph shrugged. "Oh, I don't recall *what* she said, exactly. Anyway, here I am." He spread his arms. Two couples at a nearby table goggled at him: a double date of credit-card clones. Glyph, following Pippa's eyes to them, waved familiarly. "See you at the séance," he called.

"Shh," said Pippa. "You're terrible."

"You don't know. Listen." (Leaning low.) "Your friend Judith has, you said, this house-sitting job. Does she leave a key around? Do you suppose we might just   "

"Just crash there?" Pippa wondered why she had not thought of this. "She leaves the door unlocked. Everybody does. Beats me why, it's not like we trust each other."

Glyph counted out bills and laid them on the table—an awful lot, it seemed to Pippa.

"*Always* overtip," he said, without looking up. "It's the single most effective form of good karma." He grabbed his cape and whipped it around him. The credit-card dweebs stared elsewhere, probably afraid he might shout good-bye to them. "Do they have a cab in this town?"

"One, in winter," said Pippa. "If he's not in jail for unpaid speeding tickets."

As she arose, the entire spiritous content of the brandy snifter raced to her brain at once. Her visual field filled with colored blobs, and she tottered badly enough that Glyph slid a broad, surprisingly firm hand under one armpit, providing uplift and guiding her toward the door.

Just at the tighten-the-scarf stage, cold air swirling around their ankles while they paused in the foyer, the door banged open and a giddy party of about twelve jaunted in. They paused to regroup, and Pippa recognized Brenda Cigogne among them, then Kaspian Aaby. It was the cast of *Sleeping Talia*, fresh off the stage, crowding in for what evidently was going to be an impromptu cast party. Their mood was elevated. Their cheeks, through traces of greasepaint, blushed rosily after a vigorous walk from the Opera House. Full of themselves, blinking in the atmospheric gloom of the Sea Puppy, none of them at first took note of Glyph or of Pippa.

Then, shoving his way from behind them, came Mark Portion, newspaper baron, dressed in his usual manner of the upmarket slouch. From his neck hung a camera that might have been pinched from Jimmy Olsen. His eyes shot straight toward Glyph, once-overed him, and then settled meaningfully upon Pippa.

She felt drunk and stupid. She felt embarrassed about Glyph, not for his own sake, but because her standing here beside him—with his arm tucked under her own, being eased out of a public drinking establishment—was a situation not only likely to be misconstrued, but almost impossible to construe correctly.

Brenda Cigogne noticed her next. Then Kaspian. Then everybody else, people she kind of knew and people she didn't. They all stared at her, and at Glyph, and at each other. Nobody said anything, but their silence was of the awful type that sometimes greets your arrival in a crowded room, making you think that everyone has been talking about *you*.

In the midst of all this, from the center of Mark Portion's chest, a camera flashed.

"Dear *Hecate*," Glyph exclaimed, lifting an arm to shield his eyes. "Are *you* trying to wreck me for *weeks*?"

Mark Portion snapped another exposure. For insurance.

"*Come*, Pippa," Glyph said, grandly escorting her through the scandal of thespians, who parted magically before him. In a center-stage whisper he said, "You'd think some *people* had never seen *people* before. Ah, life in the provinces!"

Pippa avoided Kaspian's gaze in the most schoolgirlish way: by glancing in his direction to determine whether he was looking or not. He was. His chocolate-mint eyes were wide and thoughtful. They seemed to be asking her something, probing for some bit of information he wanted or needed to know.

Glyph gave her no time for any of that. He pushed her gently ahead and the two of them stepped out into a moonlit December night, frozen so still it might have been cast out of composite stone in shades of gray, brown and ivory. The street was empty. The air felt like so much dead weight. Glyph pulled his cape tight and gave a shudder. "Mercy," he said. "We got out of there—"

"In the nick of time?" Pippa guessed.

"—without calling that taxi." But the way he smiled suggested he really didn't care. "Already I deduce," he said, sounding pleased with himself, "key facts about the nature of your problem."

"That's great," she said.

"And together—" tucking his arm into hers; setting off

down the sidewalk like a gender-inverted Dorothy leading
her Scarecrow "—we can turn it *right* around."

"That's really great," she said.

But what she really thought was: Just what I need. Another weird relationship.

Judith Loom sat naked in the yogic position known as
padmasana, the Lotus. She was centered, amid four stubby
candles, in an otherwise empty living room, her skin the
color of a peach where the sun has *not* brought out a pink
blush. The air was thick with Japanese sandalwood incense,
so delicious when you catch just a breath of it outdoors
during a ritual, so dense and suffocating now. There was
no music; just a resonantly click-clucking Seth Thomas
clock that lay face-forward, like Cogsworth sleeping one
off, in the dining room where all the furniture had been
dragged. Judith registered their arrival (accompanied by an
arctic draft while Pippa battered the door shut) with an
irritated twitching of the nose, but kept her eyes shut. Her
feet were exceedingly delicate. Her middle bulged not
quite to the point of sagging, in a way that had been
fashionable back in sometime like the 40's. Do men's sexual
fancies really change from one decade to the next? What
causes this to happen—the women? Or the times?—certain
decades being more conducive to, say, oral sex than
others.

Another mystery.

"How lovely," said Glyph, taking in such sights as there
were. "Look how straight her back is! And without even a
zazen pillow."

His attitude—that Judith might as well not be conscious—brought her around. That and his voice. She
flickered her eyes for a minute or so, then opened them
to consider the Creature from the Left Coast.

"Hey, Judith," said Pippa. "Sorry to break in on you. We tried calling."

Judith disregarded her. She and Glyph were busy checking each other out. She did not appear to feel the slightest degree of self-consciousness about not wearing Item 1 of clothing—which is what hitting the Pagan festival circuit will do for you, Pippa supposed.

"*I* remember," Judith finally said. She might have been reentering a conversation she had just blinked out on. "Starwood, right? In the mud? The Sending Hither of Deer Flies?"

Glyph strode more committally into the room. He whipped off his jongleur's cap and bowed low. Or tried to: stiff from the cold, he didn't make it past the horizontal, and came up wincing.

"I'll never see 23 again," he moaned.

"Why not?" Judith straightened her legs with toes pointed ballerina-style, left then right, preparing to stand. "I see it on the street all the time. In fact, I try to bring it home with me now and then."

"A girl after my own heart," Glyph said, his voice soulful. "Wait for me, darling, and we can be skyclad together." He cocked his head sideways, Groucho Marx–style, wiggling a neatly plucked brow. "Unfortunately she'll have to wait till July, when it's warm enough for me to *expose* myself again."

Judith trilled with silly laughter. Glyph helped her to her feet. Stepping back, she executed a curtsy that (from where Pippa stood) mostly consisted of a lowering and spreading out of the hind parts. Gross.

"Charmed, monsieur," she cooed.

Glyph kissed her open palm. "My darling," he said, "you have the body of a Goddess."

Pippa felt excluded and slightly bored, as though she

were missing out on a whole chain of inside jokes that weren't all that funny anyhow. She squeezed through the dining room, discovering in the kitchen Judith's familiar Ashera. The ferret raised her tiny hackles and faced Pippa in assorted defiant poses, prepared to do battle over the remains of what appeared to be day-old pizza, already long stripped of anything of interest. An odor of garlic and ferret urine hung about the room.

"Judith?" said Pippa, coming back out. "What exactly are you, um, doing?"

Back in the living room, Judith had gotten into a long-sleeved leotard with no panties underneath, and Glyph had slipped out of his cape. The heat was on full throttle: an advantage of caring for someone else's house, letting their bills pile up at the fuel-oil dealer.

"Purging," she said. "I'm observing a period of silence and meditation. At least I *was*. I was fasting for a while, too, but it didn't seem healthy. Did you know that lamas in Tibet can raise their body temperature enough to melt snow?"

Glyph shivered. Pippa had heard this too many times to think about. "Have you guys introduced yourselves?"

Judith shrugged. "No need."

And Glyph pointed a long finger back at her. "We met last summer at Starwood. Lady . . . Greenchance?"

"Shh," she pretended to scold him, "that's a *ritual* name."

One of about 30, thought Pippa. Judith looked delighted. Glyph was playing her like a hand of cards.

Pippa knew you were supposed to consider yourself lucky about certain things—that you hadn't lived during the Burning Times, et cetera—but she did not. Historical facts had never swung much weight for her, compared to, say, having or not having a gallon and a quarter of milk (whole, skim, low-fat, butter-, or sweet acidophilus), depending on whether the month's WIC vouchers were in the mail. And now even milk meant nothing. Losing her home meant nothing. Page after page of her mental dictionary was blank, until you came all the way to *W*. And then there was no definition, only a picture.

The picture of Winterbelle that Pippa carried in her mind was like this:

The hair first. The hair is in motion and swinging all around, some of it getting in your face so that you can almost *smell* it. (But not quite.) The skin that is not as soft as it looks, but baby-smooth and without a blemish. Except maybe little gravel scars from her Elf of Pickup City phase, and now maybe a burn mark from the stupid candle.

Her eyes. Looming, filling the screen in your head. So crystalline, blue with more gray than Pippa had hoped for and a little yellow, so that they could seem weirdly impersonal, remote, ageless: just a look, Pippa hoped; but you never could tell where eyes like that had been. What they had seen.

The nose, sloping, pixieish. Poor lips prone to chapping. Cherry-red when the girl had a fever. Fairy down on the sides of her neck, so warm. So warm and full of that healthy green smell of childhood.

The shoulders, shivering, squeezed in. Fearful.

The little chest, pinkish-white, tiny nipples the same color. Belly button: innie. Hips as narrow as a little boy's, but thighs so muscled and strong they surprised you, when for instance you watched the girl try to get down from someplace dangerous she shouldn't have climbed to—one leg stretching down, seeking the next firm landing, the long sinews stretched out and those fearless, purposeful feet swinging one way and another, usually shoeless, usually dirty, toenails always chipped.

Pippa glanced back across the living room where Glyph

and Judith were mugging for one another—or as it seemed, for an invisible audience *out there*, phantom eyes in the darkness. Striking poses, talking their knowing talk. Neither coming anywhere close to the question of why Glyph was in town or how he and Pippa had come to drop by, together, in the middle of the night.

Pippa slid out of her backpack. She wandered down the hallway. Judith's winter house-tending berth was in an outstandingly bland raised ranch. It was not even 50's kitschy chic. More like 70's paneled blah. The owners were a couple of aging locals who now spent from mid-November through the end of April in an equally boring house nowhere special in Florida.

But to Pippa, tonight—making probably her fourth visit—the place was different. The doors running down the hallway seemed to close upon chambers full of secrets. Halfway down, between the closet and the bathroom, she stopped to look at a little shelf, finely bracketed hardwood, that held a collection of decorative shot glasses. There were shot glasses made for special occasions (Bernard Eugley's retirement—"50 YEARS of SERVICE AND LOYALTY"—as village fire chief) and shot-glass souvenirs from destinations Pippa had never heard of, such as Lagarstad, Bavaria. To Pippa neither the glasses nor the shelf was of interest here but rather a glimpse they gave you into somebody's life. The quirky and meaningless things you do. Why collect shot glasses? And yet now here they were, and each of them, presumably, recalled some episode in an earthly existence that would presently draw to a close. (At any rate that's what wintering in Florida most often means.) It struck Pippa as so sad, so futile: no one would ever really grok this modest collection of shot glasses, what they meant in their totality to the old guy who collected them. And some year soon now they would all be taken down and boxed up and whatever meanings or memories they had encoded would be lost. Forever lost. Dissolved by the corrosive seepage of Time.

Pippa felt like crying. Of course, she almost constantly felt at the point of crying now; but *real* crying—its spontaneity, the letting loose, the breaking down—happened almost never. Something that was needed for it had gone. Yet now as she stood looking at the shot glasses Pippa felt tears streaming freely, and she thought how stupid it was, when for all she knew the old guy himself never gave the goddamned glasses a moment's notice.

Well, it was insane. Everything was totally insane. And Pippa was drunk, or something like drunk, not to mention homeless and childless and unemployed. Judith and Glyph were laughing as they arranged a short-pile burgundy carpet diagonally, which couldn't be right, on the living room floor. Arthur Torvid was probably sitting at his computer, fighting his flame war. Brenda Cigogne was giddy-headed. Kaspian had beautiful eyes. Winterbelle was shaking with fright. Pippa wandered into an unused bedroom that must have belonged to a grown child of the couple who owned the house. A boy, she surmised. She wondered what his name was, where he had gone to. Where do any of them go? Where had Winterbelle gone? Specifically: were they keeping her here in town or at some safer remove from her mother? Was she sleeping? Or had her bad dreams come back, the ones that made her afraid to close her eyes, to entrust her mind to the dark?

Pippa's eyes felt cleaned out by tears; her body felt like it weighed a thousand pounds. She trusted nothing. She feared everything, even the two people laughing at the other end of the house. Nonetheless she fell asleep as quickly as her eyes fluttered closed, and as deeply as the cherished infant everybody once upon a time has been.

*   *   *

She was the last one to wake. Sunlight glanced through the blinds of the grown son's bedroom but showed no hankering to enter. Blue LED's glowed 10:19. Many years worth of *Natural Geographic* rose in twin towers, blocking access to a closet. At the other end of the ranch, a radio was on.

Pippa rose like a patient experiencing major side effects from her medication. She bumped out to the hall and into the bathroom but avoided looking at herself in the mirror. In the shower she stood for a long time, slowly pivoting. The water could not get hot enough. Finally she put back on the same clothes she had been wearing but left her hair unstraightened, hanging every which way while it dried. The bangs partly buried her eyes.

In the kitchen, breakfast was ready. Judith handed her a plate of eggs and pecan swirls (the kind you unwind in strips and nibble your way to the center). Glyph sat at a red linoleum-topped table by the kitchen door, listening to the Ten-O'clock Block on WURS, a slot reserved for talk-oriented features, aired at a time of day when people who might object to them are busy doing something else. Earning a living, for example. And only the hard-core non-mainstreamable are hanging out nibbling pecan twirls at what, 10:46 a.m. While the sun poured happily through white ruffled curtains in somebody else's home.

"Thanks," said Pippa.

"My poor *sister*," said Judith. And she hurled herself into an upper-body embrace with Pippa, awkward in that it caused the breakfast plate to tilt. "I had no *idea*. Why didn't you call me, you poor darling? That's what we Witches are here for, isn't it? To help our sisters in times of need."

Glyph strained to catch the reply of a homeopath with a strong German accent who had been asked by an interviewer whether, in the doctor's view, conventional medicine tended to treat the sick human being like a machine whose parts needed some form of crude, mechanical adjustment.

Pippa was not sure that witches, as an uncapitalized class, were for anything. It seemed to her they just *were*.

"Thanks, Jude," she said, striving for greater conviction. She sat down in the sunshine. Judith watched while she took a bite of egg. Pippa once again had that strange delusion that she was faking it, or at least coming across that way. Like it was a performance: enter the Bereaved Mom, who will touch our hearts with her unsparing depiction of grief and loss. She just didn't feel up to it.

"Vell of *course*," the radio homeopath was saying, "it is important to consider the *bull* patient, not just these *imtoms*, in choosing the proper remedy."

"What about the whole society?" Glyph demanded of the plastic AM-FM receiver. "The context in which disease is permitted to manifest?"

Judith pulled up a chair. In addition to the sunshine, every single light fixture in the kitchen was on. The dishwasher churned. A chicken defrosted in the microwave. The exhaust fan pointlessly sucked air out of the house. Pippa wondered why the vacuum cleaner wasn't chugging away all by itself, out in the living room.

"I hate this time of year," said Judith.

"Why?" said Pippa.

"Who doesn't," sighed Glyph.

Judith studied the spirals of steam above her coffee mug, showing an Allison Bechtel cartoon. "It just kills me to see the Xians so smug and satisfied."

Pippa didn't think it cost you anything to see other people happy, but she was tired, so tired, like the prematurely senile northern gods who had lost their magic apples and just didn't feel like talking anymore. The pecan swirl was doughy, textureless.

"They have every reason to feel smug," said Glyph. "Another year, another million kids psychosexually screwed up."

Judith sipped her coffee and barely looked at him. It was amazing: like they had been roommates for years, just friends of course, and could hold a conversation on autopilot.

"Catholic school?" Judith said, not without sympathy.

"Fourteen years," said Glyph.

Judith shook her head. "And a lifetime in recovery."

"Oh! Recovery. Don't talk to me about recovery."

"Really?"

Judith scrutinized him. Really *what?* wondered Pippa. She felt like a stranger—a traveler they had taken in.

Glyph clucked. "I *just* about swallowed my gum," he said. "There I was in one of my groups and believe *me,* I have never left a *moment's* doubt as to where I was navigating from. And in front of the Goddess and Petula Clark, this *gentleman* who claimed to represent, cough cough, the Tantric community of Marin County, so much as pointed the finger at me and said, *This* is the person who I remember forcing me to learn the wiener-butt dance. Quote unquote. I do not shit you."

Judith laughed. Not *at* him, as the saying goes.

"What's the Xian connection?" asked Pippa.

"Infiltrators!" said Glyph, with drama. "Shills at every meeting. Satan this and perversion that. And all manner of Chiller Monster Horror Feature material. People claiming to have been forced to drink baby's blood. A cauldron bubbling with aborted fetuses. Mothers watching while the Devil-in-Chief fucks their daughters. Or their sons! And people *believed* it, because they heard it everywhere. Every meeting you went to. Didn't matter what you were recovering *from*. Somebody there would be a ritual abuse survivor. And you know, they're exactly like U.F.O. people except that on the whole, their stories make less logical sense."

Judith frowned. "I've never heard any of that stuff around here."

"Don't worry," said Glyph. "It'll play here eventually."

"Now, hold on," said Pippa. "You're saying, there's some kind of fundamentalist conspiracy to spread rumors of what, Satanism and child abuse, by sending people around to 12-step meetings?"

"*Conspiracy* sounds too paranoid," said Glyph.

Which was kind of Pippa's point.

"Those people don't need to conspire," said Judith. "They've all got exactly the same brain. When one of them has an idea—which isn't too often—then they all have it. And they never change it. That's why they can't tolerate dissent. They stamped out the Gnostic movement, and the Pelagian heresy, and women priests, and ecstatic visionaries, and then they went on to burn nine million Witches in the Inquisition."

The doughy mass in Pippa's mouth did not want to go down. "Nine *million?*" she said, around it. "Where'd you get that from?"

"It's a Fact," said Glyph. He switched the radio off. "And you know, when they couldn't convict Joan of Arc on charges of Witchcraft, they executed her for dressing like a man."

"Go on," said Pippa.

Glyph nodded. Solemnly. "And what's so outrageous is, Jesus Himself was gay."

"What?"

"Everybody knows that," said Judith. "Never married,

surrounded himself with men, had this weird thing about his mother. Anyway, all great shamans are gay. It's the berdache tradition—the evolutionary function of homosexuality."

Glyph said, "And *look* at Mark 14:51. Christ's last night of freedom, and he spent it in a garden with a naked boy. *That's* why he posted the guards outside. Personally I think Judas betrayed him out of jealousy. Hel hath no fury . . . "

"Wait," said Pippa. "Jesus was a shaman? A *gay* shaman?"

"Well, a magician," said Judith. "Everything he did and taught—"

"*Including* the ritual cannibalism," said Glyph.

"—came right out of the Egyptian magical papyri. The Gospels are practically a handbook of Hermetic sorcery."

"Yeah?" Pippa sipped her coffee, thoughtful. She wished she had had time to get a little more reading in. "I still can't believe the nine million."

"They weren't just burned, either," said Glyph. "They were hacked and stoned and bludgeoned, mostly by their own neighbors, once the Church had gotten everyone all worked up."

This Pippa could picture. "Yeah, but still," she said, "it's wrong to blame *all* Christians for that. They just believe what they're taught. Don't they?"

"They do that," said Glyph, as though she had been agreeing with him.

"What's wrong with the whole Xian ethos," said Judith, "is the idea of Mankind at the pinnacle of creation. Formed in the image of their male God. Commanded to rape and despoil the body of the Mother."

"They don't *all* think that," said Pippa.

"It's in their Book," said Judith.

"But it goes deeper than that," said Glyph. "It's woven into the whole structure of left-brain, exploitative, male-dominated Western culture. You could throw away the Book and you'd still have the identical set of assumptions. Take scientists. The only way they know to understand Nature is to dissect it or bombard it with electrons or reduce it to equations in a computer. *That's* what we're up against."

"We?" said Pippa.

"Children of Gaia," said Judith.

"Practitioners of Earth-centered spirituality," said Glyph.

Judith said, "Witches."

Glyph said, "People who are not afraid of living in their own flesh."

Pippa said, "Oh."

She didn't feel hungry. She was eating because it seemed like the right thing to do. She wondered exactly what she was doing here, in Judith's borrowed kitchen. Living? Waiting? Or just crashing for the night?

Glyph folded his large hands on the linoleum table and cleared his throat. "Now that we've gotten all *that* cleared up—" (provoking a giggle out of Judith) "—what say we put our heads together and come up with a plan?"

"To get Winterbelle back?" said Pippa. Striving for even the wannest feeling of hope.

"Oh, *much* more than that," said Glyph. "A plan to set this pretty little village on its ear."

Judith made a humphing noise. "Why not whack it on the head with a baseball bat?"

"Too phallic," said Glyph.

"Well . . . a frying pan, then."

The two of them laughed. Living in the moment, Pippa thought. While she was dying

a little bit more
with every breath.

"**E**verything will be fine," Judith assured her. "Tonight we'll do a little ceremony of purification to clear the obstacles from your path. I'd give you a lift, but I'm already 15 minutes late for a *fêng shui* consultation."

"You're getting a *fêng shui* consultation?" said Pippa. "For what?"

Judith was in her Dress-for-Excess mode today, as though she were applying for jobs in three separate decades. "Not getting," she said. "Giving. A friend of mine is opening up a jewelry shop in the Old Tannery and she senses some strange energies coming out of the building somewhere."

"Yeah," said Pippa. "One of them is probably my lawyer."

Judith frowned, probably assuming that she must have heard wrong. "Merry part, y'all," she called over her shoulder.

"And merry meet again!" Glyph responded from the back of the ranch house. He emerged wearing a terry cloth robe, black hair wet and long, in time to see Judith's ancient, rusted-out Volvo slipping down the driveway, which was still piled with snow. He conspicuously shivered. "How do you people *stand* these winters?"

"That's kind of a mystery," Pippa said. "You never think it's going to be so bad until you're in the middle of it. Then you tell yourself, Don't worry, we made it through the last one. Then about the middle of March you feel like you're going to die. And sometimes you do."

"You do?" Glyph stared at her, worriedly.

"Check the obituaries," she told him. "All the really old people pick March to die in. You go into the Stop 'N' Go on Thursday when the *Herald* comes out, and they'll be standing around there saying like, Look here—old Doris didn't make it over March Hill "

Glyph patted his hair without conviction and retreated to the bathroom.

Pippa felt a need to get out. She slipped on her parka and stepped on to the front doorstep and stood there a little while, getting her bearings.

By daylight, the neighborhood where Judith had found this year's house-sitting gig was unbelievably average. It looked like where the endangered middle class had come to go extinct. The houses were pretty much alike though not identical, and there were trees but not really tall ones, and everything looked safe. Safe in the sense of, you could bring your parents here and tell them, See Mom & Dad, I'm mortgaged out the gonads for this split-level, and they'd approve and give you a lawn mower for your birthday. Pippa got no feeling, standing here, of being stared at. The windows in these houses were not designed to be stared out of. Most had curtains drawn, and the rest opened into functionless living rooms that nobody had actually sat down in since Christmas—4 days ago, can you believe it?—for the ceremonial opening of presents. Pippa felt pleasantly anonymous. She dropped a pair of very dark sunglasses (borrowed from her unknown hosts, currently in Florida) into place.

She had not gotten halfway up the block when she practically slammed into Carol Deacon Aaby.

Anyway, her car. It was a Chevrolet station wagon that looked something like a hearse, only instead of black it was yellow. A weird yellow, sulfur-metallic. Carol Aaby was twisting her head this way and that, backing down an immaculately shoveled driveway, and somehow incredibly (though it figured) for all her craning around she failed to notice Pippa until she had almost flattened her. Pippa backed up, shaking her head—amused more than startled, as though even Death now were something she felt detached from—until she recognized the driver. Then she sort of slunk down inside her parka and pressed the dark glasses more firmly onto her nose.

As to Mrs. Aaby, you could not have said whether she knew who Pippa was or not. Probably they didn't get many pedestrians around here, and Pippa's presence must have seemed like some kind of mistake. She made *I'm sorry* shapes with her mouth. Then she just looked. Finally she backed the rest of the way onto the street.

Pippa was left standing on the sidewalk in front of the Aaby house. What she thought was not *So this is where she lives,* but rather, *How can Kaspian have come from a place like this?* It did not make sense: The boy so elfin and smart and enigmatic. The house so plain. White vinyl siding and green aluminum shutters. Decorative mailbox with the family name embossed.

There was no figuring. Still waters run stagnant, but occasionally something interesting bubbles up. Pippa set off down the street once more, thinking very clearly how Judith would pronounce in her dramatic big-eyed way, *There is no such thing as coincidence.* A maxim of hers, which like all the others struck Pippa as essentially useless. No coincidences: so what? So every single thing that happens is some kind of omen, she supposed.

Just then, a sound came from behind her that raised a tremble from the bottom of her spine.

It was a sort of howl, like a dog in pain. Only not quite a dog, and not quite pain. Something different and much cooler. And louder, because it seemed to have come from a long way off.

Pippa peered around, wondering. To her surprise there was a clear view of Wabenaki Mountain from this quiet, ultraordinary street. All you had to do was lift your head above the rooftops and there it was. She couldn't believe she hadn't noticed it before: the northwestern slope, rising steeply all the way up to Maiden Fell. It was rough and irregular, white and gray and brown, so massive and all-important that it reduced the neighborhood to negligibility—debris that had fallen over the years at its mighty feet.

Yet the neighborhood managed to ignore it. The direction the street ran, the angle at which the houses were set, the cookie-cutter landscaping—all of it colluded to deny the mountain's existence, or at least to keep you from turning your eyes that way. What's so great about an old mountain? the perfectly linear avenue made you think. You can still enjoy the convenience of one-story living!

The howl came again. If anything, louder. A thin, hollowed-out, keening sound that rose abruptly, like a siren, and faded all the way to nothing over a duration of 5 or 6 seconds. A long time, considering.

No, it is *not* a wolf, Pippa thought (though she desperately hoped, and almost managed to believe, otherwise).

Omens, as everyone knows, come in threes. She stood there for the longest time, just past the Aaby house, on a boring street whose name she hadn't noticed. *Waiting for the wolf to howl for a third time*—it was too hokey to admit. She must be desperate for portents. Good or bad, it almost didn't matter now. The next logical step would be the astrology column in the *Herald*, which came out tomorrow. These are the depths, she thought, to which I've been driven.

The howl did not come again. Make of that what you will.

At the gloomy end of Ash Street, two police cars stood before Aunt Eulace's house.

One of them was parked normally, while the other had been yanked over to the curb and left there at a ridiculous angle, in a coplike display of indifference. We've got more urgent business than parallel parking, ma'am—that was the message.

And the awful thing was, this time Pippa was buying it.

She did not turn away. She did not even try to make herself inconspicuous. She kind of had the idea that somehow these dark glasses made her look like somebody else. So she just went on walking until she stood across the street from what had been—until about 18 hours ago—her home.

Out of one or both of the cop cars, a dispatcher's voice sputtered loudly about a disabled vehicle southbound on the state highway. Why is it always *vehicle?* Pippa wondered. Never a car. Like it's always *alleged perpetrator* or some such thing. Never the asshole who did the crime.

Through the second-floor windows, she thought she could see movement in what was still, in her mind, Winterbelle's room. The dark glasses made it hard to be sure. After a while the movement stopped and Pippa became aware that there were other people out on the street besides herself. One of them was a lady a little younger than Eulace—say, early 70's—who, catching Pippa's eye, stepped over with a refreshingly flagrant case of curiosity.

"Whatever could have happened?" she wondered aloud. She did not recognize Pippa, and it was mutual. People here did not leave their houses all that much.

"Haven't you heard?" a man's voice said.

Pippa turned to find a gentleman somewhat younger still—old enough to join AARP but not to collect Social Security—coming up from the opposite direction. He had that recently-retired-and-restless look about him.

He said, "It's the child-torture case," his voice triumphantly cranky. "It's been all over the radio."

"It has?" said Pippa. All she could remember was a German homeopath.

"Oh my gracious," said the older lady. Her curiosity, stoked to a fervor now, caused her eyes to shine and a nice rosy glow to appear on her cheeks. Pippa guessed that a little excitement did stay-at-homes good.

The man came up beside them. Across the street, Eulace's front door opened and a policeman appeared, carrying a black plastic bag. If you didn't know better, you'd think he was taking out the garbage.

"My god!" said the woman. "Do you suppose they've got a body in there?"

The man scoffed. "No, no—they're gathering evidence. They've got to take it down and inventory and label everything."

"Evidence of what?" said Pippa.

The man did not hear her. Probably he had reached that stage where you lose the ability to perceive sound waves of a lower socioeconomic pitch.

"It was all over the news," he reiterated.

"I see," said the woman.

The policeman dumped the black evidence bag in the

trunk of Car #2, the one that was badly parked. He slammed the lid, cased the street, looked straight into Pippa's eyes (or at least her lenses), and disappeared back inside the house.

Like magic, she thought.

The man said, "They say it was Satanists."

"Really?" said the woman. She blushed further, as though the news was better than she'd dared hope. "Have they caught the, what do you call it—ringleader?"

"Devil-in-law," suggested Pippa.

The man gravely said: "Still at large. They've got a warrant out, and the Chief says they'll be looking at all the places she's known to frequent."

"She," repeated the woman, titillated.

"Some misguided kook, I guess," the man said. "Probably got caught up in drugs and lured into a cult of some kind. It happens more than people like to think."

"Does it?" said the woman. Her attention strayed, and Pippa followed her eyes across the street to where two policemen were struggling with what appeared to be a bulky piece of furniture. The woman said, "Why look— isn't that a Norwegian cupboard bed?"

Pippa whipped the glasses from her eyes. As sure as she stood there, the policemen heaved onto the front porch the very bed that Judith had jigsawed out of ¾-inch plywood and Pippa herself had painted in the folk style called *rosemaling*. To her, this was the ultimate act of desecration. Trash somebody's sacred circle: okay. Defame them in print: fine. But take away a little girl's *bed?*

"This has really gone too far," she declared.

"You're telling *me*," said the woman. She turned to Pippa with a look of passionate conviction that took 15 years off her face. "If they damage the paint job, it'll *never* be properly restored. Believe me, I can tell you that for a *fact*.

I've got a whole house full of old painted furniture, and you just can't *find* the craftspeople who know how to do that kind of thing anymore."

"It's not really that hard," Pippa murmured, because she was totally out of her mind and this woman was talking about something *real*. "You can make your own egg tempera with the kind of pigments that—"

But wait: there was Deputy Doug! He was holding up the rear end of Winterbelle's bed, and he was taking care not to scrape it against the porch railing. (Pippa would spare him.) She slipped her dark glasses back into place and turned away. Behind her, as she skedaddled up Ash Street, she could hear the man explaining how they come and recruit young kids right out of the schools nowadays.

"Wait," the woman called after Pippa, "young lady!"

She quickened her pace.

"You never know who's behind it," the man was saying. "It can be someone strange and freaky-looking, or it might be your own next-door neighbor."

Get out your bludgeons, Pippa thought.

"You are *where?*" shouted Arthur Torvid through the telephone.

Pippa had already told him quite clearly that she was four doors down from Carol Deacon Aaby. She was not going to repeat herself.

"Don't you realize," Torvid said, at undiminished volume, "the cops have been on me like a cheap suit since I got out of bed this morning, looking for *you?*"

"They haven't found me," said Pippa.

Torvid breathed heavily enough that you could hear it. "I'll tell you this, Pippa Rede," he said. "Your world is turning to shit in an awful big hurry, and if I were you, I wouldn't make things worse by hiding from the Law."

"I am not hiding." (Pippa wondered if this was true.)
"I'm not doing anything. I'm just sitting here watching,
let's see. It looks like *General Hospital*."

Glyph lifted his head from the TV. *"The Young and the
Restless."*

Pippa told her attorney, "No, it's *The Young and the*—"

"I DON'T CARE WHAT IT IS," said Arthur Torvid in
an Old Testament voice. "If I am discovered to have any
knowledge of your whereabouts, and I fail to report it,
then I face disbarment and possible jail time. Do you
understand?"

"Gosh, no," said Pippa. "Thanks for telling me how
rough you've got it."

"Pippa, *please*," said Torvid. He paused to breathe awhile.
"I am not unsympathetic. I'm your *attorney*, remember? But
it's my duty . . . I mean, fuck that. You've just got me
into a difficult situation here, okay? I mean, I'll cope with
it. But I want you to understand where things stand. Just
as an example, suppose the Feds are tapping my telephone?
It happens a lot more than people think."

"Lots of things seem to happen more than people think,"
said Pippa. Call it perverse, but her mind was being pulled
toward the television, where a twisted-looking love/hate
triangle was playing out between two guys with way-long
hair and a girl with a crew cut. "So, um, you want me to
understand how things stand? Well, how about this.
They've taken my daughter. They've taken my daughter's
bed. I've been fired. My aunt has thrown me onto the street.
I'm crashing with this witch friend who right now has
been called away to exorcise the dragon energies from
your building."

"Come again?"

"My lawyer is under the delusion that the Feds give a
shit about his phone calls. I've got this P.R. guy who

flew in from someplace he calls Califia, who is the one person I've ever met who is *guaranteed* to have something about him to offend *everyone*. Now I can't even go back to get my things because the police have got the house staked out. The man on the street thinks I'm a Satanist. There's a warrant for my arrest. Mark Portion took my picture half-drunk last night and I'm sure it's going to be all over the *Herald* in the morning. Am I leaving anything out?"

"Mark Portion what?" said Torvid. "Half-drunk? He's supposed to be in recovery. Wait'll *this* gets around."

Pippa didn't care enough to correct him. "And one other thing: I'm four doors down from a decent Christian mom who wants me stoned to death. Hey, did you know that Joan of Arc was a cross-dresser?"

"Of course she was," said Arthur Torvid, very carefully, as though convinced Pippa was losing it altogether. "Now Pippa Rede, try to calm down. Take a few deep breaths. Pop a little yellow pill. Do something to relax. Let's see if we can figure something out."

"Right." Pippa took the phone away from her ear, which needed a rest. It had had a long day so far of listening to very strange stuff, and hadn't even made it to *General Hospital*. Arthur Torvid's voice came out of the earpiece. "Hey, listen," she said, cutting him off. "You said you'd accept payment in kind, remember? Well, what kind of payment do you figure that's going to be? Huh? Maybe I call you up from jail and shout at you every now and then? Because so far that's about all you've done for me. If you can't help me, then—then—"

She couldn't think then what. So she hung up the phone.

Glyph sprawled across a goodly part of the sofa, watching her with big, calm, absorptive eyes. The better to remember her with.

"Would you mind turning that damned TV off?" she said. "I get enough of that at home."

His eyes opened a bit further. He made no move.

It was too much.

Really too much: all of it.

Pippa grabbed the arms of her mouse-colored sweater and yanked with all her strength until the wool began to part. The shoulder seams ripped first, then the hem around the neck. Pippa tugged and tugged, stretching the fabric until it tore, then adjusting her hold and tearing it again. She pulled the wreckage of the sweater over her head and seized it between her fingers and shredded it into pieces which she threw down at her feet. Finally there was nothing left larger than a Kleenex, and Pippa's fingers were raw, and she stood there in a bra that could have been whiter.

"I *hate* them!" she shrieked. "I fucking *hate* them! And I don't *give* a fuck if witches aren't supposed to hate. I'm a witch and I *hate them* so much, I—"

How she got on the floor she did not know. There she was, and she was crying now. Crying again. All she ever did, it seemed like.

"Oh, fuck," she wept. "I've lost everything."

Glyph was above her, reaching down with big hands, stroking her shoulder. She accepted the comfort of his touch.

"Sweetheart," he said to her, soothingly, like a parent to a child, "why don't you go lie down? There's nothing you can do right now—nothing for your little girl. Nothing for you. The best thing is to rest. You've got to take care of yourself—hear me? You've got to be strong. Or *get* strong. I'm here to help you. Okay?"

She decided to obey him. It was the easiest thing to

do. But after this, she thought, laying her head down on some grown-up kid's pillow, there would be no more easy things.

Only hard things
from now on.

Glyph and Pippa sat across the living room from one another, early next morning. Judith had not come home last night. The TV remained off and they were listening to the morning show on WURS, which featured uplifting spiritual readings by a guy whose purring, holisticker-than-thou voice raised Pippa's stress level, news of Native Peoples around the world, and the daily trivia challenge.

"Back in 1970," said the announcer, "the average C.E.O. earned 15 times as much as an average worker on the factory floor. What is the ratio today? Is it A, 30? B, 50? Or C, 70? The first correct caller wins a pair of tickets to tonight's performance of *Sleeping Talia.*"

"B," said Pippa, picking automatically the one in the middle. That way if you were wrong at least you didn't look stupid.

"C," said Glyph. "Trust me. I don't know from economics, but statistics like that are *always* worse than you think they could possibly be."

"That would be going some," said Pippa.

The announcer slipped on a ballad called "The Green Fields of France," concerning a visit to the grave of one Willie MacBride, age 19. A real pick-me-up.

"Where could Judith have gotten to?" she wondered aloud.

"Something must have come up," Glyph charitably supposed.

"Yeah—I bet I can tell you what, too," said Pippa. "Somebody's penis."

Glyph batted his eyes. "I can't believe I *heard* that."

Pippa couldn't either, actually. Something weird had happened inside her brain. A switch had gotten turned.

Glyph said, "Well, you know what the Goddess says. *All acts of love and pleasure . . .*"

"Are my rituals," said Pippa. "Right. Judith says that all the time."

"Just *saying* it isn't enough."

"Listen," said Pippa. "I can't stay here any longer. This isn't fair to Judith. Or to you, either. I mean, doesn't me being here sort of make you an accessory?"

"An accessory to what?" Glyph said, sounding bitter. "The worst injustice in the history of like, the *world?*"

"Not the worst, probably." She propped her head back on the wing chair and stared up at the swirly-textured plaster of the ceiling. "The worst would be, I don't know. Some innocent kid getting mowed down in a drive-by shooting."

Glyph thought about this. You could practically hear him. "How about, a whole *bunch* of kids that get mowed down by some A.W.H.M. with an assault rifle?"

Before she could ask he translated: "Angry white heterosexual male."

Pippa knew she could top that. "Okay: how about *all* the kids who have to *live* in this shitty country, where every lunatic who wants to can own a whole *arsenal* of assault rifles?"

"All the kids *everywhere*," said Glyph, rising to the challenge, "who are born into the world with no hope of a decent life. And nothing left to believe in. No Savior to come gather their little souls into his shopping cart."

"Ooo," said Pippa. "That's a big one."

They sat for a while. It was too depressing to go any further.

"Yeah, well," said Pippa finally, "the world does suck. But you have to believe in *something*. Don't you?"

"I don't know," said Glyph. He looked at her thoughtfully. "I can tell you what *I* believe in. But I can't say you have to believe in it, too. It gets to be sort of a mind game. And I get tired of mind games. I'd rather get up and *do* something."

"Like fly up here to rescue a damsel in distress."

"Not *fly*," he said, in make-believe self-pity.

I like this guy, Pippa realized. She didn't remember exactly when or how she had gotten to like him. But she did, now.

"Well, thanks," she said. "Thanks for coming. Thanks for wanting to help. But I guess it's a little too late for that. Anyway, I better get going."

"Where?" he asked her. Carefully. Not pressing. Just wanting to hear.

She shrugged. "Anywhere. Nowhere. I've got to just, you know—vanish. *Poof.*"

"That'll be quite a trick," said Glyph. Then he slapped a hand across his mouth, as though catching himself in a faux pas. "But what am I thinking? You're a Witch, aren't you?"

It was nothing to joke about. "Not a very good one."

Glyph cocked his head. "Now, just as—as a *thought* experiment—what do you think would happen if you were to go turn yourself in? Make a big show of it. Invite the media, as they say. I could help you. We'll draw up a manifesto, protest your innocence, swear to carry the fight all the way to the Supreme Court."

"Or all the way to the stake," said Pippa. She took about two thirds of a second to contemplate this. "I've got a lawyer who believes the government has no constitutional authority to interfere with the lives of its citizens. So like, I kind of have the feeling we'd end up with a hostage situation at the Old Tannery building."

Glyph laughed but caught himself.

She sighed. "Oh, I don't know. I'm just afraid . . ." She stopped because her throat felt clogged. "It's just, with Winterbelle and all . . . He told me I'd lose her one way or another, if things got this far. And now they've gotten this far. So I don't—I guess I don't want them to get *me*, too. Because then they'd have us both. We'd be in their power. We'd each be a prisoner, in a different way. At least out here, I can try to do something."

"Like what?" said Glyph. Then he lowered his head. "I'm sorry. I didn't mean to empower the negative."

"Don't worry," she said to him. "It's empowered enough."

So she stepped out in broad daylight, the morning of December 30th, onto the street where Carol Aaby lived, without so much as a borrowed pair of sunglasses. Trees Cracking Moon was well into its second quarter, and right now would be high overhead, though invisible. Pippa could almost hear a voice narrating, *And on that fateful day* . . .

From the doorway, Glyph told her, "Blessed be," forlornly.

"Peace," she replied, flashing him the old hippie two-finger salute.

Nobody caught her. In fact, nobody seemed to notice her—at least not during the time it took her to walk out of that boring neighborhood and across the river on a one-lane bridge to an older and quirkier part of town, where, among other things, the George Burroughs Elementary School was situated. Houses here had been built a hundred years ago for workers at the textile mill. They were modest for their era, but today were far beyond the reach of employees at the credit-card center that fleshed out the old mill's shell. Some were still owned by very old people who had lived here for decades. The rest had been bought up by a new class of gentry—retirees and young professional types—who had expanded and Jacuzzied and privacy-fenced the neighborhood into something quite different than it had been. Pippa liked it anyway. She liked the age of the trees, the odd shapes of windows, peculiar details like the ornamental brickwork of chimneys, sidewalks swallowed up by ancient junipers, pergolas sagging under grapevines. The place had good bones.

She turned up Church Street, which was wider than most, so that the snowplow had buried cars along both curbs. The oaks that lined the sidewalks had taken a hit from gypsy moths two summers ago, and some of their huge weakened limbs had crashed down in the last storm. This gave the street an abandoned, half-wild look that to Pippa was engaging, almost irresistible.

She stopped walking. Church Street, she thought.

It rang a bell. Someone had told her once something about Church Street. Someone who lived here.

Drop by and see me sometime, a person had said. But who?

Pippa looked up the street and down, trying to figure out who she knew that might live in a place like this. She looked at the house she had stopped in front of: a Queen Annie sort of thing with bay windows big enough to walk upright through. A weathered brass placard by the door said

MALLARD

Of course. Mad Mallard, the friend of Brenda Cigogne. Who had bumped into Pippa (or rather the converse) while walking her dog one day. And offered a vague and unexpected—but apparently genuine—invitation.

Drop by and see you, thought Pippa. By the Goddess, I will.

She had to guess where the sidewalk might be. The snow lay unshoveled without even boot tracks to guide her. For all Pippa knew the house was empty. Yet it did not look that way. Something about the place hummed on a subtle plane, a frequency that maybe only witches would receive, with motion and purpose and life.

On the front porch Pippa raised a massive knocker shaped like the head of a duck. It was a cartoonish, nursery-rhyme duck, wearing a bonnet turned lichen-green with verdigris and sporting a pair of granny glasses halfway down its bill. The sound it made was like a hammer banging a metal spike.

She did not catch the instant in which the door was flung wide.

Suddenly warm air billowed out and Mrs. Madeleine Willoughby Mallard was standing there, her presence larger than her physical body, motioning Pippa to come in. She looked merry and not at all impatient. And not in the least surprised.

"Pippa, my dear!" she exclaimed. "You must be *exhausted*."

What made her say that? Pippa squeezed past her into a wide entry hall, lit from high above by a cupola. A long wool runner led the way to a distant kitchen.

The front door shut with a thump and that was that: winter was outside, and in here all was warmth and sunlight and smells of baking.

"*This* way, if you please," Mad Mallard said, moving quickly down the hall toward a pair of glass doors through which Pippa glimpsed rather much of the color pink. "Come out to the morning room, it's where I *live* at this time of year. I'll get you some tea."

By the time Pippa made it through the double doors, Mrs. Mallard had already slipped in and out again— through a side door to the kitchen, from which direction Pippa heard crockery being heedlessly knocked about. She eased her backpack off, then her parka—it seemed only natural to do so—and took advantage of being left alone to try to orient herself.

Mrs. Mallard's morning room was the most truly marvelous place she had ever seen. Many windows stood at the east and south, and through them sunlight gushed onto dozens of lustily blooming geraniums, in shades ranging from virginal pink to voluptuous fuchsia. The colors did not match but their clashing was vibrant and somehow acceptably tasteful. What little you could see of the walls had been painted dark green, but most of the surface was taken up with bookshelves, a rolltop writing desk, an upright piano, paintings of landscapes and dogs, and a sideboard offering an impressive variety of booze. Dozens of rugs overlapped and piled atop one another. There were chairs of which no two were alike, tables assorted in function, and a giant fringed velvet ottoman. Pippa chose a plump armchair close to the ottoman and plopped down, sinking to the depth of one thigh.

Into the room then breezed Mad Mallard bearing a mahogany tray weighted down with a nanny-style teapot, two cups, a platoon of scones, a jar of red jam, a pint of clotted cream, linen napkins as large as crib sheets, and two narrow vases each containing one perfect pink rose. It was the most civilized tableau that Pippa had ever beheld. Her consciousness seemed to be transported into a Louisa May Alcott novel, some place of perfect girlish happiness.

"I do think tea is particularly welcome at this time of year," said Mrs. Mallard, setting the tray down on the ottoman and pouring for both of them. "Don't you?"

Pippa felt unable to speak. She closed her eyes and let warm sweetened jasmine-scented tea roll down the back of her throat. Tears filled her eyes and she was ashamed, but unable to stop them.

"I know, poor dear," Mrs. Mallard said. "I know it's been terrible. Here, try one of these scones. And do take *lots* of cream. I feel it's so . . . *fortifying*."

Pippa cried without making any noise, and she ate, and she sipped. She did feel fortified, but at the same time, paradoxically, weakened, utterly feeble. Unable to move or to explain herself, or in any way even to begin to get her act together, conversation-wise. Mrs. Mallard took no notice. She stuffed herself happily with her own goodies, and looked none the worse for it. Her floppy knotted-wool fisherman's sweater looked about 40 years old and seemed the kind of thing Katharine Hepburn would wear. It was like the two of them, Mad and Pippa, were in together on some wicked great secret (—but what?—).

Finally, intoxicated with the easefulness of it all, Pippa managed to say:

"Hey, I love your room."

"Why, thank you, dear. It was *intended* to be a sort of studio. I used to paint a bit, you see. And my good Mr. Mallard did his *best*, poor thing, to convince me that what a painter wants is *northern* light. A cool, neutral, *revealing* light, is how he explained it. But of course I wouldn't dream of such a thing. Neutrality, for one thing, I quite abhor. And cool light, in a climate like this? As for *reveal-*

ing—well, if you have nothing to hide, then take a photograph, is what I say. Painting is all about *omitting* things, isn't it? Selecting a certain aspect of reality and putting that down on canvas. I mean good heavens, why would one want to *reveal* more than is necessary?"

She sighed. A trace of sadness came into her eyes.

"I'm afraid I wasn't really a very good artist. More of a tinkerer, really. Anything to keep the hands busy. But not *that* busy."

She peeked into Pippa's teacup, tipped the last of the pot in, and rose to her feet.

"I shall have some more, I think. How about you?"

Pippa didn't know what to say. She couldn't imagine what more you could want, having gotten all this. She didn't think in her whole life she had begun a sentence with the words "I shall." Someday she would. She promised herself.

"Why don't I put some *music* on?" Mad Mallard exclaimed, as though the inspiration had irresistibly seized her.

While the older woman, radiating cheerful energy, shuffled through a stack of well-used vinyl recordings, Pippa gazed languidly about the room. She thought that any one of these paintings could hold your eye for days at a time. Then her eye fell (by accident) on the *Weekly Herald*, half-folded on the rolltop desk. At almost the same moment, Mrs. Mallard called over to her:

"You're welcome to take a look at the paper, if you like. It just arrived a little while ago."

Arrived how? Pippa wondered, recalling the absence of footsteps out front. She approached the *Herald* warily. The crease down the middle of the front page concealed the main headline, as well as half of an overblown and underexposed cover photo. Shouldn't have fired that photographer, Pippa thought. Then she thought of Mark Portion with the big camera dangling from his neck, and she reached out for the newspaper with fingers that already were starting to tremble.

There she was. Pippa Rede: bleary-eyed, plaster-skinned, right at the top of page 1. Her eyes looked like something you glimpsed paralyzed in your headlights, just before the *splat*. Glyph had been cropped out, mostly. All you saw was his arm intertwined with hers, the long fingernails like talons, an indistinct sparkle of rings. Underneath the photo a bold-faced caption ran:

The suspect currently being sought by police in connection with a widening cult scandal.

What do you know, thought Pippa. At last, I'm famous.

She lowered herself into the saggy armchair. A rush of blood swelled her temples. Out of an old amplifier with two big glowing tubes, choral music of Hovhaness transubstantially flowed. Pippa did not recognize it and found it sort of weirdly ethereal—like Hildegarde von Bingen, whom a lot of women she knew listened to, but with maybe some Pink Floyd thrown in.

The *Herald*'s headline said:

HOLIDAY SHOCKER: LOCAL MOM,
CALLING HERSELF "A WITCH,"
NAMED IN RITUAL ABUSE PROBE

I am not going to read this, Pippa thought.

And she did not.

Yet the poison seeped into her veins. Words flew up at her eyes by their own malevolent power.

Alleged to be Satanic in orientation.

That asshole Mark Portion, she thought. *Head of a shadowy ring thought to have.* He knows this is a bunch of lies. Doesn't he? *Operating behind a veil of secrecy over the course of months or years.* I could just kill him. (She canceled the thought, but half-willingly.) *Perhaps as many as dozens of local children.*

No, she thought. NO.

Noted expert on cult-based patterns of abuse Allison Rhinum.

People will believe this, Pippa realized.

Memories that can sometimes take many years to surface.

They won't know any better.

Parents are advised to be calm in questioning their children and to refer any doubtful cases to trained professionals for evaluation.

Then pick up some nice heavy stones.

So-called "Witchcraft," which authorities say may consist of a mélange of beliefs drawn from many occult or esoteric sources.

And stone the evil woman. Stone her till she's good and dead.

At the bottom of the page, a little boxed insert said: ONE SURVIVOR'S FIRST-PERSON ACCOUNT—See Editorial Page.

Pippa felt like screaming. She felt like running out of the house, burying herself in a snowbank, and waiting to die. But at the same time she thought that now, at least, it had come to a head. Her situation had gotten as hopeless as it was going to get, at least until she was caught and dragged before the howling mob. The realization gave her a peculiar, almost transcendental sense of immunity. She felt like she was floating above it all, an out-of-body presence looking down on her own life, her own methodical dismemberment.

So she turned to the Editorial Page. Why not? She even felt almost calm—insanely calm—as she sought out and found (you could hardly miss it) the article outlined in a bold black box.

ONE SURVIVOR'S STORY, it was called, and the author's name was given as "Michelle," in quotes. It began with a note from the Editor.

Although it is not the policy of the Herald to publish unsigned articles, an exception has been made in the following case for three reasons: First, in view of the extremely personal and painful nature of the experiences described. Second, "Michelle," a young woman currently attending college, comes from a family that has been known personally by the Editor for many years. And third, the events related herein are consistent with other accounts made known to the Editor through his contact with the local Recovery community.—M. P.

Pippa sensed that she was about to have a revelation. She could almost make out the shape and texture of it. She could imagine the voice, the actual voice, of this so-called "Michelle." This was her first experience of anything like clairaudience, or whatever it was.

Despairing, exhilarated, beside herself, she started to read.

> *I am a ritual-abuse survivor.*
>
> *It's taken me years to be able to make that statement, but I'm able to say it now. And I'm able to say that even though the things that have happened to me have been so terrible that I tried to forget, and for a long time I did block out all the hurtful memories, today I am able to acknowledge what's happened to me, and I know it was not my fault, and I know that I am a survivor.*
>
> *For those of you who have never heard of QROST or Quasi-Ritualized Occultic Sexual Traumatization, I should tell you that there are many informative resources available in which you can find out about this terrible underground movement that has been preying upon the most vulnerable members of our society for many years.*

Now I come to my own experience. I do not know how to begin because I do not know what the "beginning" was in my own case. One of the things I have learned is that a belief in Satan and worship of him goes back at least several generations in my stepfather's family. My stepfather is dead now and I do not wish to speak ill of the dead, but I must truthfully say that it was not until after his passing that I began to encounter some of the strange lapses and bad dreams and other upsetting experiences that I now understand to be part of the pattern of a returning memory. Evidently I had managed to suppress the true reality of what I had suffered for as long as my stepfather was alive, possibly because in my immature and vulnerable state I still desired as all children do to have their parent's approval and love. But after a while I began to notice (this may sound like a small thing to you) that I was unable to pay attention in math class. There would be days when I could just not remember anything that had happened there. Now, my stepfather was a math and science "freak." Anything to do with them or with computers, etc., would get him very excited. I believe this may have been part of his own searching for something to believe in since he had so long estranged himself from God. But this is only my opinion.

From there I began to have periods where I couldn't sleep at all. I would lie in bed at night with my whole body trembling. And whenever I closed my eyes, sometimes little brief snatches of scenes that I couldn't completely make out would occur before my eyes, but never anything I could quite remember or put into words.

I never examined fully what these things might mean, and it was not until I went away from home to attend my first semester at a large out-of-state University that things really came to the point where I was forced to seek help. And that was because I experienced a major post-traumatic crisis with physiological abreactions, to use terms that I have since grown tragically familiar with. Unable to attend classes or cope with eating regularly or communicating with my peers, I was referred by Student Health to a specialist in recovered memory who quickly stated that these symptoms I was experiencing—social withdrawal, confusion, eating disorder, inability to concentrate, and a chronic anxiety state—were suggestive of unresolved childhood trauma. And it was through this patient and nurturing individual that I first dared to confront what soon became a trickle and then a flood of understanding of what unspeakable things had been done to me.

I feel anger, of course, as well as shock at the extent of my stepfather's deeds and those of others whom I barely know. Those feelings will be with me for the rest of my life and I accept ownership of them. My job now is to not be a victim any longer.

When I first began to allow the memories of my past to surface, I did not understand how such things as rape and participation in rites of devil worship could happen without you fully remembering. I realize at this time that it is much more common than anybody thinks. There are citizens right here in this Village of ours who have perpetrated such evil acts, and who even now continue to victimize the most innocent members of our society, ruining lives and even entire families in their lust for power and other selfish ends. Probably most of these people were once like myself, lured unknowingly onto the path of Darkness by someone whom they trusted or loved, perhaps an admired older person or even a family member. A small number of others, who are the most dangerous, are like my late stepfather because they have been born into this secret tradition and indoctrinated at the earliest possible age in the belief system of the Satanist, who says: "There is no Authority higher than myself. I am equal to God and whatever pleases me is my Godly right to do."

The things that were done to me over a period of many years are still too painful and the wounds raw and unhealed for me to speak very much on this subject. But I will say that I have personally attended more than one hundred Black Masses, which usually occurred at a hidden place in the wilderness, because the true Satanist fears the eyes and ears of his neighbors and is at *home only among wild beasts which are his spiritual kin. At some of these rituals I was made to participate in orgies which would go on for hours, often involving children of a very young age who would scream in pain and confusion not knowing what was happening to them. In my memories now I can hear these screams again, and sometimes I even feel the pain of when it was my turn. I see my stepfather's face commonly in these memories, which are similar to tape clips where only certain things are visible in front of the camera, and I believe now that he was present at all or nearly all of the rituals I attended. But other people were present as well. The most common number of members of a "Coven," as it is known, is 13. Many of the faces I cannot see clearly enough to identify beyond a reasonable doubt. And I have been advised by the Police and others in the Legal profession that I am putting myself at personal risk of retaliation if I name any of the people who committed the deeds of which I speak.*

It often seems as if our system of Justice is designed to protect the perpetrators and punish the innocent, or at least allow the victims to continue to suffer from wounds they have received because there will always be loopholes that allow the guilty to go free. I am also convinced (though I cannot prove this) that certain highly placed members of society whom I will not name for the reasons above, may be more deeply involved in these matters than they wish to be known. But I will say no more about that until I have gathered further proof.

Of course, I am only speaking from my own personal history. I have been told by experts in this field that often the way young people are lured into these traumatic rituals is by first attending what they think are harmless "New Age" workshops or other activities where they are introduced to thought-control techniques which in turn make them more receptive to what will come later. Step by step their minds are invaded by new ideas which seem exciting at first but are really just the foot in the door of something that is more horrible and cruel than they can possibly imagine.

This is not what happened in my particular case as I have said. But I pass it along as a warning to others who may be at risk. Is it really worth it just to feel "enlightened" or "one with nature"? Ask yourself that.

You may be wondering why I have waited until now to speak of my experience and to warn others. The reason is that I have been too afraid. I know that my stepfather was connected with people in very powerful positions of authority. By speaking out like this, even with the protection of not revealing my name, I make myself the target of revenge which these people are masters of. And I have been afraid also of not being believed. But when I came home from college for my Christmas break, and I discovered that once again, our Village has been shaken by stories of unspeakable acts perpetrated against children, I realized that the time had come to reveal the things that I know.

In addition, I have only recently, since being back home, had a new memory which may have resulted in being again in the place where my initiation into the Dark Path occurred, i.e., my stepfather's home. On one of my first nights I had a dream where a face appeared which I did not recognize at the time. But then a day or two later I happened to be in a store where I was applying for a job, and this very person appeared there. As soon as I saw this person, I knew that my memory was real, and that this was one of the members of my stepfather's Coven and perhaps even the person he designated himself to be his successor when he died. This person's correct title in the Coven would be Priestess or High Priestess if my guess is correct. I will not say more now because I know there are legal proceedings under way in which I may be asked to testify.

So now I have spoken. I never thought I would find the courage to validate the truth of my own memories by taking this step. But I hope that by doing so others like myself—maybe even some of you who are reading these words—will become empowered to step forward and declare, No More Victims! Then someday we may truly say that Good has triumphed over Evil, and the healing process can finally begin.

Mad Mallard said, "It positively makes the jaw drop, doesn't it?"

She seated herself beside Pippa. A fresh pot of tea lay steaming on the ottoman.

"It seems clear," Mrs. Mallard went on, in a chin-up, that's-the-spirit voice, "that poor Mark Portion not only has taken leave of his senses, he also has dismissed the last remaining staffer who knows how to parse a sentence."

"It does sound pretty stupid." Pippa creased the *Herald* into a tight little packet, which Mad Mallard removed discreetly from her hands, carried to the fireplace, and dropped in.

"I thought you *should* read it," Mrs. Mallard said. "But there's no sense dwelling on a thing like that. It drags one's quality of awareness down to *their* level, and life is too short for that. We have arrangements to make, after all! So many things to do! Have another scone—and try the raspberry preserve, this time. I scavenged the berries myself from along the old railroad track."

Pippa obeyed, and yes, the preserve was delicious. Only a small part of her mind seemed able to focus on that, however. The rest was playing back the "Michelle" piece again and again. She wondered how to make it stop. She also wondered why it was that everyone she talked to seemed to have plans they wanted to make, while she herself had none at all. In fact she had not much belief that there was going to be any future in which plans could be carried out.

She was dolloping clotted cream out of its bowl when, from the front hallway, loudly, came the resonant whack of the duck's-head clapper. Mrs. Mallard looked up, her neck tall and thin, in obvious puzzlement.

The knock came again. Insistent.

"Well," Mad Mallard said, "I wasn't expecting *that.*"

The normally unperturbable older woman walked briskly to the door of the morning room then hesitated. She turned back to Pippa and said:

"Dear, perhaps you should grab your coat. And your knapsack, don't forget that. I've slipped a few extra things in. If you just go right through that door you'll find yourself in the kitchen, and I'll meet you there in just a few moments."

The knock came a third time and Mrs. Mallard bustled off down the hall.

If nothing else, Pippa had learned by now not to be overly bothered by the fact that this or that event made no sense. It was the things that *did* seem logical (for example, that a mother and daughter might be allowed to live together in peace) that were likely to crumble to dust on you.

Therefore, wasting no time thinking things through, she grabbed her parka and then her backpack (which seemed heavier, a bit), and she hurried into a kitchen that was much like the one at Eulace's house, only infinitely better appointed. In place of the cranky old cookstove there stood a huge green-and-beige enameled Aga. This great object, from which steady and comforting heat emanated, boasted half a dozen separate ovens, including one large enough to shove a plumpened Hansel into. From the direction of the front hall she heard a man's firm and business-like voice.

"I'm sorry to disturb you, ma'am," he said.

It sounded like Deputy Doug.

"One of your neighbors reported seeing a person entering your home here who looked like—" (sound of paper being unfolded) "—*this*."

"Like *this*?" Mrs. Mallard's voice replied, full of hauteur and incredulity. "Young man, I have never known anyone in my life to look that *that*. Why doesn't that fool hire a professional photographer?"

"It's just a little overexposed," said Deputy Doug (it had to be him), politely. "Maybe what they need is just some better processing equipment."

Mrs. Mallard made a sound like *ffsshhh.* "He'll never spend the money. He told me once in plain English that people don't buy a newspaper for the *contents.* They buy it for the *advertisements.* It's something he memorized from a seminar."

"Yes ma'am, I see." (Sound of feet scuffling.) "So may I ask you, have you seen this person? Would you mind if I just take a quick look around the house?"

"I should mind that very much. In fact, I should mind your remaining here in my hallway for so much as a moment longer. The very idea!—barging into someone's house on the basis of a *tip* from some busybody neighbor who has *nothing better to do than pry into other people's business.*"

She shouted the last several words, apparently for the benefit of any neighbors within earshot. Pippa smiled in admiration. A weird little titter slipped out of her.

"What was that?" Deputy Doug said.

"What was what?" said Mrs. Mallard.

"It sounded like somebody laughing."

"Perhaps it was my pet wolf," Mrs. Mallard said blithely. "I keep him for protection, you know. He's trained especially to attack strange men wearing uniforms. Have I asked you already to leave, or must I do so now?"

There was silence, then Deputy Doug said, "You know, it's possible to have a bench warrant issued on the basis of a radio call. Only takes about 15 minutes, if you can find a judge."

"How progressive. So nice to have met you, then. Cheers."

(Sound of a door being closed in someone's face.)

By the time Mrs. Mallard appeared in the kitchen, Pippa was waiting in open-eyed admiration. "Aren't you worried about getting in trouble?" she said. "I mean, thanks a million. But couldn't you get arrested or something?"

"Oh, I do hope so," Mad Mallard said. Her eyes were bright and she looked festive. "I do want to feel that I'm doing all I possibly can. Now here—take this and then you really must get moving. I shouldn't imagine it will take them long to return."

She handed Pippa an ancient-looking key—large and rusty, attached to a strip of leather that appeared to have been whacked off a belt. Pippa took it, feeling approximately like someone who has been handed a fortune in Confederate currency.

"My family owns a cottage," Mad Mallard explained, "up on the mountain. We kept it, when we deeded the land to the state. Nobody's used it in *ages*. I trust the road is still passable. If you pick it up just below the bridge, it should take you there eventually. I'd say *you can't miss it*, but the whole point is that it's so *easy* to miss, which makes it perfect, don't you see? Now don't lose the key because if I remember correctly, the lock is rather stout."

Pippa stared at the key and at Mrs. Mallard. She didn't know what to say. Or do. Fortunately Mrs. Mallard felt no such impairment.

"Your coat has got to go," she pronounced. She took firm hold of Pippa's parka and lifted it out of her hands. "Too distinctive. Whereas—" she reached behind her "—they'll never recognize you in *this*."

Into Pippa's arms she dropped a load of dead weight that was exactly what you might expect a sack of coal to look like: dark, shapeless, and coarse.

"It's warm enough, at any rate," Mad Mallard said. "Be off, now."

Pippa poked at the mass of rough wool, looking for armholes. The garment drooped about her like a gorilla costume. It smelled like wet dogs.

"*Ideal*," ruled Mrs. Mallard. "Don't forget your knapsack."

Pippa would never, ever have forgotten that. Mad Mallard prodded her toward the rear of the kitchen. A mat there was damp, as though snow had been tracked in not long ago. At the back door the two of them paused and looked at one another.

"I don't know how to thank you," said Pippa.

"Nor I, you," the elegant older woman said, with a smile that suddenly took on shadings of *tristesse*, world-weariness. "It's been so long, I've nearly forgotten how much this sort of thing riles the blood. But that's exactly what someone like myself *needs*, don't you see. Otherwise one just sits around and the fire goes out, and before you know it . . ."

"The wolf is at the door," muttered Pippa.

Mrs. Mallard stared at her as though this were a most remarkable observation. "Good-bye, my dear," she said. "You have all my blessings."

"You've sure got mine," said Pippa.

Then the two of them—rather out of character for each—quickly embraced, and as quickly separated. Mad Mallard threw open the door. Air as brutally cold as on a mountaintop slammed against them. Pippa yanked the ill-fitting coat as tight as it would go. The top button was missing so she had to hold it with one hand below the neck. She stepped down to a small back porch.

Mrs. Mallard quickly closed the door behind her. Pippa

was once more alone. She turned around to get her bearings.

Snow stood in great drifts everywhere. From the porch, stairs led down to a tiny, oval-shaped clearing in the midst of what must have been (once upon a time) an elaborate formal garden. At the center, a statue of a graceful, slightly built young woman—a wood nymph?—stood frozen in the act of twirling about. Dark clipped yews made a moody backdrop. Oaks leaned inward, their arthritic limbs sheltering rhododendrons, hydrangeas clutching papery brown flowers, maple-leaf viburnums, a few broken boxwoods, mountain laurel, and hinoki cypresses twisted to the ground by the snow. The backyard merged without delineation into a woodland that pressed up from behind. If the neighboring houses had not stood so close by, you could have imagined yourself already safe in a dark forest.

Pippa heard a car door slam, then a man's voice. Not Deputy Doug this time. Fear grabbed her and she stepped down from the porch; then she noticed tracks in the snow.

The tracks led from the porch in a straight line across the clearing and into the woods. At first Pippa thought, Aha—*that* explains how the newspaper got here. But looking more closely she saw they were not boot tracks; they appeared to have been made by some kind of large animal. Not a cat or a dog. Bigger than that. She bent low but the exact shape of the print was hard to make out. The animal had gone back and forth repeatedly, so that the trodden path was nearly continuous.

The idea gave Pippa pause. Could it be that some dangerous forest creature had made its den underneath Mrs. Mallard's house? She glanced back nervously, and noticed for the first time a large bowl placed to one side of the kitchen door. From where Pippa stood she could see a wisp of steam curling up from the bowl into the frigid air.

Oh, great, she thought. Mad Mallard has made the Beast a nice pot of broth.

Well, the illogical is all you can depend on, right? She turned and set off down the path worn familiarly into the snow, and detained herself no further wondering what kind of creature had made it. The only thing that mattered was that

> the path was there,
> and she was on it.

The path took her very efficiently through the woods. As animal trails will do, it shaped itself in snug accord with the contours of the land, deftly skirting places where you might get stuck: thickets, fallen logs, patches of ice dangerously thinned by water seeping below. Pippa knew she was somewhere near the center of the village, but had she not—had she just woken up here after a nice 100-year nap, which she could use about now—she might easily have mistaken this for genuine wilderness.

But that line of thinking led her around to the question of what creature it was whose paw-steps she was following. So she just lowered her head and hurried on, and in a few minutes she saw a clear space opening ahead. She proceeded more cautiously until at last, to her surprise, she realized that she was approaching from behind the old Yew Street cemetery.

Her sense of direction was not so great. She guessed it must make sense that the cemetery abutted *something*, and it might as well be the neighborhood where Mrs. Mallard lived. In fact this seemed fitting, though she could not have said why.

She trudged out into the open space and stood among limestone grave markers, smoothed by erosion. The track more or less vanished. Snow drifted before a wind that came sharply out of the west, dragging ominous clouds behind it. Already the sun (a feeble thing) had disappeared. It would not be long, she guessed, until dark. Even if right now was no later than midday, dark would come soon enough. These were the longest nights of the year. Longest and coldest and most desperate. And she was awfully alone.

Far across the cemetery, out on Yew Street, a police car drove by. It looked small and unthreatening from here. Pippa almost waved. But she was not stupid, even if she was insane and exhausted and drained of hope. She possessed, at the very least, one important thing, and that was a destination. The destination was a cottage to which she carried a rusty key. All she knew was that the cottage was "on the mountain," and that an old road (which was no longer a road) ought to take her there. The road began, if she understood correctly, just under the bridge.

Of course, a town with a river flowing through it has any number of bridges. But Pippa guessed probably she knew which one Mrs. Mallard meant.

It takes a while to thumb a ride when you're wearing a coat that makes you look like a gorilla. Pippa made a point to remember this, in her next life. There was not much traffic to begin with, at this time of year, and what there was was mostly old ladies heading back home after some excursion into town. Having lunch and not leaving a tip, for example. Pippa had been a waitress and knew all about it.

When somebody pulled over finally, it was two kids in a pickup truck. A boy and his girlfriend. Pippa experienced some tawdry feeling that might only have been punctured vanity, thinking how she must look to them. She knew it was almost too trite even to remember this, but not all that long ago she had been exactly like these two kids. One of them anyway. When the boy asked where she was going and she said, "The bridge," the two kids exchanged smiles, and that made everything worse. The boy put the truck in gear and skidded off, oblivious to the shitty road conditions.

Pippa understood. Pippa remembered how it had been. She had ridden down to the bridge many times, even on afternoons like this. She had been there once during a blizzard in a Ford Fairlane with chains on all four tires. While she and her boyfriend of the moment (not Winterbelle's father) had dallied there, with the motor running, beneath the arched concrete span—because that after all is why you went to the bridge and why it was just called *the bridge*, as opposed to *the bridge by the Old Tannery* or some such thing—snow had piled up three feet high all around, so that getting the Fairlane out was completely impossible. It hadn't mattered. She and her boyfriend joked and smoked cigarettes and finished the bottle of wine and then made love again. She could almost taste the cheap wine, right on the edge of her tongue—Wild Irish Rose or something equally atrocious—but try as she might, she could not see the boy's face or remember his name. For sure, he was gone now.

The boy and girl let her off and kept on cruising. While she stood there working up her resolve, a tractor-trailer roared by, spraying her with rock salt. She laughed at it. Actually laughed. *Cackled*, practically. It was just so absurd. Everything had gotten so crazy that you might as well laugh. Or you might as well cry. They were just about interchangeable.

Here she was, an old woman of 28. She was returning to the scene of ten thousand teenage orgasms, a few of them her very own. She was fleeing from the law. She looked like a witch. She even *felt* like a witch, which was something that for a while, a long while, she had really wanted to do. Now she did not. What she wanted now was to wake up in Florida and not even be able to remember this ridiculous dream. She wanted to wake up and not be Pippa, not be cold, not be frightened, not be standing on the bridge in the middle of winter.

She wanted to laugh again. To laugh as she had laughed only a minute ago. Laugh in the face of all of it, and just not care.

But she could not.

So she guessed it was time to go.

She left the highway. She scrambled down the embankment, taking a shortcut to the graveled space under the bridge where kids had always gone and would probably always go, until the Say No to Everything brigade came along and blocked the drive with a huge mountain of Bibles. It could happen any day, she guessed.

All the times she had come here, she had never noticed an old roadway leading off into the state park. Probably she wouldn't have seen it now, except that Mad Mallard had told her it was there. And *thwang*, as if by magic, the road appeared: two shallow ruts with the tough stalks of last summer's goldenrod in the strip between them. The entrance was blocked not by Bibles but just as ineffectually, with a chain stretched between two 6x6 pressure-treated posts. You could see where kids with ATV's had blazed a sort of alternative on-ramp, bypassing the chain and cutting through the woods a little farther down. Recent snowmobile tracks made the way absolutely clear.

Pippa guessed there was no turning back. It was funny: she had not given a thought to turning back until now. She remembered how good and safe she had felt (even for just a little while) in the raised ranch where Judith was house-sitting. Then even more fleetingly in Mrs. Mallard's morning room. She wanted so much to be in either of those places again—or really, anyplace at all. The balcony of the Opera House. A booth in the Sea Puppy. Aunt Eulace's parlor, with the Magnavox on full groan. In comparison to those places she was nowhere at all.

She took a step onto the abandoned road. Nothing happened. She felt neither better nor worse. She took another step, then another. Her heart failed to pump up with resolve. She guessed that she was going to have to do this in the absence of any good feeling whatever. No favorable omens, no gritty determination. Not even a really good idea of what she was trying to accomplish, beyond possibly dying of exposure before the mob could track her down.

Well, so be it.

She started walking.

The road climbed gradually at first, then steeply, up the side of Wabenaki Mountain. The snowmobiles had left caterpillar tracks that were easy to follow on foot, like a narrow stairway. But after a while the tracks veered off southward, back toward the village, and Pippa saw nailed to a tree one of the bright orange arrows that identified an official snowmobile trail, maintained by a club of local enthusiasts. The trail went one way and the old road continued another. With a sigh, she let go this one remaining connection with the orderly, human domain.

After that the road became more overgrown, with baby spruces and white pines. Sometimes she could only follow it by raising her head and looking up at the taller trees and figuring out where the cutting had been done, a long time ago. It was as if she was making her way by reference to the sky, or what she could see of it, rather than the land.

Soon it started to snow. Or perhaps on the mountain it had been snowing all along—this happened sometimes—and Pippa had just climbed high enough to walk into it. The snow swirled thickly all around her, leaving her already shaky sense of direction just about shot. She kept going anyway. Really, what else was there to do? It was that or just sit down and die.

She walked for hours. At least it felt like hours. Maybe it was months. Maybe she had already crossed the line into the Otherworld, the ambivalent realm of Faerie, where time lost all ordinary meaning. The light kept dropping until there was hardly any difference between the shadows under tall evergreens and the open space that she hoped was still the road and the empty patches of sky that were nothing but clouds so close she was probably almost as high as they were. She supposed this land was too drab and featureless to be the Otherworld, which was generally described (by those few who managed to escape it) in pretty vivid terms. Even Hel, she gathered, was reasonably well lit. Just misty, and dismal, and cold.

Pippa was so tired that it was all she could think about. She quit wondering how far she had come, how far was left to go. The snow fell too thick to see more than a dozen strides into. She was following *something*, but it might not have been the road; just as likely it was a path stamped out by a bear. Or by whatever wild thing found its way regularly to Mrs. Mallard's back door. Pippa shuddered.

It was almost night. There would be no moon. Her nose had been running for the past couple of hours, and the thin discharge was caked and frozen over her lips. Snow had gotten into her boots. The backpack weighed more than she did. She stopped and walked some more and stopped again. You could hardly tell any difference between them. Every sensory connection between herself and the physical world—even that part of the world consisting of her own body—was numbed to the point of being lost.

Pippa closed her eyes and opened them: there was still a distinction, though a faint and attenuated one. Keeping them closed felt more comfortable, and she was together enough to recognize this feeling of comfort as a danger sign, a warning that hypothermia was setting in. She had to fight it even if she couldn't remember why.

On she went. In no direction at all now. Just on. Just moving, so as not to be still. Being still and being dead sort of faded into one another in situations like these.

All of a sudden, for no reason, Pippa came to a halt. Her body seemed to have quit moving of its own accord— not out of weariness, but as though it was reacting to something.

She strained to see in the gloom that was everywhere around her. She listened but could hear only a ceaseless whirring of wind. Then she heard a single other sound— like a big piece of snow dropping behind her—and she spun quickly.

Too quickly. One boot caught in deep snow and she lost her balance and fell sideways.

She blinked; she looked blindly around. Snow collected on her face. She tried to prop herself up but only managed to thrash in a disorganized way. Her backpack weighed more than the Moon. Her head was filled with stars.

She felt the Beast nuzzle against her cheek, and smelled the rancid heat of its breath.

She tried to scream. Only small noises came out, like whimpering.

The Beast grunted. Its breaths were labored, as though it were weak and exhausted too.

She felt its snout pressing against her side, under her flailing arm, deeper, into her ribcage. Burrowing for her heart.

The final effort she made was in her mind alone—she wanted to see and to understand this thing that was happening to her. If only for an instant. If only in the last instant that remained.

So she blinked her eyes and she stared hard at the Beast and she made one final effort to concentrate. And her mind rewarded her with a single thought:

Wolf.

And then she was lost to herself
and everything was
black.

III

as ebony

Oh sisters, too,
What may we do
For to relieve this day?
This sad youngling
For whom we do sing,
Lully, lully, lullay.

—*"The Coventry Carol"*

Pippa opened her eyes and she saw nothing—rather she failed to see, her eyes were inoperable—and knew right away that she was dead.

Then she felt an ache in her back—the unyielding sort of pain you get from lying still in a very wrong position—and even the certainty of death drained away. She tried to raise her head and succeeded. She pressed a hand to her body and touched the coarse wool coat. She was not dead, but she would be soon, of exposure. Focusing all the strength that remained in her, she forced herself upright, and understood that she was in a sheltered place, tucked against a wall.

Snow fell lightly around her and onto her. She made an effort to remember where she was and what had happened. Her only memory was fear. Fear and cold, and blinding white. Then sleep. Sleep that should have lasted forever.

It seemed to her that something had awakened her: some definite thing. A noise. A sense of being touched, prodded at.

She remembered the Beast.

The fear grew stronger. It lifted her and pressed her against a surface that was hard and flat. Her hands explored this and she realized at last it was a door.

And she had a key. Though surely this could not be *that* door. (Could it?)

Pippa reached across her shoulder and found her backpack still snugly in place. She wriggled it off and pawed at the clasp, graceless as an animal. Her fingers barely responded and she worried about frostbite. But such a worry is almost an indulgence, under the circumstances. The backpack fell open and the key on its strip of leather lay right at the top.

The door was hard as iron, rough as unpolished granite. She ran the key up and down, back and forth, until it clinked metal-upon-metal. It took what seemed like several minutes, thrusting sightlessly, to find the handle and, under that, a hole. Finally she got the key through and it seemed to jam in place. She tensed her arms, ready for a struggle; but to her surprise—no, disbelief—the lock turned with an infinitely satisfying *clunk*. The door refused to open, but Pippa did not want to hear about that. She kicked until it gave way, then more or less fell through and rammed it shut behind her.

Inside now.

No darker here than out. Quieter, though—with a strange echoey quality, as though she were breaking a silence of ages. Sepulchral. Pippa took a step into the blackness and her feet struck stones, making a clop, as if she were wearing Gretel's wooden shoes. The noise frightened some animal that scurried frantically, off to one side, around knee level. A small thing, like a squirrel.

One step at a time, one stone to the next, she crossed a room whose size was unfathomable. The air was so still and icy, it was like being inside a freezer. Pippa wished she had thought to count her paces. In case her vision did not return, she would need a mental map. Vexed, she stepped carelessly, and her head banged something so hard she almost fell down again.

She groaned and staggered, rubbing her brow; then reached out and her fingers touched stone and she said:

"The hearth."

It had to be. Huge and perdurable, built of rough-cut blocks. With her head throbbing she groped around the thing, sizing it up, and this is what she deduced: one and a half arm-spans wide, slightly taller than your average witch, with an opening huge enough to park a snowmobile in. And *logs:* there were logs piled inside it.

On a whim—sort of testing the Norns, which can be risky—Pippa straightened up and ran one hand along the mantel. Her fingertips touched a little box. She picked it up and heard the most beautiful sound in the world—wooden safety matches rattling on cardboard.

Her hands were shaking so badly, with cold but also partly now with excitement, that she dropped the first match and failed to light the second. The third astonished her, flaring like a miniature explosion.

Her eyes worked again. She lowered the match toward the open hearth and not only were a dozen logs stacked there—dry and splintery, gray with age—but beneath them was a great mass of yellowing newspaper. Pippa could hardly believe it. The match burned down and scorched her fingertips and she yelped, but at this point even pain was a welcome feeling. Feeling itself was welcome.

She squatted and lit another match. For the moment, her curiosity was stronger than the cold—she reached with her free hand and tore off a corner of the newspaper. It was dated more than two decades ago. This fire had been laid while Pippa was still a tiny girl. And never lit. But why?

Who cared? She lit it now.

The old newspapers coughed into flame and the long-seasoned wood caught right away and burned hot. Pippa barely managed to locate the damper handle and yank it open before smoke filled the room.

She turned in front of the fire with her arms raised, defrosting. At the same time, by dancing flame-light, she scoped out her surroundings.

A cottage, Mrs. Mallard had called it. But from inside, you would describe it as something even humbler than that. A hunting cabin, perhaps. It seemed to consist mostly of just this one room: squarish, with exposed roof trusses blackened from years of smoke. There was no insulation, but on the walls hung giant furry hides that Pippa guessed had belonged to moose and bear and (maybe—if they were old enough) caribou. Over the door an iron peg supported a pair of enormous, gut-strung, Yukon Cornelius snowshoes. Pride of place, directly over the mantel, belonged to the stuffed head of a very large wolf. Its yellow glass eyes stared out with an accumulation of rancor.

It was not a comfortable room. The only furniture comprised a table too large for the available space with a plain wooden bench on each side, pressed against one wall, plus a single stuffed (or formerly stuffed) armchair angled toward the fireplace from an opposite corner—and *this* appeared to have been converted to a squirrel lodge. And yet for what it was, the little cabin was perfect. It made Pippa feel enclosed and protected. She stared at the fire, blazing lustily now, and seized by an impulse, began pulling off her clothes.

The old coat, soaked now with melted snow, dropped in a heap. She hooked it on a big nail above the hearth to dry. She took off her gloves and her boots and her scarf. She tugged off her sweater. She slipped out of her jeans. Eventually she stood naked and had to turn quickly, around and around, because the part of her that faced the fire was very warm and the other parts were freezing.

It was cool, though. Cool in the sense of spontaneous and fun. Pippa's body temperature rose steadily. As she got warm she also got sleepy. Exhausted, to be exact. She put back on her shirt and jeans and looked around and saw that two rooms opened off this one, on either side of the hearth. To the left was a bunk room with rotten mattresses and blankets filigreed by moths. To the right was a room stocked with cordwood, mostly beech. The whole thing was a mystery: as though the lodge had been provisioned for winter, more than twenty years ago, and then abandoned.

Pippa lugged armfuls of wood back to the main room. The old beech logs were light as cardboard. She tossed them one at a time onto the fire until it became huge and roaring. The lodge creaked as heat loosened its timbers. The stones of the hearth grew warm to the touch. Pippa checked for air leaks and found a frigid draft seeping through a knothole near the floor. She stuffed a sock there and wiped the first drops of sweat off her forehead.

Pleased now—especially to find herself sweating—she took a closer look at one enormous black bear hide. The fur was not as rough as you would expect. The leather was stiff but pliable. She lifted it off its hooks and let it flop to the floor. Then she dragged it over to the fireplace, and she thought: *There.*

Already she had begun the process of building her little nest.

She took down one of the smaller hides that she was determined to think of as caribou—a near relative of reindeer, therefore perhaps magical as well—and lay down with it on top of the bearskin, folding it around her like a sleeping bag.

Before she had time to think about how wonderful it felt, she fell asleep.

In one of the many dreams that drew her in like whirlpools, deeper and deeper, Winterbelle walked ahead on a path through the forest. The girl was 5 or 6 and wore bulgy snow pants and an Icelandic sweater knitted with a reindeer motif. Her little legs moved energetically in rapid short strides. Her hair swung around her like sunlit hay. Pippa's heart felt big and full. She tried to run and catch up with her daughter but gained no ground.

Afterward—a different dream, or the same one many weird turns later—the girl was calling and calling but nobody answered. She might have been lost or might have just wanted somebody there with her. You couldn't tell from the quality of her yelling, which was insistent but blank, hollow, as though she were calling from deep down a well, or inside an empty church. Pippa tried to reach her but got lost in the folds and turns of dream space.

Another was nothing but darkness. Stars overhead— seven, she counted—nothing more. A sensation of dread.

Pippa opened her eyes and it was still night. The fire was burning, though the logs were down to orange embers. The wolf's head was only a shadow. She slept again.

Daylight leaked through faded curtains depicting an Old World hunt: wild boars with fearsome tusks, Lithuanian bison, slavering hounds, an idealized Dark Wood. The hunters themselves were nowhere in sight. You were meant to project yourself into the scene, Pippa guessed. Sort of like guided visualization. The curtains caught you in an alpha state, just waking, when your imagination is purest, most nearly attuned to the ground wave of universal consciousness.

She rose shivering. The fire had burned to ashes, some of which had drifted out onto the caribou hide. Pippa noticed things that had eluded her the night before. A heavy-duty poker, for starters. She used this to prod the ashes until dull red coals appeared, then heaped on wood until the fire was snapping again.

The second thing she saw was a makeshift kitchen in one corner of the room. It did not amount to much— battered aluminum pots and semiusable utensils, an empty water jug, a collection of canned goods that looked like leftovers from somebody's fallout shelter. Pippa might have been numb and jaded and all that, but you really had to marvel at the concept of *canned okra*. And cream of barley soup. Calamari, in genuine olive oil. Succotash. Vienna sausage, swollen botulistically. And what in the world is hominy? Why are there 3 large cans of it? It was enough to make you laugh. And the really funny thing was, there was nothing to open the cans with.

In the back room where wood was stored, she found an old enameled chamber pot, deep as a cauldron, a thin book by M. F. K. Fisher, and a long-handled, rodent-gnawed broom.

She hefted the broom, which did not look much good for sweeping, but seemed *just* the sort of thing you'd want to fly on. Now, she thought, all I need is a black cat.

She sat on a bench in front of her fire. She was not displeased. She was not pleased. She was not anything that she could find a word for. Well, *alive*—that was one thing.

The fire crackled gamely. Old wood that had once been part of living trees (and still was the home of zillions of microbes, industriously metabolizing its constituents) became vapor which became thermal energy. Watching it, Pippa was lulled into a content-free awareness that she guessed was probably Zen or something and probably therefore good for her.

She supposed she needed time to recuperate. Not *heal*. Heal means *become whole*, and she would never be whole without Winterbelle. Nor would she ever come to accept things the way they were. That would be like accepting that life was pointless, hopeless, a complete waste of time. You might as well be dead. In fact, the dead were probably a lot more personally committed, more seriously engaged in the business of being dead, than that.

She supposed that if she was planning to live here for any period of time—if she was planning to *live*, period—there were things that needed to be done. Cleaning, for instance. Opening the curtains, letting a bit of daylight in. Venturing outdoors to collect snow to melt for drinking water.

Pippa did none of these things. She did as close to nothing as you can do. Only breathed; and now and then shifted her position on the wooden bench. After an un-measured period of time the fire burned low again, and she roused herself to heap a *lot* of wood in the gaping hearth, then lay down on her bear-hide mat and drew the coverlet of caribou fur snugly around her. Visions of rein-deer filled her mind.

Leaping, prancing reindeer. Ranging down from the Arc-tic; passing in great herds through the winter forest. Wild and magical and free.

She slept on and off for all of that day.

When she woke up, everything was black again.

The night was not silent. Close: but if you listened intently (and here, everything Pippa did or thought was intent) you could hear air moving at changing velocity across the roof and past the walls of the little cabin. You could hear a great horned owl coo in 4-note syncopation. You could hear branches creak, and snow that melted off the roof drip down to patter around the footings. Those were clear sounds that were easy to interpret, but there was another category as well.

Pippa believed for a while she heard footsteps. Or paw-steps. But it could have been nothing; or it could have been one of the miscellany of noises made by the fire. Finally it was gone and she wondered if perhaps it had been only a sound produced by her own body. A realignment of bones.

Another time, something like tap tap tap . . . tap tap tap. Then pause; then tap tap tap again. It came from so near it was hard to think she was only imagining it. Yet again, the harder she listened the fainter it seemed to grow. Maybe it was a small animal attracted by the warmth of the cabin, wishing to come inside, to keep her company. If she had known that for sure, she would gladly have invited it in. She was not exactly lonely, or at least she thought not. But a witch likes to have her familiar. Like Judith's silly ferret.

She smiled, but with no warning at all, her eyes flooded with tears. She hugged herself inside the caribou skin.

"Oh, Winterbelle sweetie," she sobbed. "Where are you, sugar? Are you warm enough? Your mommy misses you so much."

She was not at all hungry for the longest time.

Suddenly—this was in the middle of the night—she decided that she needed to eat something *right now*, and from that instant she felt ravenous.

Her backpack had sat there all this while, right where she left it, to one side of the fireplace. She remembered Mrs. Mallard having slipped in a little something extra, and her mind filled with thoughts of day-old scones. Raspberry jam. Hungrily she raised the flap, and on top of her other things she found a small leather pouch. She picked this up and squeezed it avidly, but it did not feel in the least foodlike.

What in the world, she thought.

The pouch opened with a draw-string. Inside she found an assortment of items she *never* would have chosen to bring along on a flight from Law, Order, and Decent Christian Society.

There was a tube of mascara: kohl-black. A jar of gloppy facial cream, the kind you smear on at bedtime, when no one will see you. Lipstick: deep, purply crimson, almost black, like a withering rose. Exceedingly dark sunglasses. An ivory-handled comb, two dozen hairpins, and a length of black silk ribbon.

What's with this *black* thing, she started to wonder.

Delving, she pulled out an ever-so-slightly torn scarf, and lastly an ill-used pair of panty hose. These too were black as sin, and by this time Pippa was done with feeling exasperated; she was starting to grow amused.

For reasons known (if at all) only to herself, Mad Mallard had given Pippa an entire makeover package—a do-it-yourself Crone kit.

Pippa laid it all aside. From lower down she pulled out the remainder of what she had carried so long and so far: 1 toothbrush, 1 cake of soap (unopened), 1 t-shirt (oversized), 2 paperback romances (neither of which she felt like reading anymore), tampons, 1 extra sweater, 2 pairs of socks, a wind-up alarm clock, her sewing kit, a butane lighter, a wooden pestle, and a mortar of cast stone. Household-goods-wise, it did not add up to much. There was also the Santa Fe knife, which she took from her pocket and tossed on the pile; and, holiest of holies, the little frog fetish Winterbelle had carved for her. Gingerly she held this, unwrapped its swaddling of cotton, kissed it reverentially, and laid it with great care upon the mantel.

Now, then. She was *here*. The hunting cabin was now, officially, a witch's cottage. Deep in the Dark Wood. Where the wild things are.

Hunger, once acknowledged, would not go away. And now that she came to it, Pippa guessed she was thirsty, too. *This* at least had an obvious solution. She picked the largest pot from her kitchen corner and took it to the door.

There she stopped.

Was she ready for this?

It was only a door. But the idea of pulling it open was not as straightforward as it ought to have been.

For a whole day and night, she had found refuge in this sturdy little hiding place. She had been warm and she had felt safe here. Protected, as if by magic. It seemed that she had penetrated to the heart of Something—the forest, the mountain, Nature Herself—and that to open that heavy door would be to crack the seal of protection.

She understood that these ideas were irrational, born of emotion or instinct. But rational or not, they were *real*. They were as real as the fact of Pippa being a witch, which was also as totally crazy as it could be. Yet look at the trouble that had come of it. Two whole lives down the toilet. All because of a *word*. How much more irrational can you get than that?

Pippa backed away from the door.

There is a way of opening a magic circle, if you need to. Small children and cats can go sneaking in and out, but grown-ups have to be more deliberate. Pippa went back to the modest pile of her belongings and she picked up the Santa Fe knife.

She advanced upon the door, ritual blade lowered.

"I cut a hole," she announced. She moved the blade, surgically, counterclockwise. "I cut a hole and I pass through it. The web of concealment is not broken. The circle remains intact."

She grabbed the door and pulled it hard. It came open with a whoosh of freezing air.

Funny: she had forgotten it was winter. Or no; the memory of what winter *meant* had left her mind. Temporarily. It came back now. Pippa stepped out onto a carpet of firelight, cast across the snow.

The carpet had bumps and hollows. One deep shadow marked the place where her body had lain the night before. And beyond that, a trail of prints led away, recording the journey that had brought her here.

Shivering, she stepped farther out, into enveloping darkness. The tracks were like tiny valleys, yellow up one slope and blue down the other. She craned her neck and found Trees Cracking Moon suspended high, a day or two short of full, brushed by clouds that swarmed like cobwebs at the end of a broom, still bright enough to cast shadows. Pippa stared, amazed by its beauty, its serene and distant remove. Then she bent low and studied her own trail, because it was there, closer to the Earth, that the mystery seemed concentrated.

She was sure of this: the tracks through the snow had not been made by boots. They had not been made by human feet. What you could see of them appeared to have been made by very large paws, with three or four lobes, bluntly clawed. But none of the prints was clear, partly because snow had drifted over them, mostly because something had been dragged along the path, smudging things.

The way it looked to Pippa was that some very large animal had come right up to the cottage door, dragging a heavy burden.

The burden had been Pippa. What else could it have been?

As to the creature that brought her here, all she could think of was the one whose tracks led back to Mad Mallard's back door. *My pet wolf*, the old lady had said.

That was impossible, of course.

On the other hand, here Pippa was: impossibly alive, after having collapsed in a blizzard.

Somehow she had gotten here. Not died of exposure. Not stayed lost on the mountain. She might never know how this had come to be. But it *was*.

"Thank you," she said aloud. To the night; to Trees Cracking Moon; to the mysterious, blessed, magical Beast. "Thank you, I mean it. I'll try to pay you back. But anyway you've earned some heavy-duty karma points."

She pressed her hands together and made a little bow.

The night did not reply. The Moon looked on impassively.

From deep in the black woods, a raven uttered a throaty call that ended in a sputter. It sounded like an aging orator getting off to a bad start. Then it was over and did not resume.

Pippa decided not even to think about it. Certain things you just have to accept. Maybe all things. You accept them and you go on. She scooped a heap of snow into the aluminum pot. Back in the cottage, she closed the door tight and punctiliously resealed the circle.

For a few minutes she stood in front of the fire, shaking all over—from cold, from exhilaration, and from a peculiar kind of fear: a feeling that she was standing at the very edge of the Mystery:

> the dark and marvelous Thing
> she had groped for
> all her life.

She looked for food.

One entire day of her life—from its frozen, ice-white, sun-dazzled beginning on the hard floor of the cottage to a black and bone-weary end, staring between stars into the deepest pockets of Time—Pippa spent scrounging and gathering and hunting for and not finding enough food. Like a desperate animal, beyond all question of pride. Like the great-great-grandmother of every little girl who ever lived: an ancient hunched-over unspeaking scavenger haunting the secret places of the forest, communing with beasts, bargaining with the Powers that rule there.

Pippa hadn't eaten for almost two days. Not since tea-time at Mrs. Mallard's.

Fasting is good for the soul et cetera; but Pippa's soul was not the immediate concern.

She started with the old tin cans. Cream of barley soup: the most appealing of the lot. She positioned it between her feet and smashed it hard with the poker—knocking the can sideways, spilling soup out a hole the size of your thumb. The stock was pale and cornstarchy. Pippa dribbled it into a pan and shoved it close to the fire. Then she backed off, and without really thinking, she plopped into the old rotten armchair.

It felt different than she expected: lumpish, hollowed-out. She bounced up and down a couple of times, then bent to examine it more closely.

The chair was a squirrel's nest. It was stuffed with straw, dried leaves, bunches of twigs chewed to size, and about a thousand acorns.

Acorns. Pippa blinked.

What can you do with acorns?

They are edible, surely. The squirrel had been planning to eat them. Pippa thought she remembered hearing of acorn pie.

She picked up a single acorn and rolled it between her fingers. It was large, fatter than a thimble. *The mighty oak,* she thought.

She tried biting it. Too tough.

She placed it in her mortar and crushed it open with the heavy pestle. Its insides crumbled to fibrous bits.

She brought one of the larger bits to her mouth and chewed reflectively. The texture was disagreeable, like decayed wood. But the flavor was okay. Sort of like a raw nut.

Well, I guess it *is* a raw nut, she thought. Or something.

A sizzling, sputtering noise interrupted her. The cream of barley soup was boiling over. With a yelp Pippa dashed across the cottage, but the soup was scorched beyond salvaging. The pan was not looking good either.

She moaned: "Awww, shoot."

For an instant, Pippa glimpsed herself in her own mind's eye, the way she would appear to someone else: the stuffed wolf, maybe, peeking down from its place above the mantel.

"Go ahead," she told the wolf. "Laugh."

The wolf continued to stare in its sour fashion. So Pippa had to laugh for it. To laugh for *her*, she corrected herself; because it seemed to Pippa (not for any reason she could think of) that the wolf was a female.

"Tough luck, Sister," she told it.

Acorns are satisfying in their way: you can make a mush of them and fry them up, and you end up with something vaguely granoloid. But Pippa needed more than that; she needed to get her strength back. Why, she wasn't sure. But you *never* hear about a witch feeling too run-down to lay a spell on you.

Pippa determined to make a serious forage.

She took it on faith that there would be something out there to forage for. People had been food gatherers for a long time before they became farmers and livestock keepers (let alone comparison shoppers). In fact, witchcraft itself, like other magical belief, arose in those days when there *was* no daily bread, because there was no domesticated grain. Instead there were ever-moving herds to outmaneuver, fruit to pluck at the perfect time (and birds to beat you to it), herbs to harvest, roots to dig, scurrying critters to trap. You had to be smart and you had to be plugged in to the rhythms of the larger, nonhuman world. Because there could be no pretense of control here. Everything was connected and *you* were connected, too—just one strand of the web, and not the biggest or the strongest one, either. In those days, bears had been gods, and so had brutal winds, and life-giving sunshine. The Underworld lay close at hand—for every day you saw how new things unfolded from it, and how old things returned to its depths.

It was hard to get uppity, knowing all that.

So Pippa proceeded with caution. She bundled herself

in all the layers of clothing that would fit beneath Mrs. Mallard's old coat. She took the empty backpack as a satchel, though she fretted that this might produce contrary results, like taking an umbrella to make sure it doesn't rain. Magic is pesky that way. Then she stood for a little while before the hearth, gazing at the little frog fetish, then higher at the wolf's head, which looked angrier than usual. That time of the Moon, maybe.

"Please," she said, addressing the wolf, but really hoping to connect with something larger, the Womb that the wolf had sprung from. "I'm really hungry. I've got to find something to live on, if it's okay with you. I *promise* I won't take more than I really really need. So please, let me find something."

She strapped on the Yukon Cornelius snowshoes. They made her legs splay apart, so that she could only move by lifting and plopping and heaving herself along. But once she got the pattern down it was kind of fun, like walking on a totally deranged planet—especially when she waddled out into gray cold morning, and the shoes lifted her up on the blanket of snow, and she felt both weightless and klutzy, like a fledgling fairy nowhere ready to fly.

A change had come into the air. The clouds had thickened. They zipped by so fast, in bulbous clusters, with deep ultramarine fissures between them, that for many seconds Pippa stood there watching them endlessly going by. Then, laboriously, clunking the snowshoes together, she managed to turn around, and for the first time she got a real look at her little witch's cottage (née hunting cabin) from outside.

It was cozy and small. Its eaves were decorated with Victorian gingerbread, pieces of which were missing as though they had been nibbled at. All around it ran a wooden slat fence with lathed finials, its whitewash chalked down to gray, from which many boards and the entire gate were missing. The stone chimney, with doves' nests tucked into its sides, protruded through a roof whose shakes were heavily colonized by moss. White smoke puffed out. Above the door a moose head was mounted, its massive rack askew. Over the years the skin had been gnawed away, exposing the skull.

The whole scene could hardly have been cooler, or spookier. The cottage sat in a clearing between giant, widely spreading trees—white pines mostly, but also red oaks and a stand of aspen whose branches quivered before the steady, southwesterly wind. The air brushing Pippa's cheeks felt unseasonably gentle. It was as though Nature had gotten bored with the routine of winter and was trying something new. Not spring: too dark and omen-laden for that. Not autumn either because it lacked a sense of finality. Something different. Unforeseen.

Pippa found everything—cottage, forest, mountaintop— overwhelmingly beautiful. Also lonely, and a little sad, yet in a lively way, like Irish music. But the day would be short. All days were short now, and the nights were going to be hungry ones if she didn't get a move on. So taking a deep breath, she plodded on showshoes through the gap where a gate had been, and entered the Dark Wood.

A trail of four-lobed tracks led one way. Pippa went another.

The snowshoes made a crunchy noise, mashing down, and when they came up again their tails flipped snow against the backs of her legs. It was hard enough work that her breathing came heavily, but pretty quickly she found a rhythm, and covered perhaps two miles over the course of an hour. That is a much bigger deal than it sounds like. And at last she came upon a stand of winterberries.

Winterberries are head-tall, deciduous hollies that hold their little red fruits high, at the branch tips, mostly out of deer-chomping range. Birds pick them clean by spring, but it takes a good long freeze, and then a thaw, to soften the berries up, so there were plenty still there for Pippa to rake into the backpack. She took a couple of pints, leaving many times that behind, and felt reasonably satisfied. It wasn't enough, but it was something.

Higher up the slope loomed a stand of oaks, the largest of them wearing big puffy clumps of a lichen called old-man's beard—pale green, like things that glow in the dark. Pippa heard a woman once on the community radio station say that you could use this to make a soup stock. It was rich in something, Pippa didn't remember what. At the time she hadn't cared. But anyway the lichen was easy to harvest and there was plenty of it.

She scraped around in the thin snow beneath evergreens, hoping to uncover some ground nuts. There was nothing but partridgeberry, which tasted like bitter toothpaste with a texture of wax. Ick. In the process she uncovered clumps of tan, bambooish grasses, but their seed heads were so tiny you couldn't even think of threshing them for grain. There were standing spore cases of cinnamon fern, but those were probably poisonous or something. Pippa grew discouraged. And with each trudging footstep, exhaustion was coming on.

By now a couple of hours must have gone by—the light had changed in complicated ways, which made it feel longer—and Pippa had so *little* to show for it. One truly strange meal, perhaps; and even that was assuming that the winterberries turned out to be palatable. Still, she guessed she better go back. The last thing she needed was to get overtaken by darkness out here.

It took like, *forever* to find her way back to the cottage. Long before she got there Pippa guessed she had burned off more calories than she could ever replenish with the stuff in her pack. When at last she came in sight, and caught the sweetly acrid smell of woodsmoke, her relief was as sudden and visceral as a drug kicking in. She halted outside the ramshackle fence and just stood there. Letting her breath slow down. Feeling alive.

She noticed, from here, some remnants of an old garden (for there must have been a garden, once upon a time) along the fence. There were stalks that looked like short, withered sunflowers, their blackened heads drooping, seeds stripped by birds. The plants had spread to form a wide stand, crowding out everything in their path. Pippa tried to think what these flowers might be, to picture how they would look at the height of summer, blooming their invasive little heads off.

She got it almost right away: Jerusalem artichokes. A misnamed plant, neither an artichoke nor remotely Middle Eastern. You see it occasionally in gardens, especially older ones, though nowadays people grow it more for its bright yellow daisies than for its thick, starchy, and allegedly delicious rootstock.

If only Pippa could figure a way to get the damned things out of the ground.

Ah, well. It would have to wait until morning. Tired as she was, she would make do tonight with what she had.

"I'll be back," she promised, wagging a finger at the stand of *Helianthus tuberosum*.

Then she dragged herself the last few steps to her door. And there, as she was bending to unstrap the snowshoes, she encountered the fresh, bloody carcass of a rabbit.

A big rabbit. White with gray markings around the fallen ears.

Pippa was grossed out and wonder-struck, at once. The rabbit's eyes were wide open: brown, smallish, wearing a look of surprise.

Well, Pippa was with the rabbit on that one. She squatted down awkwardly, poked at the carcass—yes, it was well and truly dead—and cautiously lifted the head to expose the wound that had killed it: at the throat, a single bite, sundering both jugulars.

Pippa guessed the rabbit had died quickly enough. She hoped so. Closing her eyes, she uttered a little invocation of thanks to the poor animal, for giving its life so that she could have a dose of high-quality protein.

Then she reflected that, of course, the rabbit hadn't exactly *given* its life. Its life had been taken from it, quite suddenly, by a predator. If there was any giving involved, then it was part of some murkier, infinitely stranger transaction. From the predator to Pippa. The sacred gift of food.

Understanding this made her feel slightly sick.

She glanced around toward the woods, where night was now undeniably closing in. The thick trunks and long, sweeping branches seemed to crowd together, as though they were sneaking up on her, like the forest in that play you aren't supposed to say the name of.

"Well, hey," she said, "thanks. Thanks a lot. I guess. No, I mean it—thanks a million. This is exactly what I needed."

The forest did not reply. Trees Cracking Moon was invisible behind the clouds. Pippa saw no yellow eyes staring back at her. But she imagined them. So clearly, it was not much different than actually seeing them out there, staring back.

*   *   *

The body of a hare features a great thick loose covering of fur, and beneath that a layer of fat; and in the middle a big gob of yucky guts.

Once you get all those things out of the way, it's meaty and delicious. *So* delicious. Pippa had spent a couple of years as a vegetarian (this was before Winterbelle came along, and she lost that special concentration you need), and she could hardly believe herself now: elbows on the table, stuffing greasy bits of this like, *dead animal flesh* into her mouth. But there she was. And she didn't feel bad about it, either. When she was finished she spooned out a big bowl of lichen soup that had been simmering for more than an hour. That was good, too. It could have used a little salt, and maybe some rosemary.

The winterberries sucked. She put them aside.

At last she leaned back on the bearskin and she experienced a lazy feeling of all-rightness. She knew that all was *not* right; but it certainly felt that way.

The feeling made her witchy antenna vibrate. Because she recognized that this was the sort of moment where you carelessly prick your finger with an enchanted needle and plunge into a hundred-year nap.

She figured that she ought to take precautions.

The remains of the hare, for example, ought to be properly attended to. Pippa gathered them up in a pan, skin and bones and entrails, then slipped on Mrs. Mallard's coat and opened the door.

Already outside, she realized that she had forgotten her little door-opening ceremony. But then she thought, That's okay. If anybody is reckless enough to fuck with a *witch*— let alone a witch hunkered down in her gingerbread cottage, way in the middle of the Dark Wood—then let the fool have at it.

She imagined the look on the face of this hypothetical

fool, when he realized what he'd stumbled into. Eyes popping out of his head as he stares at the grinning skull of the moose. Beads of sweat forming on his brow as he hears the cackling from within.

"Come on," she said to the night—loudly, heedlessly. "Here I am. Come get me."

She felt absolutely full of herself: charged up with strange, possibly magical energy.

It was a new feeling for Pippa.

She stood there under the starless, moonless sky, listening to wind whispering secrets in the trees, with the bloody remains of a sacrificial animal in her hands, and she thought, Wow—I guess it's really happening.

I guess I'm really
turning into
a witch.

She woke early next morning, and lay beneath the caribou hide watching dawn change color at the windows.

It began lavender-gray, faint as the afterglow when you turn off a TV in a darkened room. This became cooler, paler: neurotic blue, a color you might paint a laboratory. As the luminosity increased it shifted toward pure white. Then, just as Pippa was about to get up, declaring the day officially begun, the sun found a chink in the forest and shot one pumpkin-yellow ray toward the cottage. Outside the window it struck an icicle as thick as Pippa's forearm, hanging low from the eaves, as organically warped as a stalactite. The ice broke the sunlight into fragments of every imaginable hue. When you moved your head, the colors moved too; the icicle changed shape like a hologram. Pippa stared and stared at it. She was entranced.

That's a funny word: entranced. Pippa remembered the way Winterbelle (who *loved* icicles, loved to snap them loose and bring them inside and lick them like Popsicles) would stare through the kaleidoscopic accretions of ice with a look of such total fixation that it *might* have been a sort of trance. A state of innocent reverie.

Winterbelle, her magical elf. Her poor beautiful lost little girl.

Abruptly, without thinking, Pippa threw off the caribou hide and rose quickly and crossed the room. She opened the door and stepped outside in her bare feet.

The sky was clear; the rising sun was yellow; the shadows of the pine trees were long and deep green, almost black. Pippa scooted around to the side of the cottage, where snow melted and dripped from the low eaves and froze again in weird, tapering columns. She grabbed one—maybe the same one, probably not—and tugged sideways against it until it broke free of the roof and fell to the ground. It was hard to lift—heavy and cold and slippery. But she managed it. In a strange way, in her mind, she was bringing it inside for Winterbelle.

She slammed the door. The icicle was as long as her arm. She looked for a place to put it and finally set it thick-end-down on the table, its skinny end propped against the wall.

By the time she got the fire stoked up, melting ice had already formed a puddle on the tabletop. The puddle was almost perfectly round and looked like a shallow glass dish. The icicle looked like glass too—hot, molten glass—especially when the firelight swirled and refracted inside. It looked . . . how, exactly? Alive. In motion. Whorling, forming vortices and funnels. Pippa sat on the bench, fire to her right, warming her body, the icicle near her face. She tried to call to mind exactly how Winterbelle had looked at such moments: how she had rested her firm and determined chin between her two dry-skinned, usually scraped-up, occasionally dirty little hands. The way her cloud-blue eyes became opaque, distantly focused, unblinking. And her untroubled mind seemed to float.

In a trance, Pippa thought. Feeling her own mind drifting out there. Caught in a frozen whirlpool.

Fire trapped in ice.

Motion in stillness.

Magic—

in which the impossible, the things you understand cannot really happen, do happen, become real, acquire irresistible momentum, explode outward from your consciousness through the layers and layers of external reality, and in due course—if you're lucky, if you truly get your wish—change every single atom of the world. Just a teeny bit. For good and for all.

Inside the icicle, shapes and colors danced.

In Pippa's heart, a little girl stirred sleepily, shifted under her covers. Halfway awoke.

Winterbelle, sweetie—the thought rising from deep inside Pippa, like a bubble of pure feeling. Reaching her throat chakra, the energy center that mediates between *inside* and *out there*. Then becoming a different thing: not words: a pulse: a spreading wave of maternal love.

In her distant bed, under a polyester comforter with scratchy hem stitching, the little girl stirs.

Mommy, she thinks.

Pippa's heart swelled, stayed open a second, then contracted hard. Her eyes were locked on the icicle, but she could no longer see it now. Only a brightness at its center. The world at large was well lost.

Winterbelle opens her eyes. Warily, flicking them sideways. The other girl, in the bed across the room, still asleep and unmoving. The door to the hall almost shut:

only a narrow band of yellow, the beginning of sunlight, visible up and down the crack.

Winterbelle rolls slowly, carefully, to the inner edge of the bed, the chilly cavity next to the wall. One slender forearm pokes out from beneath the comforter, trailing a pink flannel nightie. The hand gropes lower, sliding down the wall, finding the bottom of the mattress. Twisting, digging under. Probing.

Making contact.

Pippa drew in her breath.

Winterbelle's fingers lock on to a small wooden box. She tugs this gently, moving it by millimeters outward. Checks again behind her, finds her roommate (an older girl called Cherrille, stupid and coarse) still reliably asleep. Turns back.

And pulls out the tiny dollhouse. The witch's kitchen, made by her mom out of a bunch of itsy bitsy stuff inside a jewelry box. *So awesome.* And awesomely secret, too. Because they will punish her all over again if they ever find it. Just as they punished her the first time when she managed to hide it from them. Only probably worse next time around.

Winterbelle holds the box tightly in both hands, close to her heart, with its lid still closed.

In truth she hardly needs to open it anymore. She has stared so hard so many times into that shrunken-down, fairy-tale-perfect room, all its details are pressed firmly into her memory. The bunches of herbs dangling from a Popsicle-stick rafter. The stove made of shards of real brick. The cauldron made out of a thimble.

The only thing missing is the witch.

And that, of course, is what Winterbelle cries about, every time.

Because she knows who the witch is. And she knows how much the witch loves her. And she believes, truly believes, with all the force and purity of a nine-year-old heart, that the witch will use all her magic, all her secret powers, to come and rescue Winterbelle someday.

Winterbelle takes a breath. She lets it out too loudly—glances hastily behind her toward Cherrille. But the other girl is still completely out-of-it, in a way Winterbelle almost wishes she herself could be. (But she cannot. She will never be oblivious. It is her curse.) So now she turns back to the dollhouse. It is time for her little private ceremony.

Being a witch's daughter, you learn certain things. You learn mostly by observing them. Witchcraft is not about words, Winterbelle has noted. It is not even about feelings. It is more (she has deduced) about connections. Between things, between people, between this time and another, one place and someplace else.

Winterbelle believes that this box connects her in some magical way with her mom. So she has made up a little ritual—tiny and secret as the dollhouse itself—to go along with it.

She closes her eyes now, feels the box pressed inward against her ribs, only an inch or two from her heart. She takes a single long breath, holds it, then utters her wish. Her great and only wish. A secret that anybody with half a brain could guess.

Then she opens her eyes again and lifts the lid off.

In the Dark Wood, the witch's cottage quakes. Its beams rend and snap. Where its roof had been, Pippa stares up through cobalt infinity.

*   *   *

"Mommy," whispers Winterbelle—so very quietly the words are almost inaudible even to herself. "Mommy, I miss you. And I love you. And I'll see you soon."

Then she snaps the lid shut and twists sideways and thrusts the box back deep into its hiding place. And lies flat again, while the tears dry slowly on her cheeks. Listening to the slow, sluggish breathing of the fat idiot across the room.

Pippa felt numb but intent. Freaked, but focused. She stood before her cottage (its roof miraculously restored) whanging away at the brittle ground in which Jerusalem artichokes were trying to hide from her. *In vain,* she wickedly thought. The poker came down again and again, so hard it made a whole chain of motor nerves jangle.

The sun still hung low—Pippa felt eye-to-eye with it, on her mountain—but so diamond-bright, glancing off the snow, that she slipped Mrs. Mallard's dark and old-ladyish sunglasses on.

The ground broke up in solid chunks. There was no way to separate helianthus roots from the rest of it, so she laid the chunks aside and kept whanging. She had read somewhere like *Organic Gardening* that getting the dirt out of the tubers could be a bitch; but in that case it would be an even match, wouldn't it? One bitch to another.

The new sound—unknown and yet familiar—went on for some time before she allowed it to interrupt her. By that time it had gotten loud and alarmingly close.

Pippa straightened up. She listened hard. It was a machine noise, she thought—a small engine, like a chain saw or a lawn mower. But it was moving, too, which made it peculiar. It moved *quickly,* coming at her through the trees, getting closer all the time. What on Earth? she thought, raising her poker defensively.

It was a snowmobile.

A gleaming black & silver Arctic Cat, sliding over the white mantle and tossing a plume of snow behind it like a comet's tail.

It leapt right out of the woods heading straight for where she stood. Just shy of the fence it skidded sideways, knocked a bunch of snow up against the slats and braked to a halt. The motor died. The driver—a compact man, wearing an olive-drab all-weather suit and a motorcycle helmet—looked *much* more surprised than Pippa.

Then he shook his head, removed his helmet and grinned at her.

His face was round, open, copper-tan. He had a long black ponytail, and in one ear he wore a cluster of white and black feathers wound together with gold wire. His eyes, though squinting in the glare, were sharp and bright, and there was about him a quality that Pippa believed was known as *presence*.

She judged him to be okay. Not a dangerous or hostile person. She judged him to be about 30—just a bit older than herself. She judged him to be at least part Native American.

She could not help wondering what he thought about *her*—standing alone here in the middle of the woods, hacking away at the frozen ground, unbathed and unkempt and wearing an old lady's sunglasses.

"Morning," the man said then.

His voice was deep and rather still.

"Hey," she said back to him. And added, without a moment's thought, "How did you *find* this place?"

He kept smiling, though his eyes pointed mostly away from her. Which was good, because it allowed her to stare at him without seeming rude. His skin looked both leathery and smooth, even boyish, as though he hardly needed to shave. His nose was flat, and there were small friendly creases around his eyes and his mouth. It was somehow a *decent* face.

The man said, "I followed some big old snowshoe tracks." (Pointing back across his shoulder.) "Yours, I guess. Back there along the ridge." He glanced toward her and then away again. "Anyhow I've been up here before."

"To this place?" she said. "Really?"

He nodded and they looked at each other straight-on for a long moment. It seemed to Pippa that things were twisted around—that this guy was acting more comfortable, more at home here, than she felt herself to be. She resented this. She twirled her poker.

"This where you live?" the man asked her.

What could she say to that? She shrugged. "For a little while, I guess. It belongs to a friend of mine."

The man nodded. "Mrs. Mallard."

"You know Mrs. Mallard?"

He looked down at the snow, absently cocked his head; not like he was evading the question; more like this was a matter of habit with him. "Not really *know* her. I do some work for her. She gets me to come up here sometimes, keep an eye on the place. Especially right around New Year's."

Pippa wondered why. "The cottage looked kind of deserted when I came," she said, fishing a bit.

The man gave that smile again, a nice smile, but with a sly, almost secretive expression wrapped up in it. "Mrs. Mallard doesn't ask me to *do* anything," he said. "Just keep an eye out. Like now."

This made Pippa a tiny bit uncomfortable. As though she were being spied upon.

"Yeah, well," she told the man, spinning her poker, "everything's fine here. Okay?"

This was an invitation for the guy to crank up his snowmobile and leave. Either he didn't get it, or he wasn't ready to go yet. He gazed past Pippa, toward the little cottage. Taking things in. Thinking them over.

Then he said abruptly: "My name's Spear." He stared down at his Arctic Cat, like it was an animal, requiring attention. "I might be coming out this way again, so . . . if you need anything, from in town or anywhere, maybe I could bring it to you."

Pippa knew the name Spear. It took her a few moments to remember from where. "Ah," she said. "You're Jacques'—"

"Cousin." He grinned up at her with his head tilted a little bit sideways; it gave him a knowing, foxy kind of look. "I guess you must be Pippa."

She could not very well deny it. It confused her, though. And it pissed her off. Now her cover was blown. Now she had to trust this guy, this almost total stranger—on a *snowmobile*—not to go mouthing off to everybody in town.

Well, it was done. And besides, wisely or not, she *did* trust him. There didn't seem any reason not to. She trusted him, but she was not really happy about it.

"You know what I *could* use?" she said, impulsively. "I could really use a good cup of coffee. Nice and hot."

Spear gave her the grin again. Like a fox's. He tugged off one of his thick gloves and reached into a pocket of his all-weather suit. The hand came out with a Drum tobacco can. He shook the can like a rattle.

Pippa had spent enough of her life in the kitchen to recognize the sound of dancing coffee beans.

"Never leave home without it," Spear said.

Then he was climbing right off the snowmobile without

so much as a *May I come in?* He stepped right through where the gate ought to have been (to keep intruders from barging in like this) and headed for the front door. The moose skull grinned down at him like the two of them were old hunting buddies.

"I guess you've got something to grind these with," Spear said over his shoulder.

At least, Pippa noted, he had the courtesy to stop at her doorstep, giving her time to catch up. She surrendered; she jammed the poker in the snow and said:

"Yeah. I'm pretty sure I do."

It was good to have an excuse to use her mortar and pestle, she supposed. Otherwise she would have lugged them all this way for nothing. She sat at the table pulverizing a handful of dark, heavenly-smelling coffee beans while Spear hunkered down in front of the fire, bringing a pot of melted snow to a boil.

"Don't have any eggs, do you?" he asked.

"Where would I have gotten eggs?"

She didn't mean to sound impatient, though it came out that way. It was a little hard for her to adjust to the sudden advent of this Indian guy in her life.

Spear shrugged. "I can pick some up for you. See, what you do, you toss a couple eggshells into the pot with the coffee, and it helps the grounds settle out."

She wondered if this was some authentic bit of Native American wisdom.

He winked at her. "Read that in a detective novel. Ross Thomas." He glanced around the room and said, "Looks like you can use some reading material, too."

"I've got books," said Pippa, defensively. For reasons that were unclear to her, she felt a need to straighten things out with him. She did not wish to be underestimated. "There's one called *How to Cook a Wolf.*"

Spear looked at her as though she could not possibly be serious.

She laughed. "No, really. It's not actually about cooking wolves. I don't *think* it is. I mean, I haven't read much of it, but it seems like it's some funny old lady's experiences during a war."

"Which war?"

She didn't know. "Why? Are you like, a veteran or something?"

He nodded. "Of the Gulf. Navy Reserve."

She found this moderately interesting but didn't know what to say, how to ask about it. Silence returned, to be broken a minute later by water spuming over the sides of the pot.

"You ready?" he said.

"Ready." She reached over with the mortar and scraped the grounds in. "It's kind of fun to do it this way. Primitive. But effective."

"*I* think so," he said. "Makes kind of a ritual out of it."

She shot him a look at the word *ritual*. And she was positive he caught the look, even understood it. He looked back with an expression of . . . what? Stillness and calm. Not unfriendly or anything like that. Just very private, very quiet.

They sat for a while, letting the coffee steep. Pippa was better at silences than some people—than Judith, for instance—but she was no match for this Spear. He gazed into the fire as though he could have gone on doing that for the next couple of days. In the end she caved; she just came out and said:

"So what are you doing here, really? I mean, you *can't*

have just happened to come by. You knew my name, for starters. Did Mrs. Mallard send you? Or what?"

Spear did not look at her right away, but seemed to consider the various aspects of what she was asking him, meanwhile giving the pot of coffee a gentle shake.

"I wondered," he told her finally. "Wondered about you. I wanted to see you for myself. I knew they must have gotten it wrong in the paper, but I wondered *how* wrong. In what way. I wondered if maybe you were for real."

"What do you mean?" she said. "What do you mean, *for real?*"

Spear shrugged. He stared down into the coffee as though looking for an answer there. "The witch thing. I wondered, is it like, something New Agey? Or is it like that movie? Or is it different? I was just kind of curious."

It did not seem to Pippa as though he were posing this as a question. He wanted to explain himself to her, not the other way round. So she said, "Well? Have you figured it out? Was it worth the trip?"

"It was worth the trip." Very earnest, as though it were important that she should know this. "Definitely I'm glad I came. I like you. You're a nice person, I think. And you . . . you're very pretty."

Pippa thought of something Glyph And/or had said: *I just about swallowed my gum.* She couldn't remember any guy, all the way back to Winterbelle's dad, laying down a line like this. And yet you couldn't look at Spear, the way his face was so open and his eyes unblinking, and believe he was bullshitting you, angling to get laid. It was as though he were speaking to somebody else, not you. Maybe a separate part of himself.

"Here," he said. "Java's ready."

They divided it between two smaller pots, because there were no mugs in the cottage. Pippa sipped at the hot liquid and wondered what came next. Spear looked away again. The silence was just starting to feel awkward when he began speaking. This time not so slowly, but in a manner that suggested he knew exactly what he wanted to say.

"I dropped out of law school," he told her, swirling the liquid in his little pot, "because I looked around there, and I could tell most of those guys—and I mean, the women also—they had some kind of motivation I didn't have. I not only didn't have it, I didn't *get* it. There was sort of a focus to them, a way they looked at one thing and that's all they could see—it's hard to explain. But I was never going to have it, anyway. I knew that. And what I figured was, this thing was what you needed to be a lawyer. So I quit. And everybody was disappointed. They had their hopes pinned on me, I guess. But I came back home, and nobody said anything. They just sort of looked at me like they didn't understand, and by that time I wasn't sure I understood either. You don't have any idea why I'm telling you this."

Pippa shook her head.

He nodded. "That's okay. The thing is, I could have been a lawyer—the first one ever from the Passamaquoddy people—and suddenly I wasn't going to be. And since then, I've spent a lot of time thinking about how it is that you decide what you're supposed to do with the life you've got. Do you do what feels right to you, or do you do what you figure you ought to be doing, or maybe what you have some kind of special aptitude for? There's any number of possible approaches. But I guess what I've done is, I've never been able to choose between them. I've just been *living*. It's not bad, it's what most people do. And I guess I'm still young enough to start again and do it differently. But anyhow."

He took a deep breath. He glanced sideways at Pippa, then away again.

"What's happened is, I've developed this special personal interest in people who are doing something that doesn't make sense to anybody else. Who are just, you could say, *guided* along some path through life. It's very intriguing to me, how that happens. So when I read in the paper that there was this witch—I mean, a *witch*. Imagine that. And everybody is saying how awful this person is, and we've got to take her daughter away, and she's been molesting children and sacrificing cats and whatever. I just had to wonder, where does that come from? What is it that she believes, or she wants, or she feels drawn toward, or however it might be, so that she's watched every single thing in her life get smashed up and ruined right in front of her eyes?" He paused and looked at her, eyes open and deep. "Who *are* you, I guess, is what I was curious about. Does that make sense?"

Pippa nodded, somewhat to her own surprise.

"All I wanted to do was meet you," Spear added, a little hastily. "I'm not asking you to explain anything to me. Now that I've met you, though, I'm kind of thinking a little differently than before. You're not exactly what I was expecting. Not that I was expecting anything particular, that's sort of my whole point. But now that I see how you are . . . I wonder maybe if there's something I might be able to do for you. Something to help."

Pippa reached over and patted the guy on the shoulder. "The coffee's nice," she said. "That's a help. Maybe if you come out this way again you could bring some half & half, and a couple of mugs. No styrofoam, though."

She meant this to be a little joke, to cut the tension or awkwardness that had built up. Spear nodded seriously, memorizing it.

"I've got a couple ideas," he said. "But it'll take me a little time to chase them down. What does day after tomorrow look like for you? Would it be all right if I came back then?"

"I don't think I've got any plans," said Pippa, dryly. "Come on, Spear—look at me. Do I look like my social calendar is full? You can come back any time you want. If I'm not home, just hang out and keep the wolf company."

He glanced up at the head mounted above the fireplace. "That wolf," he muttered.

"Yeah," said Pippa. "She's a tough one."

A tough one like me, she thought. A hard one to figure. She looked at Spear, and she wondered whether he really understood what he was getting into. Or whether she did either. He drained off his coffee, returning her gaze in silence. Neither of them was sure.

"Hey," she said—weirdly, but meaning it—"I love your earring."

He grinned, and he looked shy. "Thanks. It's from a loon. Magic-bird, the old people called them. I was following behind this one in a canoe, and it must have been shedding its feathers, and I just scooped them up."

"Cool," said Pippa.

"Cool, yeah," said Spear. "Cool and magic."

His face was impassive again. Opaque. Kind of maddening, Pippa thought.

She was sorry when he left.

It seemed to Pippa that she ought to do a little ceremony. An observance of the Full Moon, or something. Anything.

Maybe it was the way Spear had left her, the thing he had said about magic. Maybe she was feeling restless and cooped-up. Maybe the time was simply right. In any case, it seemed to her that she ought to attempt a bit of witchcraft.

After all, witchcraft is what witches do.

And after all, there were things that she still hoped for, wished for, dreamed of—although from here, from now, they seemed impossible to attain.

And there were blessings, many blessings, for which to thank the Goddess Freya, provider of good earthly things. Food, and warmth, and unanticipated allies. Plus other things that Pippa might not even know about. Blessings are not always obvious, especially in black times like these.

Then there was an evil enchantment to break. (Maybe Hella could help with this.)

And of course there was Winterbelle. Winterbelle to watch over. Winterbelle to worry about. Winterbelle to fight for. (A petition to the Valkyries might be helpful here.)

Anything else?

Too many things else. All the terrible fucked-up things about the world down there, below her mountain. The whole strange web of circumstance and personality and conflict and cooperation that made up a life, anybody's life. Winterbelle's sad little life. Pippa's own. Too much to do, or even to think about, in one magical working.

But that, she supposed, is where belief comes in. Faith, humility, surrender of the self—all those things you need in the single instant when the spell is cast, your wishes sent out into the ether, and the magic is left to run its deep and subtle and unknowable course.

Pippa guessed she would have to work on that.

Meantime, there were worldly matters to attend to. Jerusalem artichokes to thaw and clean. Pots to scrub. Holes in her stockings to mend. And however chewed-up the broom might be, this place desperately needed to be swept.

These chores kept her occupied—almost happily, in that she lost herself in the tasks, forgot for a time things that she never believed you could ever forget—so that before she knew it, the day had ended. Another long night had begun, and she was tired and ready to lie down and embrace it.

Life is a witch, Pippa thought, dozing off. (She was quoting Judith's favorite bumper sticker to herself.)

Life is a witch, and then you fly.

What woke her next morning—early, before dawn—was a noise so violent, so deafening and so close, that the echo of it, rattling through her consciousness, left her curled up inside the caribou hide, panting hard. It had sounded like lightning, striking very nearby. But it could not have been that. There was no storm. Everything now, in its aftermath, was extremely still, bizarrely silent; not even a rustle of air across the mountain, or a crackle of embers in the hearth. Pippa lay for what seemed a very long time, unwilling to move from her place of safety. Eventually (betrayed by her body: *again*) she needed to get up and pee.

The cottage was colder than she could remember. Overnight the temperature must have plummeted. It was about 6:00, she guessed, from the soft dusting of blue at the windows. The rounded edge of the chamber pot was rimed with icy condensate.

She piled logs on the fire but they seemed to have little effect. The flames leapt up bright but as though at a distance, or seen through thick glass.

Something strange had happened. She felt a sense of massive energies having been released, some enormous wound-up tension sprung.

She supposed she must open the door and look out. She must investigate. After all, she was a witch; this was her clearing in the Dark Wood; nothing must happen here without her knowledge. But Something out there felt scary, even so.

She pulled on every piece of clothing she owned. Layer upon layer, and still she was cold. Her fingers trembled buttoning her jeans, lacing her boots tight. For an instant, at the door, she hesitated. Then she yanked it open and went outside.

At first she saw nothing. Indistinct shapes of trees, the wooden fence, a sky so clear and pale that the stars looked dangerously close, like strange bright insects swarming around her. Trees Cracking Moon was just setting; she could glimpse it partly, a fat bright melon-yellow globe, in a gap between ancient oak trees. It looked full, but it must not be quite yet, or it would still be a few degrees higher. *Tonight, then,* she thought. Tonight she would go out and dance and howl beneath the bulging moon.

Then, in the place where the moon was going down, she saw what the loud noise had been. The shattering, violent, tension-venting clap that had wakened her, and stilled the forest.

One of the great, twisted oak trees had broken in two. Split cleanly through the trunk: one half remained standing as it had stood for maybe two hundred years; the other half lay sprawled and doomed—dying, though still frozen into dormancy—across a wide patch of her clearing.

It had just *happened*. Nothing had made it happen. No wind, no shuddering of the mountaintop. At a certain instant, for reasons only Nature Herself could know, the great oak had broken in two. Tons of living wood fell down upon the Earth—and nothing more. It was not the end of a story nor the beginning of one. It did not convey a meaning or a moral. It was a singular event, with no context at all.

Pippa went back into her cottage feeling shaken and strangely unmoored, as though her connections to the world, to all normal and reassuring features of human existence, were pulling loose. She wrapped herself in caribou hides and huddled in front of the fire for most of that day, simply trying to keep warm. Now and again she dozed, and she dreamed of Winterbelle, and she woke up sobbing, but unable to remember why. Where had she gone, in those dreams? What heartbreaking scenes had she witnessed there?

On the other side of the Earth, in secret,

Trees Cracking Moon waxed to its greatest fullness,
drawing all the waters of life
unto itself.

Witching hour.
Shape-switching hour.
Poisoned needle stitching hour.

An opening for madness, mirth and mercy.
Moon-dancing. Mother wit. Winter's fury.

Double, double, legal trouble.
Read the skies like Hoyle and Hubble.
What does Pippa know for sure?
Where do Life and Story blur?

The old tales are clear about this: a life is not crowded with bliss.

Mother is dead.
Father is absent, silent, old.
Mom's stand-in wants to ditch you in the cold.

Someday your prince will come
inside of you.
Then you won't be just a princess.
You'll be two.

Be kind to all eccentric Crones.
They might have magic in their bones.

The Beast is not what he may seem.
(What is he, then?)
The Woods are dangerous,
but not as much as Men.

Women's talk is sly and spiced with lies,
corrosive, full of molten freakish power.
But just as running water takes the easy way to ground,
seeks its level, wears the mighty mountain down,
so lies are often code
for things too terrible to say
yet real
as shadows are
in sunlit lands—Califia. Midday.

    Other things the tales recall:
Good girls sleep where ashes fall.
Brooms don't hang there on the wall;
they zoom.
Plus help you sweep the room.

Fairies don't favor the already blessed.
Godmothers come to the poor and distressed.

You can get so hungry you want to eat
gingerbread trim. A genuine Dark Wood treat.

A cauldron simply means a pot.
The only kitchen thing you've got.

Witches are ugly, yes:
from malnutrition. Badly dressed
and unbecoming,
they seldom bathe because they don't have indoor plumbing.
Wild-eyed and thin,
they'll never fit in.
The righteous Village takes this for a sin.

There's nothing like a rousing mob
to make you miss your slave-wage job.

Dresses might have monsters in them.
Or maybe not.
Trials are nice if you can win them.
Be thankful if at least you've got
   1 pot to pee in
   1 door to lock
   1 yard where you can dance at 12 o'clock,

the witching hour.
Bitching hour.
Hidden treasure snitching hour.

Throw roots and berries, all you can gather,
into the pot. Stir lightly. Boil until a lather
forms at your mouth.
Then strip your clothes off.
Fling your arms wide.
(This might freeze your toes off
but it toughens up your hide.)
Show the Moon your body.
Feel the blood that surges through your veins

run down and melt into the Earth.
(Never mind about the stains.)

You've had your Ball.
You took your fall.
It's only midnight for an hour.

Then, too soon, The End.
No gowns left to mend.
No needles to prick;
no distaff to stick
in someplace dark and sour.

Is there a moral here at all?
Life is a bitch.
Don't fuck with a witch.

> *She's just a crazy woman, maybe.*
> *But with power.*

In the east, for Freya—goddess of plenty, of sexual pleasure, of soft mattresses and summertime—Pippa laid a pile of winterberries, gathered from the forest. Red as blood.

In the south, for Joulupukki—"Yule-buck," the white-maned shaman, bearer of gifts and dispenser of punishment, the *real* Santa Claus—she set down her little frog fetish, the most precious gift she had. White as snow.

In the west, for Frey—the male twin, a right jolly old elf, stroking his eternal hard-on, spurting fount of fertility—she arranged sprigs of mountain laurel, still hanging on to last summer's withered seed heads. Green as holly.

And in the north (the quarter of danger), for Hella—queen of mist and fog; keeper of terrible secrets and lost souls; outcast and enemy of those blustering warrior gods with alcohol-dependency issues—Pippa cautiously set down a scrap of oak wood, snapped from the mighty broken tree, into which she had carved and stained with soot the elder rune *Hagalaz*:

N

— a symbol variably taken to signify hail; the Hag; the Underworld; reversal of fortune; the dark aspect of Woman; mortal danger; and witchcraft. Black as ebony.

"Take that," Pippa said, addressing all the deities at once, because she felt hurried and self-conscious. "Accept these gifts, and please listen to what I'm going to ask you. Please. It's really cold out here so like, if I forget any proprieties or whatever, I hope it's okay. So. Anyhow."

She pulled out her butane lighter, moved clockwise at a rapid shuffle from one quarter to the next, and finally— due north—she turned to the center, where she had built a pyre of fallen branches as tall as her hips. She declared:

"I light this fire in the name of my beautiful little elf Winterbelle. May its light shine brightly so that her spirit can find its way through the darkness."

The butane flared and the freeze-dried wood caught readily. As flames gathered force, she added cuttings of white cedar, for their fresh and pungent smell.

"Unfriendly Beings," she called sternly, "be gone from here. Let my circle be cleansed and purified. Now go."

She picked up the old broom from where it lay and swept the air with it. White smoke swirled, like a galaxy in the early stage of formation. The night air was as clear as ice, almost perfectly still. Snapping sounds from the fire shot out through it like tiny detonations.

"Now I call upon helpful Beings to draw near, to enter this circle and join with us. Join with me and Winterbelle.

Bring your strength to share with us and accept the gifts of our magic and our *prana* and . . . I guess that's all I can think of right now. But please, *come.*"

She went clockwise around the circle again, partly to keep moving, partly to build up a magical charge. The right-hand turning, called by witches *deosil,* is supposed to concentrate subtle energies. The left-hand turning, *widdershins,* disperses them. You go deosil to cast a spell and widdershins to lift one. Beyond that, Pippa wasn't sure of the proper ceremonial order of things. When she had done rituals with women friends she always felt like the person who gets picked last for the softball team. Some of the women would be given roles in the ceremony—invocations to offer, magical tools to deploy—but never Pippa. Because as soon as the ritual got started she would grow spaced-out and disoriented. It was almost like getting seasick from being heaved around by a boat; only here it was the Earth itself that was moving, motion rising out of the ground.

She knew she was strange that way.

Tonight she felt no different. Just colder; and more profoundly alone.

The fire rose as high as her head. It was hot, but not with the penetrating, cozy heat of a fireplace. More a wild, raging heat, leaping out at you. Slightly dangerous, out of anyone's control. Like magic; real Magic. Do you dare to approach it? Then hang on to your ass.

Pippa took off her clothes. She started from the top, warmer parts first: hat and coat and sweater. Then boots. Then blouse. Skirt. Long wool socks. Underwear.

Skyclad now. Wrapped in nothing but deathly blackness. She became a Night Thing once more. Her body slipped into a dance of fear and excitement and hope and trepidation, twirling and hopping deosil, always deosil.

"Dance with me!" she called to whatever helpful Beings

may have gathered. (She was aware of none; but you can't assume too much about your ability to perceive such Things.)

Her naked feet in the snow became numb with cold, and a couple of times she lost her balance. Losing your balance, of course, in the largest sense, is exactly what you want to do. She leapt and spun with greater abandon and tried to think of a song to sing, a melody, even a bare rhythm of syllables. She reached hard into her brain and out popped a short tune from one of her Christmas Revels tapes. (Christmas again. No escaping it.)

"Light in darkness," she shouted, not very musically, *"let us sing.*

> *"Brightness now returning.*
> *Dum, da dum da, dark and cold!*
> *Now with hmm mm burning!"*

She remembered *most* of it. She hoped the Higher Powers would cut her some slack.

> *"Da da da da, empty,*
> *And its fire forever spent,*
> *Then the flame sprang up anew,*
> *For da da dum, yearning!"*

A rousing good tune—though if she remembered correctly, the original lyrics had something to do with danger from a strange armed man.

She sang it again. And again and again.

The fire leapt and Pippa danced. The fire danced and Pippa leapt. And her limbs grew distant, her skin felt more a part of the outer night than her inner, genuine self. Her hair flew all around her head.

Suddenly she stopped. She stood with her back to the cottage, staring through the flames into the blackness beyond.

She thought she felt the presence of something new. Or maybe someone?

"Hello?" she said, too quietly. "Is anyone there?"

Then she thought, Of course *Someone* is there. She had spent the past half hour attracting every spirit on the mountaintop. And mountaintops are, by all accounts, the places where spirits prefer to hang out while visiting the earthly plane.

"You are welcome!" Pippa called, though her quavering voice did not sound too sure of it. "If you come in friendship, to help Winterbelle, then you're welcome to join us."

The sound came again. An indistinct sort of thing, like the muffled chime of a bell. Pippa felt a rattling chill pass through her and it was not just because the air was colder than a witch's tit. Though there was that as well.

"Hello?" again.

The Sound came closer.

This wasn't what Pippa had expected. All the many ceremonies she'd done, all the times she'd invoked beneficent gods, chummy devas, wood nymphs, brownies, pukkas— the lot—she had never really, truly, deep down believed that one of them was going to, like, show up for the party. Maybe in *spirit*. Enter your consciousness, alter your mood. But not like *this*.

She grabbed her broom. She clutched it sideways in both hands, like Robin Hood ready to stave off Little John. (And failing, if she remembered.)

From the far side of the burning pyre, out where black night merged with even blacker forest, *Something* crept in on feet much bigger than a cat's. It came with a huffling noise. The chiming sound grew clearer and louder. Then dimly, outlined by fire—insubstantial as an aura—Pippa saw a Shape. And the Shape was passing through the space where the gate had been, and still damned well ought to be.

It reached the edge of the circle, exactly opposite Pippa. It began to move around.

Pippa moved, too, circling, keeping the fire between them.

Then she thought, You chicken. What are you running from?

Was she *serious* about this? About really doing magic? Or was this whole witch thing just some kind of pathetic make-believe?

Pippa turned and stood her ground.

She was naked, clutching her broom, ready for anything. At least, as ready as she was ever going to get.

"If you've come to help Winterbelle"—this time surprising herself, her voice much steadier—"then come on over here. Let me have a look at you."

Footsteps (bigger than a cat's, *way* bigger) crunched in snow. The ringing sound came again, high-pitched and silvery. Pippa stared through the penumbra at the edge of the fire, where a blurry form was beginning, just beginning, to solidify.

One heartbeat later, she found herself looking straight-on, with nothing in between, at the huge yellow eyes of *The Beast*.

She gasped.

The Beast halted.

It was a wolf.

Of course a wolf. A big, *big* wolf. Pippa did not know how large wolves were supposed to get, but this was bigger than that.

In its mouth, like a scrap of flesh, it carried a leather strap, from which hung a silver bell—a *sleigh* bell, Pippa thought—that gleamed like a tethered star.

The Beast took another step, and for an instant its head bent low and its eyes appeared to cloud, as though that simple motion caused it pain.

It was a big *old* wolf.

Its pelt had gone silver-white. Its legs were thin except for the joints, which had swollen arthritically. Its back was slightly bowed.

Still, you had to marvel. The way it carried itself, even now: great haunches muscular yet, neck thickly furred and held proudly forward, tail glossy and thick. The Beast had a kingly bearing, and even kings grow elderly, but their power does not necessarily slacken because of that. Pippa made a little bow in its direction, a gesture of respect.

"Welcome," she told the Beast. "You saved my life before, didn't you? Thank you. Thank you so much. I've been wanting to meet you, to tell you that."

The Beast lowered its head, then raised it again, looking up at her somewhat at an angle, as though its neck could not bend up all the way. No more howling at the moon for *this* guy.

For an instant, something about the Beast struck her as familiar. The way it carried itself; the way it looked up at her from a stooped or twisted position.

"Rrrrr rrrg *aawwwrrr*," the Beast seemed to say.

So much like human words, though Pippa did not understand them.

The effort of speaking (or whatever passes for speaking among Beasts) appeared to exhaust it. Its head dropped again. The sleigh bell pealed one lonely chime. With a forepaw the Beast scratched the snow.

Like he's fidgeting, thought Pippa. Waiting for something. For . . . an answer?

"Sorry," she said—unthinkingly moving closer, leaning down solicitously—"were you asking me something? Is there—I mean, can I *do* something for you? Do you need like, help or anything?"

The Beast said, "Gwwrrr rrr *nnnnggg* wwwr."

There was no telling, Pippa thought.

Then the yellow eyes gazed up at her and her own eyes locked on, and understanding shot through her with the clarity of daylight.

"You're tired!" she exclaimed. "You're tired of traipsing around in the snow. You need to rest and warm up a little. That's what you're saying, isn't it?"

A change came immediately over the Beast. It looked relieved, or so she thought.

"You poor thing—out here all alone in the middle of the forest. Look, would you like to, ah . . ."

She paused. Did she really want to do this?

She had set out to help *somebody* tonight. And if Winterbelle couldn't be here, then maybe in some strange karmic way Pippa had been offered a substitute. Maybe.

"You want to come in?" Pippa asked the Beast. "I don't have much to give you, but at least you can get out of the cold."

The Beast made no further effort to speak. It loped slowly, though with a certain dignity, a stately bearing, toward the cottage. The sleigh bell chimed slowly to mark its passage.

Pippa scooped up her clothes and went after it. She had to hustle because

the Wolf was already
at her door.

The Beast was asleep when Spear Pollock, snowmobile enthusiast, sputtered to a halt in front of the witch's cottage deep in the Dark Wood. He surveyed the scene of last night's ritual—a mound of ashes, a circle packed by Pippa's bare feet in the snow, her four humble gifts to the Old Northern Gods. His eyes lingered on the small frog fetish for a few moments before rising to meet Pippa's.

She had been standing outside for over an hour, waiting for him.

She no longer minded the cold. The morning was sunny, the sky so deeply blue that it seemed to be molded of thick and durable acrylic.

Spear pretended not to see the change in her. He flicked his eyes back toward the Arctic Cat, pulling a manila folder out of a compartment under the dashboard and approaching her with his gaze locked downward, near her feet, where you could see the lower runs of the wretched black pantyhose. He held the folder out where she could take it, and she did. In the process, he really could not help glancing at Pippa's face, and the way he reacted—as if she spooked him—could in other circumstances have been funny.

A civil person, Spear forced a game smile. "You've done something to your hair," he ventured.

She said, "Ha."

The elder rune *Hagalaz* had worked its magic on her. (That, and Mrs. Mallard's makeup kit.) Overnight, Pippa had turned into a Crone.

With the Beast sacked out on her own bear mat, before her fire, Pippa had sat awake through all the hours of darkness. She had been too keyed-up to sleep. Besides, the Beast snored. He—of course it was a *he*—had a great big snout and he snored at unbelievable volume.

Toward dawn, she got an idea.

She took out the Santa Fe knife, her ceremonial blade, and set to work on her hair. What she had in mind was sort of a *Friends* do, except using ashes in place of baby powder. She had no idea what she ended up with. The only way you could approximate a Magic Mirror in this place was to melt snow in a flat pan and lean over it, and even then you couldn't trust the results. Water is a tricky medium—not for nothing associated with the Moon and with the loonier aspects of Woman—and who knew when some bedeviling vision might float up from its depths?

As for the wardrobe, that had been a no-brainer. Everything Pippa owned looked like crap now. Ditto the unscrubbed face. Triplo the banged-up fingers with dirt (and, Goddess knows, maybe rabbit guts) under the nails. Aschenputtel to the max.

Spear was being a sport, though. He nodded courteously and stood there, jiggling a hand in a pocket of his allweather suit. Like, wake up and hear the coffee beans.

Pippa reached out and touched his arm, gratefully, and—*bless him, O Ancient Ones!*—Spear didn't flinch. He shot her a smile, looking pleased, like a little kid who needed reassurance but wasn't sure how to ask for it.

She told him, "It's just this thing I'm doing today, all right?" But that wasn't quite enough, so she added: "Look, it's a disguise. Sort of. Or in a way I think it's the Real Me, and the *other* way I looked before, that's what the disguise was."

Spear eyed her thoughtfully. Then he seemed to decide that, of the various ways you could spin this in your head, the simplest and best was just to accept it.

"Check that out," he said, pointing at the manila folder. "It's something your lawyer ought to see. If you've got one. In the paper they were quoting Arthur Torvid, but I wasn't sure . . ." He trailed off, uncertainly.

"Sure what?"

Spear shrugged. "Whether he's for real or not. I mean, I don't know the guy. But my impression is that it wouldn't be past him to call the paper and *claim* to be representing you when he'd never met you in his life."

Pippa sighed. "I kind of have that impression, too. But he's my lawyer. For better or worse."

Spear accepted that, too. He pointed at the folder. "Then show him that. Or just tell him: Bonnie Abbott, Fifth Circuit Court of Appeals, Virginia. Unanimous ruling. He can look it up."

Pippa peeked inside the folder and saw about 40 sheets that appeared to have been Xeroxed out of law books, almost black with teensy print.

"Bonnie Abbott," she repeated.

"A Witch," said Spear. "Or so she identified herself."

Pippa gave him what she supposed was a demented smile. "You can never tell, can you?" she said. "Not till the Hour comes."

"I guess." He turned sideways, glancing out toward the place where the great oak had split in two. In his ear today he wore a tiny leaping fish, carved out of malachite, which made a nice contrast with the burnt sienna of his neck. "So hey—you want some coffee? I brought special stuff today. And two new mugs—FedEx from the Sundance catalog. You'll like them, I think."

Pippa felt all at once so filled with warmth toward this good-hearted man; she would have hugged him but she wasn't sure how he would have felt about that. What with the ashes and body odor and all.

"Well, to tell you the truth," she said, "I've got kind of a . . . a houseguest. An *unusual* houseguest. He just sort of showed up in the middle of the night and I took him in."

Spear glanced up at the sky. Not a response Pippa would have predicted.

He said, "Was last night the Full Moon?" Sounding worried.

She nodded.

"*Damn*," said Spear. "Hold on a sec."

He trotted back to the snowmobile and popped open a tiny trunk. Out of this he pulled a leather satchel, similar to Pippa's makeup bag, only larger. He came back shaking his head.

"One of these days I'm going to get organized," he vowed.

"You and me both," she said.

He looked at her in a funny way—as though he was seeing right through everything gross and dirty and weird about her. Seeing all the way in to something that even she was hardly mindful of. Then he faintly and privately smiled.

He said, "So, is he awake yet?"

Pippa said, "Who?" But then figured, Obviously this guy has the whole thing mapped. Deal with it. "Not the last time I checked. What's all that stuff?"

"His clothes," said Spear. "Mrs. Mallard sent them up.

If you hadn't reminded me, I would totally have forgotten. What a mess *that* would have been."

"His . . . clothes?" said Pippa. But she figured, when magic starts brewing, don't jiggle the pot. So she hung close to Spear while he marched toward the cottage. And when he opened the door, they discovered the Beast warming himself before the hearth, wide-awake now, wrapped up in a caribou hide.

Only, he was not a Beast any longer.

"Norbert Thiess," Spear said, "I'd like to introduce Pippa Rede. Although I guess you two have already met. Sort of."

"More than once," said the small, withered-up-looking, hunched-over and very elderly man.

He was dressed now in an old-fashioned suit. *Really* old-fashioned. Like out of Edith Wharton. He sat in a funny posture at the table—stiff, but with his torso bent forward in a way that suggested a tendency toward the horizontal. Pippa *had* met him before.

"Near the flower shop," she said. "Out on the sidewalk. You gave me a rose."

"And *in* the store, as well, my dear," Mr. Thiess said. His voice was very proper. Courtly. "You sold me roses, many roses. One at a time—quite a nuisance. I admired your hands. Those honest, hardworking fingers. I could tell that you had the proper spirit."

Pippa thought about this. (Proper spirit for *what?* And how could he tell by looking at her fingers?) She and Spear were hunched down by the fire, though even from there you did not exactly look *up* at poor Mr. Thiess.

Let's face it: there was an obvious question here. But Pippa did not know how you go about asking somebody if he is like, a *werewolf*. On the other hand, it was kind of hard to make small talk while this issue was hanging out there.

She tried this: "So, you're a friend of Mrs. Mallard's?"

"A friend," he said—repeating her statement, not exactly confirming it. He gave her a tolerant smile. Then he sighed—long and with evident feeling. "Her family and mine . . . have a very old, and not a particularly pleasant, association."

He craned his head upward. Toward the wolf's head, mounted above the fireplace.

"I suppose you could say," Mr. Thiess resumed, "that Madeleine Mallard has long felt a need, not on her own behalf, but on her late husband's—who was not a *bad* man, let me assure you; something of a sporting fanatic; but that is not uncommon, is it?—a *need*, as I say, to make amends."

Pippa couldn't stand it. It was like waiting for the verb in a German sentence. Pointing at the wolf's head, she asked him, "Is this some relative of yours?"

Spear winced.

Mr. Thiess appeared wistful for a moment, grave and melancholy, but the cloud passed. He gave Pippa a brief nod.

"My—as I like to say—Task," he told her, in his refined way, "is a matter of heredity. A burden we Thiesses bear. Not all of us. One in seven, or thereabouts. There is never any doubt which one it will be. The usual signs—the caul, the ominous birth, mother dying and so forth—invariably are present. But it is not until one reaches a certain age that the Task presses itself upon one. I like to draw an analogy with the Navy Reserve."

"The what?" said Pippa.

Spear made a gesture with his shoulders. "He got that from me. You know, I was telling him about my weekend-warrior gig. And the two weeks every summer when you go on active duty for training. He sort of made the connection."

"The *connection*," said Mr. Thiess, a bit huffy, "is obvious. The obligatory fortnight. One's duty to perform. Slip off the civvies, get into battle dress. Oh, yes—I know exactly."

He sighed and lowered his head. The weight of it all.

Spear and Pippa exchanged glances.

"Except Mr. Thiess goes on duty in the middle of the winter," Spear told her in a low voice. "The twelve days of Christmas."

"Christmas?" she said, incredulous.

"More or less. Actually it's a lunar thing. Actually, I don't know what the fuck it is. Mrs. Mallard just rings me up and says, *the Time has come.*" He shrugged. "Hey—it's a way to earn money in January, right? That's all I need to know."

Mr. Thiess raised his head. To an extent. And looked at the two of them. The sight of them, huddled together by the fire, seemed to cheer him. He allowed his head to droop back down and appeared to be at the point of dozing off.

"But *what* duty?" Pippa whispered. "I mean, what *do* you do for twelve days in the middle of winter as a . . ."

"You may as well come out and say it," Mr. Thiess told her, without looking up. "As a *wolf*."

"But not an ordinary wolf," said Spear.

The old gentleman gave a quite proper, modest, and exceedingly fiendish little smile, complete with rakish waggle of the brow.

"I put Evil," he said, "to rout."

Spear grinned, showing straight teeth. "He does that."

Pippa looked at the two of them. Men, she thought. Men and wolves. What's the difference, when you come down to it? Wolves have a deeper sense of family loyalty, is about all.

Spear Pollock stood up, dusted ashes off his pants, and said, "All right, cowpokes. It's about time for me and Mr. Thiess here to get saddled up for the ride into town."

Pippa stood quickly, too. She followed him to the door, barely a step behind. Snapping at his heels.

"How many people can ride on that thing?" she said.

He paused. "Two, pretty well. Why?"

"How about three? I'm small. So's Mr. Thiess. It would be like squeezing onto a toboggan. The more the merrier."

Spear frowned, mystified. "You going somewhere?"

She gave him her best witch's smile. "Over the river and through the woods," she said. "To my lawyer's apartment. What do you think I got all dressed up for?"

Once the Wild Ride was under way, she kind of wished she hadn't thought of Edith Wharton.

There was no good way to get three people on Spear's Arctic Cat. So they settled for a not-so-good way, which involved Pippa scrunching up against the dashboard with Spear hanging all over her like a poor choice of outerwear, and Mr. Thiess compacted but relatively comfortable at the rear.

She had not expected the thing to vibrate so hard. Not at all tobogganlike. More like a tractor going *way* too fast through a bumpy field.

Still, the trip down the mountain was a blast. And a beauty. Scrunched low as she was, Pippa watched the land-scape rush by from what would have been about the level of her waist. Trees looked huge and mighty; shadows long and black. The snow was sculpted into a fantastic land-scape of hillocks and pastures and gorges; and the longer you looked, the more different colors emerged there. Pippa supposed that after a while your eyes got bored with seeing white, nothing but white, and started to amplify what tiny traces of color were latent in the microscopic crystal lattices of the snowflakes. Each one different; or was that an old wives' tale?

So you had blue in many subtle variations—her favorite among these being a soft lilac-gray that lay deep in the swales around tree trunks, where the wind had carved graceful bowls. Proof that snow is a feminine medium, as much as water in its liquid, changeable state. And ice too: because ice means immobility, which means Death, the Hag's ultimate dominion.

And you had pink. Sunset-pink at midday, in exposed places where the Sun touched down on ridges of snow, and the snow silently prophesied its falling.

And green: a startling, unseasonable tint. Somnolent green, like the cold northern sea. Some kind of crystalline memory there? Reflection of needles overhead? Another prophecy?

And deep, deep down—if you knew how to look—there was black. In the midst of all the whiteness, black. As though you were peering straight through the snow and seeing beneath it, underlying everything, the fertile Earth, dark Womb of all things, Mother of mysteries, and your own eventual grave.

With her eyes open or with them closed, while the snowmobile raced along, and Spear Pollock's strong arms clutched the wheel around her shoulders, and the wind beat like raven wings across her cheeks, those were the things—the colors, the strange forms emerging—that Pippa saw:

At midday, darkness. The color of dried blood.
In frozen winter, the green of leaves.

Beneath the almighty Sun, trillions of frozen prisms.
Where nothing flowered, the fragile violet-blue of lilacs.

Contradictions. Vast imbalances that turn out in the end, impossibly, to be in perfect equipoise.
Such things a witch understands.
From this understanding, she derives her power.

Seeing how the snowflake absorbs the Sun—melting before it, while draining away its heat and its fury—the witch learns how to quench destructive passions.
Remembering lilacs, she believes in spring.
Sensing blood-black beneath the sheep's coat of white, she touches her hidden Self.
Perceiving green, she holds in her heart the secrets of rebirth, cleansing, new growth, a return of the good: the gifts of the Maiden.
And seeing all the colors together—their implausible harmony, their blending without distinction, their blurring, their abundance, their beauty—she knows that no matter how *little* she knows, however small and weak a thing she is, however low and fallen her place, she nonetheless stands firmly

upon the Ground to which
all things must
in the end
flow.

Pippa passed through the village in the harsh light of a winter afternoon.

Spear had let her off at the edge of the state park, where the plowed roads began. Mr. Thiess rode a bit further. To where? No one asked, or said. Pippa guessed it was part of the Mystery. She guessed it was more fun that way.

The streets were crowded—or seemed so, after the profound solitude of the mountaintop. People drove by in their Troopers and their rusted-out winter-beaters. They hurried along the sidewalks toward their separate destinations—heads down, single-minded—as though each were acting out his or her part in a long and complicated drama. Only they seemed unaware that it *was* a part; a single thread in the cloth. They had forgotten (or never known, or even wondered) what the greater, all-encompassing Drama was about. How it had started, where it would end. They had played their parts so long and so dutifully that they no longer made a distinction between their costumes and their true Selves, hidden inside.

Pippa had been like that. Exactly like these people around her. The only difference, maybe, was that her own

333

role never had been more than a walk-on—no speeches to make, no plot twists to set in motion. And you couldn't really take such a role too seriously. But now she had shucked off even that, and left the theater in midact, and traded her costume, such as it was (Minimum-Wage Shop Girl), for a witch's rags.

Now she was free to walk these enchanted streets unencumbered. To breathe the air flowing off the magic mountain. To live the precious and irreplaceable Life that she had been gifted with. Simply to *be*.

Pippa felt such a sense of freedom, of unboundedness, that she wanted to step up to one of her fellow pedestrians (anyone, picked at random) and give that person a whack on the arm. And shout, *Can't you see it? Can't you feel the Magic?* But she figured this was just a sort of temporary high; a run-in with the law would bring her right down again. Anyway, the tool of choice for such awakenings probably was the wand (preferably hazelwood), and she wasn't packing one of those.

She had to chuckle.

What strangeness! she thought. What marvels! What horror!

A couple of people looked sideways at her, but they turned their heads away again immediately.

They were scared of her.

Maybe they thought she was going to hit them up for money. (She could use it.) Or they were afraid she was infested with some unsavory hygienic embarrassment. (It was possible.) Or else they simply wished not to see her, not to know that such people still existed in the world.

No doubt about it: Pippa was one scary, ugly-as-sin, black-cloaked, hunched-over (because of the stuff in her backpack), crazy-eyed (because she did, indeed, feel crazed), curse-uttering specimen of a witch. And nobody wanted to get anywhere close to *that*.

It was as good as being invisible, without the fuss and bother of actually dematerializing.

It was Magic, of a very sneaky sort. The kind Pippa was best at.

She crept into the old house at the gloomy end of Ash Street without knocking, taking no special precautions. The Magnavox rumbled in the parlor, and Pippa figured she had an even chance of making it upstairs and out again without getting caught.

The dining room table was covered with dishes from at least four separate meals, along with dozens of ants. "Chew your food carefully," she warned them.

The kitchen was lifeless and cold.

The back stairs creaked, but Pippa didn't care. Maybe she was getting carried away with this feeling of invisibility. Maybe at this point nothing really truly mattered to her. Or only one thing—the same precious thing that had always mattered—and it wasn't the risk of discovery.

When she reached the door of Winterbelle's room she stopped.

She said, "Oh, *no*."

The room lay in shambles. Drawers had been yanked out and their contents spilled all over the floor and left lying there. The cupboard bed, of course, was gone, as well as the contents of the bookshelf—fairy tales, Dr. Seuss, a few years worth of *Highlights* and *Ranger Rick* and *How About Magic?* The closet was ransacked. Pictures had been yanked off the wall, and at least one of them (a beautiful reproduction of *Titania Among the Fairies*, by J. Simmons) was missing.

So this is how it works, Pippa thought. They bust in

and they steal pieces of your life away to use as evidence
against you. *Here, Your Honor,* she imagined the prosecutor
saying, *you see a bunch of totally naked little demons. Proof that
this unclean woman has a compact with Satan, not to mention
unnatural sexual appetites.*

She tiptoed through the wreckage trying not to care. It
was hard, but in her new, invulnerable condition she could
almost manage it. From one pile of clothes she plucked a
nice plaid wool dress, from another a pink silk blouse—
both Winterbelle's. And a pair of little tights, and satin
ballroom slippers.

This was insane but it was of overriding importance
to her.

If she meant to bring Winterbelle home—and she did
mean that, no matter what kind of magic it took, no matter
where "home" turned out to be—then the girl was going
to need something warm and pretty to change into. Something that the wicked fingers of her captors hadn't
touched.

Pippa stared down into her daughter's mirror, propped
at a weird angle against the far wall, and she pointed her
witch's finger at it, and she commanded:

"So may it be."

The witch in the mirror looked as though her mind was
pretty well made up.

From behind her, out in the hall, a voice said:

"I should have known."

Pippa turned to see her great-aunt Eulace standing there
with the remote control in her hand. Eulace was breathing
hard, perhaps from the exertion of mounting the stairs.
Her face flushed red, and her fingers were white and
trembling, and if Pippa had been in the mood, she would
have urged the old woman to sit down and breathe a little
until her blood pressure dropped.

Eulace said, "I *told* them you'd come back." She gestured with the remote control as though to render Pippa helpless by means of the dreaded PAUSE spell.

Pippa smiled (which appeared to spook Eulace). She said, "I bet they were happy to hear that. Now if you'll please just *get out of my way*, I'll be leaving again."

Eulace gasped. Pippa's voice seemed to drive her backward, up against the wall, making it difficult for her to breathe.

"I'll call the police," Eulace choked out. "I'll call them right now."

"Tell them I said Hi," said Pippa, breezing past, into the hall.

She reached the stairway. Eulace was lurching off in the opposite direction—toward her bedroom, behind whose drawn curtains she kept a telephone programmed to speed-dial 911.

"*Stop,*" Pippa said.

Eulace shouted, "You won't stop me!" But she stopped anyway, clutching the doorframe, panting.

"And tell them also," Pippa said, quiet and cool, "they shouldn't have taken my daughter's bed. Tell them that's *way* bad karma. Okay?"

Eulace's face was so puffed-up with blood and fury that tears squeezed out of her eyes. She opened her mouth and closed it, like a fish fatally breathing air.

When Pippa reached the back door she found her old broom standing where it had always stood. She ran her fingers along the worn, comfortable handle, and it seemed to her that she could feel a definite energy there.

"Okay, old girl," she told the broom. "Time to fly."

She moved at a deliberate pace (so as not to look like a fugitive), using the broom as a walking stick, through the neighborhood behind the old mill, where some of the houses were gentrified and others were dilapidated. She passed elderly ladies shuffling out for the newspaper, and children racing home from school. Dogs barked at her. She shook her broom at them. One woman gathered in three small children like a mama bird enfolding hatchlings under her wing and bustled them out of Pippa's path.

"They look so *tasty*," Pippa told her.

The woman shooed her children around a corner.

In the distance, a siren wailed. Pippa paused and glanced around and then started walking again, no faster.

In front of Mrs. Mallard's house, she hesitated. The police had come here before. This might be one of the first places they checked.

She burrowed into her backpack, which was now stuffed with Winterbelle's clothes, along with everything else. The siren fell quiet. Then, almost immediately, another one started up—a different vehicle, racing down yet another street. Her fingers found (at last!) the stout leather strap that held the key to the cottage. She ran up the sidewalk and jammed it into Mrs. Mallard's mailbox. Then—sheer impulse—she hoisted herself on tiptoe until her face was at a level with the door-knocker: the verdigrised duck with its drooping spectacles. She closed her eyes and whispered.

"Bless you—bless you a million times"
and kissed the door knocker softly
and got out of there.

For a time—long enough to walk three blocks to the river, then turn left onto Park Street—Pippa heard no sirens. There was very little traffic, and she guessed the shift change at the credit-card center had ended and everybody was back home, safe and snug (or tucked in their little cubicles, dialing up people who were trying to cook dinner, asking them why their monthly payment was late. *Just to piss you off*, Pippa wanted to tell them).

I've got to get rid of this anger, she told herself.

But the anger wasn't ready to leave her yet. It was like a force unto itself, an autonomous Power, and it had a few more butts left to kick.

The sign wagging in a cold, westerly breeze—nothing that a tough witch like Pippa even noticed—read:

ALLISON RHINUM
CERTIFIED THERAPIST
ABUSE AND RECOVERY ISSUES
"IT'S NEVER TOO LATE TO HAVE A HAPPY CHILDHOOD"

Pippa found that the snappy little slogan made no sense to her now. Once childhood is over, it's over. You've got exactly one chance to get it right—or two, if you count the next higher whirl of the spiral, when like a shaman you leave your child's body behind and morph into a mommy. And then it's not *your* childhood anymore.

So, Doctor Allison Rhinum, thought Pippa. You have made an important mistake here. At least one.

She lifted her broom and gave the sign a good clean thump. Like a pane of glass, the signboard shattered into fragments, each one no larger than the tiny dollhouse the Doctor had stolen out of Winterbelle's hands. And Winterbelle, true to her elf self, had stolen back again.

Pippa turned away. She left this place behind and vowed never to come back, forever and ever. (But you know how that goes.)

She passed on to the center of the village, where a footbridge spanned the dark, churning river, and there she crossed over to Tannery Lane. Behind her a heavy truck rumbled by, scattering rock salt. The salt would melt the snow, creating a briny residuum that would sluice off into people's yards and do serious harm to their evergreens.

She must have gotten distracted, fuming about this. (That anger, still.) Stepping across the road, over to the side where the Old Tannery cantilevered perilously over the riverbank, she failed to hear a Jeep Cherokee scrunching up behind her, until it was too late. *Much* too late to get out of its way. The driver blasted the horn—he had been blasting for several seconds, now that she thought about it—but until this very instant when she froze in place, staring across her shoulder and locking eyes with the guy at the wheel, he seemed never to have considered the possibility that she would fail to hear and to prudently yield the right-of-way. Now he was facing a potentially serious liability situation as his Cherokee (off-white, windows covered with decals from numerous ski resorts—strange what details you fix on at these moments) went into a skid and hurtled toward Pippa while slowly, gracefully spinning counterclockwise. Widdershins, the direction of banishment.

Pippa recognized in no time at all two very distinct things:

1. There was no way she was not going to get hit.
2. The driver of the car was Mark Portion, the newspaper guy.

It was neither of these individually, but rather the two of them together, that really irked her. Run over and killed by *Mark Portion*, of all people, who had already done his best to screw up what there was of her life. It was just too much.

(Bear in mind: a Jeep Cherokee is VERY QUICKLY

skidding straight at Pippa during the time it takes her to think this.)

She plunged her broom down, handle-first. She threw her weight onto the shaft like a pole vaulter, kicking off with her feet—focusing every smidgen of her anger and her stubborn resolve and her love for Winterbelle and her resentment of Mark Portion into a single, concentrated exertion—

and she flew

up over the hood of the Cherokee

as it slid beneath her,

its fender snapping the broom like a wooden safety match and

its windshield slamming painfully into her shoulder,

hurling her higher through the air

then down

into a small mountain of snow and rock salt at the edge of the street;

while in the meantime, the Cherokee kept on spinning, sliding, horn blasting, Mark Portion cursing, across the street, over the curb, onto the sidewalk, through a flimsy guardrail,

and down

into the black

and rapidly flowing river.

It was baking hot inside the Old Tannery and all the stairwell lights had burned out. Pippa had to grope her way to the third floor in nearly total darkness. Her element precisely.

She suspected her arm was broken. Or at least severely sprained or contused or whatever happens to arms when Jeep Cherokees slam into them. With every step, a bolt of agony shot up from her elbow to her shoulder and then straight into her brain.

"*Ohhhh*," moaned Pippa, dragging herself from step to step.

She felt deeply, profoundly honored.

Like Tyr, the old purveyor of justice, she had sacrificed an arm for the Higher Good.

Like Odin, the all-wise, blind in one eye, she had become asymmetrical.

And like Hella, poor thing, she looked worse every minute.

She shoved open the door to Arthur Torvid's office-cum-apartment with her good shoulder, stepped inside, and bumped it firmly shut.

It was about 4:00 p.m. The almightily smug Sun had been taken down a peg or two since Pippa climbed off the snowmobile. Now it was reduced to a grody orange blur outside the window. Inside, the office was quiet except for the hum of a computer fan, and dark except for the glow of its screen, across which fractal patterns elaborated themselves like mutant snowflakes.

"Arthur?" Pippa spoke into the gloom.

The gloom seemed to whisper or to rustle a bit, as though trying to avoid a direct answer. She tried to be patient; but then figured, even if she *were* completely invisible, purged of anger, and marked by the Old Gods—and she had no assurance of any of these things—there were, nonetheless, *cops* on her trail.

"*Arthur*, damn it," she said. "Are you back there or what?"

She inserted herself through the narrow gap between a filing cabinet and the *Easy Rider* poster, into a hallway. The air hung still and damp, smelling of aftershave and undone laundry. Pippa saw open doors but no lights. She stepped into the first door she came to.

The room consisted mostly of one wide bed. The bed was covered mostly with the unclad bodies of Arthur Torvid, her attorney, and Judith Loom, her problematic friend. The beast with two fat backsides, Pippa thought.

Torvid and Judith looked up at her, aghast. In the process Arthur twisted his neck and clutched it with both hands, groaning.

"Sister," said Judith, unsteadily. "Are you . . . well?"

"Pippa Rede," said Torvid, rubbing his neck. "You look different."

"Thanks," she said. "Here, I've got something for you."

She bent over and shook her backpack off her shoulders. The injured one did not move as it was told, and the pain made Pippa want to faint.

"Do you need help?" said Judith.

"*Shh*," Pippa said through gritted teeth. It was not a shushing noise, but the beginning of a curse. Her backpack flopped onto the mattress and Judith reached over to open it while Arthur rose and poked about on the floor, discreetly seeking his boxer shorts.

"What am I looking for?" said Judith, pawing at the jumble in the pack.

"Bonnie Abbott," said Pippa. Tears of pain ran down her cheekbones, tinted ash-gray.

"Who?"

From down on the floor Torvid said, "Name's familiar. Ouch." (Massaging his neck.)

"Virginia," said Pippa. "Fifth Circuit Court of Appeals. You can look it up."

Torvid straightened up and stared at her, evidently forgetting now about his thick circumcised penis which had retracted into his abdomen in such a way that it pointed out at you, like a tired cannon. Pippa simply could not see what all the fuss was about.

"We have *you* to thank for all this," said Judith, uncharacteristically blushing like a maiden, indicating with one coy hand herself and her hairy bedfellow. "I was just getting done with my exorcism—"

"Your what?" said Pippa.

"*You* remember. Weird energies in the building? Then Arthur showed up, and—"

Torvid found the manila envelope inside the backpack. He tore hungrily into it, paging through the sheets with a somewhat frantic efficiency. "Yes yes yes," he said, "all right all *right*." He slapped the paper down on the bed.

"Pippa Rede," he announced, back to himself now, "I've got news for you."

Pippa felt more like lying down in the middle of the state highway than getting into a major conversation with Arthur Torvid. "Tell me later," she said, turning to the door. "Like maybe in the next life."

He followed her out into the hallway, en route slipping an XXL Utah Saints jersey over his head.

"I've been reading up on this QROST business," he said.

"Me too," said Pippa. "Very good article about that in the *Herald*, wasn't there?"

"No, really," said Arthur. "Judith and I got in touch—"

Pippa stared at him and he shut up. She just didn't want to know any more about Judith and Torvid getting in touch. The whole idea was upsetting to her, somehow. Not the sexual angle per se. More like, the thought of herself up there freezing on the mountain while the two of them . . . well, who cared, though. *All acts of love and pleasure*, right?

"Enjoy," she told him. "And hey—try to work some of that legal stuff in when you get a minute. Okay?"

Torvid looked unsure how to respond. Pippa left him

that way: speechless, bare-legged, and in front of the computer.

Right where you want to keep them, she figured.

The village nestled into darkness with a practiced, comfortable air. Yellow lamps glowed inside people's windows. Stars winked in the gaps between streetlights. Pippa strolled down Mill Street, which was deader than her former trusting and innocent self. In the plate-glass window of Rose Petal & Thorn, a couple of halogen spots gleamed with unnatural intensity at a New Year's display featuring a galvanized tub full of champagne bottles surrounded by holly branches and—dangling from monofilament thread—oodles of silver balloons that were supposed to represent bubbles. They looked to Pippa like hailstones: the weapons of Hella, and a perfectly suitable form of self-defense, when you thought about it.

I'll have to tell Brenda how much I like it, she thought. Yet it seemed to her that probably this had not been Brenda's idea. Too Lawrence Welky, or something. For Brenda it was Guy Lombardo or get out of here.

The thought made her smile and she decided that maybe the anger *had* left her, because she no longer harbored bad feelings for her boss. Or ex-boss. It had been an okay job, while it lasted. All jobs end sooner or later. Anyway, Brenda still owed her a paycheck.

By the time Pippa turned onto Trim Street, where Judith had the house-sitting gig, her entire upper arm was swollen so severely it did not move at all, in any direction. This was convenient in a way, because the arm chiefly hurt when she allowed it to swing while she walked. Now the stabs of agony, with moments of relief in between, sort of averaged out to a lesser, chronic level of pain that was something she could live with. It was not different in quality (except in being located on the gross material plane) than the unceasing hurt she had felt since the night of Yule, when they took her daughter away.

My poor beautiful daughter, she said to herself. *I miss you so much.*

She halted on the sidewalk. Down the street, from the opposite direction, a police car rolled slowly, high beams blazing, sending shadows into wild flight across the vinyl siding of ranch houses. Pippa turned away from the light, because it hurt her eyes. There was nothing to be done. Either they would see her or they would not.

During the *very* long time that the police car spent rolling up the street (you could hear its studded snow tires crunch, the big motor confidently growl), Pippa stared at the house that she had stopped in front of. She wasn't surprised to see that it was the home of Carol Deacon Aaby. And Kaspian, of the chocolate-mint eyes. And wasn't there a mysterious third?—a girl called NoElle Deacon, a.k.a. "Michelle."

Pippa did not know how to feel about this family. It was as though the three individuals had gotten tangled in a conflict so ordinary as to be archetypal—the obsessive stepmother, the favored daughter, the odd kid out—but somehow it all had gotten blown into a higher dimension; the name of a well-known Dark God had been invoked; a black hole had formed into which other people's lives got sucked.

Well, these things do happen. And it's kind of hard to blame people for acting according to type. Even a Bad Wolf has got to have a meal now and then, and if your cherished little girl happens to be skipping through the woods at the wrong moment, is that the Wolf's fault?

Yes & no, Pippa guessed.

Behind her, the police car rolled past. Its headlights

moved on to other ranch houses, other wildly fleeing shadows. Pippa exhaled heavily—who knew she had been holding her breath, or for how long?—and in the act of doing so, she felt a peculiar sense of having let go of something more than stale air. A different kind of thing altogether that she had held locked inside her chest. Fear, perhaps. Self-doubt. The last unhappy residuum of her childhood. And now with the letting-go she felt a new thing: a kind of purposeful serenity: the realization (which she hardly dared acknowledge, even to herself) that Carol Deacon Aaby had *not* succeeded in destroying her, nor even in banishing her to the wilderness. All she had done was to drive Pippa down into the deepest levels of her being—into the Dark, face-to-face with the Mystery— where Pippa would never have found the courage to go unless everything, truly everything, had depended on it. As of course it had.

So Pippa had gone there. And now she was back.

And now it seemed to her that Carol Aaby was not her enemy anymore. Because Pippa had changed; she had passed beyond that. She was the buddy of the Beast— what did she have to fear from an angry stepmom?

Yes, she knew this was irrational. But so what? The whole world is crazy. Everyone is snared in the web. Only witches—and air sprites, and fairy godmothers, and other implausible beings—are really free.

Pippa walked up the sidewalk to the Aaby house for no reason at all. Because she was free, and she wanted to.

She was not clear about what she was doing. She simply understood that this narrow (and badly shoveled) suburban sidewalk was her own yellow-brick road, her rainbow bridge, the dangerous path to her destiny. All her years of cringing and weakness and self-abnegation, followed by her crisis of grief and exile, had brought her to this moment of unassailable strength. She thumped on the door, and in a few seconds Carol Deacon Aaby responded to her summons.

At first she did not recognize Pippa—who after all looked a complete fright. Carol Aaby stared not in fear but in bafflement, as though wondering if she had gotten her holidays mixed up, if this was still Halloween.

Then, getting who it was, she fled. She ran through her living room and through the open-plan dining area and into the sanctuary of her kitchen.

Pippa followed her. She found Carol Aaby frantically pawing the buttons of a phone. But something was wrong; she stared in dismay and then hurled the phone across the room at Pippa. It yo-yoed back on its twisty cord and smacked the wall and hung there, emitting static.

Pippa stood at the kitchen door. She caught scattered details of her surroundings: a television's murmur in some distant room; wallpaper with a repeating pattern of tiny pink roses; the smell of roast beef and potatoes. Carol Aaby backed herself against a counter, as far away from Pippa as she could get. Groping behind her, her fingers seized a pair of wooden salad forks. She held these out between herself and Pippa, approximately forming a cross.

"Woe to those who call evil good, and good evil," she said. Or rather intoned: singsongy, like an operatic recitative. "Who substitute darkness for light and light for darkness."

Pippa laughed. Not exactly the greeting she had expected. Carol Aaby's face appeared to morph into something not quite human. She spoke more loudly:

"Though your sins are as scarlet, they will be as white as snow. Though they are red like crimson, they will be like wool. If you consent and obey, you will eat the best of the land; but if you refuse and rebel, you will be devoured by the sword."

Pippa guessed this was a curse, of sorts. Though as curses went (in her well-informed opinion) this one lacked specificity.

Still brandishing her salad forks, Carol Aaby droned on: "And He said, I hate your new moon *festivals* and your appointed feasts. Your incense is an abomination to Me. I have called My mighty warriors, My proudly exulting ones, to *execute* My anger."

"Is that all you can do?" said Pippa. "Play back stuff you've memorized? Have you ever had, like, an actual *thought?*"

"Wail!" Carol Aaby fairly shrieked. "For the day of the Lord is coming: cruel, with fury and burning anger, to make the land a desolation. And He will exterminate the sinners from it. Their little ones also will be dashed to pieces before their eyes; their houses will be plundered and their wives ravished."

Pippa thought, This is indecent. She took a breath and gathered herself up, ready to do something Really Terrible. Deliver the big karmic payback.

Carol Aaby's voice dropped to a hoarse incantation. "Everyone is wailing, dissolved in tears."

Pippa felt herself becoming larger, towering over this woman, who seemed to shrink, cowering before her.

"Surely the grass is withered," Carol Aaby said. "The tender grass is died out. There is no green thing."

And in that instant—as though indeed the biblical formulae had worked a kind of spell on her—Pippa's vision cleared.

She had not known it was clouded. But suddenly she looked at the woman before her and she saw two versions of Carol Aaby, superimposed. One of them was a little girl—a girl about Winterbelle's age—who was scared to death of everything: the complicated world at large, the confusing business of growing up, the deathly chasm of sexuality that yawned ahead—in essence, every single thing they hadn't told her about at Sunday School. Pippa knew, as soon as she saw this girl, what it was like to be Carol Deacon Aaby. She felt the unreasoning terror that informed this woman's view of the world. She felt the impulse to flight, to denial, to seeking refuge in comforting certainties.

"Those who go down to the Pit," Carol Aaby said, "cannot hope for His faithfulness. The Lord will surely save me."

Pippa sighed. She felt cheated by her own understanding. Because you know how it is: To get it is to let it go. Just let go of it; forget and forgive.

Only, she didn't understand *everything*. And vision or no vision, she was not in a forgiving mood.

"Though the wicked is shown favor," Carol Aaby said, "she does not learn righteousness."

"Would you *shut up?*" Pippa asked, with reasonable courtesy.

She flexed her shoulder, trying to twist the backpack around. Not all the way: just enough to pull out the silver sleigh bell. With her bad arm, it was more than she could manage.

She asked Carol Aaby, insanely, "Look, could you give me a hand here?"

Insanely, Carol Aaby gave her a hand.

"Thanks," said Pippa.

Carol Aaby appeared disoriented, knocked off her Old Testament rhythm.

Pippa found the leather strap with her good hand and

she tugged hard at it, freeing the bell. Its chime pierced the kitchen with the cold purity of starlight.

Carol Aaby gave a soft cry.

Pippa shook the strap, ringing the bell again. The beautiful note seemed to shatter the present into pieces, multiple facets of reality, as though Time itself were made of ice

"Where . . . where did you get that?" Carol Aaby asked.

Pippa rang the bell again. Carol Aaby stood dumbly. Transfixed. Entranced.

Bewitched, thought Pippa.

"This bell was meant for *you*," she said. She let it hang, silent, in her hand. "Wasn't it? Your present to yourself."

Carol Aaby said nothing. But she started to lift one hand—outward, palm up, toward Pippa. Then she caught herself and stopped the hand and left it stuck there, suspended.

"Here," said Pippa. With her good arm she handed Carol Aaby the bell. "You wouldn't *believe* where it's been. But take it. And have a happy childhood."

Then, as Carol Aaby's fingers closed around it—in the instant when the weight of the silver bell shifted from one woman's hand to the other's—Pippa added:

"Now *give me back my daughter*. You hear me? I want her back. You're a mother, so I know you can understand. If you just let yourself. I'm not kidding about this. *I want you to free my daughter.*"

Carol Aaby stood there frozen. Then she let go of the bell as though it were a fatal charm. It dinged on the floor, rolled a bit, still ringing in a muffled way. But it was too late: as far as Pippa was concerned, the pact was made; she was already halfway through the living room.

Were they only her imagination, those chocolate-mint eyes gleaming out of the shadows, deep in an unlit corner?

Or was she simply accustomed to living in the Dark Wood, where spying eyes are everywhere?

No, it was Kaspian, she was pretty sure. But she did not turn back. She reckoned it was too late for that now.

All she wanted was a bath. Was that too much to wish for? She hadn't bathed in any meaningful way since the last night she spent in this house where Judith was encamped for the winter. Out at the little cottage she had sweated in front of the fire and rubbed her face with snow. But if you can accept that as a real bath you are made of more spartan stuff than Pippa Rede, do-it-yourself witch.

Most of the lights were on when she arrived, running up a stranger's electric bill, and the heat seemed to have been cranked to 90.

"Glyph?" she called, dragging herself like a zombie into the living room. "Hello? Anybody home?"

No answer. No sounds except the rattle and hum of the refrigerator.

Pippa was glad. She no longer wanted to interact with human beings, to dispense witchy energies, or to think. If she had known how to accomplish it, like the old *rishi* dudes in India, she would have shut down her autonomic functions and just kind of chilled out in a state of suspended animation.

Until what? she wondered. Until the Handsome Prince shows up and screws me in my sleep?

Until some miracle happens to make the world a gentle and orderly place?

Until the poisoned thorn gets sucked out and I wake up and the whole thing was just a gonzo dream?

She pulled her clothes off carefully in strong but survivable pain. Her shirt was a problem, because her shoulder had swollen up so much the sleeve did not want to come off. Finally Pippa decided she didn't care. With the shirt flapping half-on and half-off, she bent over the bathtub and cranked open the tap that said H—which, as it was inscribed in the porcelain handle, bore a striking resemblance to the elder rune *Hagalaz*. And the mist that rose from the water and filled the air of the bathroom did resemble (or so she imagined) the eternal shroud of fog hanging like spiderwebs in the abysmal reaches of Hel. The place your soul goes if it hasn't been invited anyplace better, and sort of just hangs out, awaiting developments. Because who knows? Someday your Valkyrie might come.

The water was so hot that it made her cry out in surprise. She willed her nerves to knock it off, and told her body that the torrid water felt *good*, damn it. Her body molded itself to the shape of the bathtub, and she closed her eyes, and the fog crept into her brain.

The water continued to rise. It gurgled through the overflow valve. Pippa didn't notice. She lay there while the bath turned the filthy gray of cinders. Her skin became parboiled white; her arm puffed-up and purple; her eyes closed but darting all around beneath the lids—

fleeing from Wolves,

or watching Elves dance at the edge of a clearing,

or scanning a field of snow for any sign of the deadly Frost Giants.

Or just staring in unashamed, limitless love at her only daughter, her little air sprite, bounding up and leaving the ground

and *flying*

free and pure, unapproachable as a bird

calling down

Look at me, Mommy!

Look at me—I can fly!

"Of course you can, sweetie," Pippa sobbed. "Mommy

always knew you could. Oh, sweetie—your mommy always knew."

But that was only a movement of the lips; not even a murmur. Nobody heard but her imaginary Winterbelle, and Pippa sank deeper and deeper into the swirling mists. She felt a strange sort of bliss, a bodiless ecstasy, rising up to enfold her, and she supposed this must be the blessing of forgetfulness.

Thank you, she thought.

And then came a Faerie
who took her into his arms

and laid her in a soft place
where she slept for
100 years.

IV

as holly

Green grow'th the holly
So doth the ivy;
Though winter blasts blow ne'er so nigh,
Green grow'th the holly.

Green grow'th the holly
So doth the ivy;
The God of life can never die,
Hope! saith the holly

—*Attributed to Henry VIII*

In the east the sun rose, red.

In the south snow buried the backyard in ambivalent whiteness, like a blanket of pure spider's silk.

In the west, yews hunched overgrown and stubbornly green outside the windows of the raised ranch.

And in the north, a coal-black shadow fell upon the door stoop. A hand tried the door knob. It was always unlocked.

Pippa dreamed of spring.

A stream gurgled fast in a rocky bed through gentle woodland. Along its banks thousands of yellow-green cross-shaped flowers bloomed. Winterbelle must have run off ahead somewhere because Pippa couldn't see her. She tried to call but in the dream she was mute. In the dream she was a mere witness, a bystander.

In the dream.

Pippa was deeper in the woods. Sunlight fell in scraps like shorn-off pieces of golden cloth. Pippa looked in every direction—north and east, south and west—but only saw paths that forked and reforked. Like branches. Like antlers.

Down one of the paths, an elfin figure approached her.

Winterbelle, the dream Pippa tried to cry. But her head kept turning, one way then another, and when she looked back the wood elf was gone.

No: there. Again, the figure moved again. A different path now. Coming closer.

Not Winterbelle. A boy.

There were shouts in the distance; the ululation of a horn. Footfalls on damp ground. Snap of winter-fallen twigs.

Pippa looked about in alarm, and when she turned back she saw that the boy had grown into a handsome prince. He wore a costume Pippa remembered having cut and stitched herself. Not too big for him after all.

He stood beside her. The clamor in the woods drew closer. From one velvet pocket the Prince removed something small and green. An *animal?*

And with a quick bob of his head—hair flying everywhere from beneath his crown—he kissed it. Then he laid it gently on the floor of the forest and a hunter's horn blew very nearby and he was gone.

Pippa tried to call out for him, but instead she woke up.

A telephone was ringing and from the bathroom Judith Loom yelled:

"Would somebody pick up the damned horn?"

—the first words Pippa heard upon awakening into this strange new century. This afterlife.

She lay flat as a corpse on the bed of someone's grown-up and long-gone son. One of her arms felt cold and she turned her head to discover an improvised ice pack: one huge and gaudy beach towel, in which armfuls of snow had been wrapped. The snow was melting, of course, and the blankets were soaked, along with much of Pippa.

But the arm hurt less.

But it still hurt.

Already, not even yet fully awake, Pippa was beginning to recognize in this squeaky-clean century some of the disappointing features of the old one: the impermanent and less-than-ideal nature of things.

She let out a protracted sigh. She blinked at the sunlight creeping insidiously through the venetian blinds. No rest for the weird, she thought.

Footsteps thumped in the living room. The voice of Glyph And/or said angrily, "Just *what* do you think you're doing, you little sneak?"

The phone rang again. There was scuffling. A kid's voice said, "Wait, I'm on your side!"

Then Pippa—realizing that she was awake, that she could talk now—called out:

"Kaspian—is that you?"

The phone shut up. For a couple of moments, everything was quiet.

Then Judith Loom came barging out of the bathroom, skyclad as the night she was reborn, and glanced into the bedroom where Pippa weakly propped herself up. She felt as though she had been asleep for a long, long time.

"All that falls shall rise again!" Judith proclaimed. "As a former lover of mine used to boast."

Glyph crowded into the breach, dragging Kaspian Aaby by the scruff of his scruffy neck. "A *friend* of yours?" he asked Pippa, arching one high mascaraed brow.

Kaspian looked helpless. Helpless but cute.

"You can let him go," Pippa told Glyph. "I don't think he's going to hurt anybody."

Kaspian, freed, glanced repeatedly sideways at Judith's frankly displayed body. Pippa could not help noting that he was not wearing a coat. Only a floppy sweatshirt that said QUESTION MICROSOFT. She shook her head.

"He *must* be on our side," she said. "He isn't dressed sensibly."

Glyph shivered in his maroon pajamas. His long hair was braided into cornrows. Obviously he had had too much time on his hands. He said, "There is no *way* to dress sensibly in this climate."

"I'll tell you what," said Pippa. "Let's put on a nice pot of hot coffee and we'll sit down and have a talk. I kind of have a feeling that people have a little bit of explaining to do."

Judith frowned at her. Having difficulty, perhaps, with the concept of Pippa taking charge of the situation. Any situation. But you know Judith: never say no. She squeezed past the others and wagged her butt out to the kitchen. Pippa started to rise from the bed when she noticed

(a) that she herself was not wearing any clothes, having been pulled out of a bathtub the night before and probably thereby saved from drowning, and

(b) that a small green frog was sitting on the edge of her bed. A frog fetish, actually. Looking somehow familiar, with tiny coal-black eyes staring up at her, and some sheets of white paper ripped from a spiral notebook underneath.

Kaspian was staring at her, and when she met his gaze he blushed.

"You dropped it last night," he said.

"I did?" she said. Not getting this.

"The head broke off," he went on hurriedly. "I glued it back together, but like, the glue I used? It dried this kind of reddish-brown color and you could see where the crack was. So I figured I'd paint over it. Is green okay?"

Pippa pressed a blanket against her breast and picked

the frog up for closer study. It was not for her, she thought, to decide whether green was okay. But somehow she didn't figure Winterbelle would mind. She said, "I guess it's the color frogs are supposed to be, isn't it?"

"Not *all* frogs," said Glyph. "They are actually quite diverse."

"Not all *real* frogs," Pippa corrected him. "But fairy-tale frogs. Sure, sweetie," she told Kaspian (who frowned at being called *sweetie*), "I think it's fine."

The papers underneath the frog looked like a kid's hand-scrawled book report.

"Don't read that now!" said Kaspian, cringing.

Pippa glanced up at him, then down again. On the top page she read

WHY I KNOW "MICHELLE" IS LYING
by "A.k.a. Spin"

Pippa smiled. Then she frowned. "What is this?" she asked him.

Kaspian's eyes had lowered a few degrees and he did not seem to be listening. Pippa realized she had let the blanket drop. Her breasts, which she considered no big deal, were partly exposed.

You have to pity men, she thought. They are so utterly helpless. Really and truly.

"Wait for me in the living room," she commanded him.

And of course he obeyed her.

Who would not?

When the phone rang again Judith answered it. She listened for a long time and spoke very little, for Judith. Then she giggled and said, "I bet I can think of *one* circumstance that's extenuating." Then she made a slurpy kissing noise and held the phone out to Pippa and said, "It's your lawyer."

Pippa lowered the spiral notebook papers. She had read through them about seven times. She glanced at Kaspian, who slouched on the living room floor watching an old movie on TBS. Glyph lay on the sofa, shrouded in a comforter.

"How's your neck?" she asked Arthur Torvid on the telephone.

"Pippa Rede!" the voice in the handset exclaimed. "It hurts like hell. Listen! These papers you brought me. Fascinating stuff. Where'd you get this?"

"Friend of a friend of a werewolf's," said Pippa. "So, is it something we can use?"

"Well . . ." Arthur Torvid shuffled documents, off-mike. "It's certainly *applicable*, I'll say that. Bonnie Abbott v. Commonwealth of Virginia. Case involving custody of a minor. The court finds that matters of religious preference, however exotic or eccentric the religion of choice may appear from an outside perspective, are properly beyond the purview of governmental bodies, including the judiciary. An analogy was made to Jehovah's Witnesses."

"Jehovah's *Witnesses*?" said Pippa.

"They're kooks, okay? But it's *legal* to be a kook in this country. Especially a religious kook. That's all the court is saying here. Of course this is not a binding precedent, coming from Virginia and all. But it's the kind of thing a judge can hardly ignore. Only . . ."

Pippa waited. She had kind of figured there would be a *but*.

"I'm not really *sure*," said Torvid, choosing his words with evident caution, "that this is the line we want to take.

For one thing, it does entail abandoning our initial impulse here—"

"*My* initial impulse was to hire another lawyer," Pippa reminded him.

Arthur Torvid gave a pained cough. "And it does leave the State some wiggle room. They can argue for example that witchcraft is not a religion per se, but rather, a *lifestyle*."

"Sure," said Pippa. "Like being born queer, right? Just *do it*, Arthur. Do whatever it takes. Have me officially legally declared a kook, if that's what it takes to get Winterbelle back. Okay? Just, whatever you do, do it *now*. Because I'm probably going to get arrested any second now so like, let's not waste any time."

She hung up the phone. Kaspian and Glyph were staring at her.

"Why did you say that?" Kaspian asked. He sounded stricken. "That you're going to be arrested."

She said, "Well, *you* found me, didn't you?"

He shook his head like she wasn't getting it. "I *followed* you. I heard you arguing with my stepmom, and I sort of snuck out after you when you left. Then I went home and fixed the frog, and this morning when my stepmom left for work I came back again."

Pippa glanced at the little frog, whose green skin was starting to grow on her. And that scrunchy little smile. Like there wasn't a thing in the world to worry about.

Judith Loom stepped out of the kitchen. "What did Arthur say?"

Pippa shrugged. "I'm never exactly sure. It sounds good, though. It sounds like we've got a strong case."

"Of *course* we've got a strong case," said Glyph, his voice muffled by layers of down.

Judith grandly sighed. She stood propped in the kitchen doorjamb, holding a wooden spoon as though it were a wand, ready to thwang somebody with. She was draped in a black caftan emblazoned with orange spirals. "If *only*," she declared, "there were some way to draw attention to our cause."

Pippa stared at her, replaying this comment in her mind. Could Judith really have said this? Could Judith Loom, the original Day-Glo Goddess, actually be wondering aloud how to *draw attention*?

"Judith," said Pippa, "why don't you go like, stand out in the middle of the village green?"

Judith looked at her in puzzlement. And Pippa supposed that maybe it was true: maybe Judith truly did not appreciate what a high-bandwidth, graphics-intensive person she was. Maybe, like every other Wiccan in the world, she had her little problems with self-esteem.

Well, I can fix that, thought Pippa.

"I've got an idea," she said.

"You do?" said Judith.

Glyph rearranged himself under the comforter, more or less vertically.

Pippa told Judith, "You go out on the green, like I was saying. Only get yourself all made up and everything first. Put on your best witchy finery, you know what I'm saying?"

Judith did not but she kept listening.

"And *you*," Pippa said, turning to Glyph. "You get dressed up, too. Like maybe a Puritan or something. And you go out there, and you tie her to a stake, and you burn her."

"I beg your pardon?" said Glyph, batting his lashes. But intrigued.

"Not for real," said Pippa. "Like a play or something. A performance. Like, you know—the *Theatre.*"

Glyph threw off the comforter and rose to his full towering height. He transported himself with campy pomp across the living room, taking Judith's arm and posing beside her, as though waiting for flashbulbs to pop. "I can see it," he pronounced. "I can absolutely see it."

"See what?" said Judith. Poor thing.

"A public burning!" said Glyph. "A shocking remembrance of things past. Sheer spectacle!"

"With maybe leaflets to pass around," said Pippa.

"I can do that," said Kaspian.

Pippa nodded. "Everybody can do something."

"But not *everyone*," said Glyph, lowering himself to his knees like a besotted suitor, flashing his eyes up at Judith, "not everyone can be the Perfect Victim."

She flicked a smile at him, uncertainly. "Well," she said, "I'm game. I guess. But shouldn't you ask Arthur about this? I mean, doesn't it seem a little . . . radical?"

Pippa shook her head. She almost said—but in the end only thought—

A witch doesn't have to ask anybody
about anything.

They told her she should skip the show.

They all told her she shouldn't leave the house, shouldn't expose herself to further danger. Pippa agreed in a way. In another way she did not. As she watched them standing there chattering in the kitchen, waiting for darkness to fall, she thought, *Just look at them:* Glyph and Judith and Arthur and young Kaspian, her whole little army of misfits and none-of-the-aboves. Judith and Glyph were, naturally, costumed to the max. Kaspian was dressed more or less invisibly, in a thrift-store parka and a ski mask, so as not to be recognized. Arthur wore a trench coat and a neck brace. And Pippa thought as she looked at them that they were all terribly sweet and loyal and wonderful. But that she was not one of them They were like characters in a story but she was the storyteller, or something like that. The director, maybe. Standing just offstage, back in the wings, looking on. And to that extent she was helpless. But to that same extent she was all-powerful. It was confusing, but she was both.

"Could I talk to you a minute?" Kaspian said. His voice was quiet, even discounting the effect of the mask.

"Sure," she said, catching herself before tacking on some momlike term of endearment.

They went out to the living room and stood by the door. Pippa could see streetlights just starting to blink on. Pink-orange sodium vapor crime-deterring lights, in a village where there was no crime. Or rather only minor and imaginary crime: shoplifting candy at the Stop 'N' Go, and quasi-ritualized occultic sexual traumatization.

"What did you think of that thing I wrote?" Kaspian asked her.

"I thought it was very brave," said Pippa. "But I don't think you should send it to the newspaper, if that's what you were planning to do."

"How come?" he said.

She could see his eyes open wide through the holes in the ski mask. Beautiful sparkling eyes. She felt like this kid's mother, though she felt like something else, too. Something a little less well defined. Like a girlfriend from a former life.

"I don't think private family matters belong in a newspaper," she said. "Not my family. And not yours either. I mean, I appreciate what you're trying to do. I know you want to help me. But getting your sister in trouble—"

"My *step*sister," Kaspian said, tersely.

"Right. Still. I don't think it's going to help Winterbelle. And that's what I care about. Not revenge or anything else."

"It *might* help."

"It might. But it will also hurt."

Kaspian nodded. He appeared to be processing these ideas slowly, one piece at a time. Pippa guessed he wasn't accustomed to moral issues being presented in other than stark, black & white delineation. After a while he said,

"How about if I give it to the D.A.'s office? Or the police? And ask them to keep it, you know, kind of secret?"

Pippa shuddered at the thought of the police. But then she remembered Deputy Doug, her old buddy. Doug would probably be okay. At least he wouldn't slap Kaspian in handcuffs and give him the third degree until he divulged Pippa's whereabouts. "Well, there is this one guy," she said.

Arthur Torvid barreled out the kitchen door. He looked like a B-movie private eye. "What are we waiting for?" he shouted. "It's show time!"

She gave them a good head start. It took a while to get into her witch's weeds—black clothes, ugly hat, unbecoming makeup. Perhaps her heart wasn't so much in it anymore. The whole dress-up, make-believe bit. What Pippa truly wanted right now was simply to be herself. To be allowed to be that and not made to suffer for it.

The evening was dark in a way that seemed radiant, as though the surface of the night had been burnished until it glowed. Naked street trees stood absolutely still. No snow had fallen for the past few days so the sidewalks were clear, everything swept and shoveled and tidy.

There was hardly anyone on the streets. It was dinnertime, roughly, but also these weeks of early January were a subdued time, a period of stillness after the bustle of Christmas. The days were getting longer but you would not really feel that until February: then it would be time to light the bonfires of Midwinter (or the mannerly votives of Candlemas) and mark another click of the wheel.

Somewhere in this village, Pippa thought as she neared the center of it, a werewolf with bad posture is sitting at home, maybe watching *Entertainment Tonight*. It is truly something to think about.

And here was something else. A small crowd had formed on the village green. Beneath the steeple of the Congregational church, mittened and booted and swaddled in mufflers, shuffling in the snow, 30 or 40 people strained to get a better view of *something*—Pippa couldn't tell what. She was over by the entrance of the Opera House, taking it in: not just the crowd but the tidy village around it, windows lit warm and yellow, the black spade-shapes of spruces, skeletal arching elms, narrow lanes that led to safe neighborhoods and playgrounds and overcrowded, underfunded schools. It seemed to her that probably not very much had changed in this place since Norbert Thiess had been a schoolboy. People were the same as they ever had been, she guessed. They either liked you or they didn't. They mostly left you alone and went about their own affairs and indulged in harmless gossip, except that now and then the gossip got a little wild and they formed a mob and chose a victim and shredded her life to tiny bits. That's the way it goes, the way it's always gone, Pippa supposed; and it was easy to regard it all from a long-range, law-of-averages sort of perspective unless the life being shredded happened to be your own.

The door of the Opera House swished open and a matronly woman stepped out. The cleaning lady, Pippa guessed: short, dark-haired, with a hint of a mustache. She was familiar, from somewhere.

"What's going on?" the woman asked Pippa, staring across the street toward the green.

Pippa remembered now. The crossing guard from George Burroughs Elementary School.

"Over there?" said Pippa, nonchalantly. "It's just a witch-burning, I think."

The woman laughed in a quiet way, inwardly, without much genuine mirth. "Well, it's been a while since we had one, eh?" she said. And she turned and walked down the sidewalk and gave neither Pippa nor the crowd on the green a second glance.

A commotion began across the street then. The crowd gasped and some people laughed and parents called to their children: a fire had been lit. Pippa could see flames between the silhouettes of well-clad bodies. She thought she could glimpse from time to time the manic, leaping figure of Glyph, who stood a head taller than most of the crowd; and once she got a clear look at the face of Judith Loom, miming horror. She almost had to smile.

Then she turned away. She walked down the sidewalk the way the cleaning lady—cum—crossing guard had gone. It wasn't that she had lost interest in the little drama, the small-town winter's tale. It was more like she was tired of living it.

The others, the performers, told her everything went great. And it went even better the next night, and better still the next. The audience kept growing (which shows how little there is to do in the middle of winter in a village like this), Glyph and Judith were overtopping one another in their roles, Kaspian had dispensed a couple hundred informative leaflets detailing Pippa's plight, and on the third night a small group of women had shown up wearing black robes and pentacles, a moving gesture of sorority. The local police, who arrived nightly to extinguish the illegal open fire, had been courteous and (thus far) made no arrests, somewhat to Arthur's disappointment.

On the morning of the fourth day, which was a Thursday, Pippa sat alone in Judith Loom's borrowed living room, her injured shoulder nestled against a hot-water bottle, dreamily staring out the side window at a corner of Wabenaki Mountain, when a loud knock came at the door.

The rest of the household was asleep. It was midmorning, a dim and blustery winter's day outside, and Pippa had tuned the small kitchen clock-radio to the community station, where a granola rap set was in progress. It takes a certain level of consciousness to relate to granola rap and Pippa was not sure she was up to it, or down with it, or wherever you have to be.

The knock came again. And a voice:

"Hello? Listen, I know you people are in there. I'm looking for Pippa Rede and it's very important. Now open the door."

Pippa thought: Deputy Doug. He's found me. The jig is up.

Doug recommenced his pounding, and at last Pippa's housemates began to stir. Judith Loom emerged first, rubbing her eyes and smearing the makeup left over from last night's show. Then Glyph, his cornrows slumped to one side. They stared dumbly at the door for a few seconds, then at Pippa.

"It's the police," she told them.

Which worked better than coffee, any day.

"Quick!" said Judith. "The sofa! Let's move it over there to block the door!"

Glyph sleepily moved to help her. Each took an end of the sofa and began to shove. Neither of them seemed to take notice of the fact that Pippa was sitting on the damned thing. Comfortably, till now. So much has changed, she thought, and yet so little.

"COME ON, GUYS," Deputy Doug shouted through the door, which was flimsy and cheap. Eminently blowdownable, if you huffed and puffed. "I CAN HEAR YOU ALL FROM OUT HERE."

"*Now,*" panted Judith, when the sofa was in place. "We

must establish a circle of protection. We need to do something *quickly* to get our magical energies up."

She and Glyph looked at one another, silently consulting. A funny expression flicked from one to the other; some unspoken understanding seemed to form between them. Glyph loosened the drawstring of his maroon pajamas. Pippa reckoned she better get off the couch.

Thank the Goddess Kaspian isn't here, was all she could think. She had witnessed some unusual stuff lately, but even so, this particular energy-raising ritual was a little bit alarming. It probably ought not to be described here in much detail.

"PIPPA? DAMN IT, ARE YOU IN THERE? THIS IS REALLY PISSING ME OFF."

Pippa headed for the kitchen, looking for the bottle of aspirin. Her arm had begun to throb again, and she felt a life-threatening headache coming on.

"*Come,* sister," Judith called after her, or rather panted, improbably managing to free an arm so as to beckon her. "Come join us—*quickly*. The charge hasn't risen enough to make us impregnable yet."

"You better *hope* you're impregnable," said Pippa.

Judith cried, "I call down all the Spirits that block and impede!"

Glyph said nothing, though his light brown skin had turned a remarkable shade of burnt sienna. He appeared to be enjoying himself.

Pippa entered the kitchen at about the same moment that Deputy Doug arrived at the back door. He pressed his face against the door panes, blinking through the café curtains like a Peeping Tom. Pippa shook out a handful of aspirin and poured herself a mug of fresh coffee. Then she just opened the door, revealing Doug in the fullness of his astonishment.

"It's never locked," she told him.

Doug hastily regathered his sense of official propriety. He stepped through the door and cleared his throat and was about to pronounce, Pippa supposed, the Fatal Words; but she said:

"Would you mind closing that, please?"

"Oh—sure, sorry about that." Doug did as he was told and then turned back again, frowning in the direction of the living room. "What's going on out there?"

"Tantra," said Pippa. "Don't let it alarm you."

She sipped the coffee, which was good, but not as good as the enchanted brew she had drunk with Spear in the witch's cottage in the woods.

"Want some java?" she asked Doug. "Or is there time for that? Do you have to like, frisk me down or anything? Would it be okay if I got some clothes on first?"

Deputy Doug stared at her. Evidently he did not take well to these departures from the script. He took another step into the kitchen and stuck his chest out and delivered the Fatal Words in a voice that was deeper than average and cop-sounding to the max.

"Pippa," he said, solemnly, "I'm afraid I have something very unfortunate to tell you."

"Oh, for heaven's sake, Doug," she said. "Don't drag it *out*, okay? You've tracked me down, I'm sure you'll get extra brownie points for it. And believe me, I don't hold it against you *at all*."

Doug frowned, looking right past her. She wasn't sure he was even listening. Briefly he touched her on the arm, then brushed past her, one hand stiffly poised near his bulging 9-millimeter, as gross and obvious a symbol as Frey's killer erection.

"Pardon me, Pippa," he said, "but I'm really worried that somebody's in trouble out there."

Pippa could hardly argue, but she felt a little irked at the way her own undoing was getting jerked around with.

From the dining room Doug uttered, "Oh my God."

"There's a goddess involved, too," Pippa pointed out. "It takes two, you know?"

At that moment, a terrible

CRASHING NOISE

came from the front door, as flimsy softwood boards splintered and fell away, and the stocky torso of Arthur Torvid appeared in the hole that he had, from all appearances, just kicked into being.

"Woops," he said. He was still wearing his neck brace.

"*Ooooooooohhhhhhhh,*" Judith strenuously mewled, in a voice that you could have heard quite clearly up the block at the Aaby house.

"What's going on here?" said Torvid, through the hole in the door. "If I may ask."

"Tantra," said Deputy Doug. "I guess."

"Yo, Officer!" exclaimed Torvid.

The sight of Doug appeared to have a tonic effect on him. He thrust himself through the hole and popped into the living room, still wearing (besides the trench coat) his neck brace. He climbed across the sofa where Judith had propped herself up on a cushion while attempting to organize her hair, and strode to greet the officer of the law. To Pippa's astonishment, the two men exchanged a high 5.

"Told you she'd be here," Torvid said.

"You did that." Doug shook his head. "I could've saved myself a *bunch* of trouble."

Pippa said, "Am I missing something? Since when is my own lawyer supposed to be helping the police arrest me?"

Deputy Doug and Arthur Torvid looked at her.

"Arrest you?" said Deputy Doug, after a beat.

"Don't be insane," said Arthur Torvid. "Haven't you seen the *Herald*?"

Pippa shook her head.

Arthur Torvid—rubbing his neck, sounding smug—said, "Well, feast your eyes, Pippa Rede." He reached into his trench coat and pulled out a whole stack of newspapers: one for everybody, including the ferret Ashera, who was slinking underfoot.

Pippa set her coffee mug down on the floor. She lowered herself next to it. A killer draft from the hole in the front door blew through the room at speeds that would make for decent kite flying. She felt right at home in it.

"If this is some kind of joke," she said, "I can tell you now, I'm not going to think it's funny. And I'll make sure none of *you* guys thinks it's funny, either."

Everyone in the room looked at her very seriously. It was not an experience Pippa was accustomed to.

And then, through the door where the hole was (and might still be, to this very day), Jacques the French-Canadian-Passamaquoddy delivery person from Rose Petal & Thorn stuck his head and said, "Excuse me. I've got some flowers here for Pippa Rede. Could anybody tell me . . . Oh, hey ya, Pip. Is it okay if I come in?"

"It was the kid that cracked it," Deputy Doug said, in his off-duty, regular-guy type voice. "The boy. I mean, it was all starting to come apart anyway. What with that little street opera out on the village green and so forth."

They were sitting together—Glyph, Doug, Torvid, Pippa—around the fire-engine-red linoleum table in the kitchen. At the center of the table lay a box, yet unopened, big enough for an Irish wolfhound to be snoozing in. Out in the living room the sofa had been stood on end to block the hole in the door, with partial success. Judith, wearing for no evident Earthly purpose a long purple cere-monial gown, was brewing coffee in a large stewpot, to which mysterious additional ingredients were added now and then.

"You know, if you throw in a couple of eggshells," Pippa said, "it helps the grounds settle."

Judith frowned but did not otherwise acknowledge her. She was half humming an old Indigo Girls song, and Pippa supposed it had been a breach of etiquette, maybe worse, to offer unsolicited advice to a Witch in her own kitchen.

Arthur Torvid said, "I'd like to think that *I* had some-thing to do with it."

Pippa patted his hand.

Doug shrugged. "All I know is, the word came down that charges had been dropped. I kind of figured it was the boy. That story of his about his sister and his stepmom . . ."

"It was the power of Art," Glyph declared.

"It was the overwhelming force of legal precedent," groused Arthur.

Judith said, "Forget about that. It was Magick, pure and simple."

Doug looked at her crossly. "What got me was, you guys never even applied for a fire permit. We had to send somebody out *every single night* to squirt the extinguisher around. It was getting to be sort of a regular public inci-dent. Out-of-towners were driving in."

Glyph sniffed. "You dragged your heels, though, that last time, didn't you? I was afraid the whole thing was going to become rather too dreadfully *serious*."

Not much fear of that, thought Pippa.

Arthur said, "But the *last* nail in the coffin was this piece in the newspaper. The exposé of this whole QROST business. Saying in essence that it's a form of mass hysteria. Like collective autohypnosis or something."

Pippa glanced at her copy of the *Herald*, spread before her on the table. The headline read LOCAL THERAPIST CHARGED WITH SPARKING "SATAN" SCARE—FAD DIAGNOSIS SHATTERS LOCAL FAMILIES.

"The part *I* love," said Judith, bending over the printed page, "is where it says, listen—'Authorities acknowledge they only became aware of the deficiencies in Dr. Rhinum's methodology after being contacted by Arthur Torvid, a local attorney who represents—' Well, you know about that. And let's see, 'unwilling to discuss what punitive action, if any, may be applied in such cases, though according to Torvid, who spoke to this reporter just prior to press time, these actions range from the rescission of Dr. Rhinum's professional certification to the nullification of contracts between herself and local agencies such as the Department of Family Services and local schools, where she has long served in an advisory capacity.' Isn't that *wonderful?*"

"It's kind of hard to believe," said Pippa.

"That Rhinum was a fake?"

"No—*that* stood out a mile. I mean, that Arthur actually *did* all that."

Far from being insulted, Arthur Torvid reached over and took Pippa's hand. "Everybody did something," he said. "Everybody who cares about you. We all did what we could to help."

"And listen to *this*," said Judith, still scanning the newspaper. "The last thing it says is, 'Roger Wemble, speaking in behalf of DFS, would confirm only that a review was being undertaken of all cases, particularly involving so-called ritual abuse, with which Dr. Rhinum had been closely involved.' What do you think of that?"

Pippa did not know. In a way, she was afraid to think anything. "What amazes me," she said, "is that Mark Portion was willing to print this. Or even assign a reporter to cover the story to begin with."

Arthur gave her a funny look. "Actually he didn't. But I guess you haven't heard."

Pippa shook her head. She supposed it was that 100-year nap. You miss out on things.

Arthur said, "Portion's in the hospital. In pretty bad shape, I gather. Pneumonia—plus evidently he almost drowned. The paper's being managed in his absence by a former copy editor that Portion fired a year ago. The piece about QROST was written by a freelancer. Some old lady, I think."

Pippa looked again at the paper and there it was: the byline read Madeleine Mallard. She closed her eyes. *Thank you,* she thought. *Thank you all so much for everything.*

Arthur went on: "They say Portion hasn't been able to talk yet. Damage to his vocal cords, they think. All he can do is sit there and listen."

Judith poured out fresh brew into everybody's mug. "Aren't you going to open your package?" she asked Pippa.

They all looked at her, and then they looked at the giant box in the middle of the table. Hesitantly Pippa picked up the tiny envelope that was tucked beneath a length of golden ribbon. The card inside, in Brenda's own scrabble, read:

> *For my favorite Seamstress*
> *and Girl Friday*

Not exactly what Pippa wanted on her tombstone. Roses? she guessed. But when she lifted the lid, she discovered a whole emerald isle's worth of shamrocks, their tiny cross-shaped flowers an unusual shade of chartreuse.

Jacques, who had delivered this, said, "I think a shipment arrived early for Saint Patty's Day. Don't tell her I said that. Oh, and also—the Stork says if you've got a little time, could you please drop by the store later on? She says she forgot to give you your Christmas bonus."

Pippa tried to process this but there was no way. It was too much, all at once. Anyway, it seemed to her that they were all forgetting something. Something very, very important.

"Doug," she said quietly. And when everybody just kept blabbing on, she said it louder, in her best witch's croak. "*Doug.*"

They all shut up.

"You said—when you first showed up, remember?—there was something you needed to tell me. Something *unfortunate*, I think you said."

Deputy Doug scanned his official memory and then—like a switch got flipped—his face turned professionally grave.

"Pippa," he said, picking right up, *exactly* right up, it was incredible, where he had left off. "Pippa, I'm afraid I have some rather bad news. Is there someplace we can go and talk privately?"

"Oh, come *on*, Doug," she said. "Just *give* it to me, okay?"

Doug cleared his throat. "I'm afraid it's your aunt," he said. "Eulace, was that her name? Right, Eulace. Anyway, I'm very sorry to tell you that your aunt passed away, a couple of days ago. Cardiac arrest. I guess she must have had sort of a bad heart, huh?"

"Very bad," said Judith. "Shitty, I'd call it."

Doug nodded, all gravity. "I guess she tried to call 911, because the call came in, but when they answered there was nobody at the other end. So you know, with this new Enhanced 911, they were able to trace where the call came from, and they found your aunt lying there in her bedroom clutching the phone in her hands. The paramedics tried to revive her, but it was too late. I'm sorry, Pippa." He paused. "At least she died in her own bed, though, huh? I guess that must be some comfort."

"A *great* comfort," said Judith. She winked at Pippa, quite evilly.

"Were there any other kin?" said Torvid. "Did she leave a will?"

"Just me," said Pippa. "And . . . and Winterbelle. I don't guess there's a will. She didn't trust lawyers, I don't think."

Torvid slapped the table. "That's *it*, then, Pippa Rede. That's the icing, right there. Of course, there's probate, but after that—hey. You've got yourself a house. A *big* old house."

"It's amazing," declared Glyph. "It's truly incredible the way things work out. It's just like a fairy . . . Wait, did I say something wrong?"

His big eyes blinked worriedly as Pippa stood and walked out of the kitchen. She walked through the living room and down the hall and into the bedroom where she had slept. She reached into her backpack, hardly noticing how much her shoulder hurt, and took out the nice clean little clothes she had packed for Winterbelle. She laid them out on the bed, which was still sodden with melted snow, and arranged them in the proper order, blouse and skirt and tights and satin slippers, until you could imagine a real girl (albeit a flat and headless one) lying there on the *Empire Strikes Back* comforter.

"It's not like a fairy tale,"
she said softly.
"Not yet."

At the height of midday, Pippa left the raised ranch with the broken door and turned onto the sidewalk where an enfeebled sun threw her shadow down before her like a fuzzy-edged carpet.

Kaspian Aaby ran out of his house as soon as she came into view. Like he had been waiting for her.

His brown hair flew in many directions at once, as though possessed by a dust devil. The sun picked out golden threads in it. His eyes were made of chocolate mint and his cheeks flushed like roses, old-fashioned round and pink roses, just starting to unfold.

When he got close to Pippa he stopped running and lowered his head, seemingly abashed, or unsure what to say.

"Hey," she greeted him.

He smiled a little.

"I heard what you did," she said. "You're really sweet. And brave, and so grown-up. I don't know how to thank you."

"It's okay." He straightened up and his teeth flashed in the sun between lips that looked like they had been chewed on. "I kind of felt like I owed it to you."

"Owed it to *me*?" said Pippa. "Owed what?"

Kaspian kicked at the snow. He saw Pippa glancing over toward his house and he said, "Don't worry, my stepmom's not home. NoElle either. They've gone to see a lawyer. I guess maybe they're in trouble. Then my stepmom's got a doctor's appointment. I'm kind of on my own for the day."

"You are." She saw that he was wearing a thick Nordic sweater with a reindeer motif. At the word *doctor*, her mind flashed briefly onto Arthur Torvid's twisted neck, and Mark Portion's pneumonia. She said, "Is your stepmom . . . very sick?"

His facial muscles twitched. "She woke up like, covered with boils."

(She *must* have heard this wrong.) "Boils?"

"You know like, super gonzo zits. It was *totally* disgusting. And her skin was this sort of *green* color. She looked like an amphibian or something. My stepmom was going on about how it *had* to be the work of the Devil."

Pippa closed her eyes, torn between trying to imagine it and trying not to. "You never know, I guess," she said.

Suddenly Kaspian blurted: "The reason I owed you is because, see, until I met you, I thought it was just *me*. I thought that if you didn't believe in all the things they told you to, you were some kind of evil wicked sinner and you were going to burn in Hell. They sure *told* you that all the time. And they just, I mean, wouldn't let go of it. You couldn't turn on the TV or say anything or . . . or *anything*, without them saying, like, the Day of Reckoning is coming real soon now and you better be ready. And it was Satan this and Satan that. I mean, I didn't really *believe* it, but it was all I *knew* about. You know what I mean? And don't even *think* about sex."

He blushed. As if coming back to himself, his ordinary reticence.

Pippa said, "Okay. I won't."

And he peeked up and saw her smiling and he sort of giggled—a little sound of relief. Pippa giggled too.

"But you've got to think about sex sooner or later," she said.

"Oh, God, *tell* me," he said, flinging his arms up. "Like, for the past year or something, I've thought about it *all the time*. I guess that's what really pushed her to the edge."

"Your stepmom?"

He squeezed his lips together and gave the slightest of nods. "I have *no* idea why my dad married her. I was only like this little kid, but even so I never got it. I think he died as soon as he figured out how screwed up it was. I was only like six years old. But I remember how unhappy he was."

Pippa said, "I'm sorry." She had a vision of Kaspian as a little kid, grieving for his father. She realized that there were warm tears in her eyes, but she supposed that by now, between her and Kaspian, it didn't matter.

"So anyway, thanks," Kaspian said, looking at her solemnly. For an instant, beside the boy in his face there appeared an early, tentative study of the man.

My little Prince, thought Pippa.

"Hey, Kaspian?" she said. "Could I ask you something?"

"Sure," he said readily.

"Did you—you know that morning when you snuck into the house? Did you like . . . kiss that frog?"

He blushed. His neck and face turned pink, which made his freckles look browner.

"Never mind," she said. She looked discreetly away, giving him a chance to summon his dignity again.

After a moment he said, in a deeper-than-usual voice, "Would it be okay if I walked you home?"

Home? she might have said. But she didn't. Only nodded. And they set out together down the snowy street.

At Rose Petal & Thorn, Brenda Cigogne was beside herself. She came hobbling out from behind the counter, knocking things down with her crutch while dragging her cast— evidently a leg had gotten broken, somehow—behind her.

"The customers!" she fairly shrieked (after scanning the sales floor for any of them; finding none; only her old comrade Madeleine Willoughby Mallard, who today had brought in a woman friend that Pippa thought she recognized from somewhere). "They can be such *pills*. You have no idea."

I don't? thought Pippa.

"Jacques has been a godsend," Brenda rattled on, "I can tell you that. I don't know what I would have done. That what's her name, NoElle, she couldn't *begin* to cope with the pressure of the holidays. You'd think the child had spent all her life in a *bubble*. I mean to say, every little *incident* just threw her into a tizzy. What could I have been thinking, giving a job to someone like that? Things really haven't been the same around here since *you* left."

Pippa thought about this (—"you left," as though she had taken it into her head to flit off to the Dark Wood one day—), and what she decided was, Brenda Cigogne being who she was, you couldn't really expect her to come much closer to flat-out saying: I was wrong. I'm sorry I fired you. Please come back. *Please.*

No way on Earth, Pippa told herself.

Though on the other hand, she guessed she could use the money. What with the big old house to heat and all.

Mad Mallard, who had been keeping herself distracted perusing the Valentine's Day display—*much* too glittery, in Pippa's not-so-humble opinion—now came forward with her friend, a lady of comparable age (or agelessness), who looked at Pippa as though trying to place her. Which made it mutual. Mad Mallard gave Pippa a comradely wink.

"You *know*," she said, in that voice that made the flimsiest subject a matter of Providential importance, "the most *marvelous* thing happened to me. I was *convinced* that the Postal Service had done something awful to my shipment of seeds from Chiltern's. *Very* rare pelargoniums, from I believe South Africa. Impossible to obtain. You have no idea. So when I saw them in this year's catalog, I fairly *pounced*. Then the longest time went by, and no seeds. I placed *many* overseas calls, but you know that famous British efficiency. Eventually I wrote the whole thing off as a dead loss. Then about three days ago, I woke up from a teeny little nap and went out to check my mailbox—did you hear those sirens, round about midday? What was all that about, I wonder?—and *there*, down at the bottom of the box, were my *seeds*. There was no other mail. Only a key that I keep in there from time to time. Now I only hope the cold has not *destroyed* them."

"They'll be okay," said Pippa.

"Oh, *good*," exhaled Mrs. Mallard, the very picture of relief—never wondering, apparently, what qualified Pippa to render judgment on such things. Which of course made two of them, or even more, as many as seven, depending on whether you counted everybody in the store. Plus the parakeets.

"I remember where I know you from," said Mrs. Mallard's friend to Pippa, suddenly. "You're the young woman I spoke with about painted furniture, aren't you? That day the police were crawling in and out of old Eulace's place. God rest her, though I doubt He'll want to get involved."

"That's right," said Pippa, remembering too. Remembering the whole scene all too sadly well.

The woman nodded with vigor. She appeared to share Mrs. Mallard's capacity for enthusiasm at the drop of a bonnet. "You *spoke*," she reminded Pippa, "as though you were rather familiar with the techniques involved. In decorative painting, that is. The exact composition of the pigments and so forth. Something about, I don't know, egg yolks . . ." She fluttered a hand, signifying impatience with details.

Pippa shrugged. "I guess I know a little. I mean, I painted that cupboard bed—the one they were dragging out."

"You *did*," said the woman (her name, we will learn, is Beatrice), opening her mouth as though nothing more astonishing had been revealed to her in her (unnumbered) decades of worldly experience. "Well, my *goodness*. That was *quite* a piece of work. I don't suppose you . . . I mean, on a professional basis . . . do restoration work?"

"My dear," said Mrs. Mallard, laying a hand on her friend's arm and eyeing her with utmost earnestness, "you wouldn't *believe* the things Pippa has restored. She can practically summon the dead back into existence."

Brenda Cigogne glanced anxiously about the store, then caught herself and laughed. "Mercy, I forgot—that poor NoElle thing is gone, isn't she? Let *her* hear a thing like that, and you'd be in for a little spiel about the occult and black necromancy and, oh, I don't know what all."

In their cages above the counter, the parakeets went into one of their periodic episodes of cheerful frenzy. Everyone looked up at them except for Beatrice, who sidled closer to Pippa and said:

"We must talk sometime, you and I. Perhaps you can come over and take a look at my collection. And *please* don't worry: I've had the honor to deal with artisans on your level before. I *know* that people never appreciate the value of your extraordinary talents. But you'll have no problem with me on that score. *I'm* quite prepared to pay you what you deserve."

Brenda Cigogne looked a little put out. She fussed about the counter, dusting imaginary contaminants off a sale basket of half-price Christmas ornaments. Pippa could not believe that you could feel sorry for a person like Brenda Cigogne. But she supposed stranger things had happened. And keep happening, every moment. It is a very peculiar world.

"Maybe I could just come in, you know, part-time or something," she said. "When things are really busy."

Brenda beamed at her, ever hopeful.

Kaspian materialized from somewhere, maybe behind a counter. (He was short and it was easy to lose sight of him. But also he had this funny elflike aspect—a way of appearing and vanishing again: *poof.*) Gallantly he told the assembled women, "Pippa's really tired, you know. I think she probably ought to get going."

"Oh, dear," fretted Brenda. "Poor thing. I hate to see you *walking* in such freezing weather."

The weather's perfect, thought Pippa. But she didn't feel like walking either. Not for the next few years, anyhow.

"Jacques!" called Brenda, turning back toward the storage room. "Jacques—is that cousin of yours still around? I wonder if he might be willing to give our Pippa a lift to her house."

Jacques emerged with a conspiratorial grin. Close behind him came Spear. Pippa hadn't seen Spear since the Wild Ride down from the mountain, 100 years and a couple of days ago. He hadn't changed much. He looked confident and healthy and just a wee bit like the cat that swallowed the canary.

"What have you two been *up* to back there?" asked Brenda.

"Packing stuff," said Jacques.

Brenda said, "Stuff?" but then got distracted by Pippa making for the door, with Spear close behind her. "Goodbye, dear," she called. "It's nice to see you looking so well."

So well? Pippa doubted it. But she caught Spear smiling at her—he was wearing the loon feather again today—and that made her a little more able to believe.

Kaspian overtook the two of them on the sidewalk. He and Spear checked each other out.

"Have you guys met?" said Pippa. Thinking, Look at them—like pack animals. They don't know whether to shake hands or bite the other guy's neck in half.

She turned to Kaspian, touching him softly on the shoulder. His hand momentarily went up to hers. For an instant, she felt again a curious exchange of energy, an immaterial tingle, that she had noticed the first time they met.

"It'll be okay," she said. "Spear's a friend. I'll be all right with him. I promise."

Kaspian nodded and he let go of her. He looked very big and very small, at once. A way that Winterbelle looked, sometimes. Trying so hard to grow up.

" 'Bye," she said. "Take care of yourself."

He nodded. Then he was gone.

Poof.

"What are you driving?" she asked Spear. Not the Arctic Cat, she hoped.

He just smiled, and led her around the corner just off Mill Street where a shiny vintage Mustang was parked. Racing green. A convertible. With the top down. In *January*.

"Are you insane?" Pippa asked him.

He had not spoken, she realized, since they left the flower shop. Now he turned and half looked at her in that funny way of his. He said, "Are you?"

"Completely," she said. "It's an occupational hazard."

He laughed, as innocently amused as a kid would be. No shadings of irony, no complications.

"Want a ride?" he asked her.

"You bet."

The Mustang was no good in the snow. Its rear end skidded around all over the street, just in the act of getting unparked.

"Wooo!" said Pippa.

Spear said, "Hang on now."

She hung. They cruised. Icy wind whipped their hair. The Mustang slipped and slid and took long, terrifying turns. Spear's feather and ponytail flew. Pippa yelped. Pedestrians gawked.

It was great.

The gloomy end of Ash Street did not, for once, look so bad.

Spear sort of miscalculated his angle of approach, and the Mustang ended up rammed at a strange angle with a couple of wheels stuck on the lawn. They climbed out and they looked the situation over, and Pippa asked:

"How are you going to get that out, do you think?" Just wondering, like. As far as she cared, it could stay until spring.

"I'll call Jacques," said Spear. "He has to yank me out of someplace all the time. He's got it down."

Then he started up the walk, evidently inviting himself into the house. He was carrying Pippa's backpack, though she could not remember exactly how he had gotten hold of this. The hedge of half-alive forsythia shook in a chance breeze and dropped a little snow on him. Against his coal-black hair, it looked striking.

Pippa pushed open the heavy door. Familiar smells came out. Then she heard it, too—the old Magnavox, booming away in the front parlor.

It struck her suddenly:

This is a house where somebody just died.

The weirdness of it swept over her. Then it passed. She stepped into the hall.

This was just a house, again. The same old house she had never really liked. Though the kitchen was nice. She had *made* it nice. She guessed she could make the rest of it nice, given enough time. Time and energy. And a reason to want to.

She stepped into the parlor and switched the Magnavox off. The silence that filled the house was almost unprecedented—in quality as well as degree. She felt a rush of . . . of what? Something like peace. An end of having to do things. Spiritually speaking, a coffee break.

Spear came in and looked around. He opened the front curtains a little wider, letting what sunlight there was in. "So this is where you live," he said.

Pippa nodded. She said, "For now. I guess."

It was beyond all understanding. Or then again, maybe it was not.

Maybe in the end, simple things like this—a house, a warm chair to sit in, a friend to talk to on long winter nights—maybe these were the only things she *did* understand. The good stuff about the world.

Kindness. Cooking. Flowers. People caring about each other.

Not the rest—the shadows, the nightmares, the haunted looks in children's eyes. Witch or no witch, she would never understand that.

Pippa laid her head back in the chair and she said, "But like, what does it all *mean?*"

Spear looked into her eyes and, for once, he held his gaze there. You could not have said whether he knew or not what she was talking about. Or whether Pippa did herself. The light in his dark irises was like a sheen on polished ebony. He opened his mouth, maybe to speak, maybe just to smile

and then came

the Knock at the Door.

"Want me to get that?" Spear said.

But Pippa shook her head. She sat still for a moment, while the Knock came again. It seemed to come from inside her as well as from without. It came from the front door but also from a very deep place, like a well, a secret well out of which the future bubbled up.

She stood up but the door opened in just that same instant.

Roger Wemble, of the Department of Family Services, stuck his head in and shouted, "Is anybody home?"

Then he saw Pippa, only a few steps away, and he exhaled loudly in relief.

"I've been trying to reach you for *hours,*" he said. "People at the office were all over me, and your lawyer's been ringing me up every 15 minutes. Don't you ever answer your telephone?"

Sweat was on his brow. Tiny drops, like spider eggs.

Pippa said nothing. She had no idea what to say to this man, but more fundamentally she felt that everything now was beyond the reach of words or even of rational thoughts. She took a step toward the door, and in her mind Roger Wemble more or less ceased to exist. It seemed probable that, should he remain standing in her doorway, she would have passed right through him.

"You may have heard," his disembodied voice was saying, "that our Department is engaged in a far-reaching internal review process. Evidence has come forth that one of our contractual advisors—a therapist, I believe you met her once or twice—may have engaged in certain, ah, diagnostic modalities that are not . . . not completely . . . Well, I'm not at liberty to divulge all the details. But I can *assure* you that the Higher-Ups are taking a *very serious* interest in certain cases in particular. Your own being one of them."

"Be careful how you talk about the Higher-Ups," Spear advised Wemble. "Pippa here is on a first-name basis with several of them."

The disembodied entity in the doorway cast its eyes toward the heavens. "*Now* they tell me," it said. "Well, then. In any case, pending of course a final resolution, which could take some weeks, it has been decided that— in the best interests of everyone concerned—and I'm speaking here both of the parent and of the dependent minor, the issue of provisional custody might best be resolved in favor of—"

Pippa flicked her hand.

There is no more to tell of Roger Wemble.

At the foot of the sidewalk, parked just behind the green Mustang, stood a small car of some nondescript grayish-brown. A wolf color. Its motor was running and there was movement, a rear door opening, a small figure stepping onto the snow.

And Pippa cried. But now, with the bracing cold running past her legs, and the small magic-mirror-image of herself racing up the sidewalk as fast as her legs would go, she cried happily. The world dissolved into a blinding oneness of joy.

And Winterbelle
raised her little arms

and they became wings,
the wings of an air sprite,
and when she shouted
"Mommy!"

she broke free of the Earth
and all its dark places, and

she flew

into Pippa's arms.

And the beautiful sprite said, "I love you, Mommy."

And the good witch said, "Sweetie, I love you too."

And the Sun exploded in thermonuclear splendor
and the snow shone like trillions of diamonds
and the world that came into being in that instant
was so perfect and clean and pure
that you had to believe everyone in it would live
happily ever after.

> So let's believe
> really and truly
> they did.

The Voice of BARD On-Line
at http://www.AvonBooks.com/Bard

READ original pieces by Bard authors.

DISCOVER the reason behind
the "Dedication."

DISCUSS the art of writing in our forum.

REGISTER for reading group information
and recommendations.

BROWSE through our list
of new and upcoming
titles and read chapter excerpts.